SPARKS!

FUTURE PURRFECT

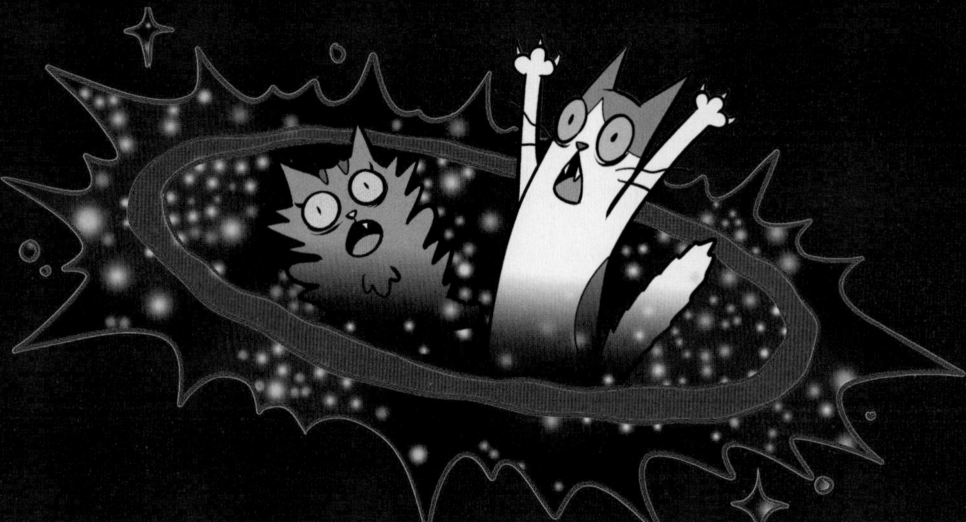

graphix

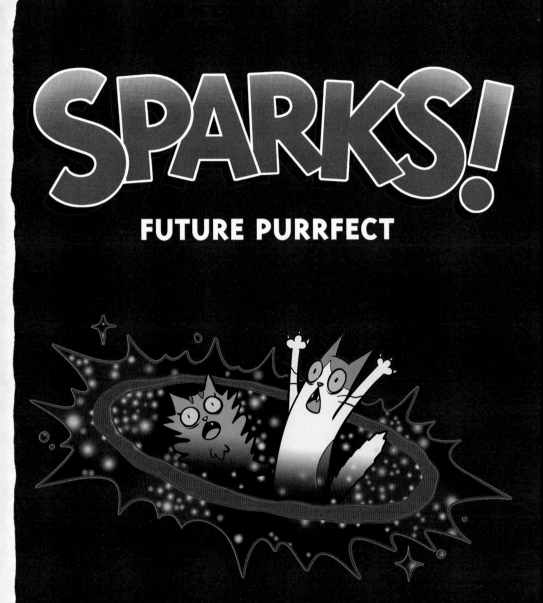

SCHOLASTIC

Photo by Nina Matsumoto

Dedicated to Louie. He likes peanuts.
— Ian Boothby and Nina Matsumoto

Text copyright © 2022 by Ian Boothby
Art copyright © 2022 by Nina Matsumoto

All rights reserved. Published by Graphix, an imprint of Scholastic Inc., *Publishers since 1920.*
SCHOLASTIC, GRAPHIX, and associated logos are trademarks and/or registered trademarks of Scholastic Inc.

The publisher does not have any control over and does not assume any responsibility for author or
third-party websites or their content.

Library of Congress Control Number: 2021936600

ISBN 978-1-338-33994-9 (hardcover)
ISBN 978-1-338-33993-2 (paperback)

10 9 8 7 6 5 4 3 2 1   22 23 24 25 26

Printed in China   62
First edition, February 2022

Edited by Adam Rau
Book design by Phil Falco & Steve Ponzo
Publisher: David Saylor

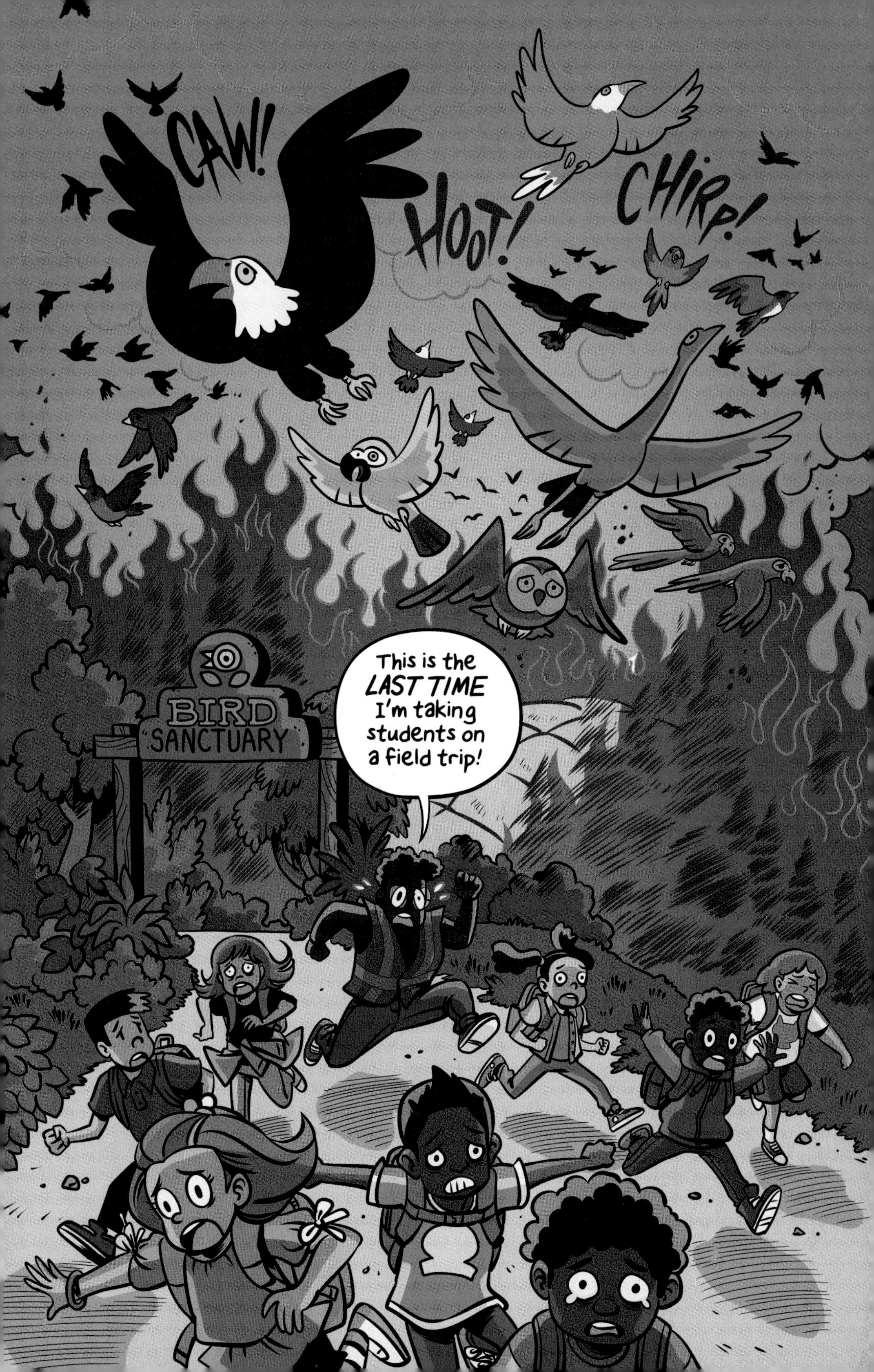
CAW!
HOOT!
CHIRP!
BIRD SANCTUARY
This is the LAST TIME I'm taking students on a field trip!

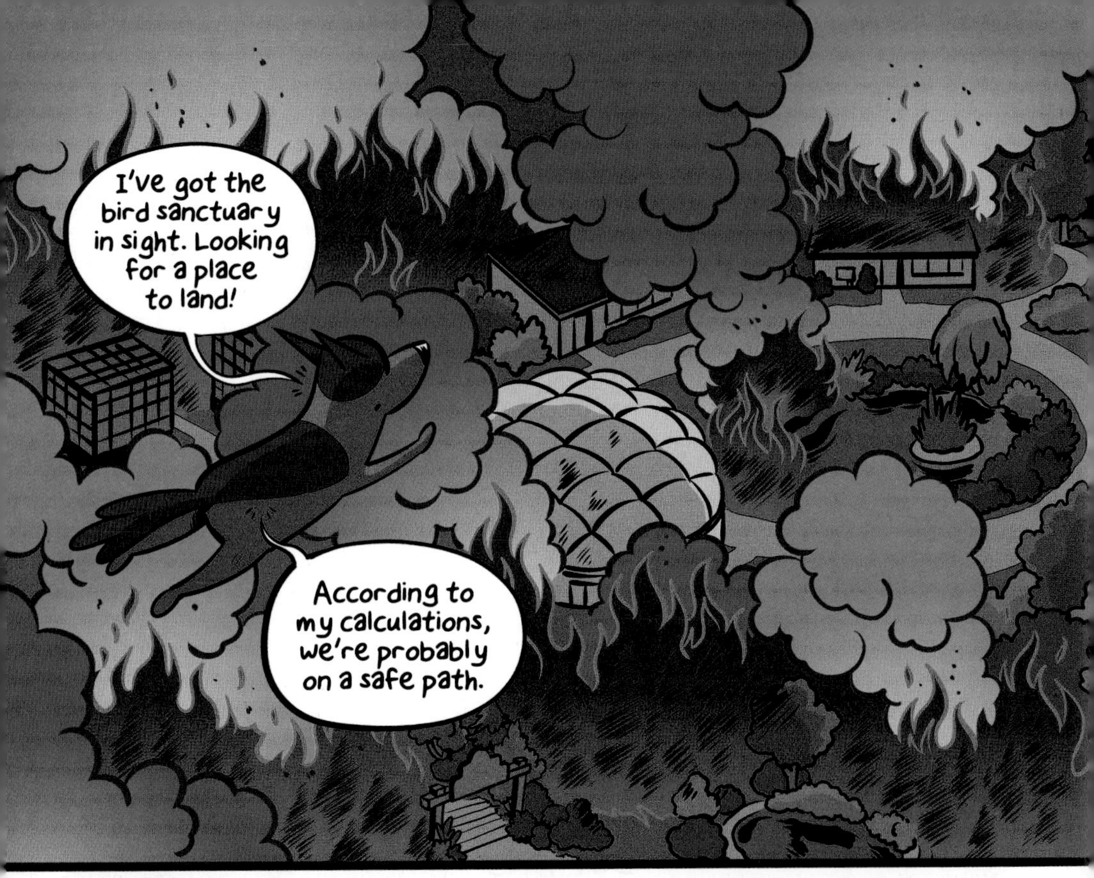
I've got the bird sanctuary in sight. Looking for a place to land!
According to my calculations, we're probably on a safe path.

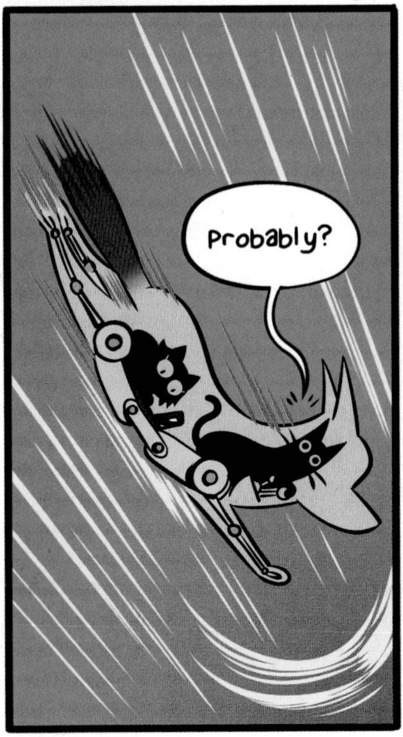
Probably?

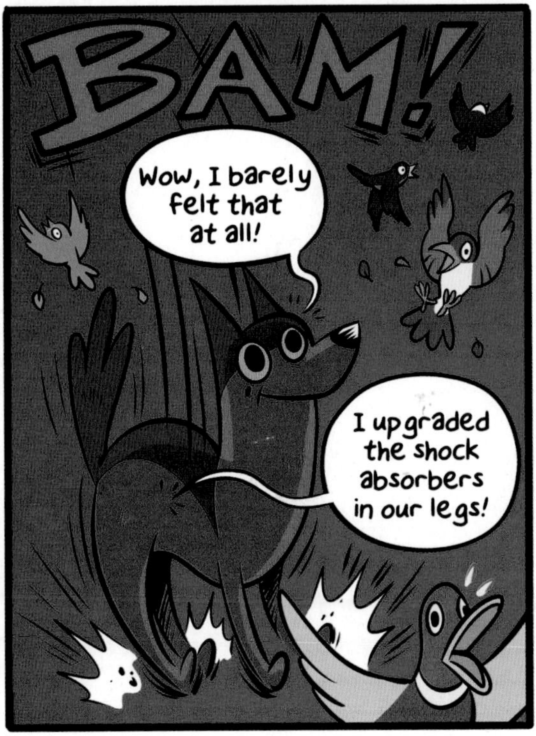
BAM!
Wow, I barely felt that at all!
I upgraded the shock absorbers in our legs!

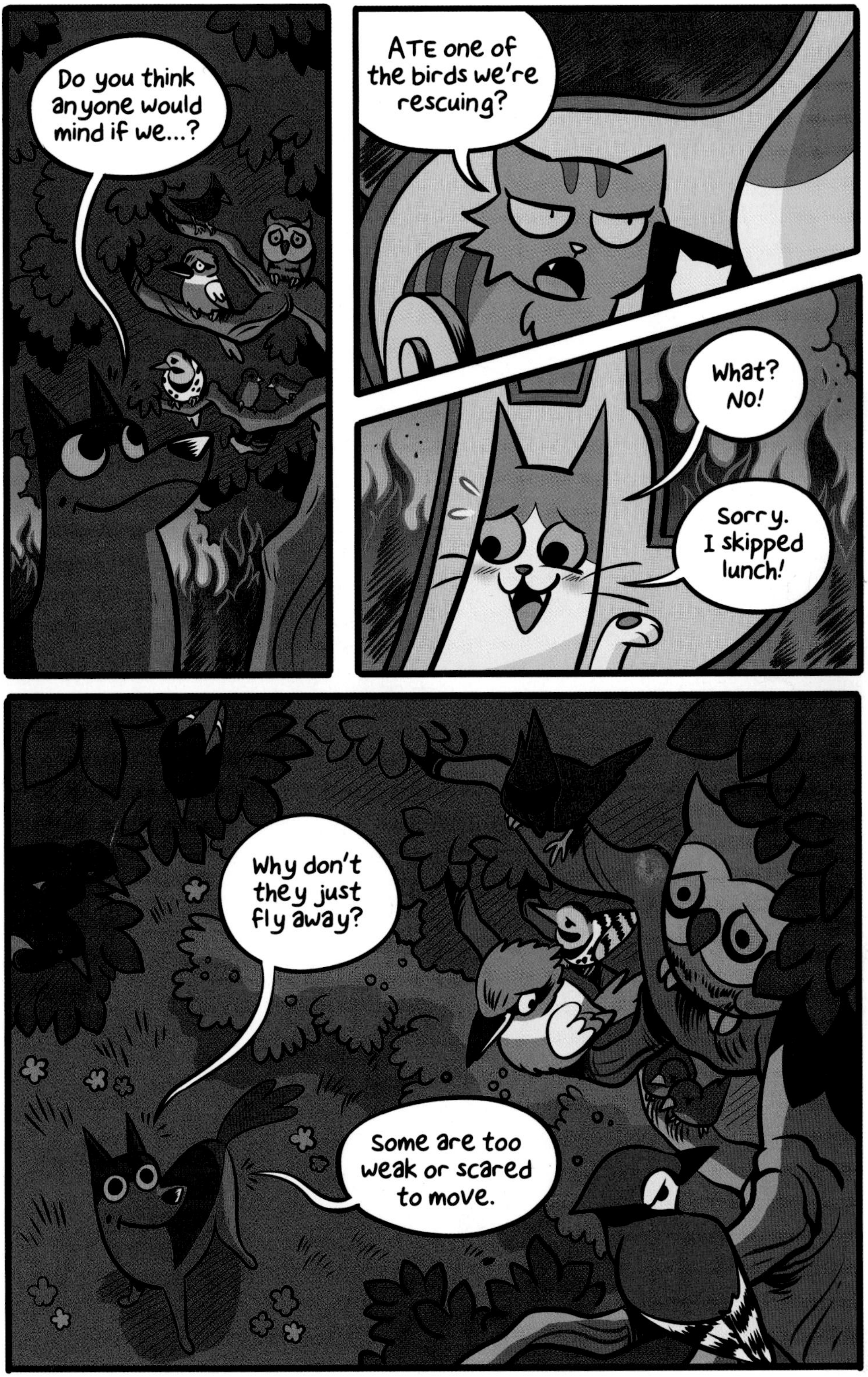
Do you think anyone would mind if we...?
ATE one of the birds we're rescuing?
What? NO!
Sorry. I skipped lunch!
Why don't they just fly away?
Some are too weak or scared to move.

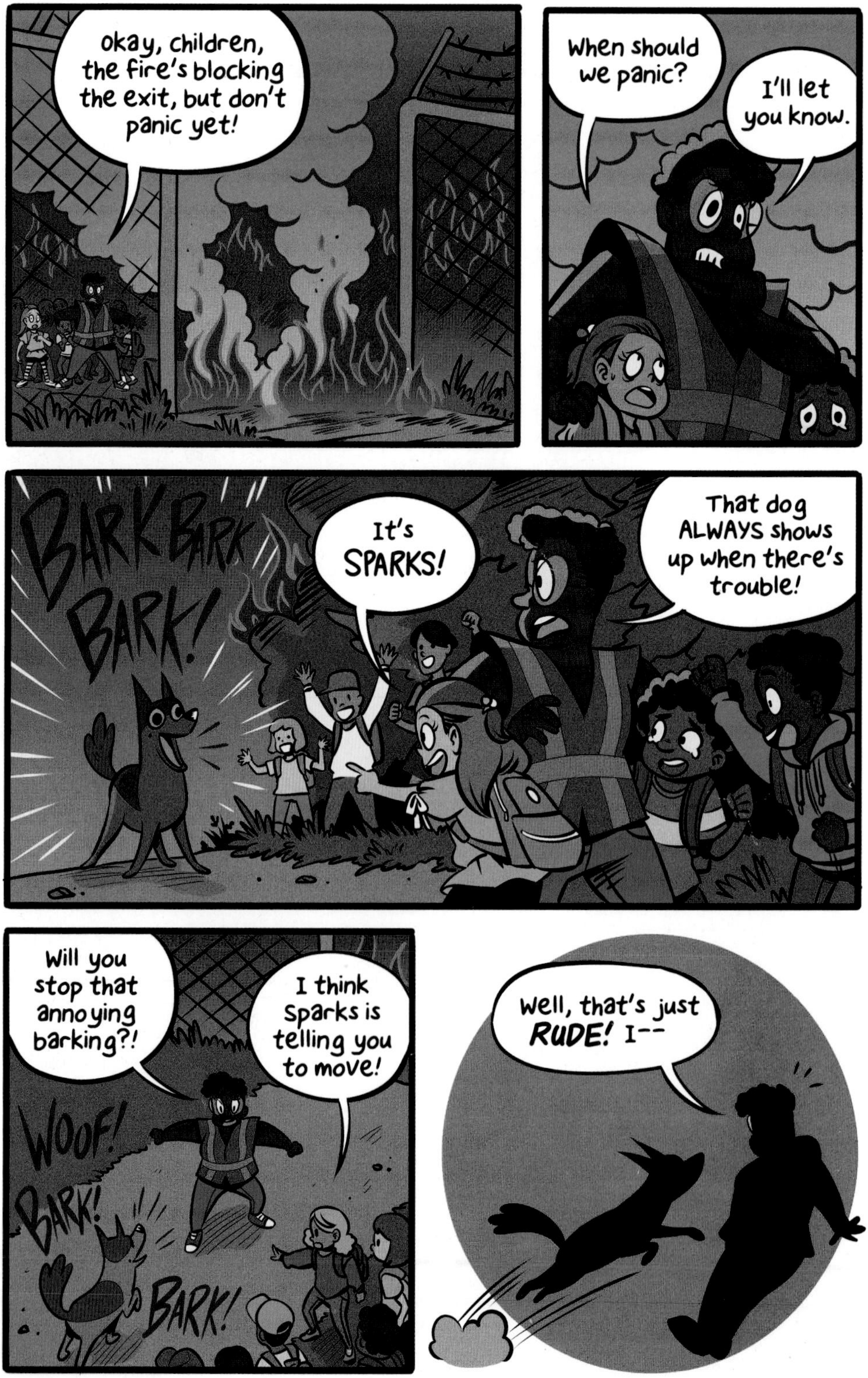
okay, children, the fire's blocking the exit, but don't panic yet!
When should we panic?
I'll let you know.
BARK BARK BARK!
It's SPARKS!
That dog ALWAYS shows up when there's trouble!
Will you stop that annoying barking?!
I think Sparks is telling you to move!
WOOF!
BARK!
BARK!
Well, that's just RUDE! I--

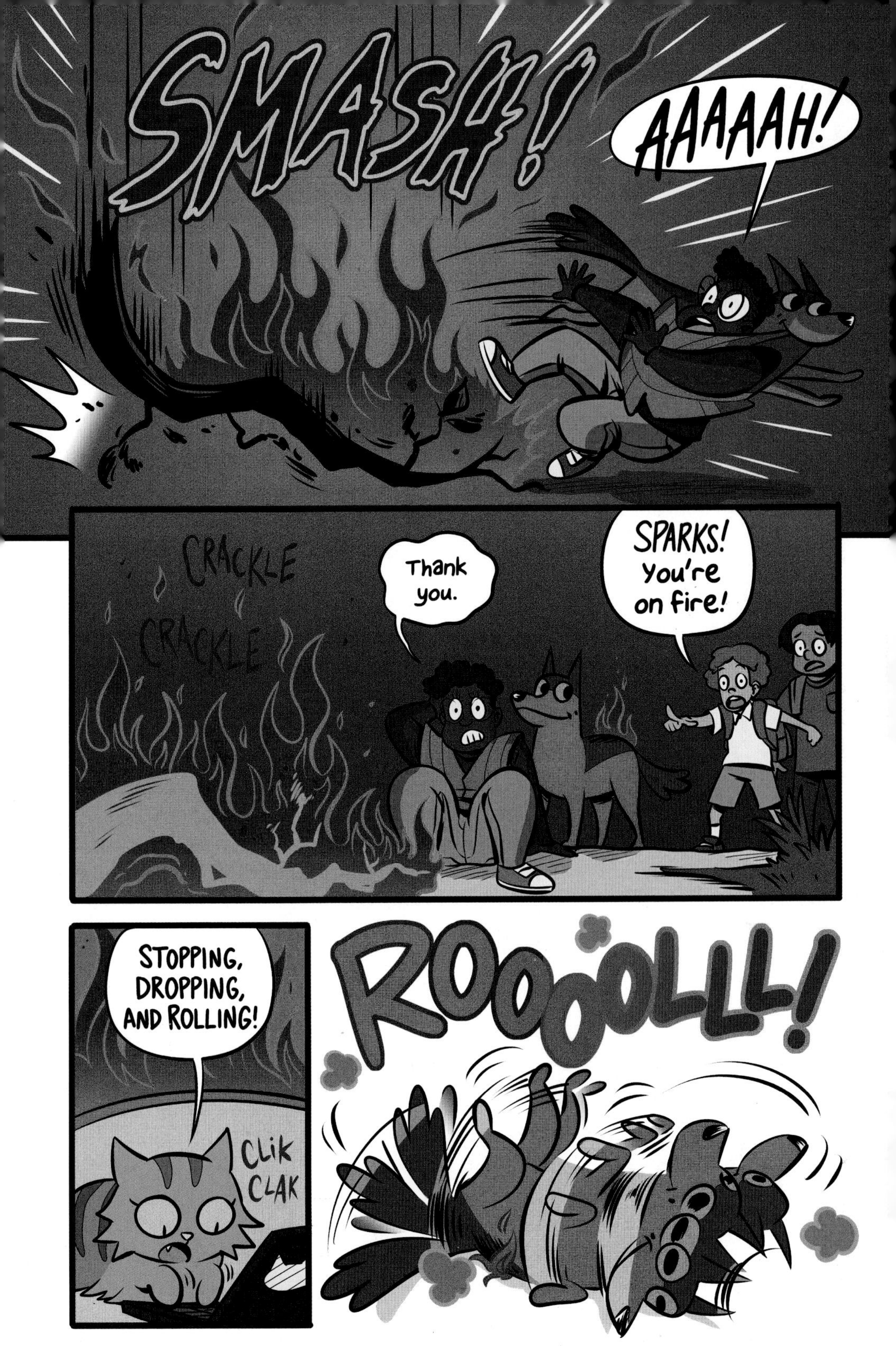
SMASH!
AAAAAH!
CRACKLE
CRACKLE
Thank you.
SPARKS! You're on fire!
STOPPING, DROPPING, AND ROLLING!
CLIK CLAK
ROOOOLLL!

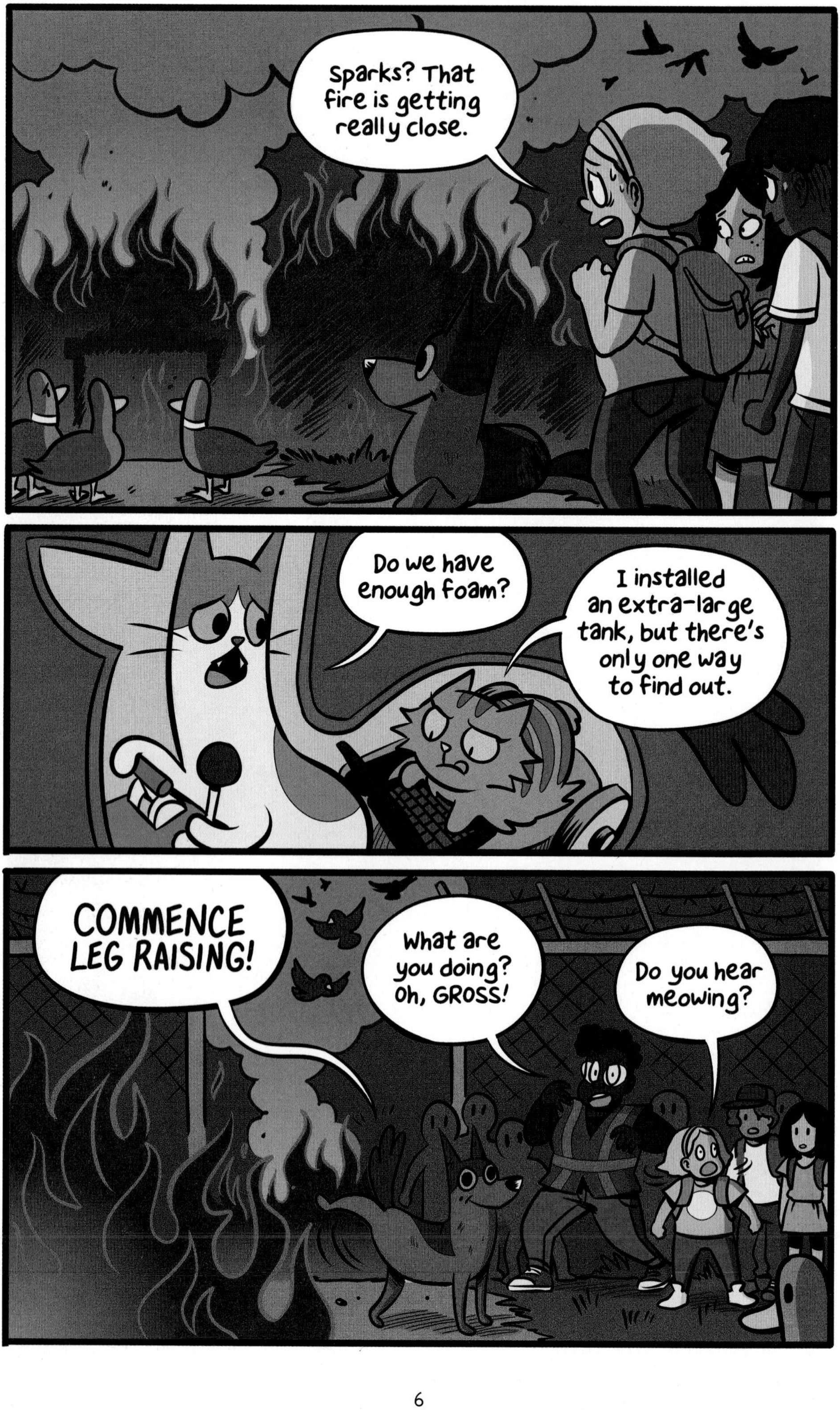
Sparks? That fire is getting really close.
Do we have enough foam?
I installed an extra-large tank, but there's only one way to find out.
COMMENCE LEG RAISING!
What are you doing? Oh, GROSS!
Do you hear meowing?

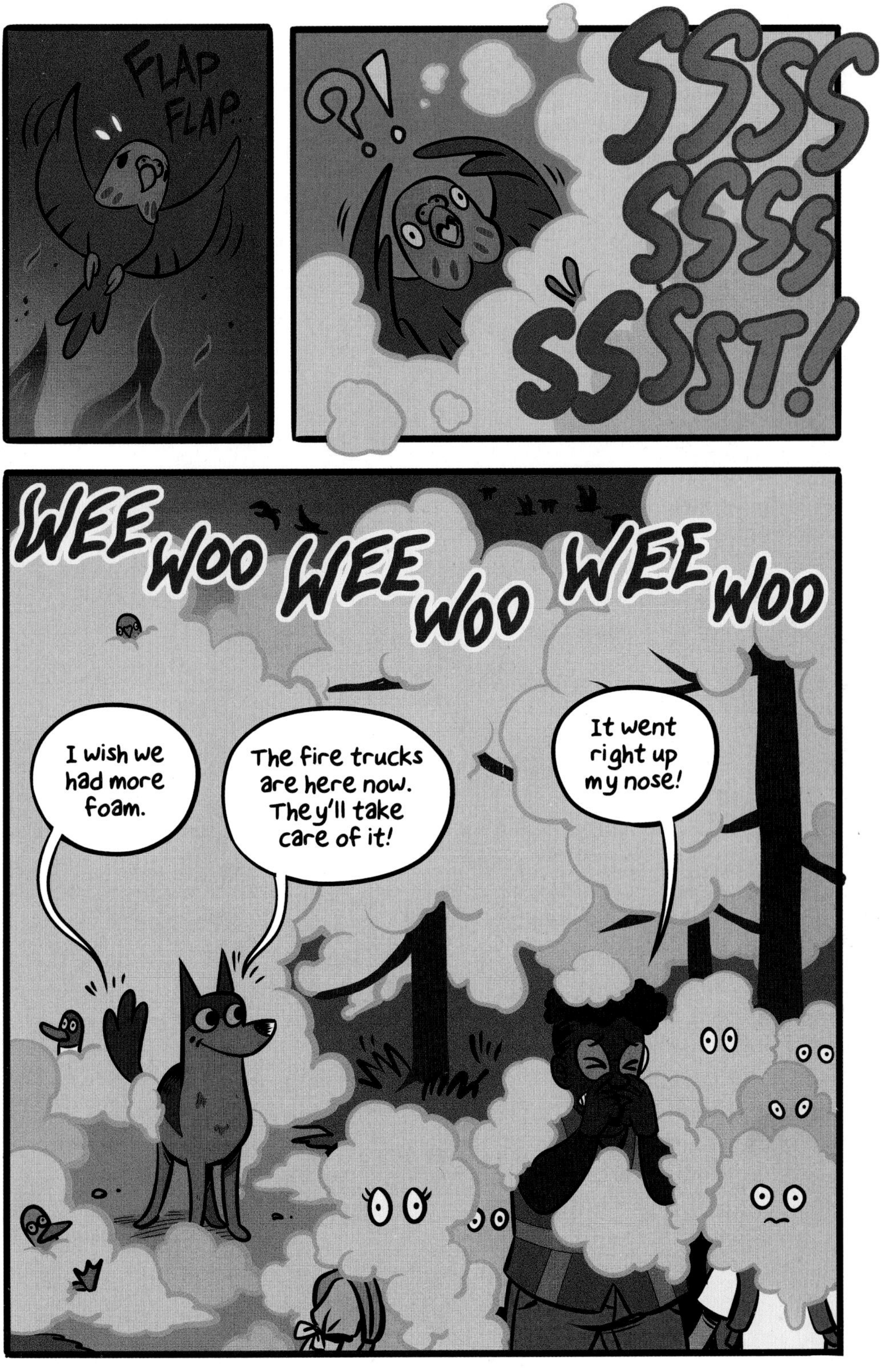
FLAP FLAP...
?!
SSSS SSSS SSSST!
WEE WOO WEE WOO WEE WOO
I wish we had more foam.
The fire trucks are here now. They'll take care of it!
It went right up my nose!

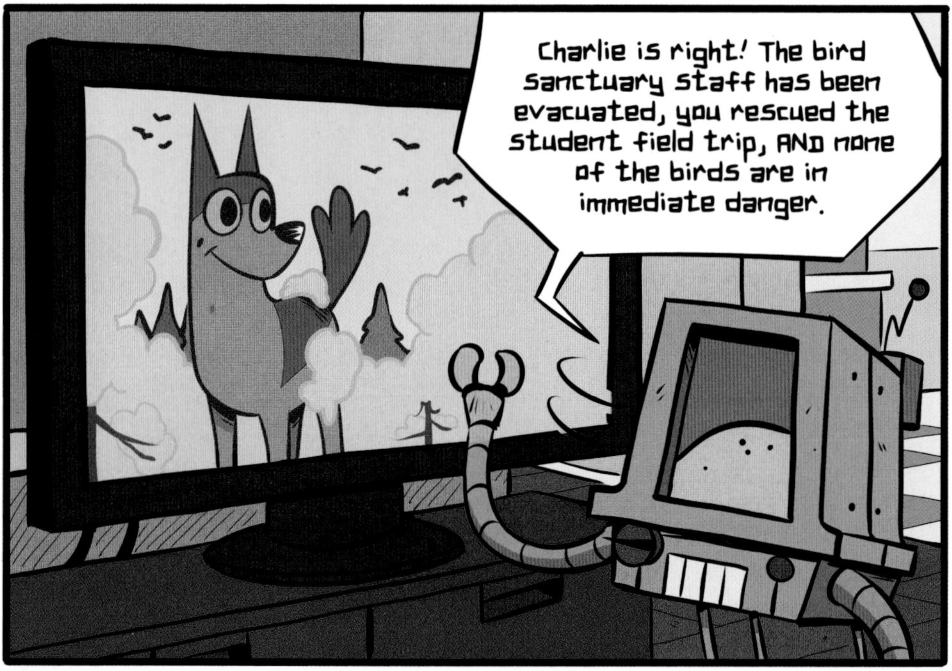
Charlie is right! The bird sanctuary staff has been evacuated, you rescued the student field trip, AND none of the birds are in immediate danger.

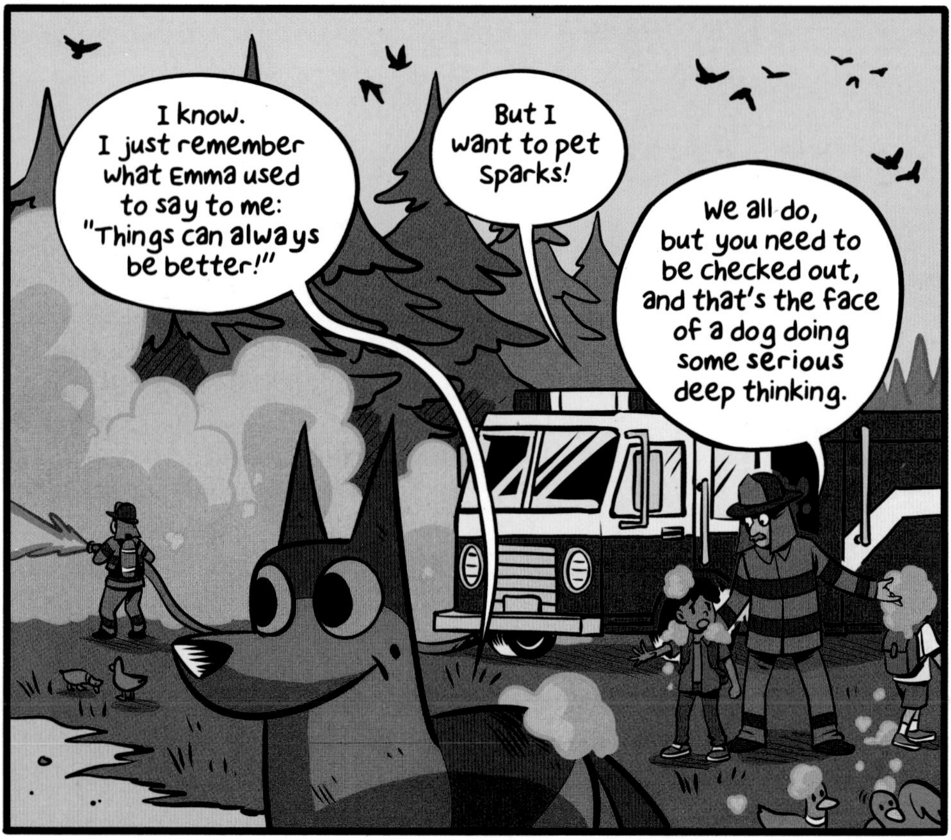
I know. I just remember what Emma used to say to me: "Things can always be better!"
But I want to pet Sparks!
We all do, but you need to be checked out, and that's the face of a dog doing some serious deep thinking.

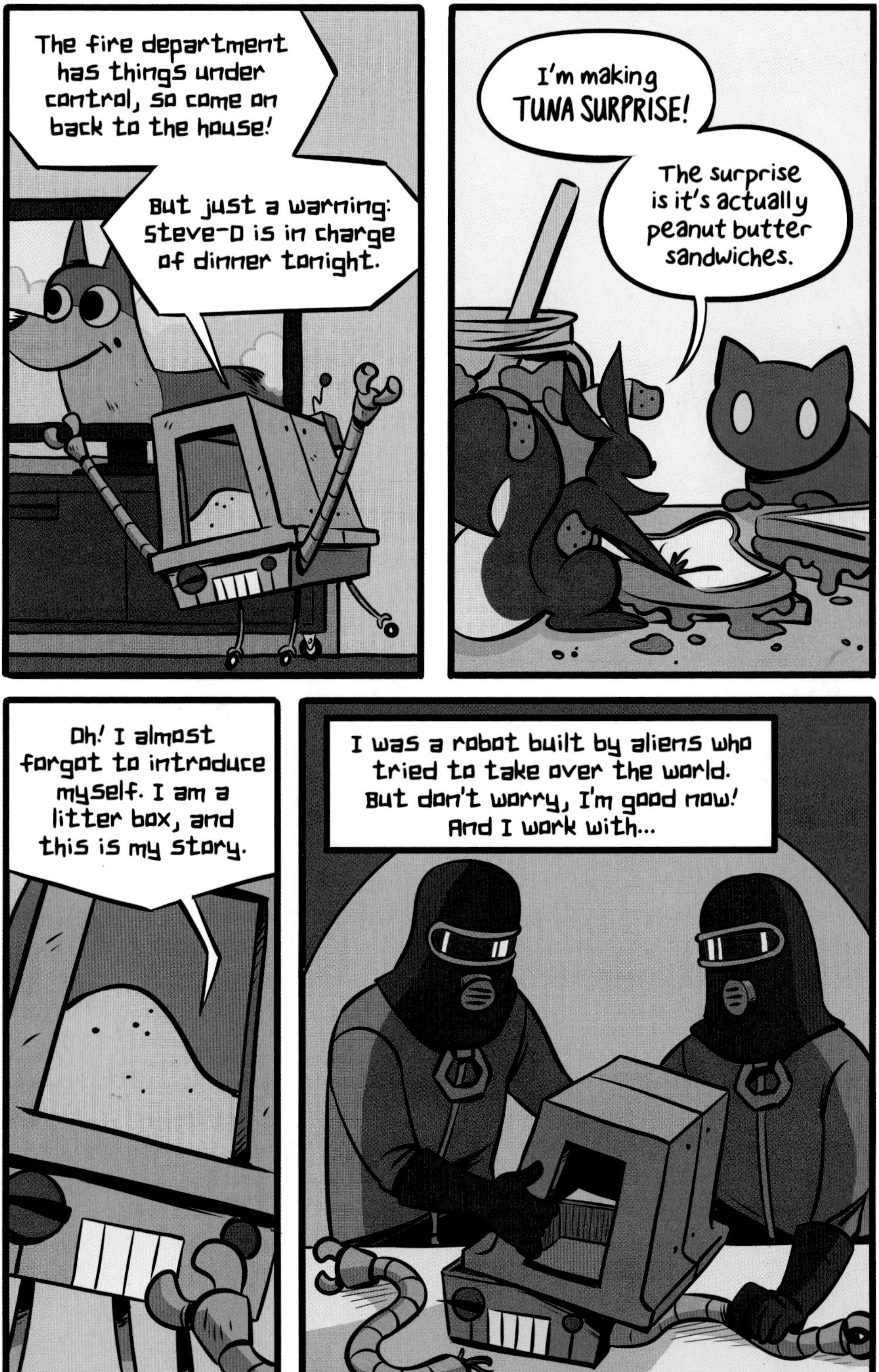
The fire department has things under control, so come on back to the house!
But just a warning: Steve-O is in charge of dinner tonight.
I'm making TUNA SURPRISE!
The surprise is it's actually peanut butter sandwiches.
Oh! I almost forgot to introduce myself. I am a litter box, and this is my story.
I was a robot built by aliens who tried to take over the world. But don't worry, I'm good now! And I work with...

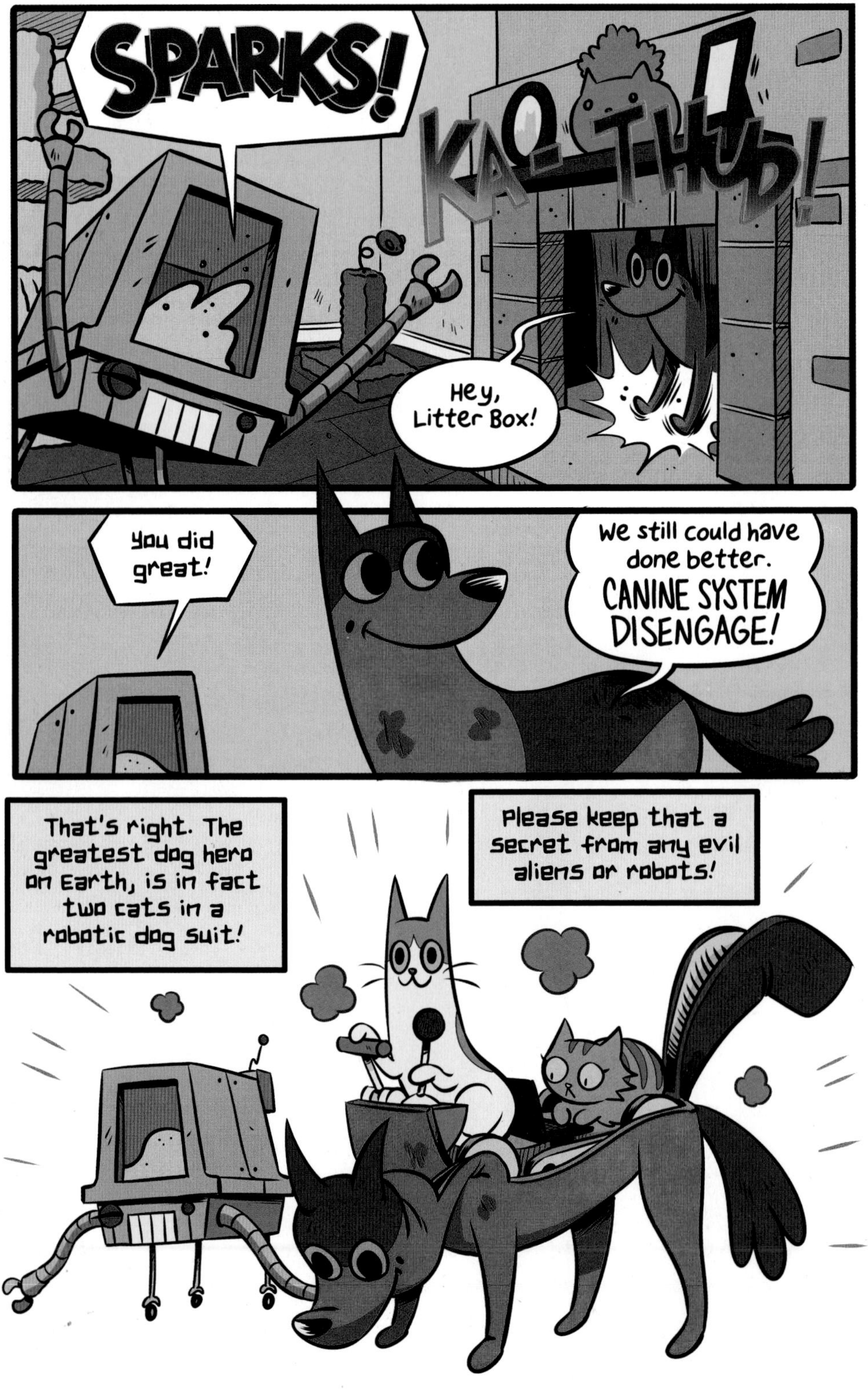
SPARKS!
KA-THUD!
Hey, Litter Box!
You did great!
We still could have done better. CANINE SYSTEM DISENGAGE!
That's right. The greatest dog hero on Earth, is in fact two cats in a robotic dog suit!
Please keep that a secret from any evil aliens or robots!

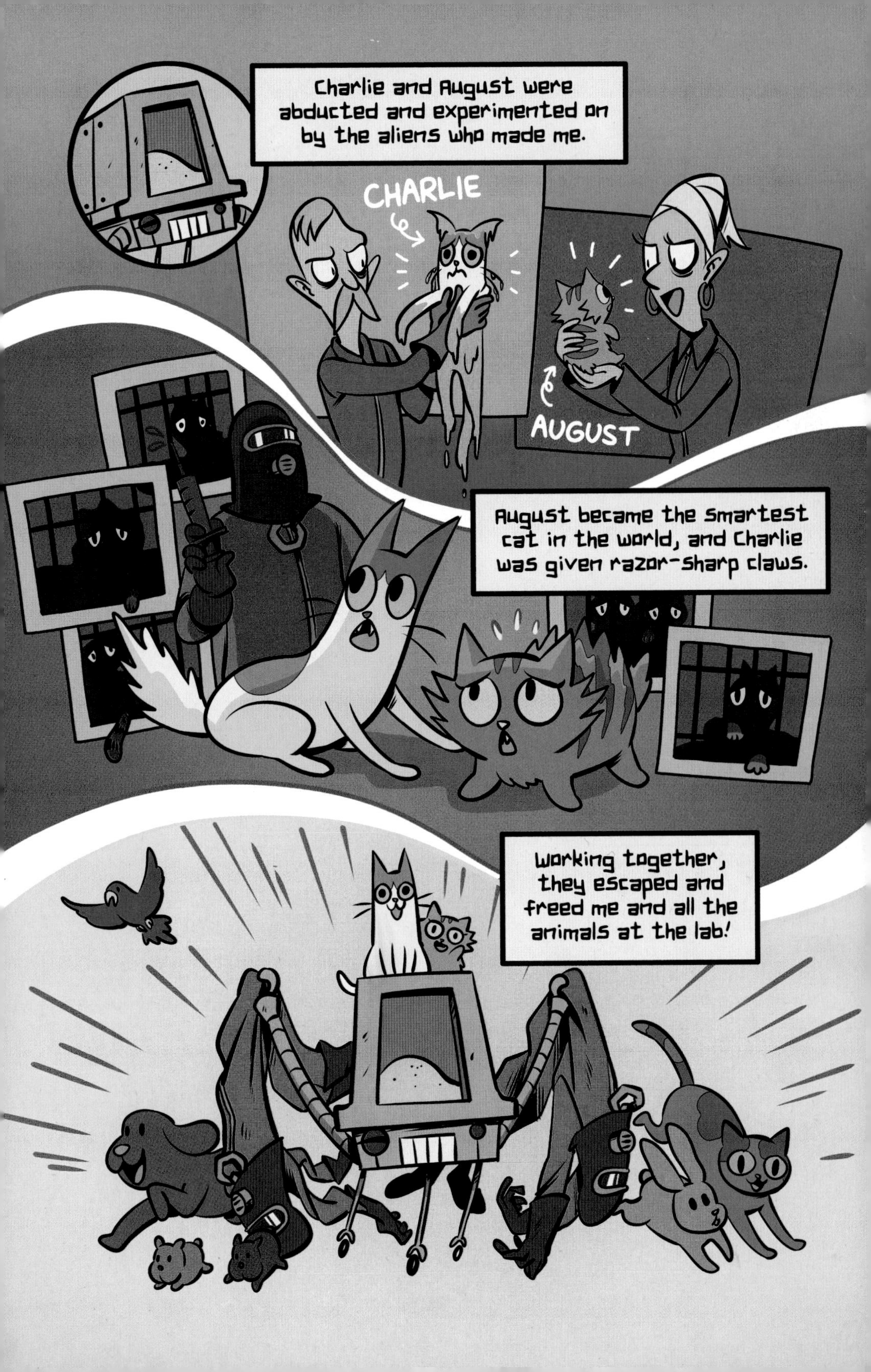
Charlie and August were abducted and experimented on by the aliens who made me.
CHARLIE
AUGUST
August became the smartest cat in the world, and Charlie was given razor-sharp claws.
Working together, they escaped and freed me and all the animals at the lab!

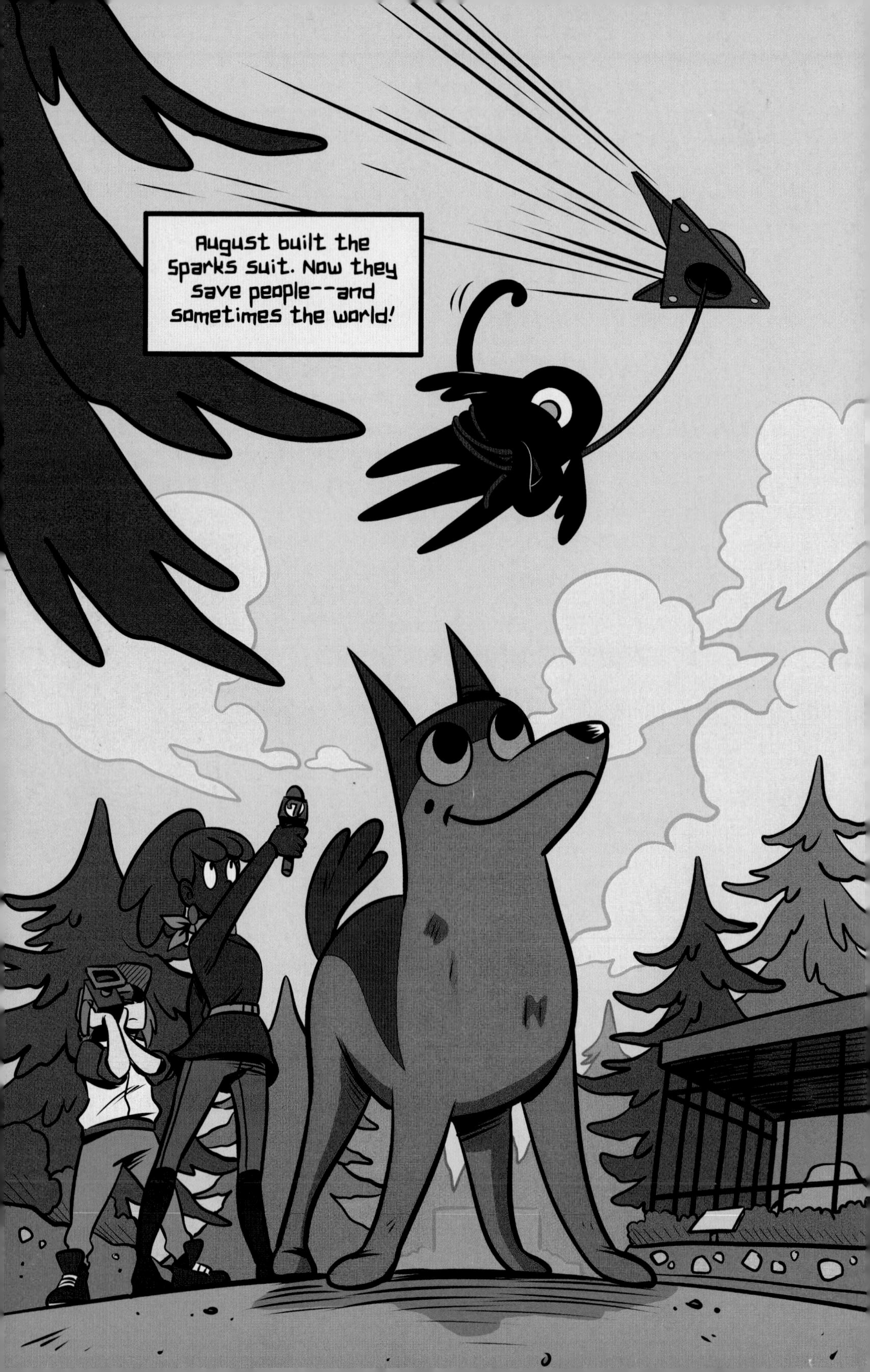
August built the Sparks suit. Now they save people--and sometimes the world!

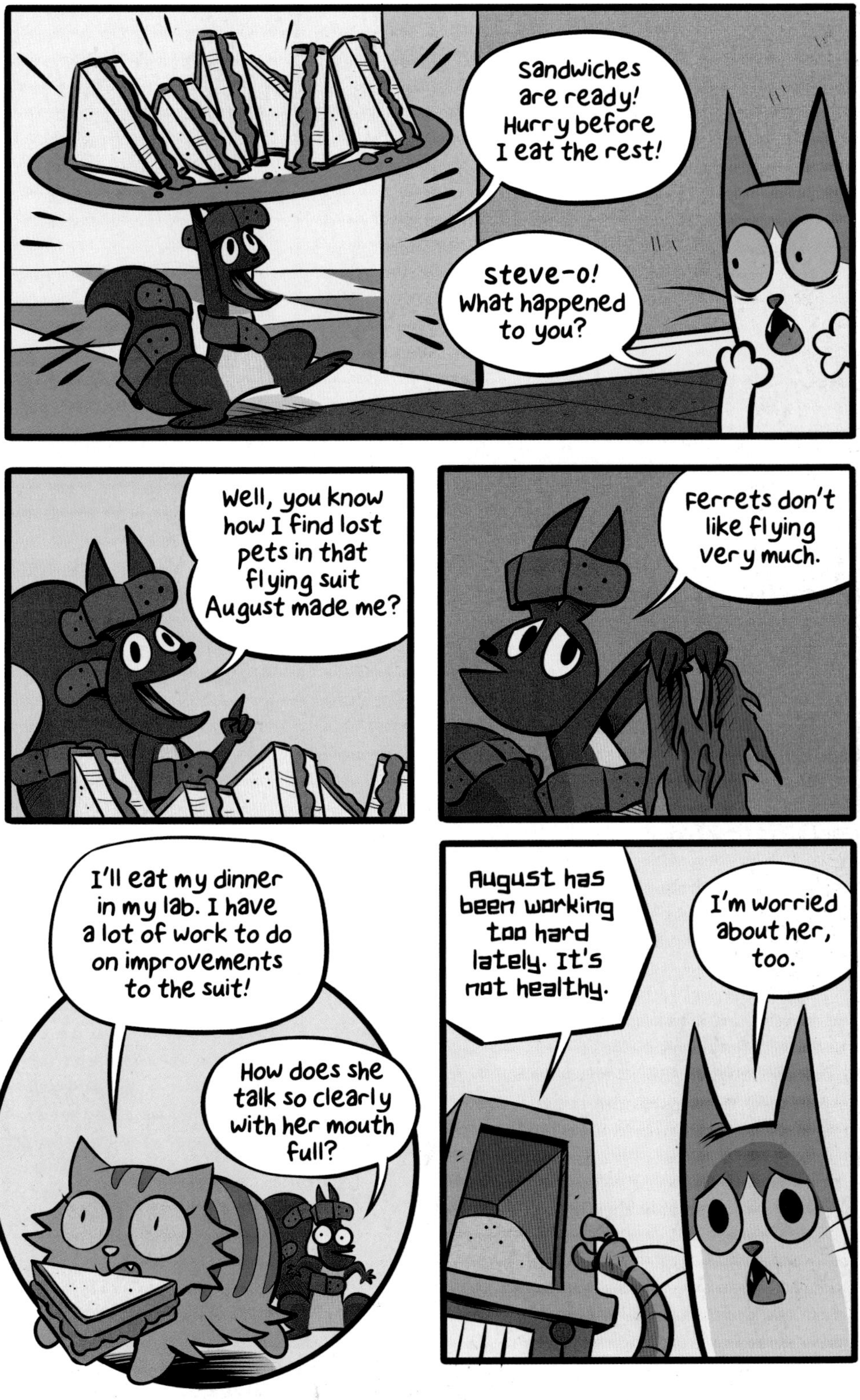
Sandwiches are ready! Hurry before I eat the rest!
Steve-O! What happened to you?
Well, you know how I find lost pets in that flying suit August made me?
Ferrets don't like flying very much.
I'll eat my dinner in my lab. I have a lot of work to do on improvements to the suit!
How does she talk so clearly with her mouth full?
August has been working too hard lately. It's not healthy.
I'm worried about her, too.

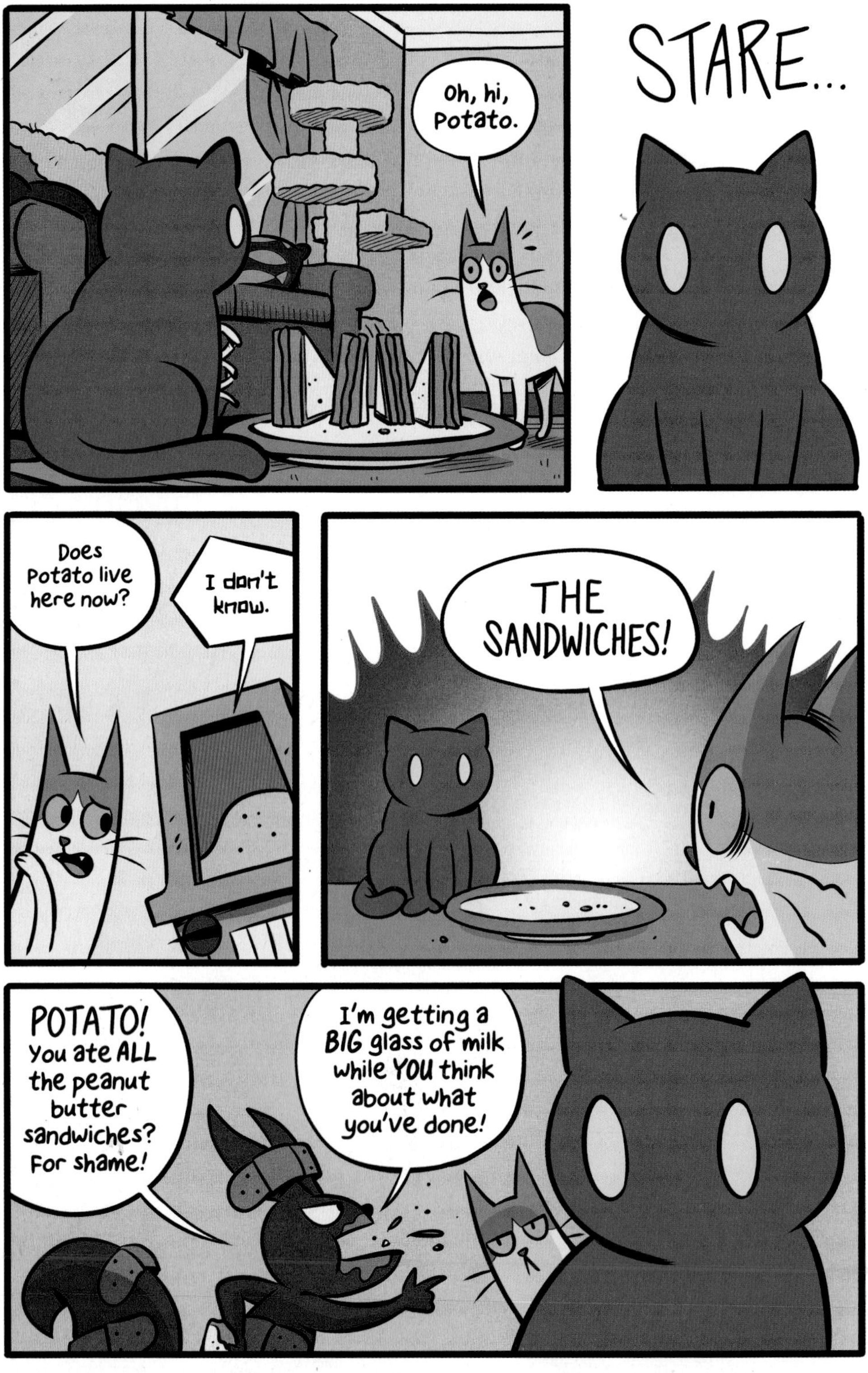
Oh, hi, Potato.
STARE...
Does Potato live here now?
I don't know.
THE SANDWICHES!
POTATO! You ate ALL the peanut butter sandwiches? For shame!
I'm getting a BIG glass of milk while YOU think about what you've done!

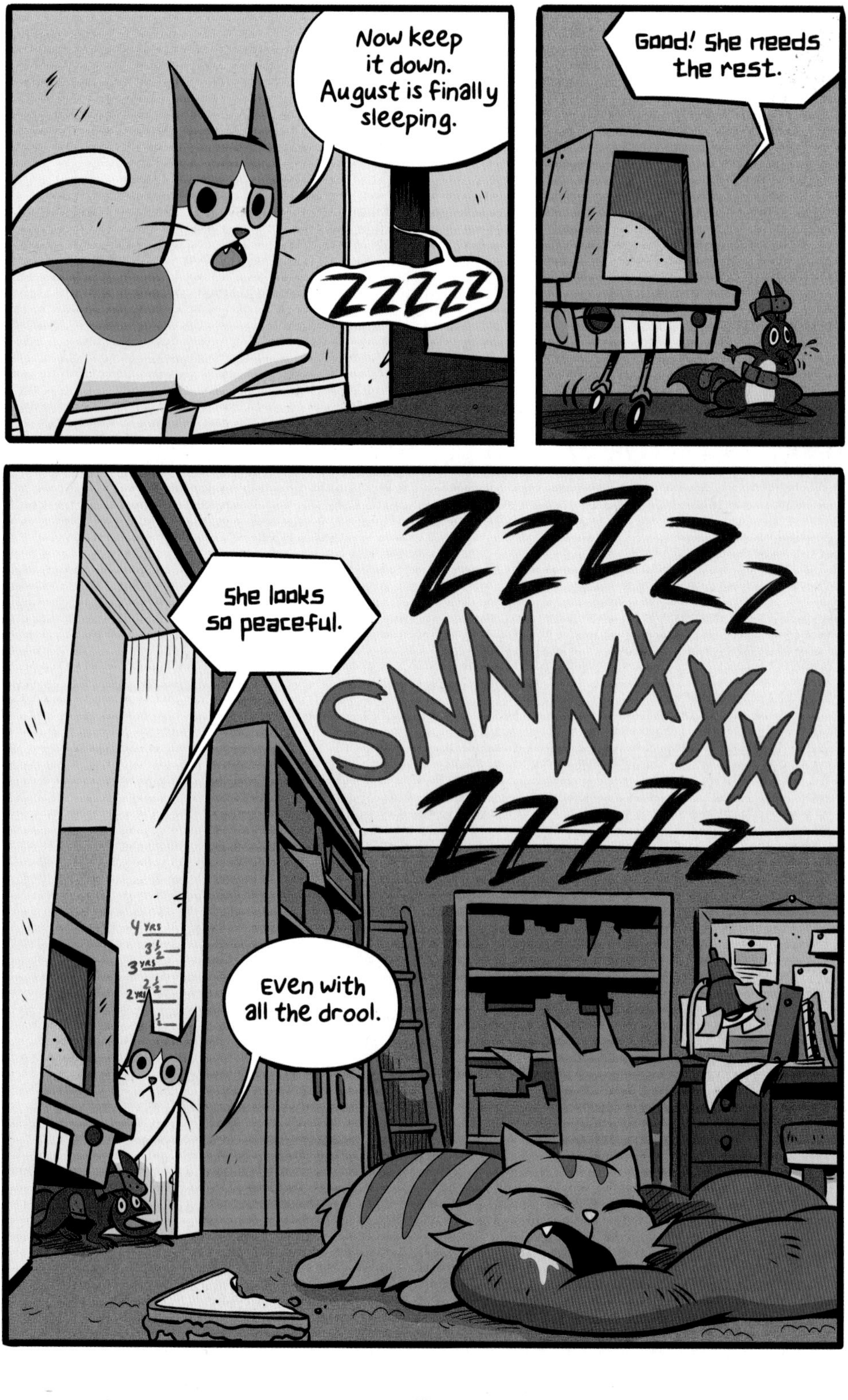
Now keep it down. August is finally sleeping.
ZZZZZ
Good! She needs the rest.
She looks so peaceful.
ZZZZZ
SNNXXX!
ZZZZZ
Even with all the drool.
4 YRS
3 1/2
3 YRS
2 1/2
2 YRS

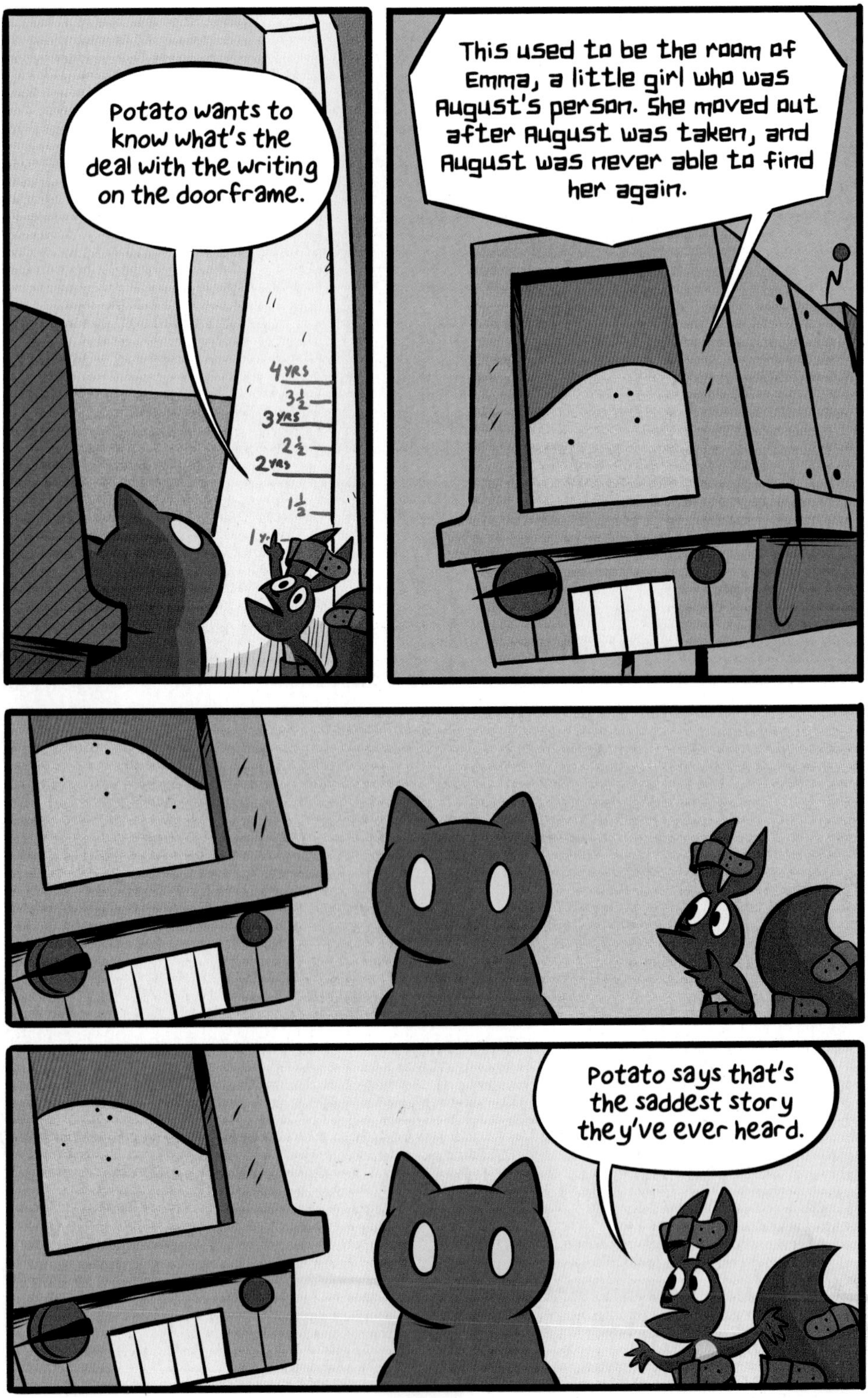
Potato wants to know what's the deal with the writing on the doorframe.
4 YRS
3½
3 YRS
2½
2 YRS
1½
1 YR
This used to be the room of Emma, a little girl who was August's person. She moved out after August was taken, and August was never able to find her again.
Potato says that's the saddest story they've ever heard.

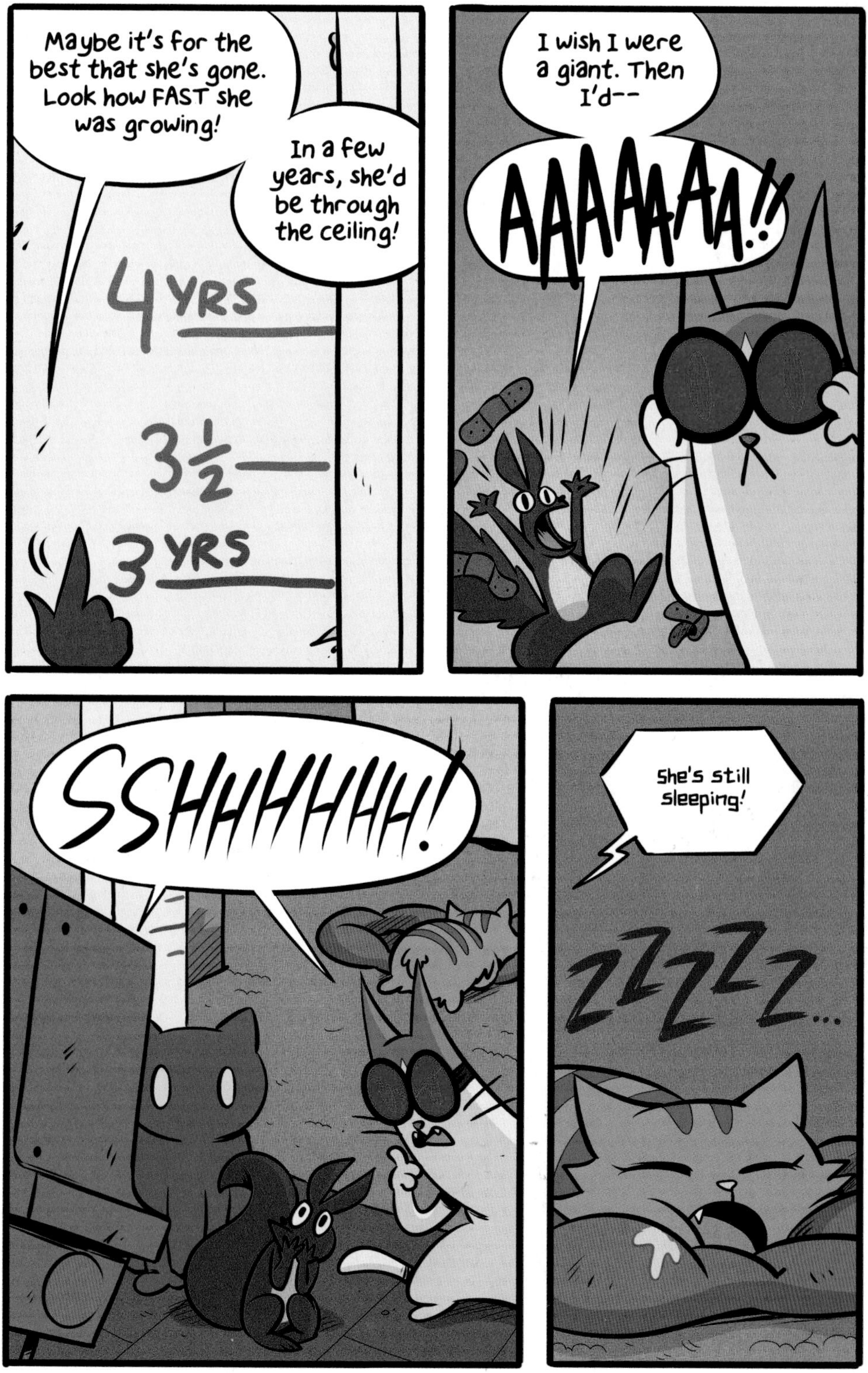

Maybe it's for the best that she's gone. Look how FAST she was growing!
In a few years, she'd be through the ceiling!
4 YRS
3½
3 YRS
I wish I were a giant. Then I'd--
AAAAAAA!!
SSHHHHHH!
She's still sleeping!
ZZZZZ...

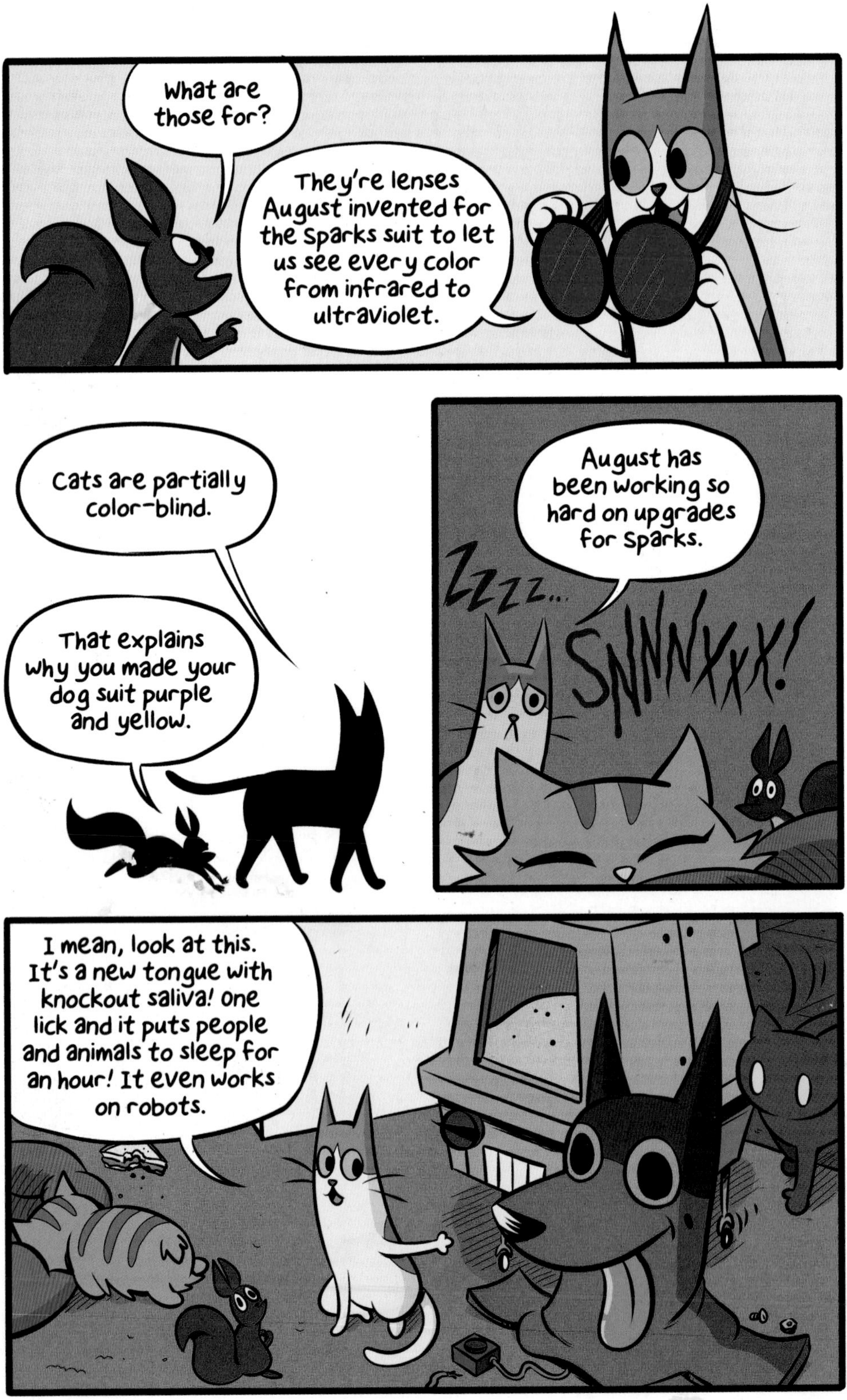
What are those for?
They're lenses August invented for the Sparks suit to let us see every color from infrared to ultraviolet.
Cats are partially color-blind.
That explains why you made your dog suit purple and yellow.
August has been working so hard on upgrades for Sparks.
ZZZZ...
SNNNXXX!
I mean, look at this. It's a new tongue with knockout saliva! One lick and it puts people and animals to sleep for an hour! It even works on robots.

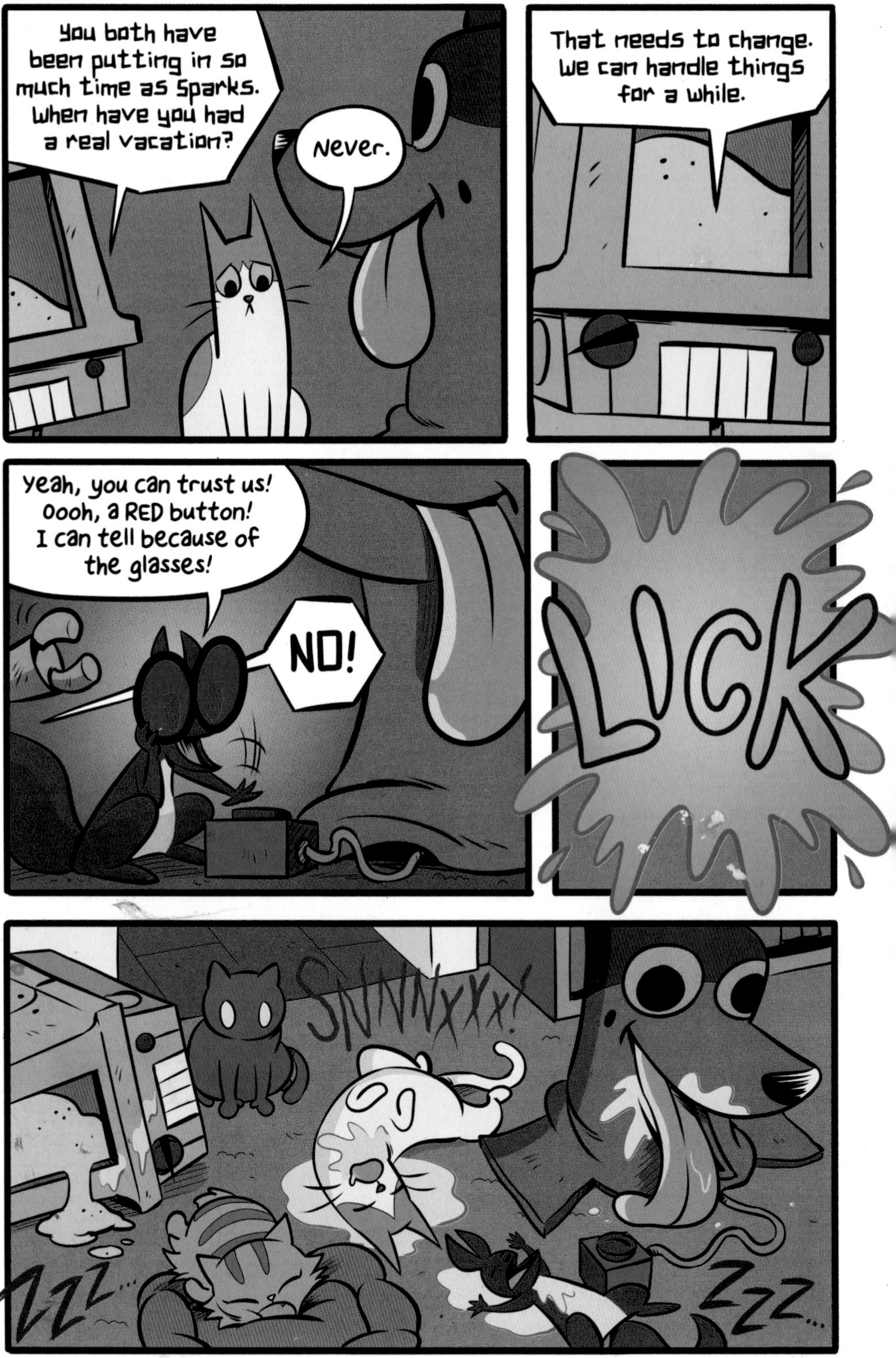
You both have been putting in so much time as Sparks. When have you had a real vacation?
Never.
That needs to change. We can handle things for a while.
Yeah, you can trust us! Oooh, a RED button! I can tell because of the glasses!
NO!
LICK
SNNNxxx!
ZZZ...
ZZZ...

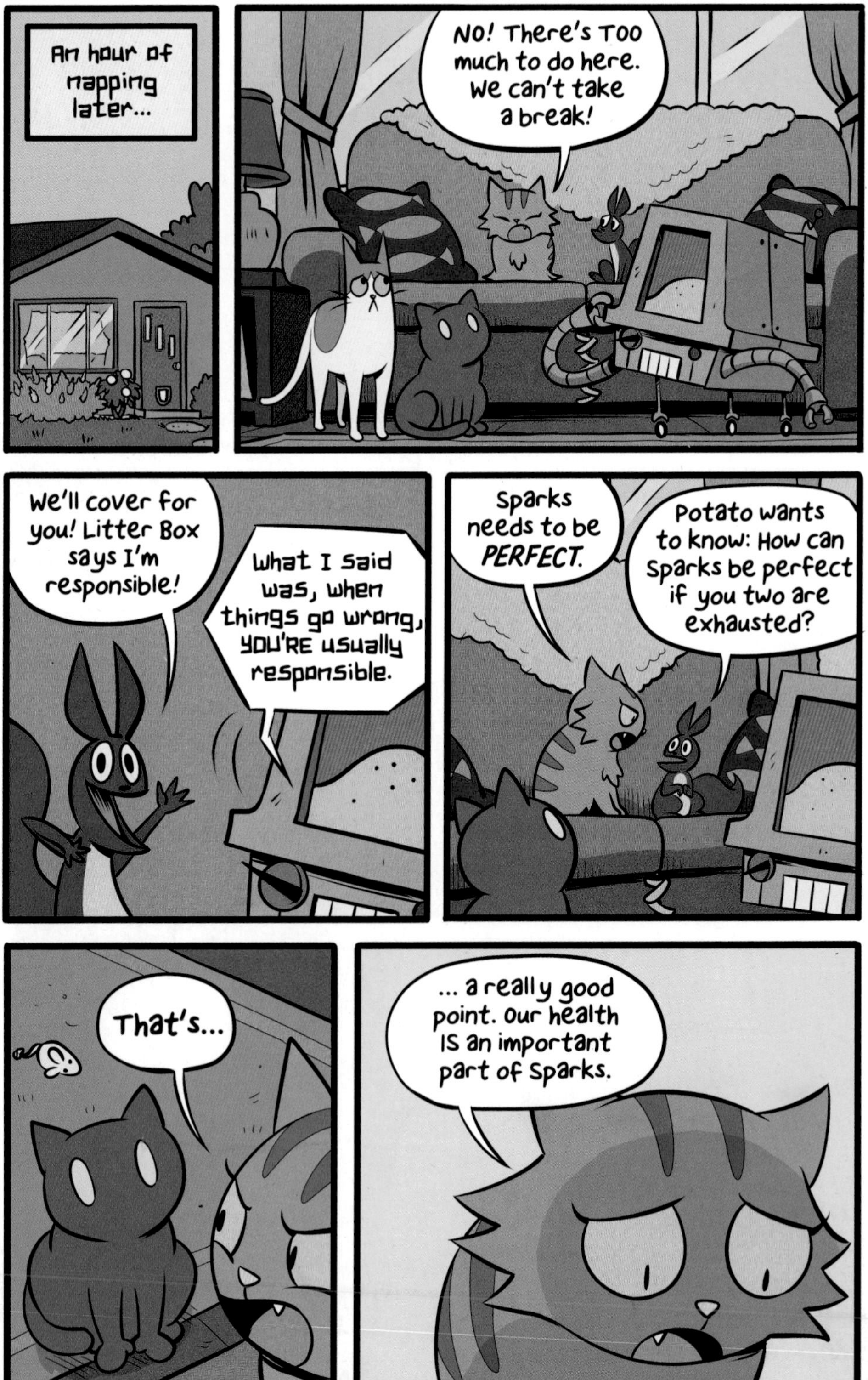
An hour of napping later...
NO! There's TOO much to do here. We can't take a break!
We'll cover for you! Litter Box says I'm responsible!
What I said was, when things go wrong, YOU'RE usually responsible.
Sparks needs to be PERFECT.
Potato wants to know: How can Sparks be perfect if you two are exhausted?
That's...
... a really good point. Our health IS an important part of Sparks.

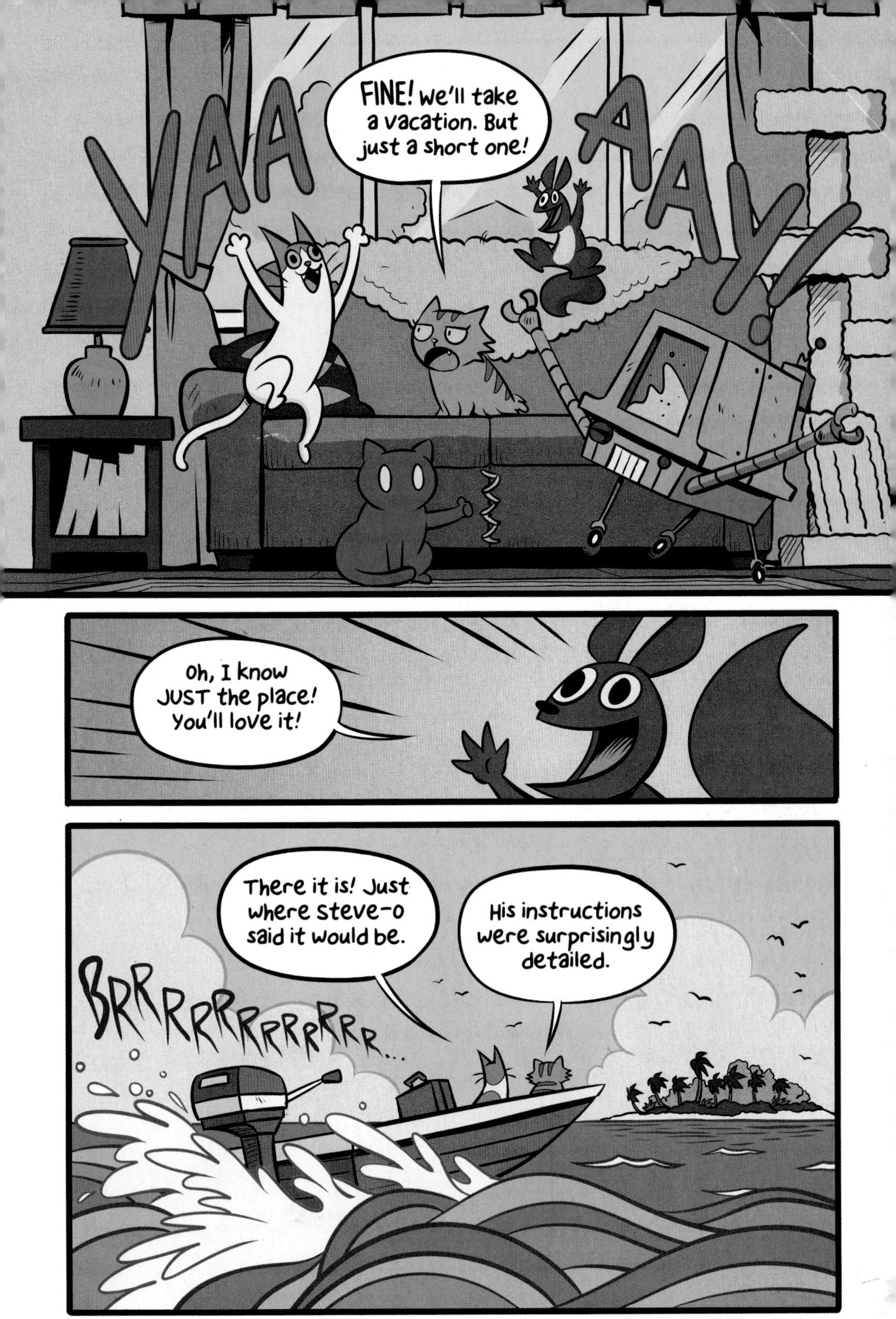
YAAAAY!!
FINE! We'll take a vacation. But just a short one!
Oh, I know JUST the place! You'll love it!
BRRRRRRRRRRRR...
There it is! Just where Steve-O said it would be.
His instructions were surprisingly detailed.

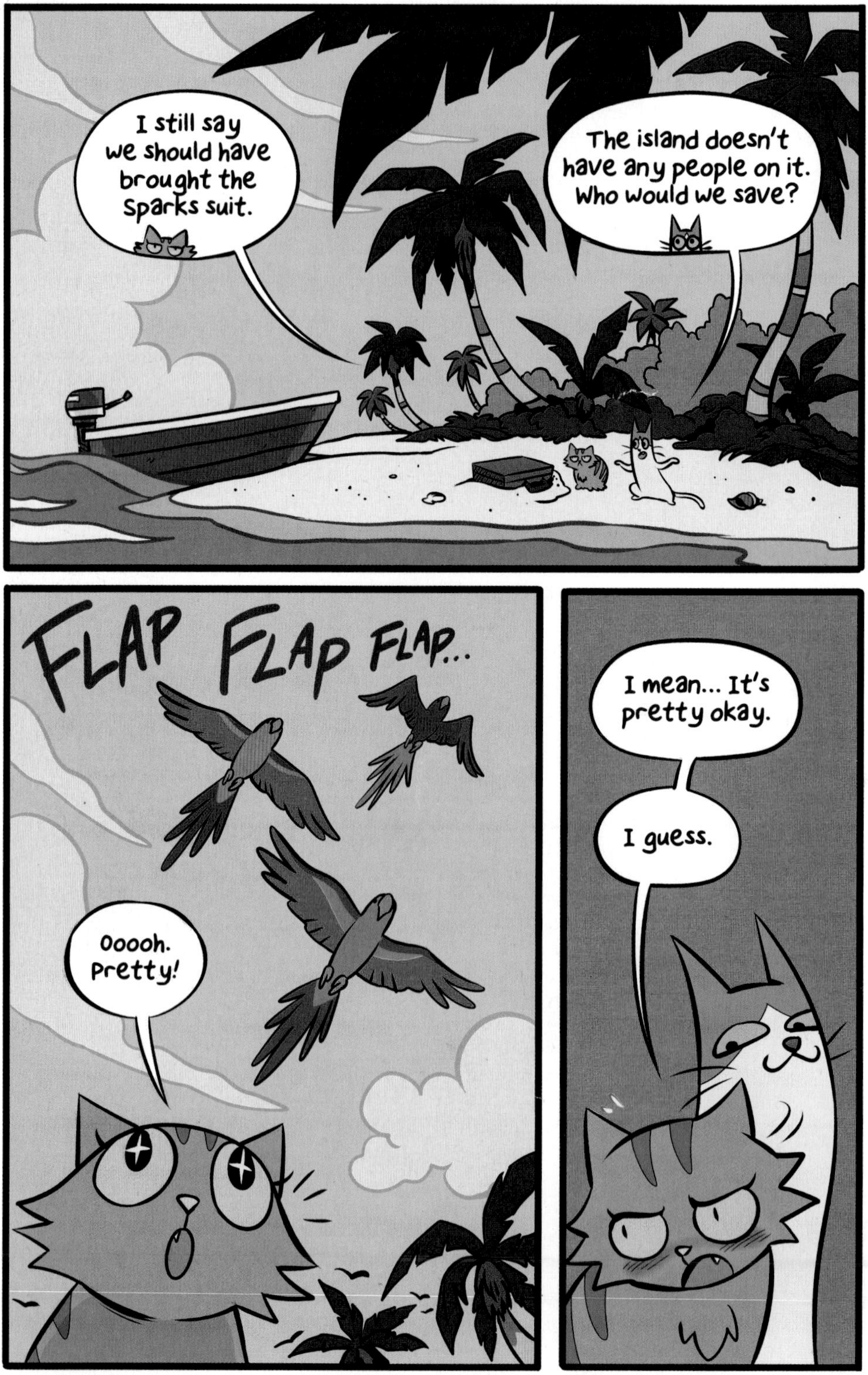
I still say we should have brought the Sparks suit.
The island doesn't have any people on it. Who would we save?
FLAP FLAP FLAP...
Ooooh. Pretty!
I mean... It's pretty okay.
I guess.

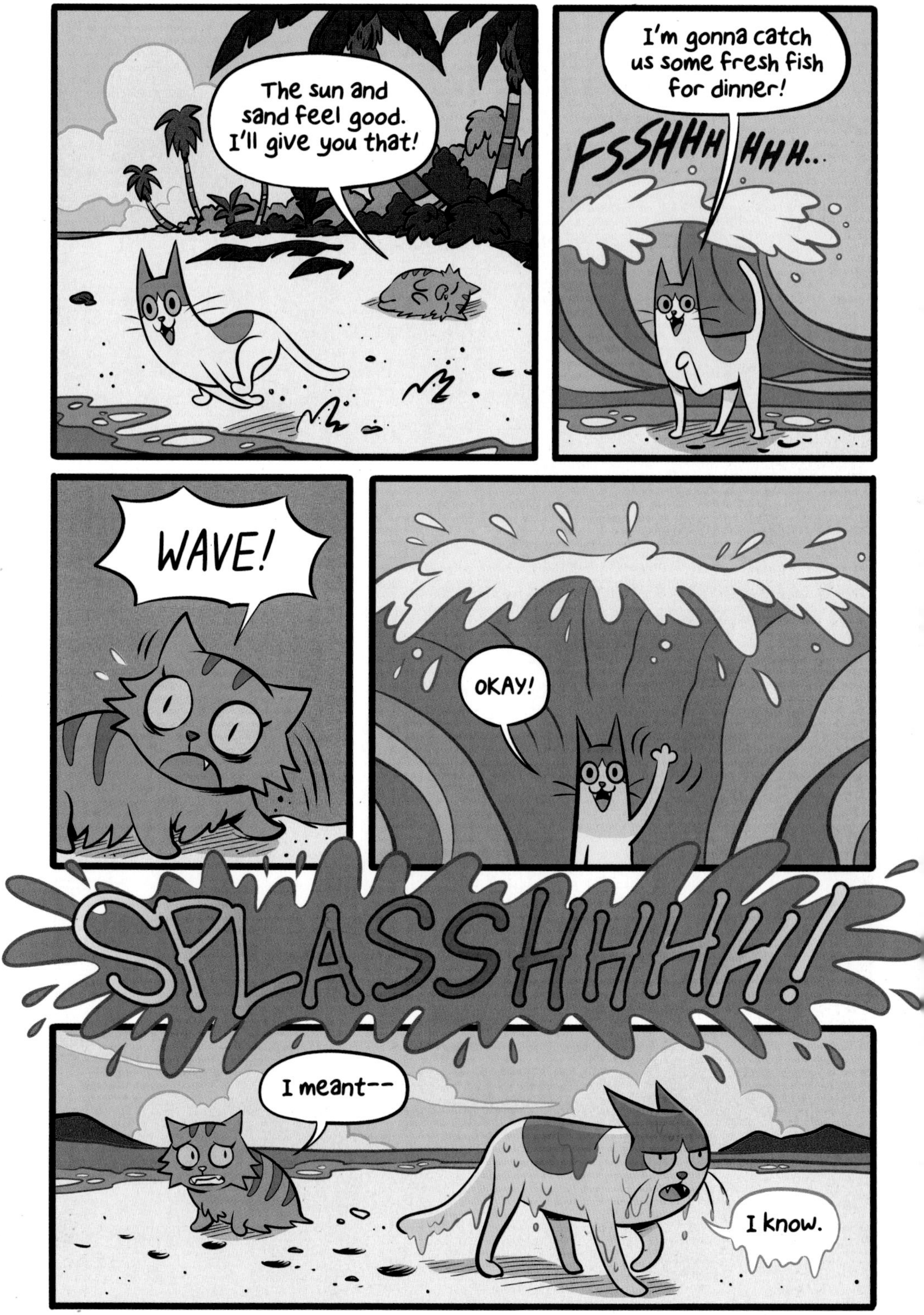
The sun and sand feel good. I'll give you that!
I'm gonna catch us some fresh fish for dinner!
FSSHHHHHH...
WAVE!
OKAY!
SPLASSHHHH!
I meant--
I know.

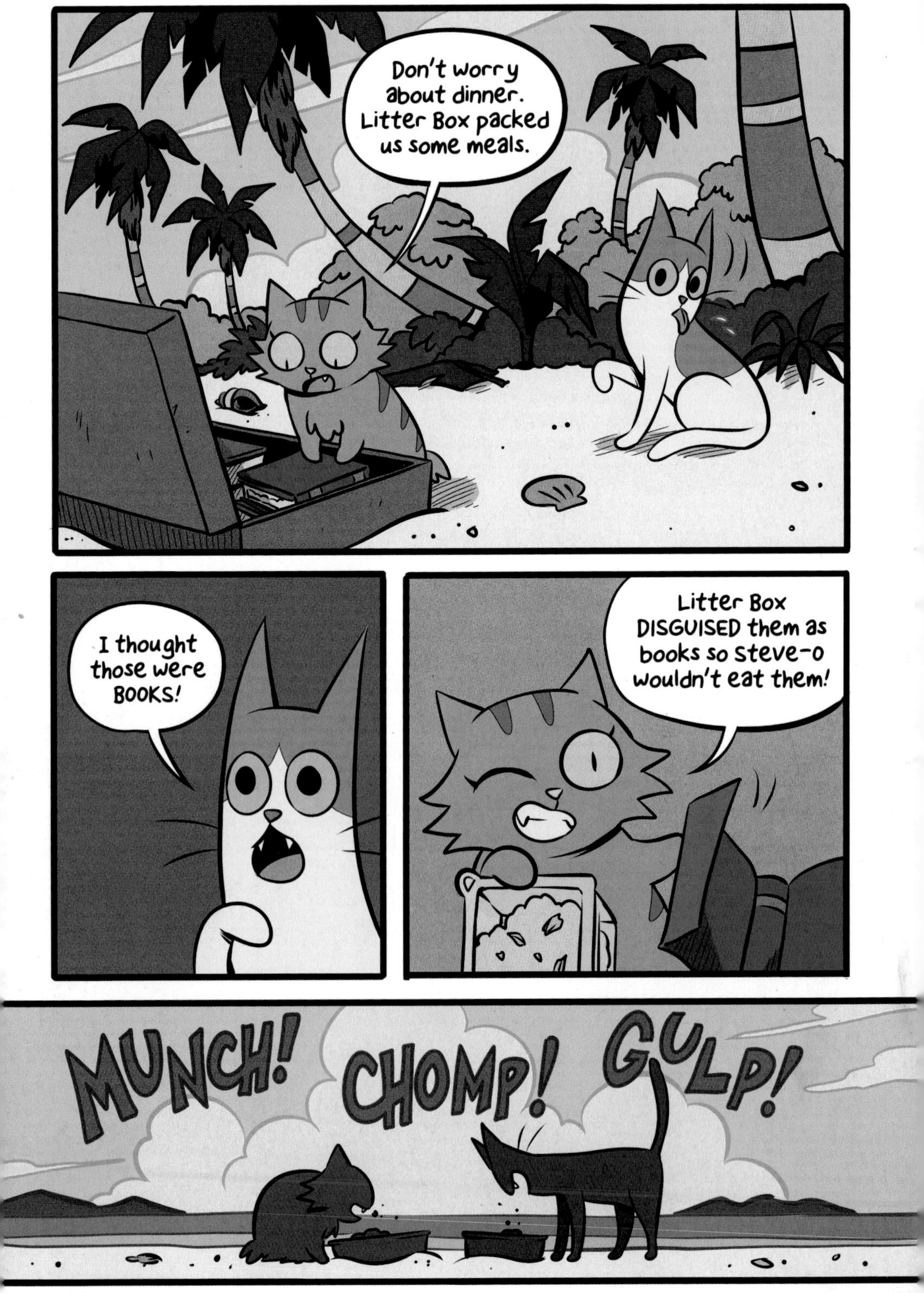
Don't worry about dinner. Litter Box packed us some meals.
I thought those were BOOKS!
Litter Box DISGUISED them as books so Steve-O wouldn't eat them!
MUNCH! CHOMP! GULP!

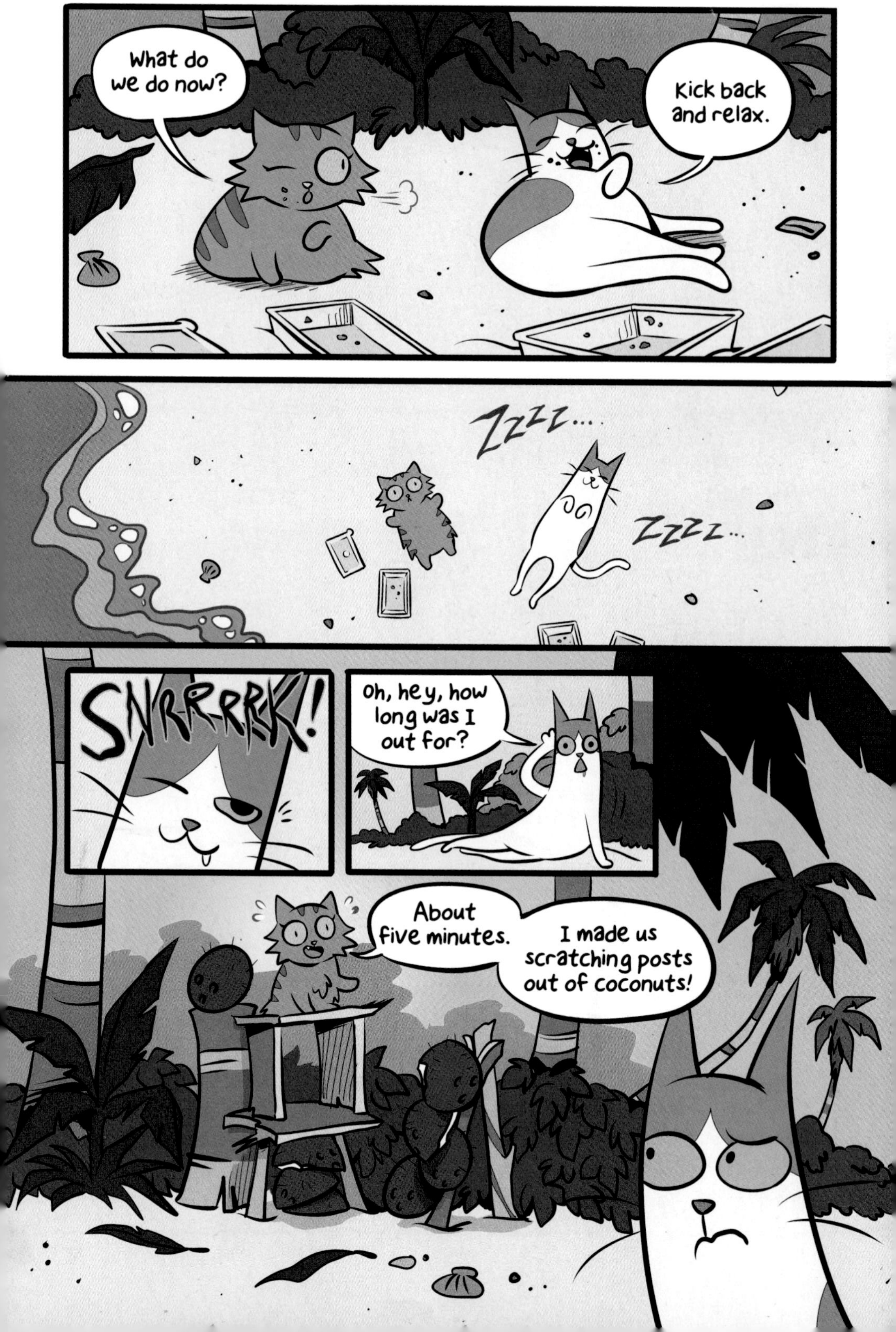
What do we do now?
Kick back and relax.
Zzzz...
Zzzz...
SNRRRRK!
Oh, hey, how long was I out for?
About five minutes.
I made us scratching posts out of coconuts!

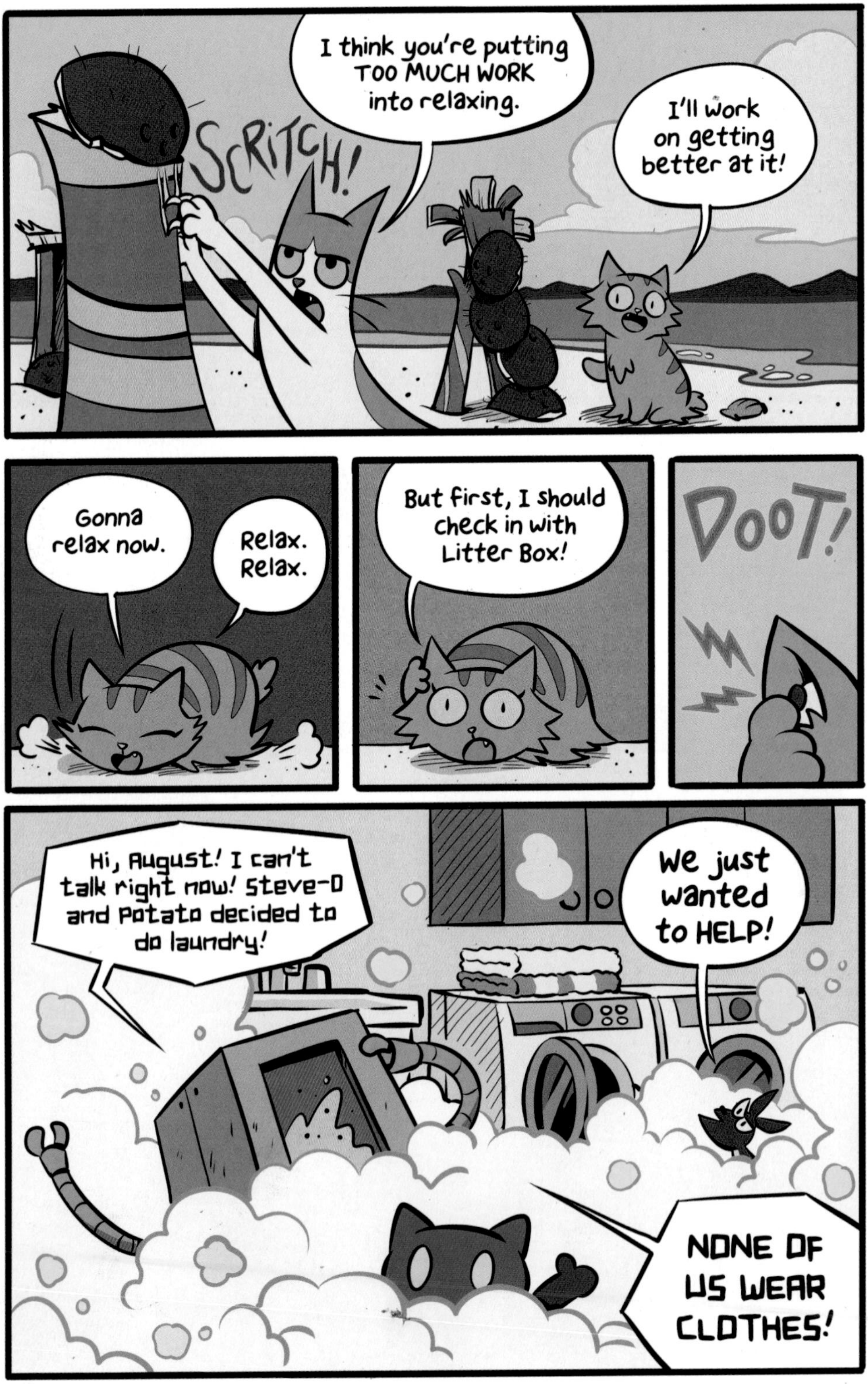

I think you're putting TOO MUCH WORK into relaxing.
SCRITCH!
I'll work on getting better at it!
Gonna relax now.
Relax. Relax.
But first, I should check in with Litter Box!
DOOT!
Hi, August! I can't talk right now! Steve-O and Potato decided to do laundry!
We just wanted to HELP!
NONE OF US WEAR CLOTHES!

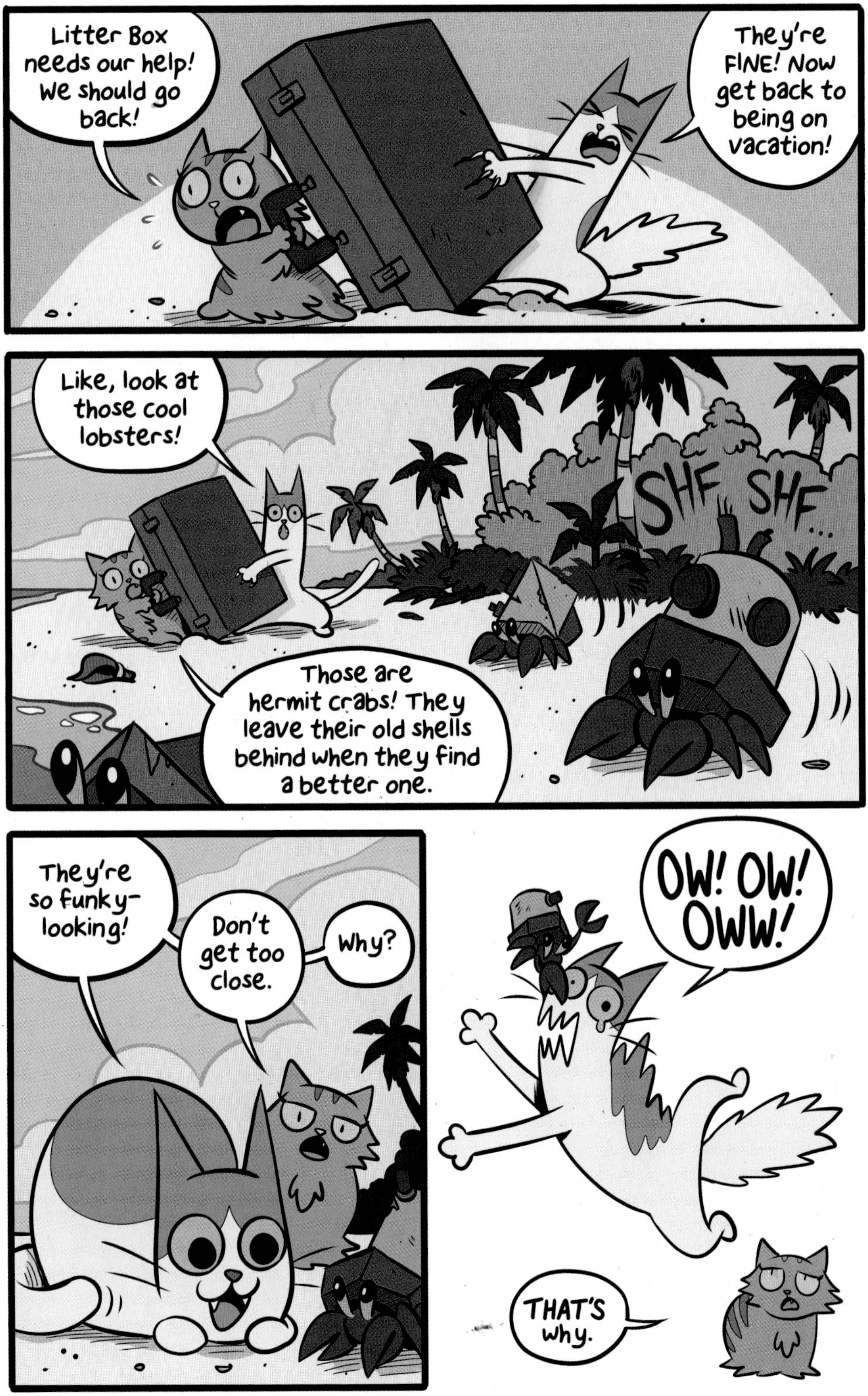
Litter Box needs our help! We should go back!
They're FINE! Now get back to being on vacation!
Like, look at those cool lobsters!
SHF SHF...
Those are hermit crabs! They leave their old shells behind when they find a better one.
They're so funky-looking!
Don't get too close.
Why?
OW! OW! OWW!
THAT'S why.

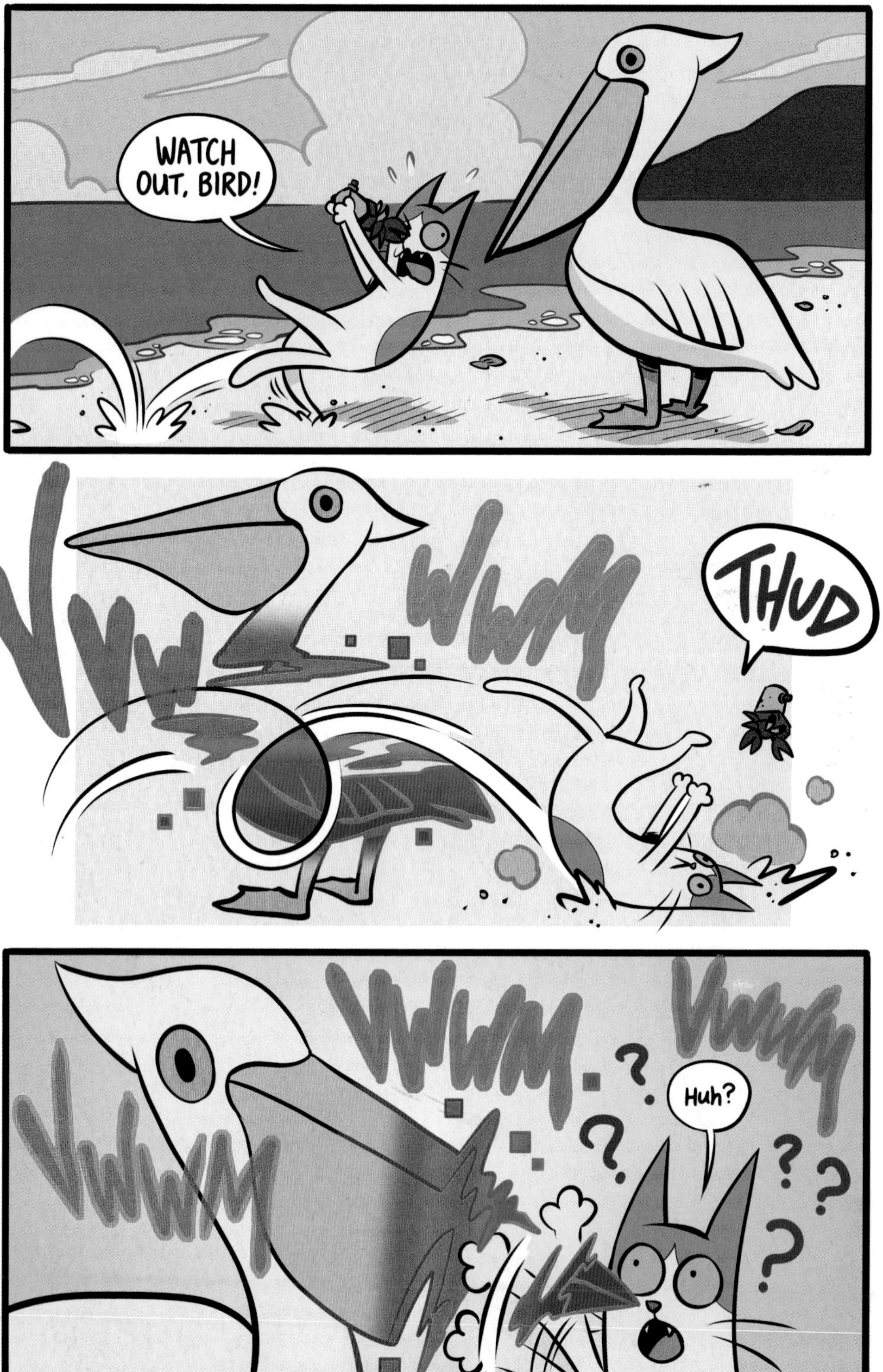
WATCH OUT, BIRD!
THUD
Huh?

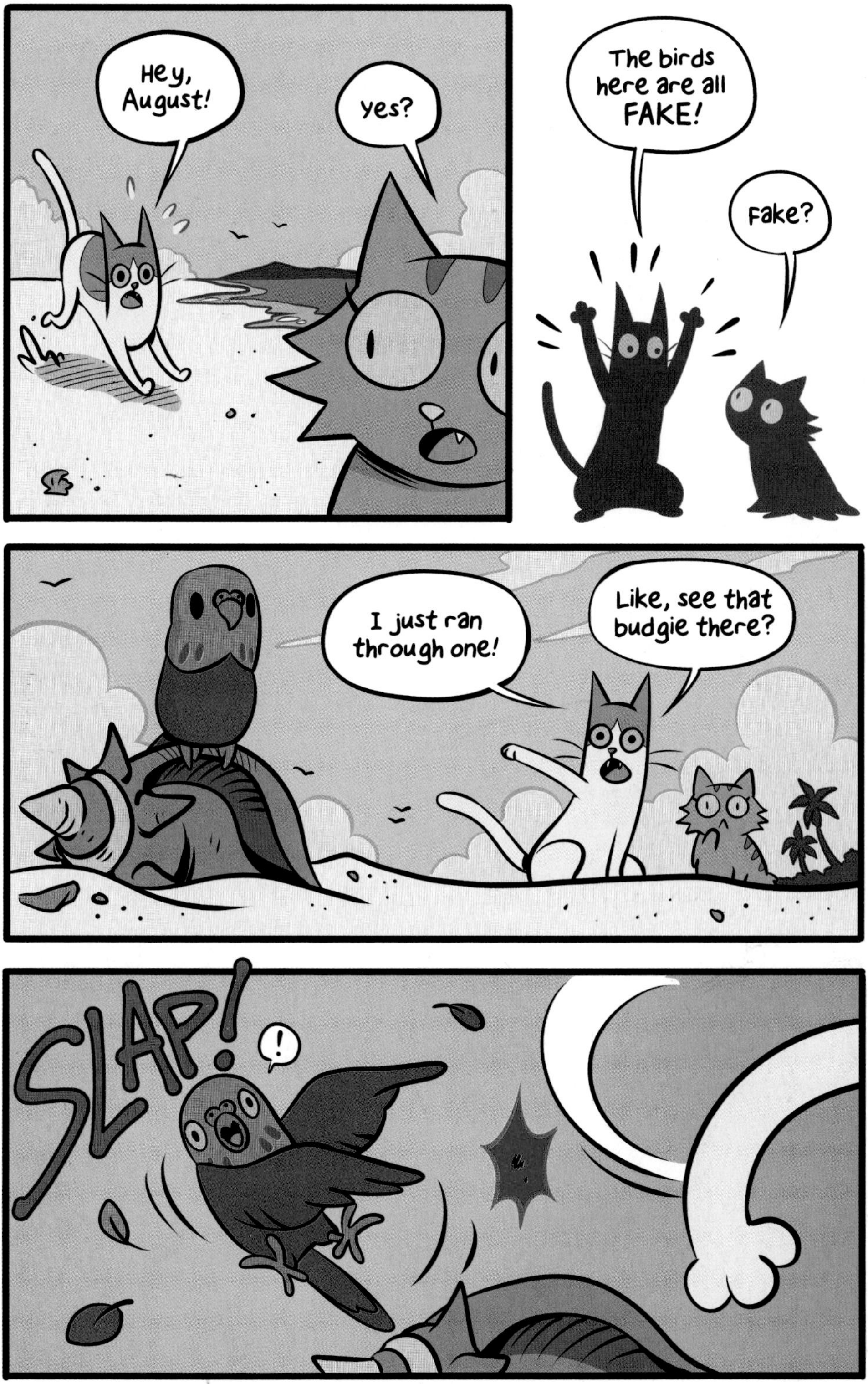
Hey, August!
yes?
The birds here are all FAKE!
Fake?
I just ran through one!
Like, see that budgie there?
SLAP!
!

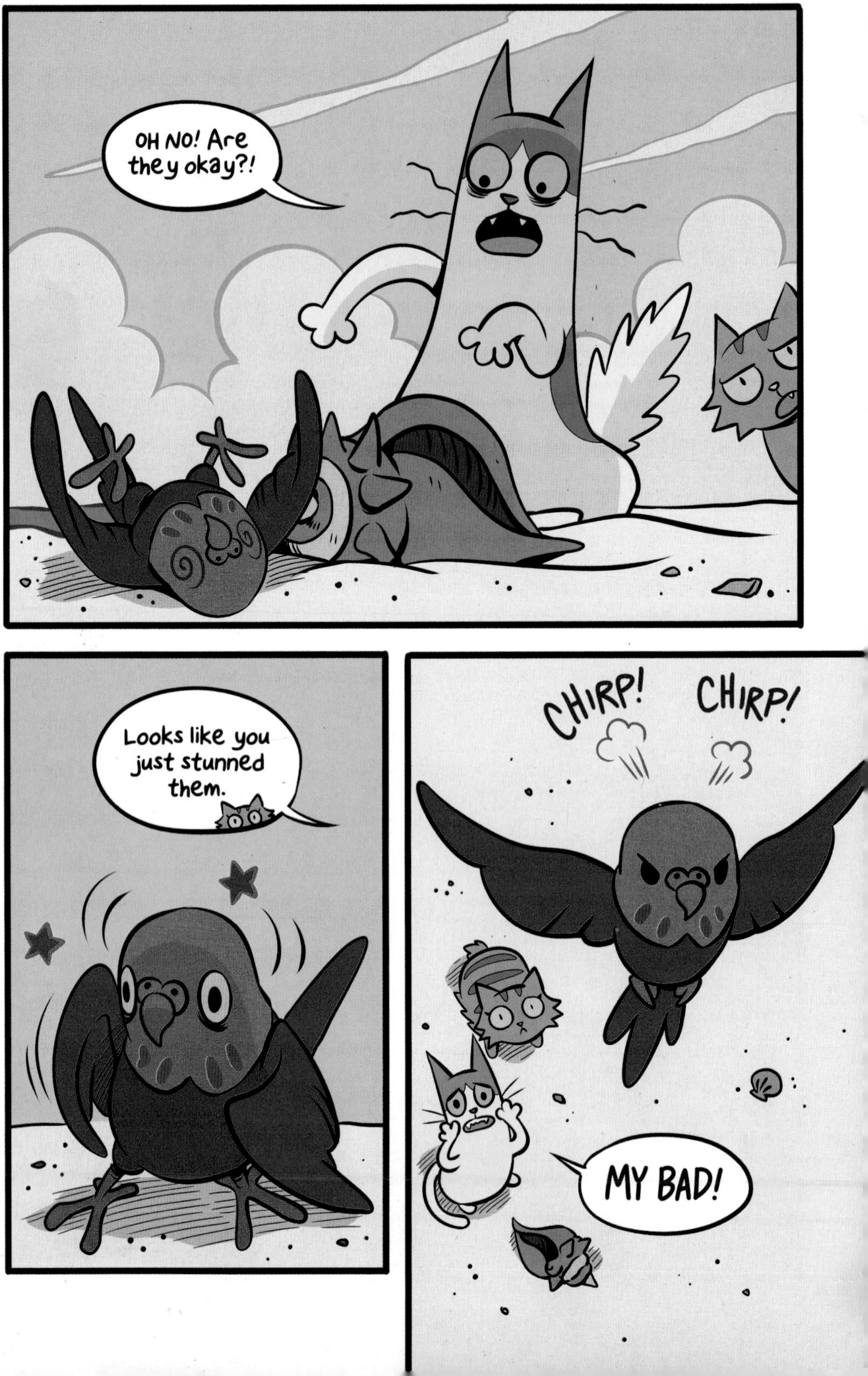
OH NO! Are they okay?!
Looks like you just stunned them.
CHIRP! CHIRP!
MY BAD!

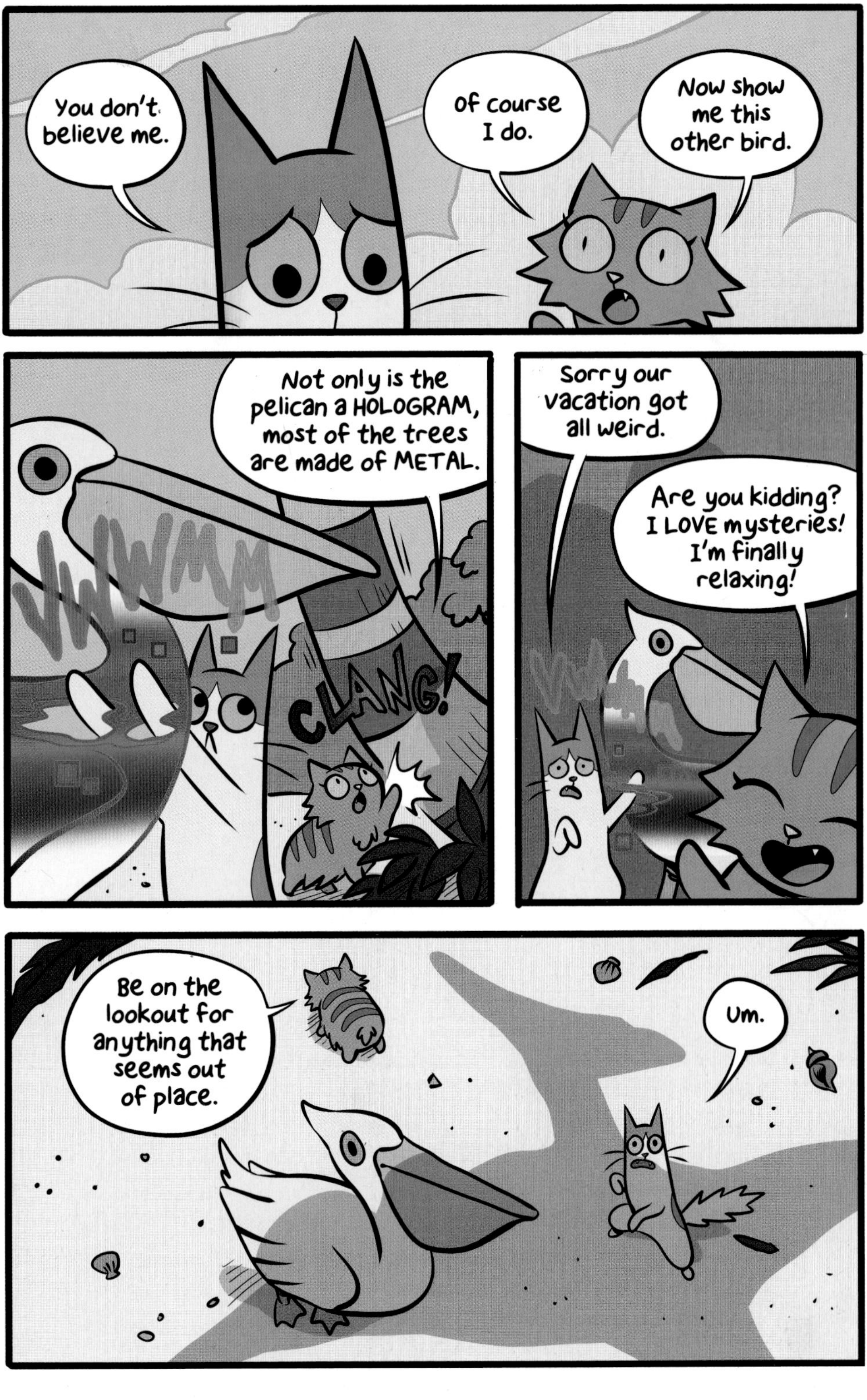
You don't believe me.
Of course I do.
Now show me this other bird.
Not only is the pelican a HOLOGRAM, most of the trees are made of METAL.
VWWMM
CLANG!
Sorry our vacation got all weird.
Are you kidding? I LOVE mysteries! I'm finally relaxing!
Be on the lookout for anything that seems out of place.
Um.

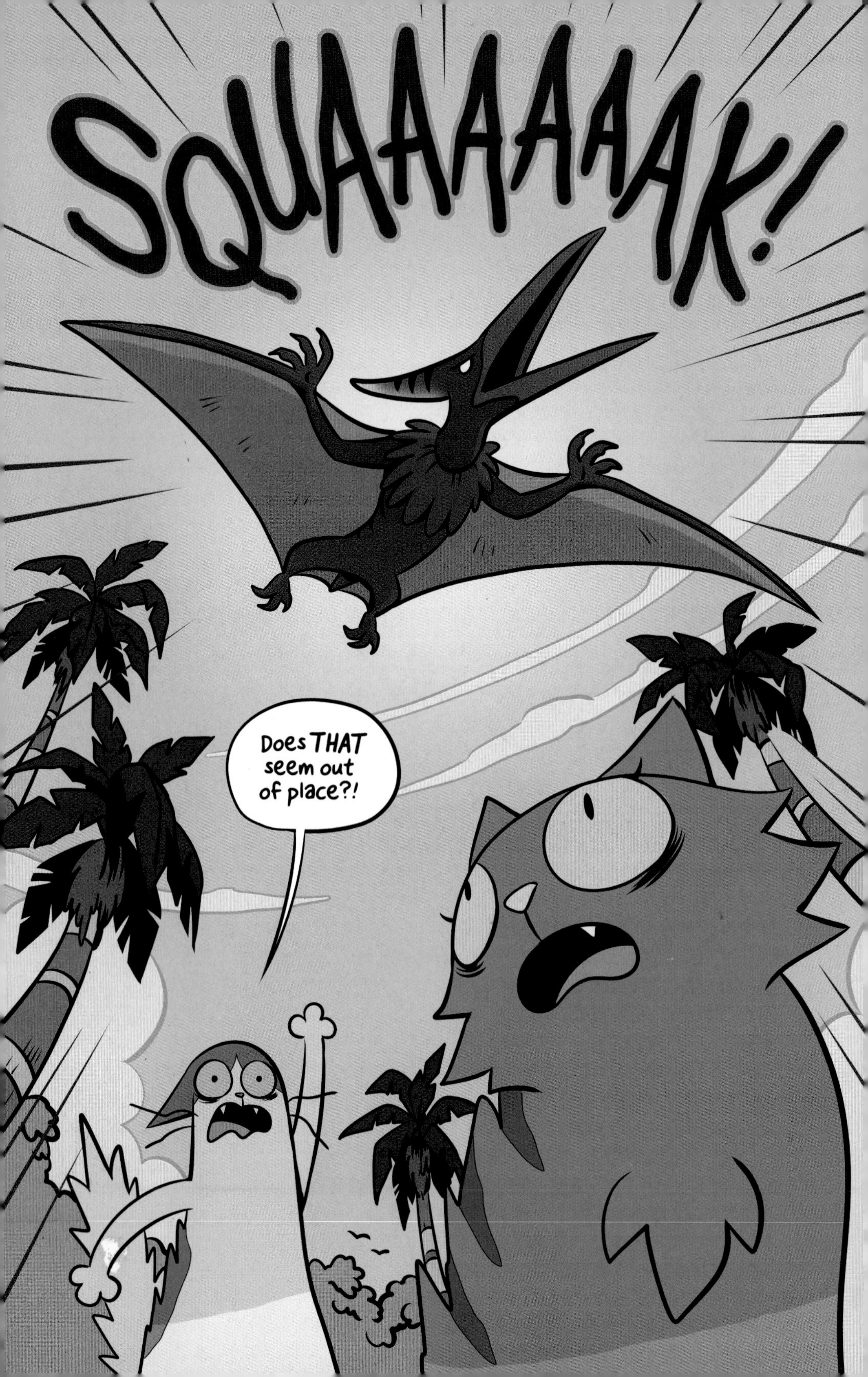
SQUAAAAAAK!
Does THAT seem out of place?!

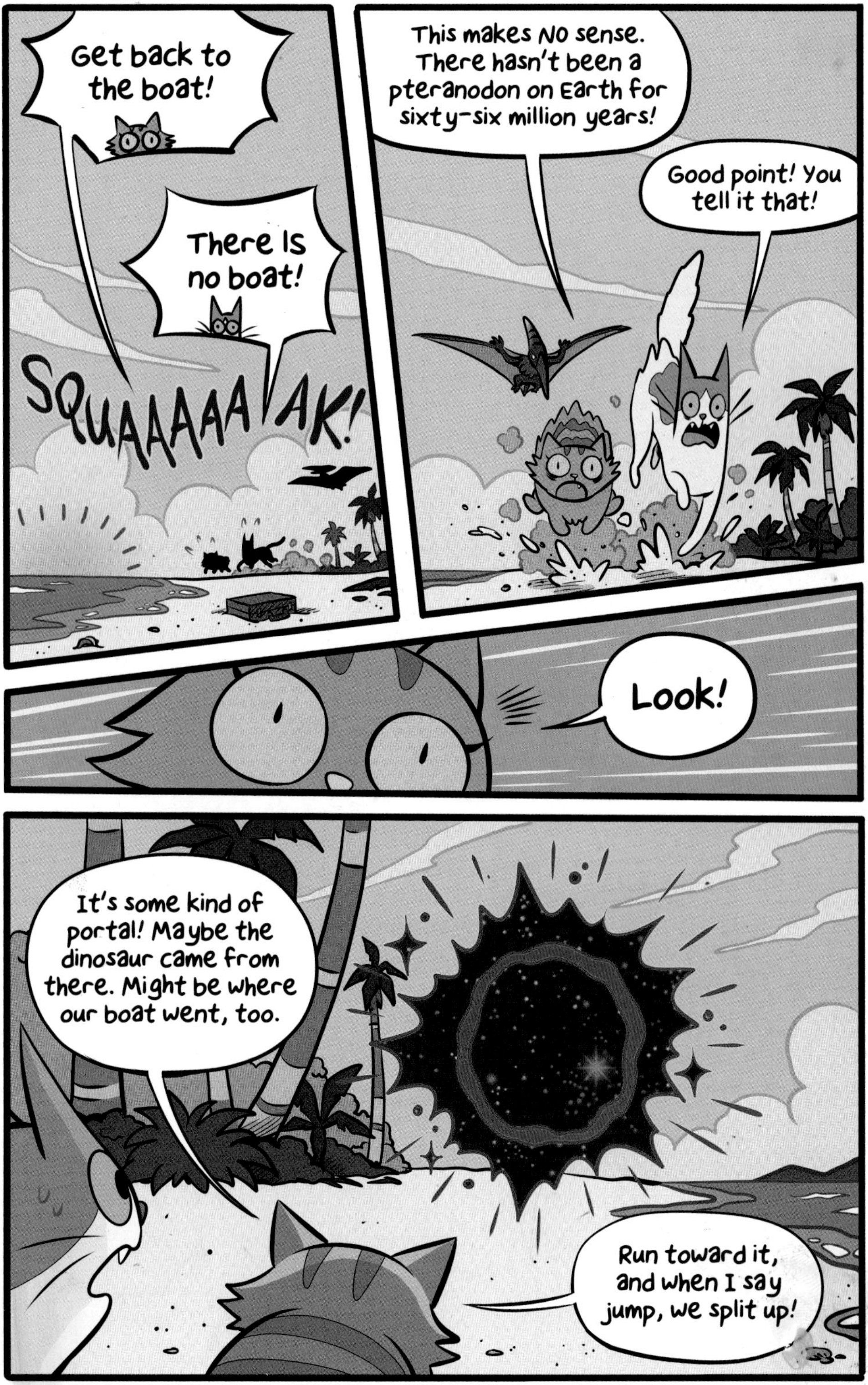
Get back to the boat!
There Is no boat!
SQUAAAAAAK!
This makes NO sense. There hasn't been a pteranodon on Earth for sixty-six million years!
Good point! You tell it that!
Look!
It's some kind of portal! Maybe the dinosaur came from there. Might be where our boat went, too.
Run toward it, and when I say jump, we split up!

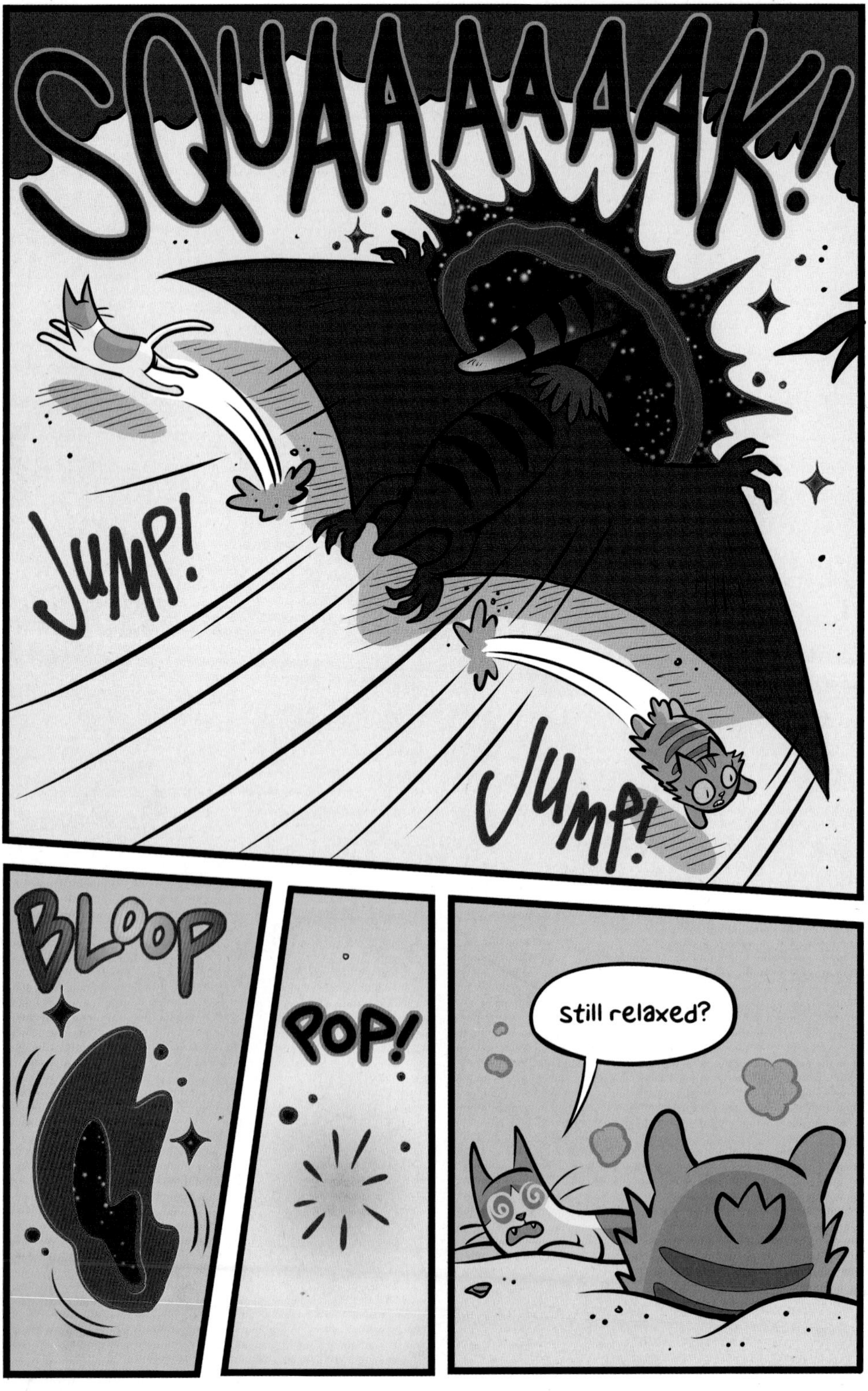
SQUAAAAAK!
JUMP!
JUMP!
BLOOP
POP!
still relaxed?

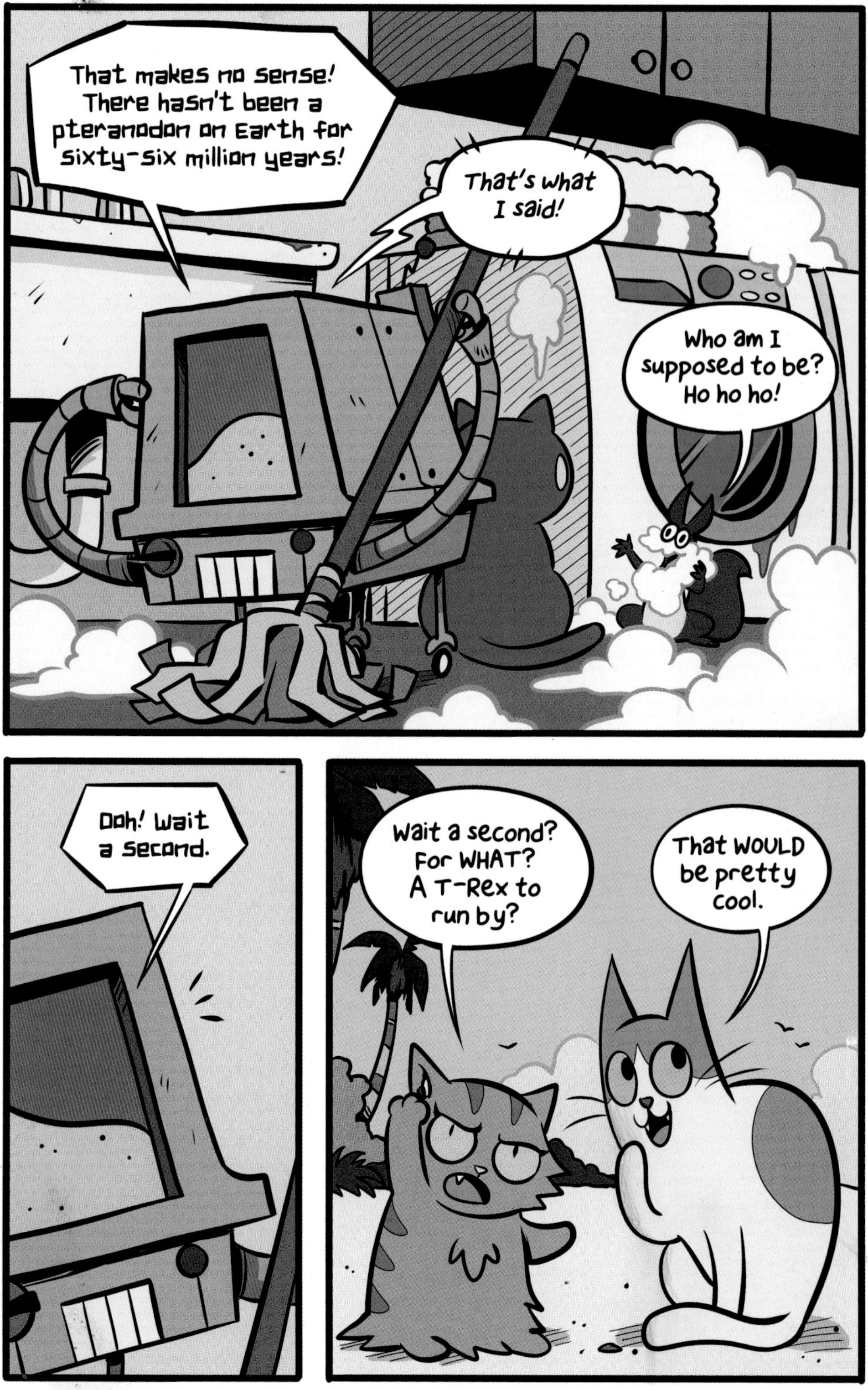

That makes no sense! There hasn't been a pteranodon on Earth for sixty-six million years!
That's what I said!
Who am I supposed to be? Ho ho ho!
Ooh! Wait a second.
Wait a second? For WHAT? A T-Rex to run by?
That WOULD be pretty cool.

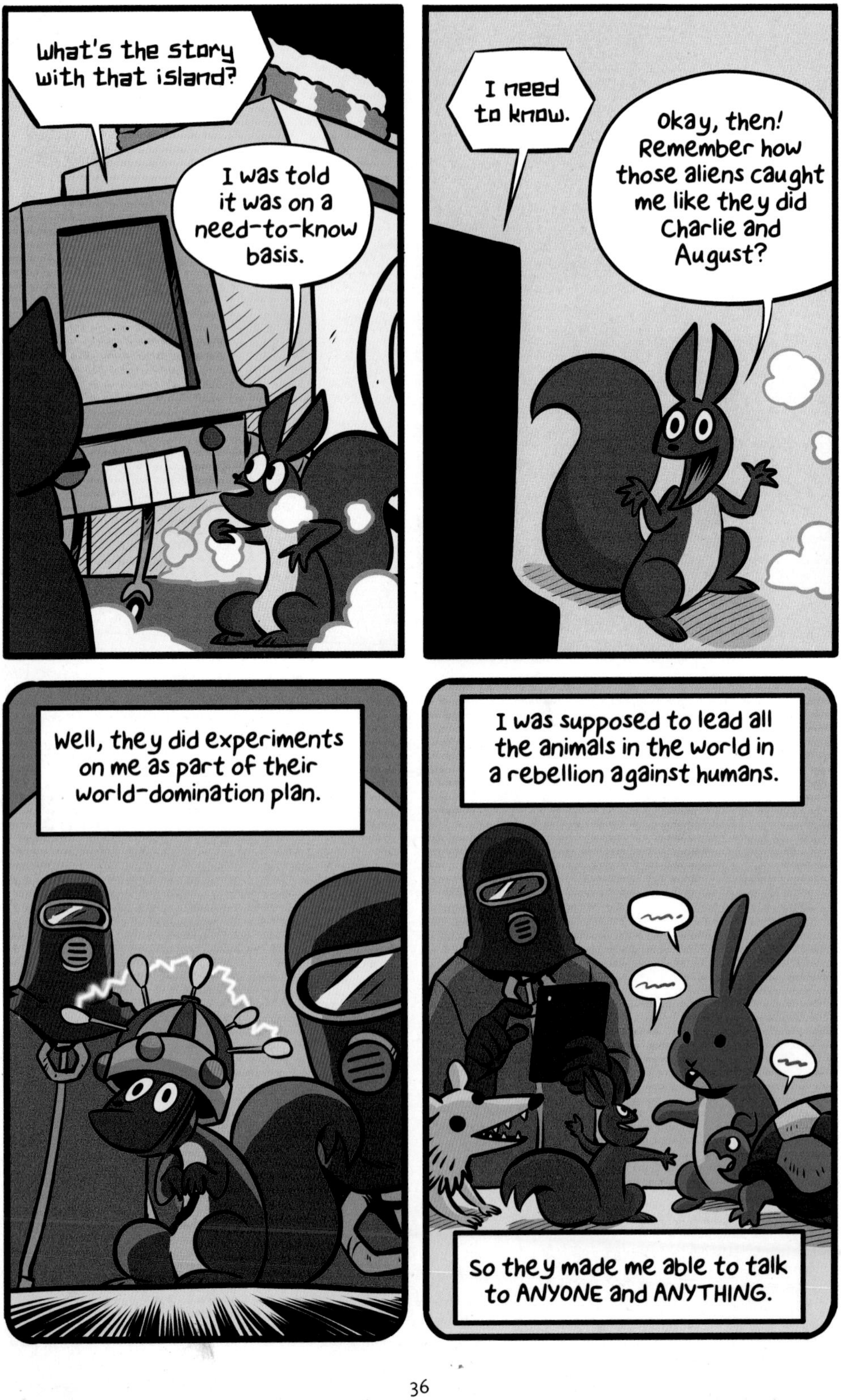
What's the story with that island?
I was told it was on a need-to-know basis.
I need to know.
Okay, then! Remember how those aliens caught me like they did Charlie and August?
Well, they did experiments on me as part of their world-domination plan.
I was supposed to lead all the animals in the world in a rebellion against humans.
So they made me able to talk to ANYONE and ANYTHING.

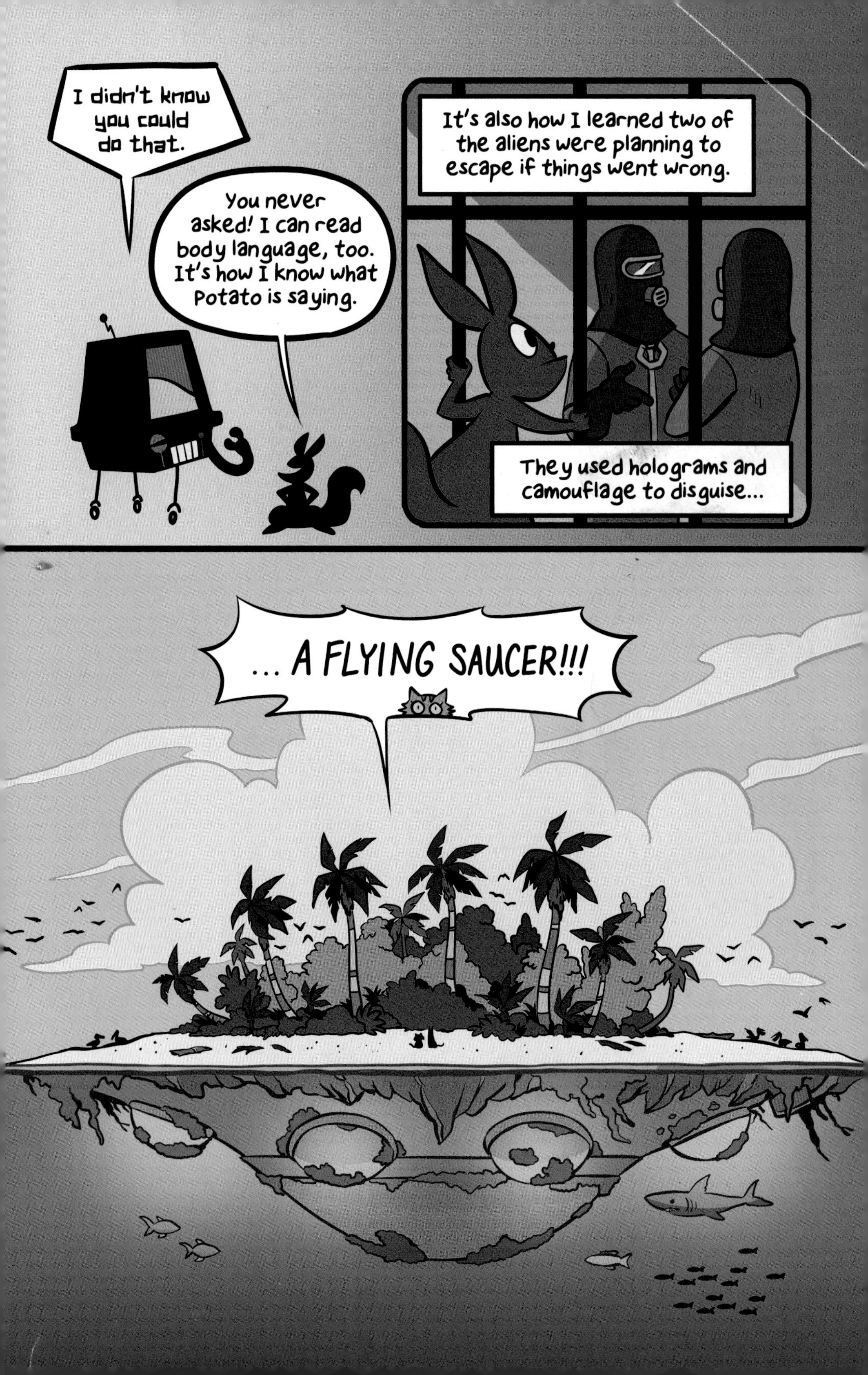
I didn't know you could do that.
You never asked! I can read body language, too. It's how I know what Potato is saying.
It's also how I learned two of the aliens were planning to escape if things went wrong.
They used holograms and camouflage to disguise...
... A FLYING SAUCER!!!

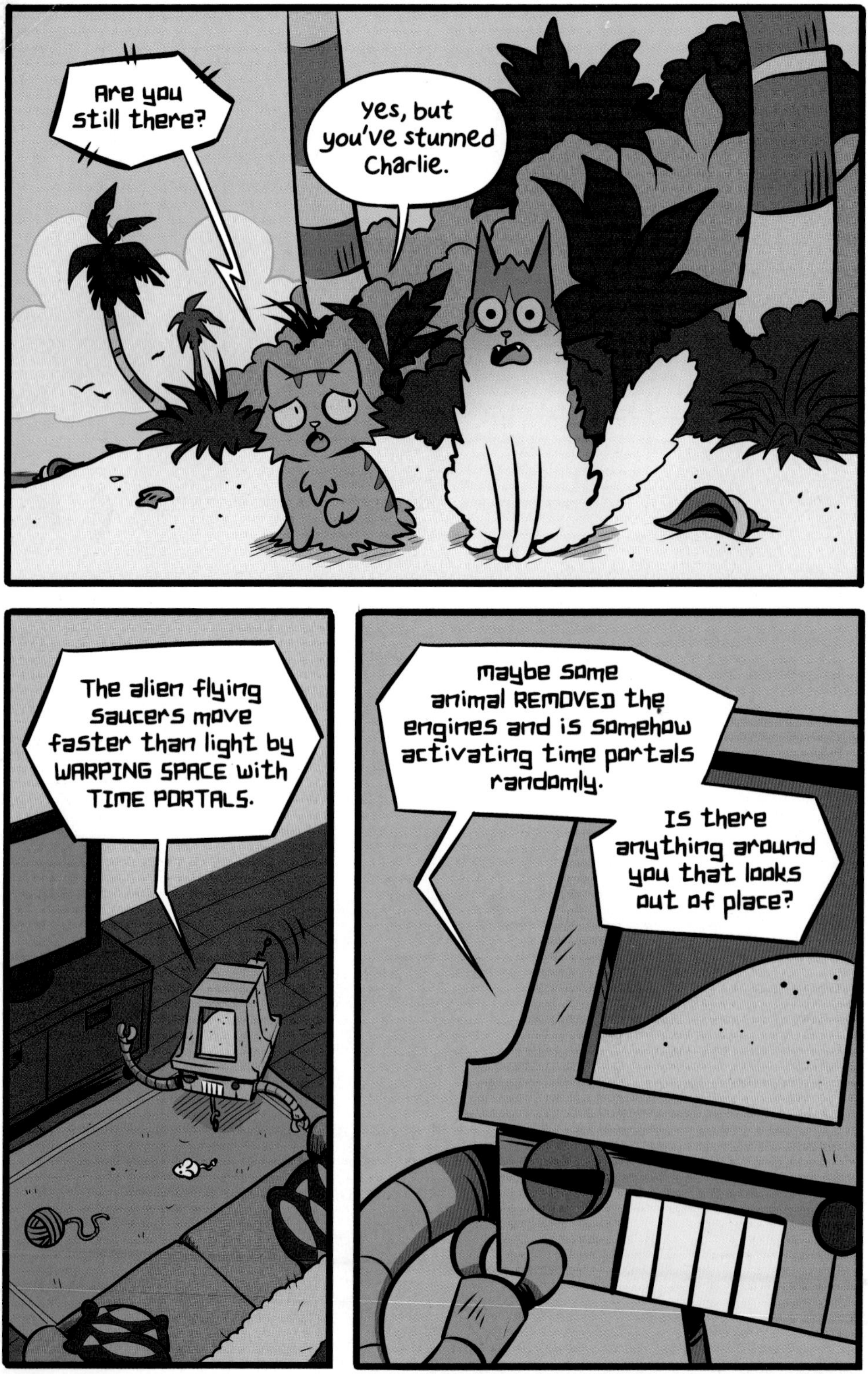
Are you still there?
yes, but you've stunned Charlie.
The alien flying saucers move faster than light by WARPING SPACE with TIME PORTALS.
maybe some animal REMOVED the engines and is somehow activating time portals randomly.
Is there anything around you that looks out of place?

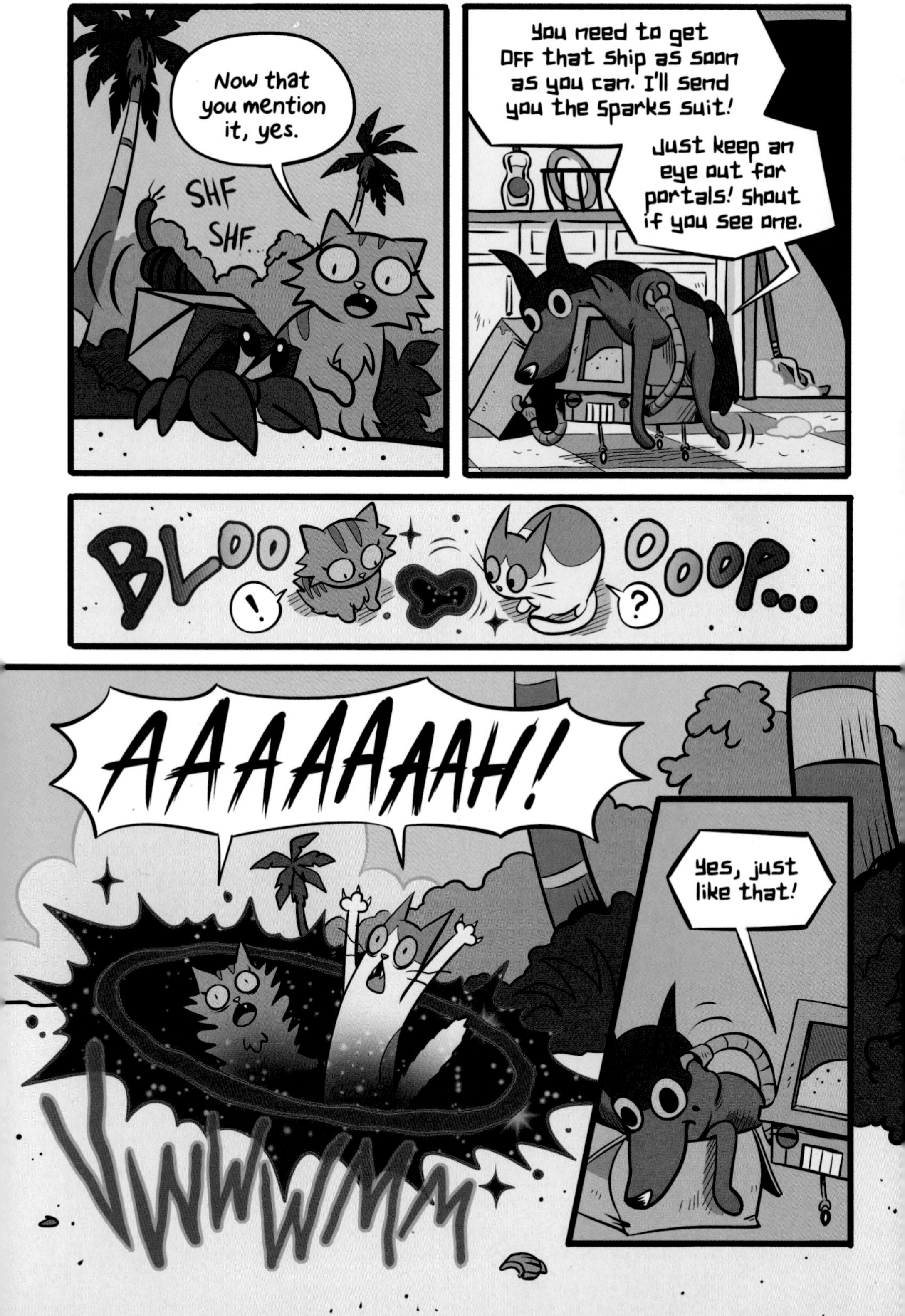
Now that you mention it, yes.
SHF
SHF...
You need to get OFF that ship as soon as you can. I'll send you the Sparks suit!
Just keep an eye out for portals! Shout if you see one.
BLOO
!
?
OOOP...
AAAAAAAAH!
VWWWMM
Yes, just like that!

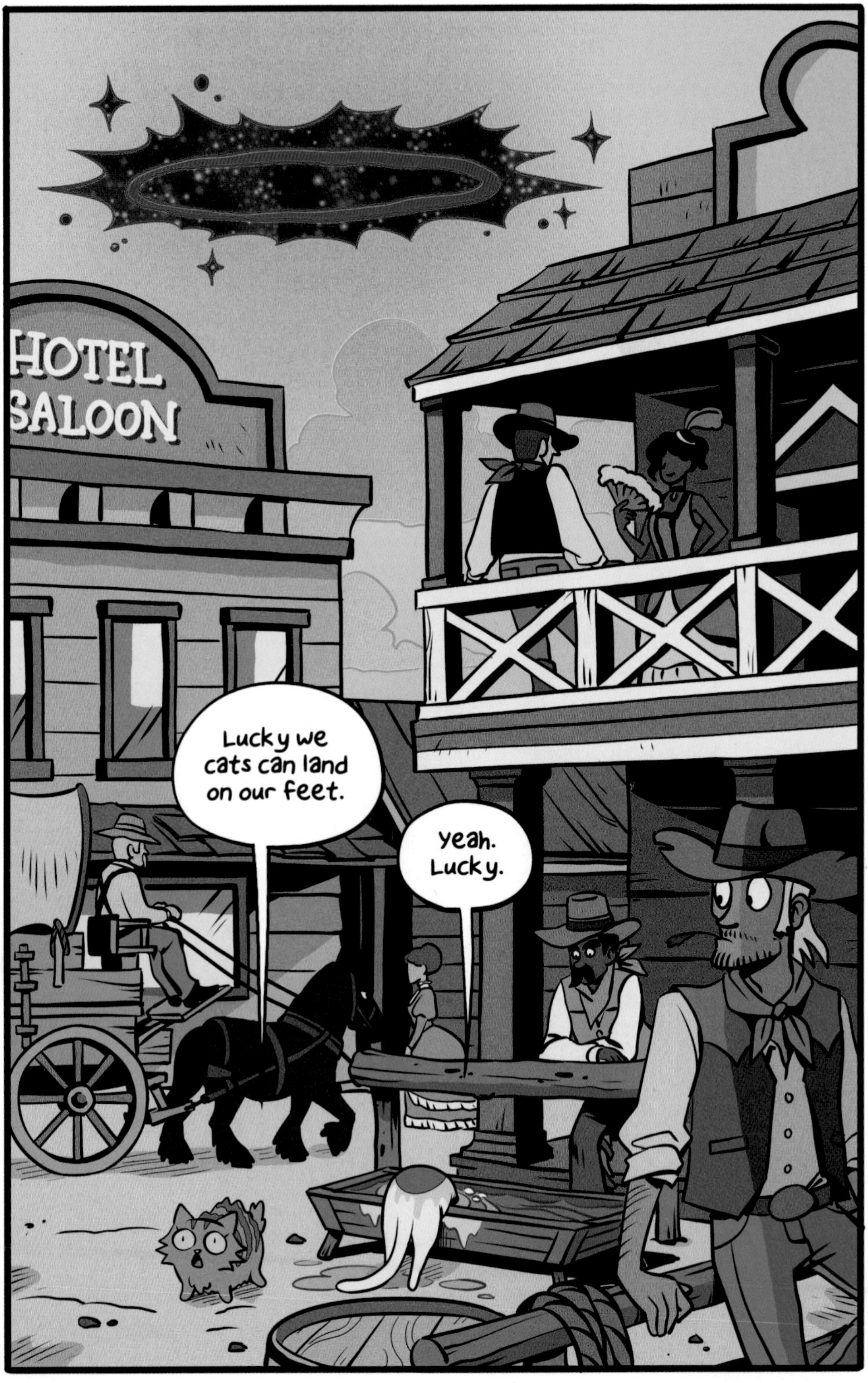

HOTEL
SALOON
Lucky we cats can land on our feet.
yeah. Lucky.

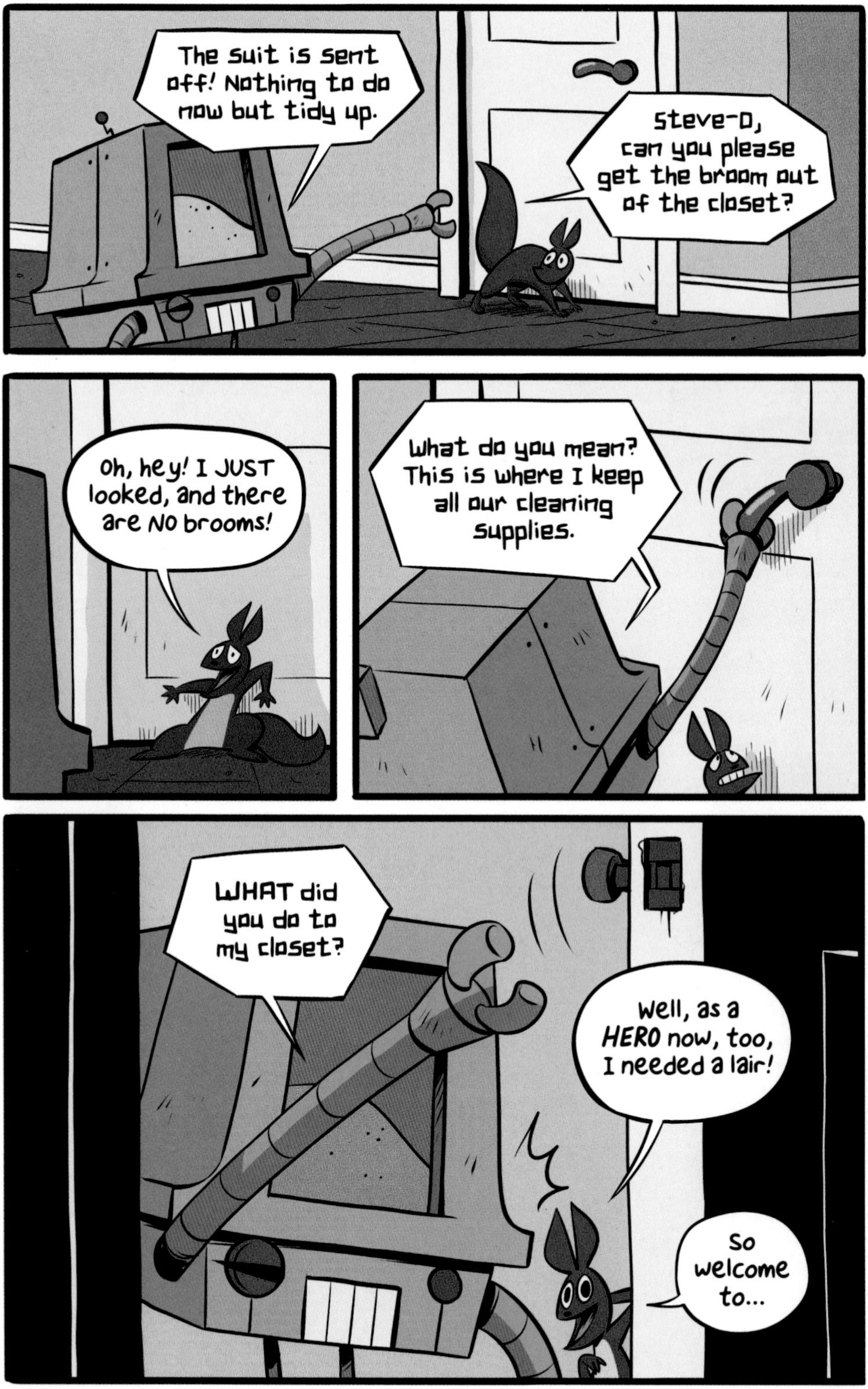
The suit is sent off! Nothing to do now but tidy up.
Steve-D, can you please get the broom out of the closet?
Oh, hey! I JUST looked, and there are NO brooms!
What do you mean? This is where I keep all our cleaning supplies.
WHAT did you do to my closet?
Well, as a HERO now, too, I needed a lair!
So welcome to...

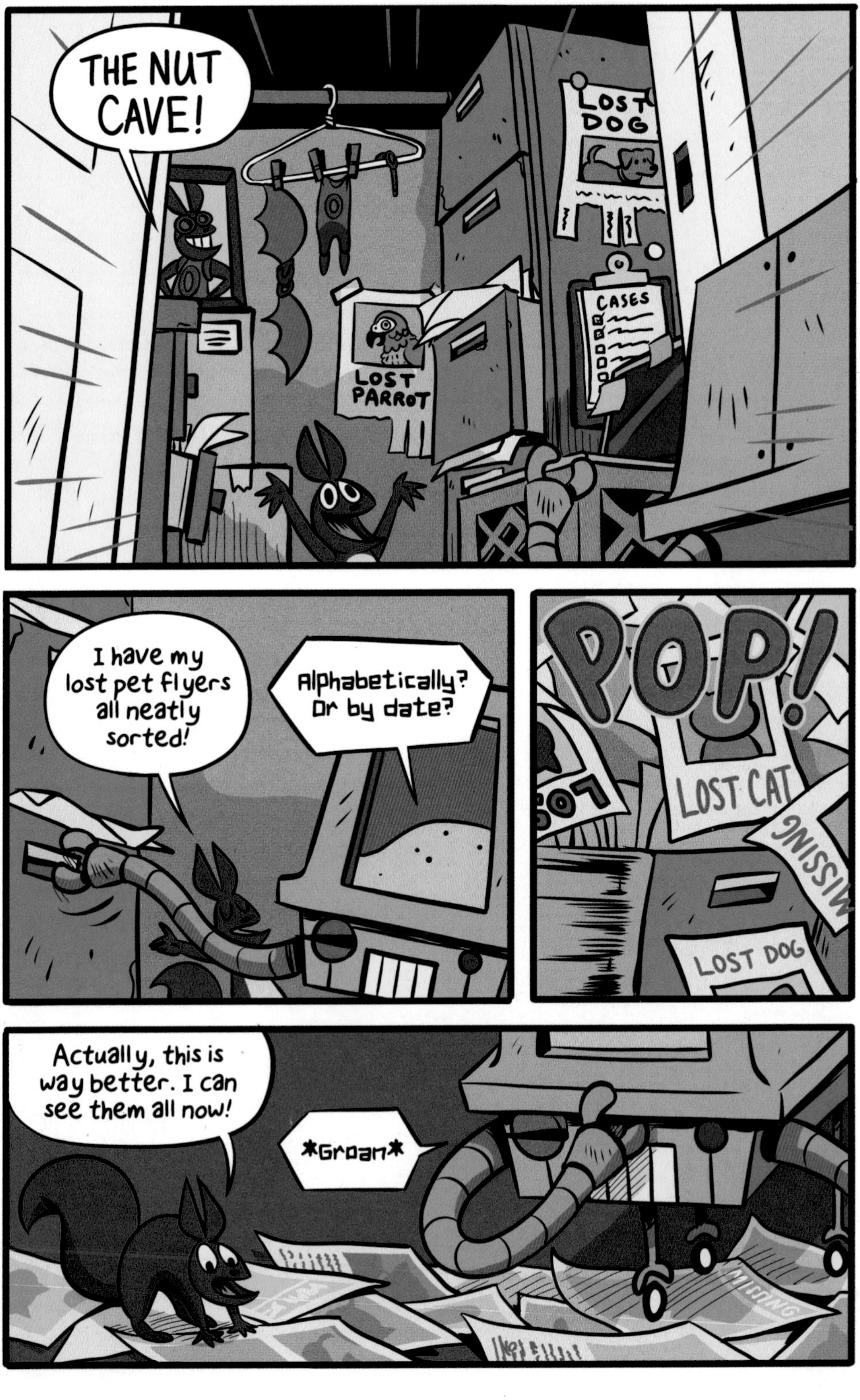
THE NUT CAVE!
LOST DOG
CASES
LOST PARROT
I have my lost pet flyers all neatly sorted!
Alphabetically? Or by date?
POP!
LOST CAT
MISSING
LOST DOG
Actually, this is way better. I can see them all now!
Groan
MISSING

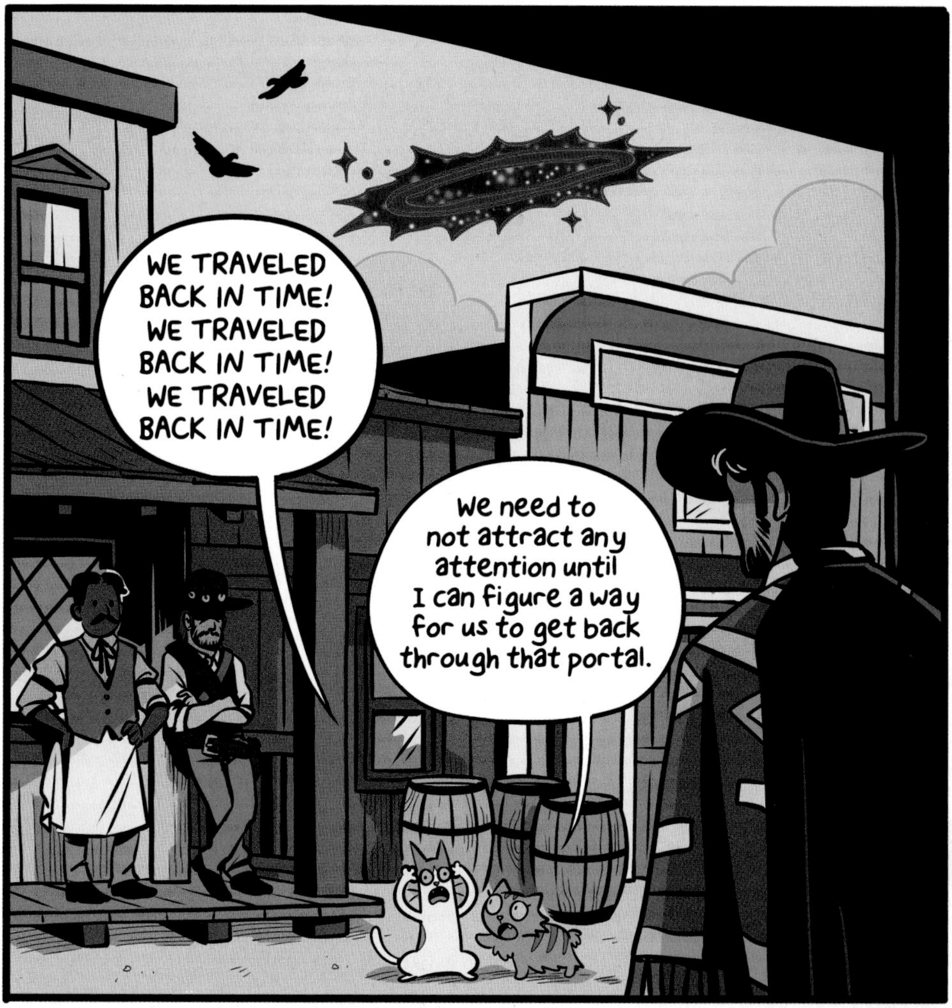
WE TRAVELED BACK IN TIME! WE TRAVELED BACK IN TIME! WE TRAVELED BACK IN TIME!
We need to not attract any attention until I can figure a way for us to get back through that portal.

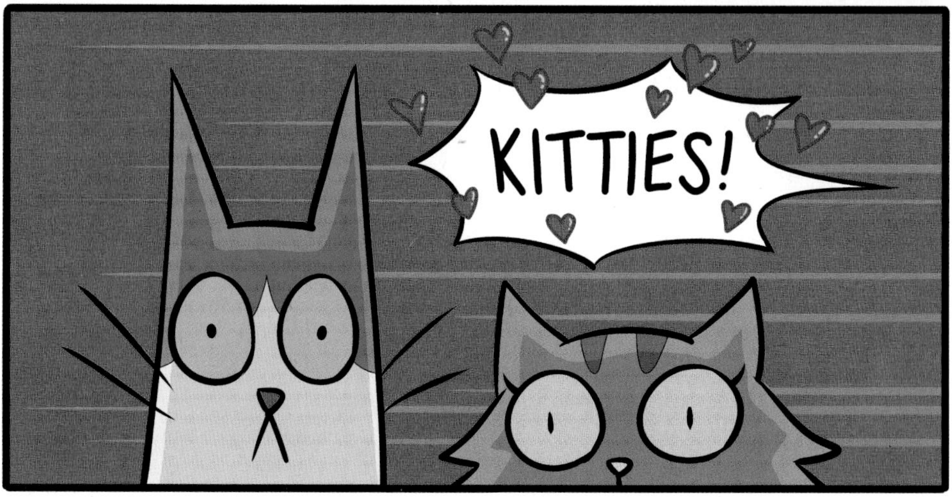
KITTIES!

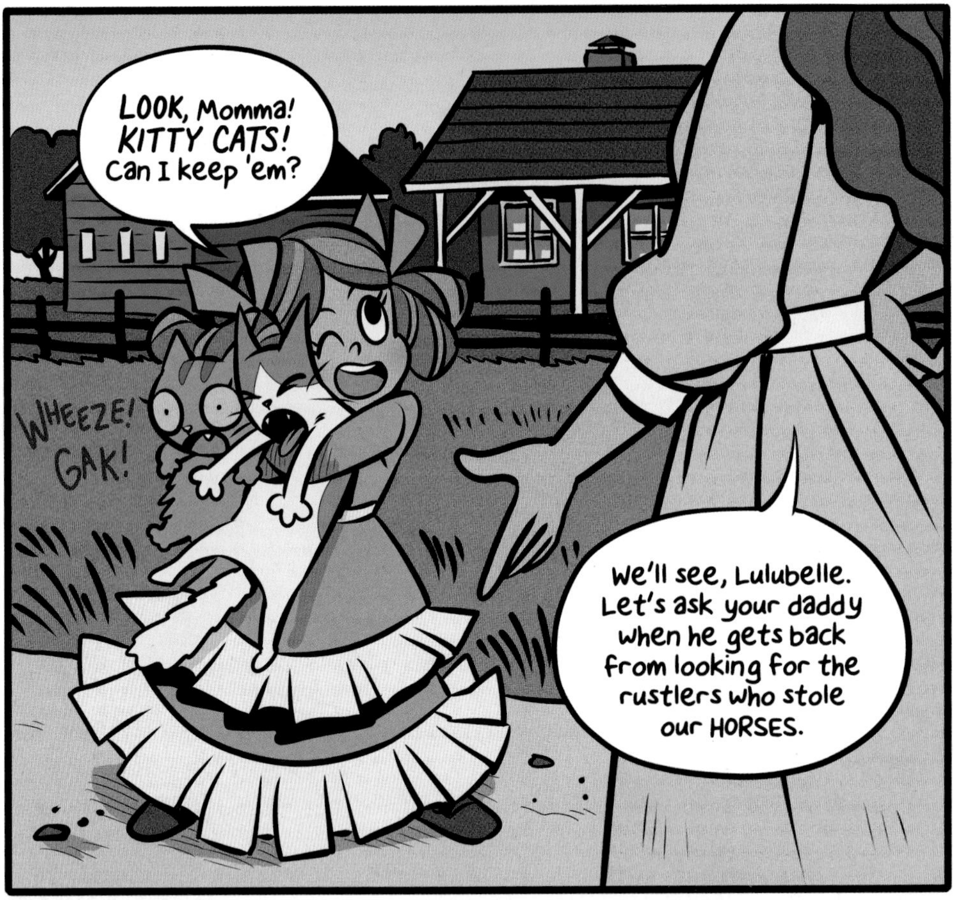
LOOK, Momma! KITTY CATS! Can I keep 'em?
WHEEZE! GAK!
We'll see, Lulubelle. Let's ask your daddy when he gets back from looking for the rustlers who stole our HORSES.

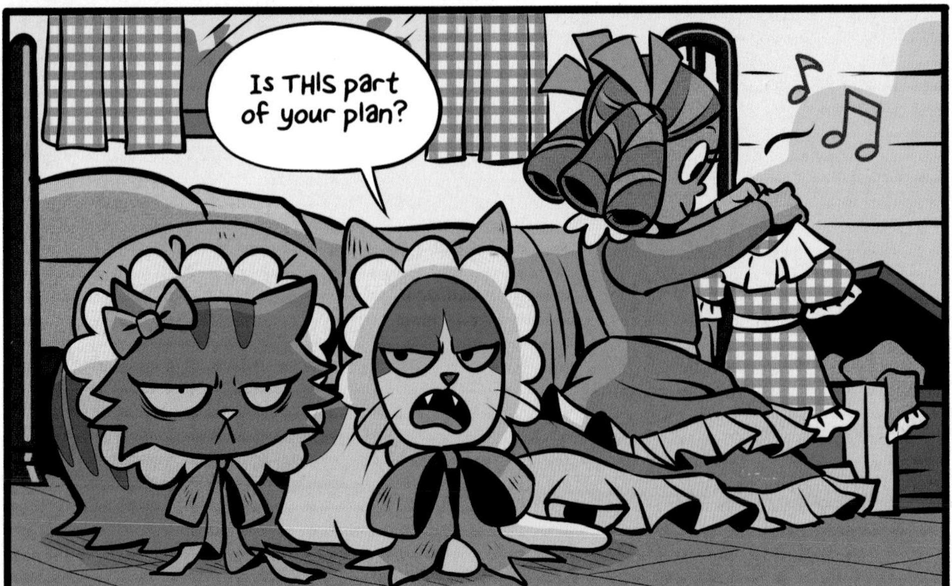
Is THIS part of your plan?

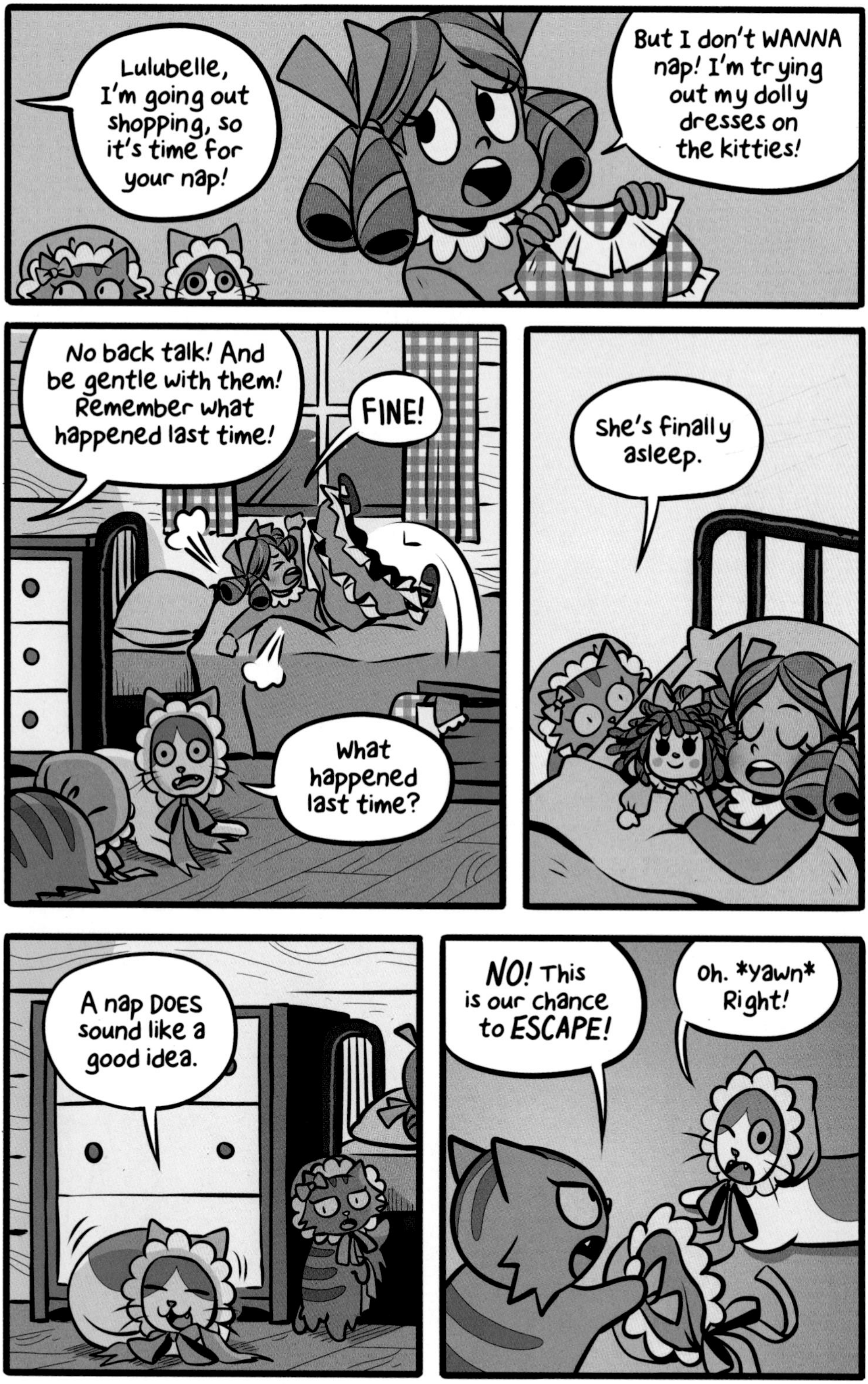
Lulubelle, I'm going out shopping, so it's time for your nap!
But I don't WANNA nap! I'm trying out my dolly dresses on the kitties!
No back talk! And be gentle with them! Remember what happened last time!
FINE!
What happened last time?
She's finally asleep.
A nap DOES sound like a good idea.
NO! This is our chance to ESCAPE!
Oh. *yawn* Right!

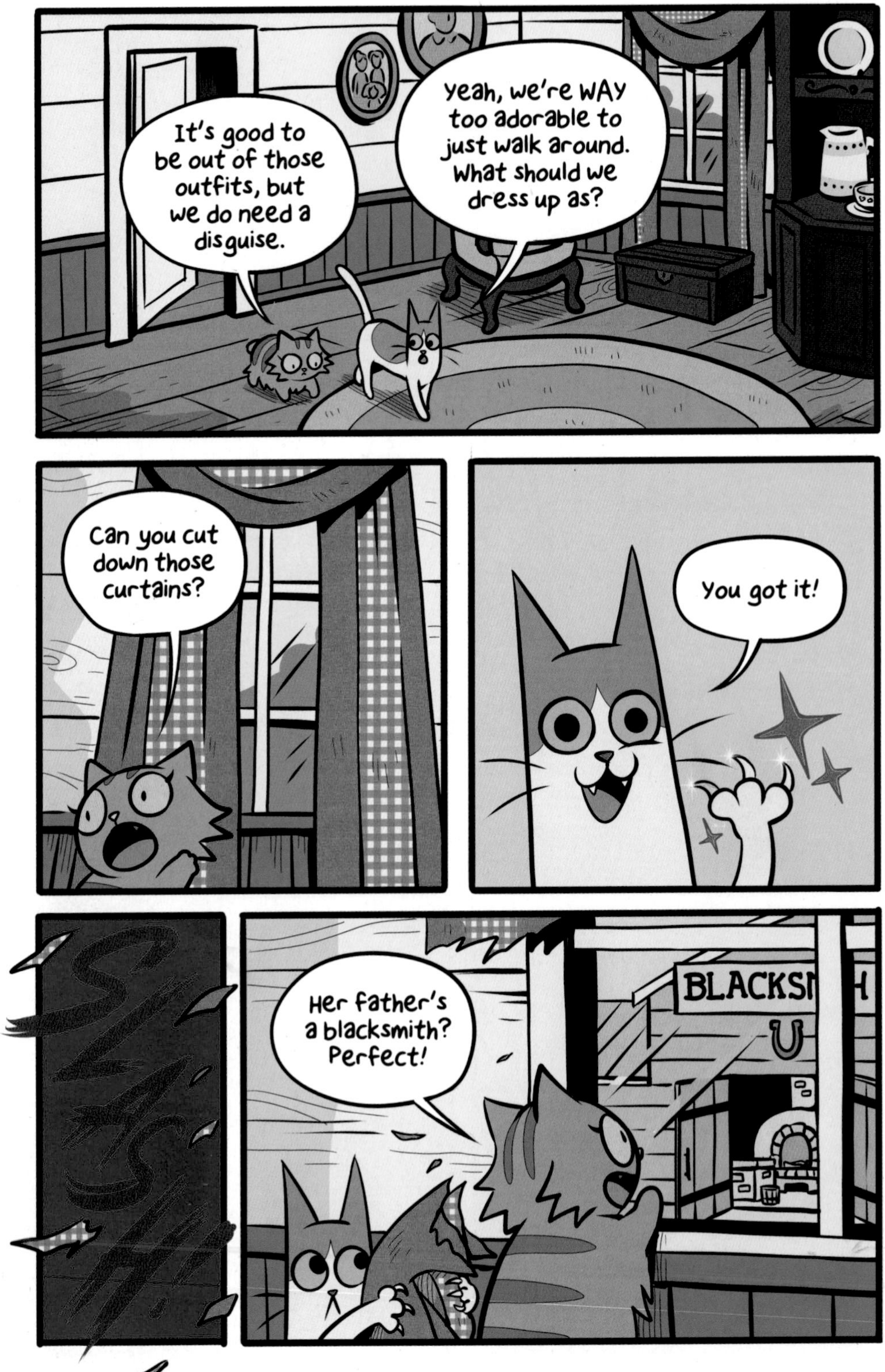

It's good to be out of those outfits, but we do need a disguise.
Yeah, we're WAY too adorable to just walk around. What should we dress up as?
Can you cut down those curtains?
You got it!
BLACKSMITH
Her father's a blacksmith? Perfect!

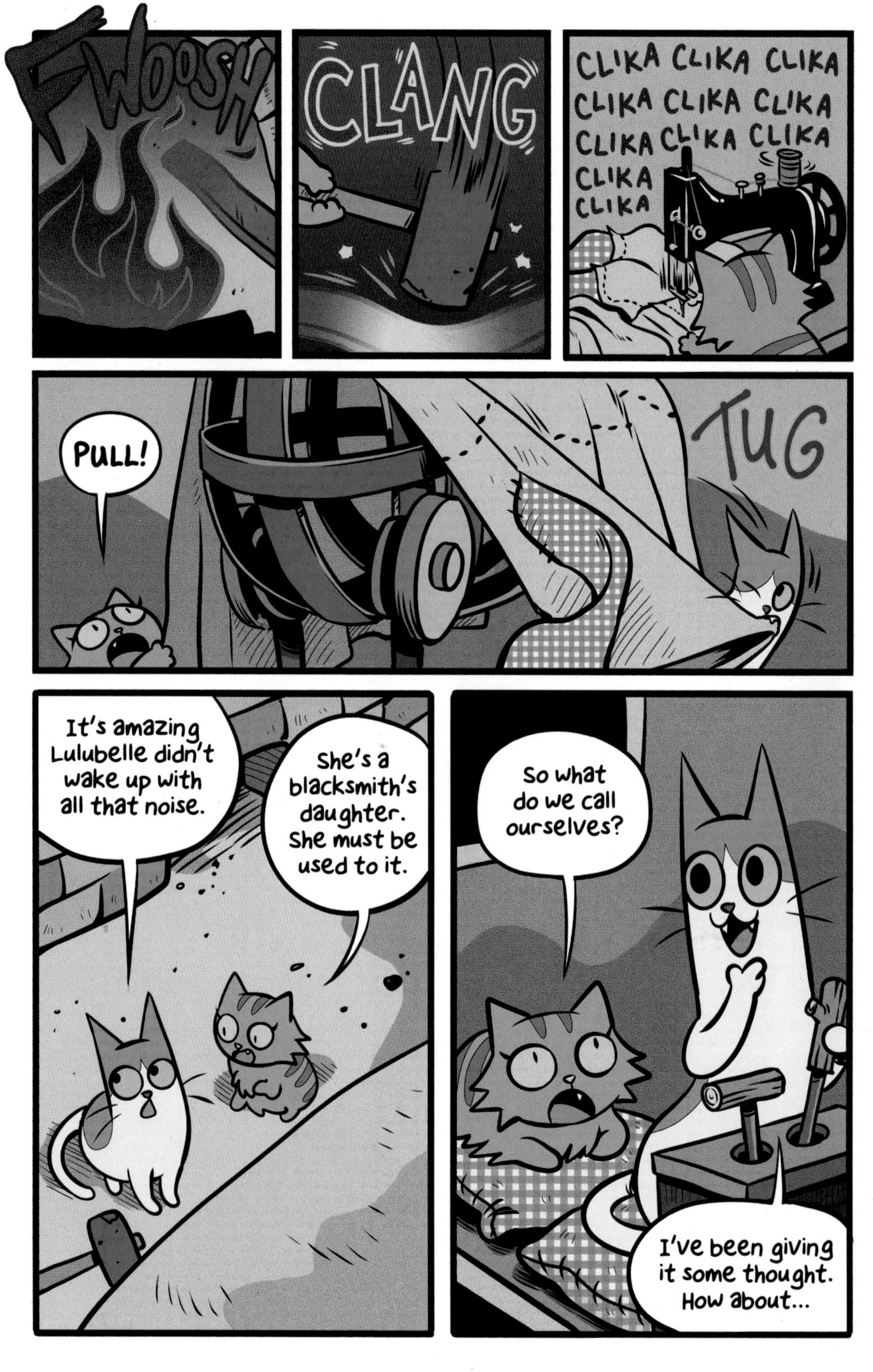
FWOOSH
CLANG
CLIKA CLIKA CLIKA
CLIKA CLIKA CLIKA
CLIKA CLIKA CLIKA
CLIKA
CLIKA
PULL!
TUG
It's amazing Lulubelle didn't wake up with all that noise.
She's a blacksmith's daughter. She must be used to it.
So what do we call ourselves?
I've been giving it some thought. How about...

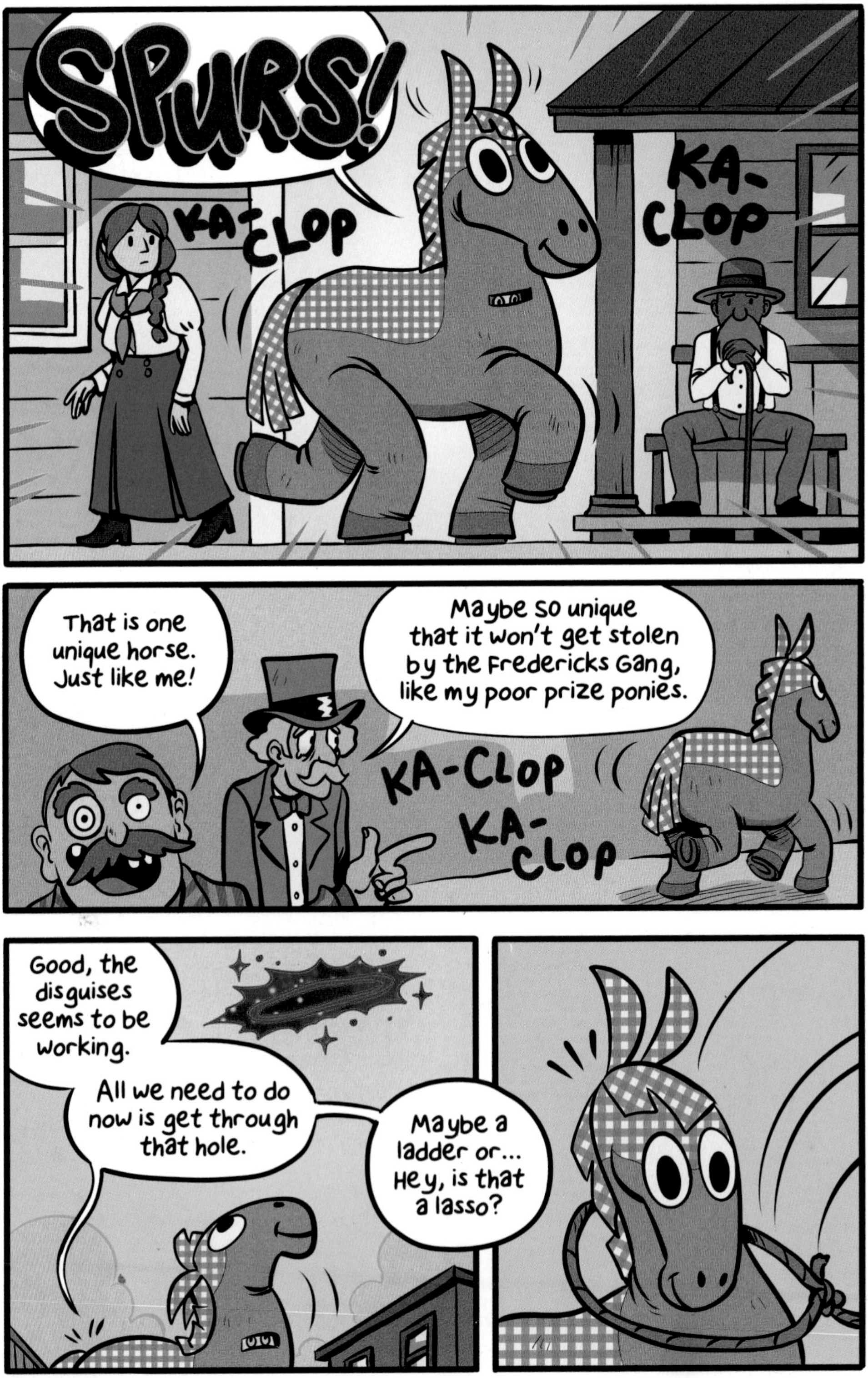
SPURS!
KA-CLOP
KA-CLOP
That is one unique horse. Just like me!
Maybe so unique that it won't get stolen by the Fredericks Gang, like my poor prize ponies.
KA-CLOP
KA-CLOP
Good, the disguises seems to be working.
All we need to do now is get through that hole.
Maybe a ladder or... Hey, is that a lasso?

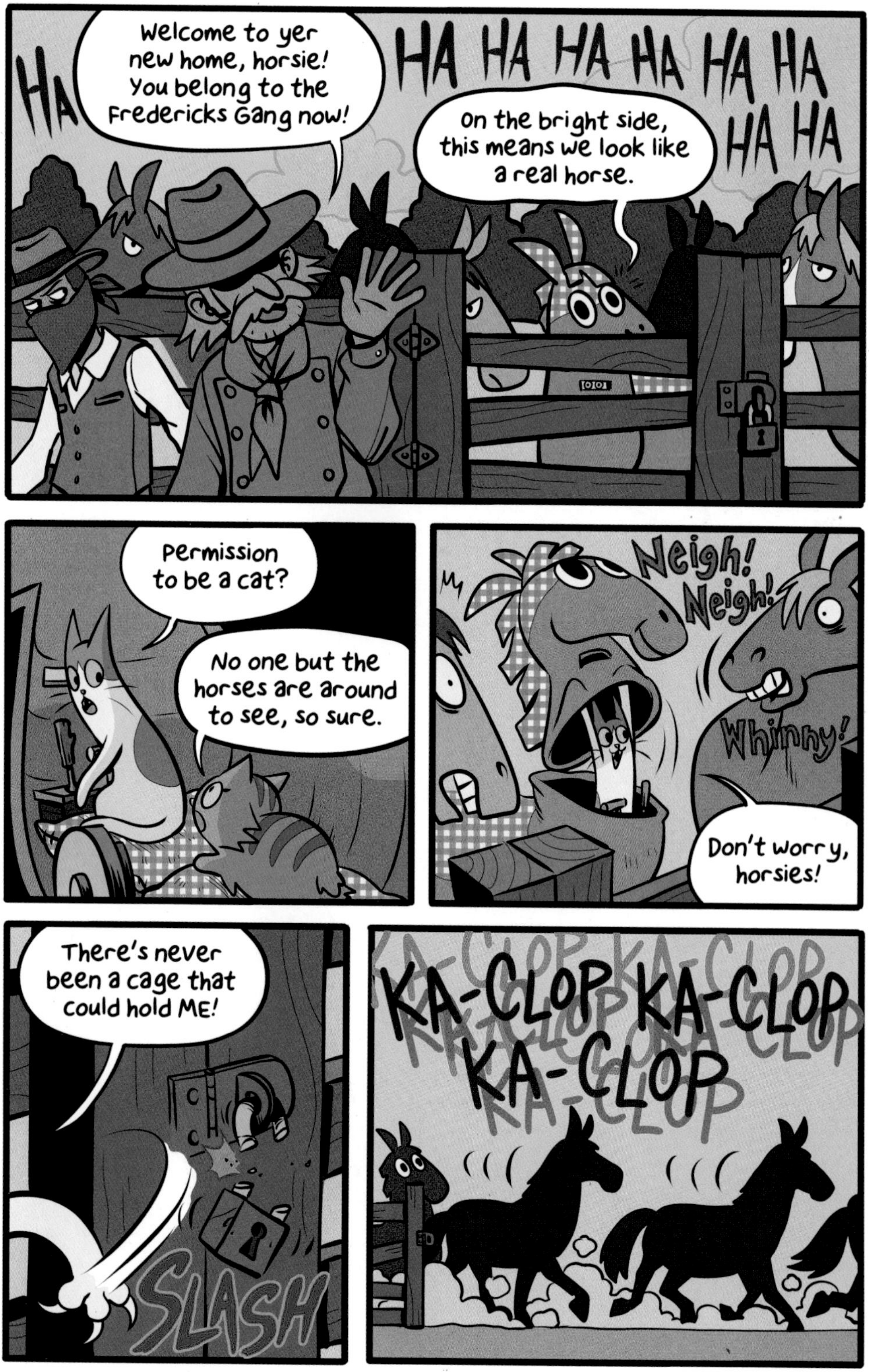
HA
Welcome to yer new home, horsie! You belong to the Fredericks Gang now!
HA HA HA HA HA HA HA HA
On the bright side, this means we look like a real horse.
Permission to be a cat?
No one but the horses are around to see, so sure.
Neigh! Neigh!
Whinny!
Don't worry, horsies!
There's never been a cage that could hold ME!
SLASH
KA-CLOP KA-CLOP KA-CLOP

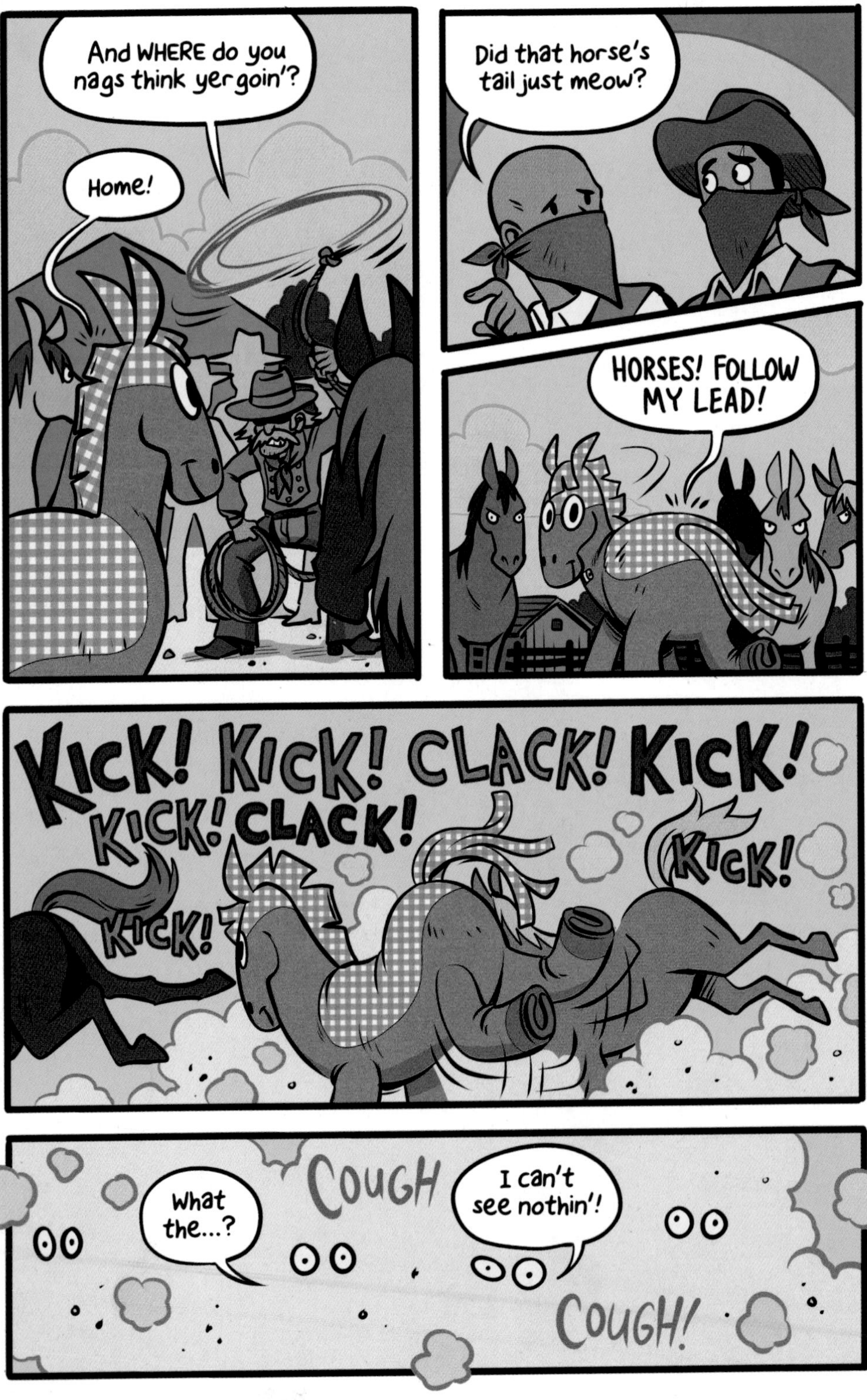
And WHERE do you nags think yer goin'?
Home!
Did that horse's tail just meow?
HORSES! FOLLOW MY LEAD!
KICK! KICK! CLACK! KICK!
KICK! CLACK!
KICK!
KICK!
What the...?
COUGH
I can't see nothin'!
COUGH!

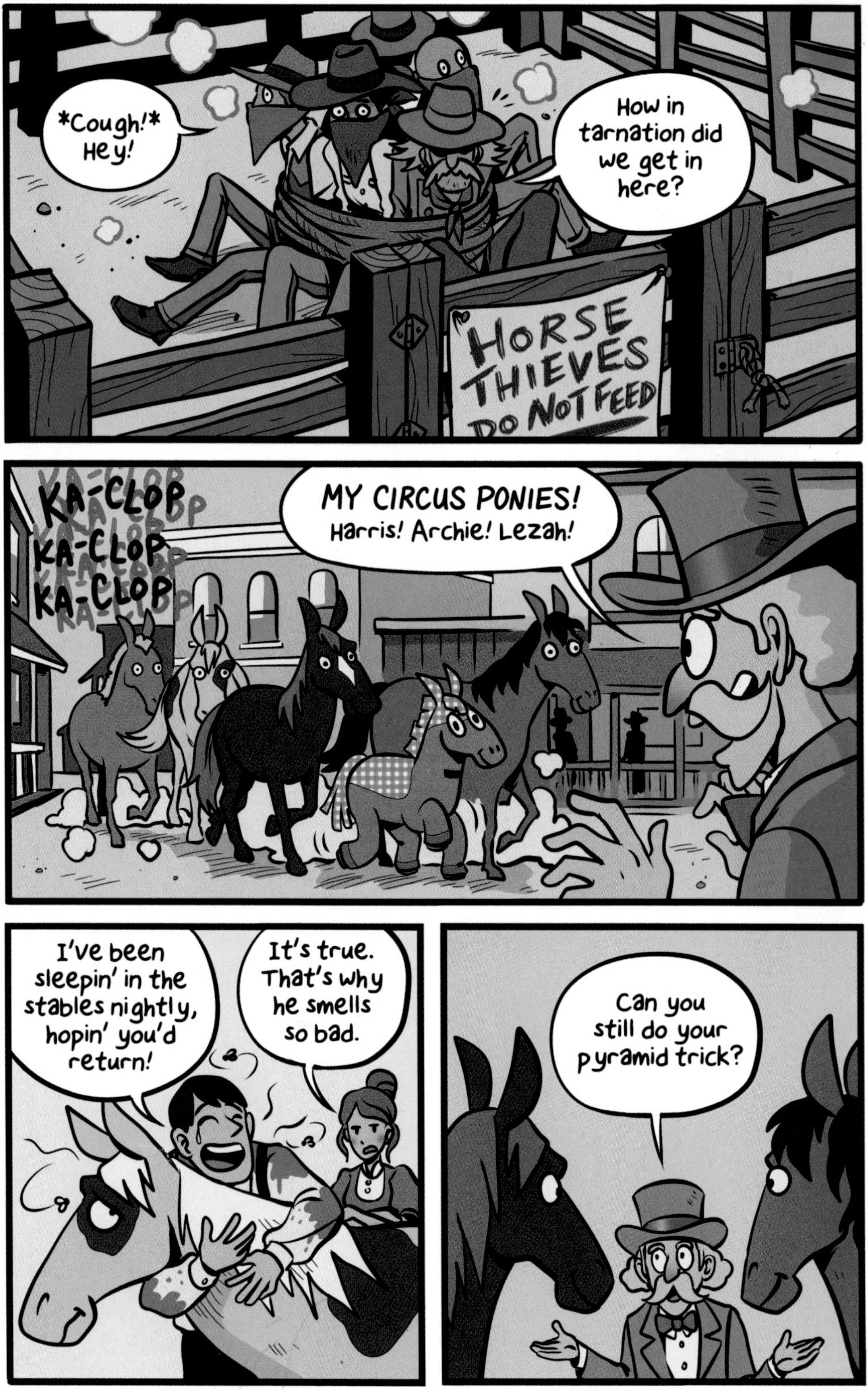
Cough!
Hey!
How in tarnation did we get in here?
HORSE THIEVES DO NOT FEED
KA-CLOP KA-CLOP KA-CLOP
MY CIRCUS PONIES!
Harris! Archie! Lezah!
I've been sleepin' in the stables nightly, hopin' you'd return!
It's true. That's why he smells so bad.
Can you still do your pyramid trick?

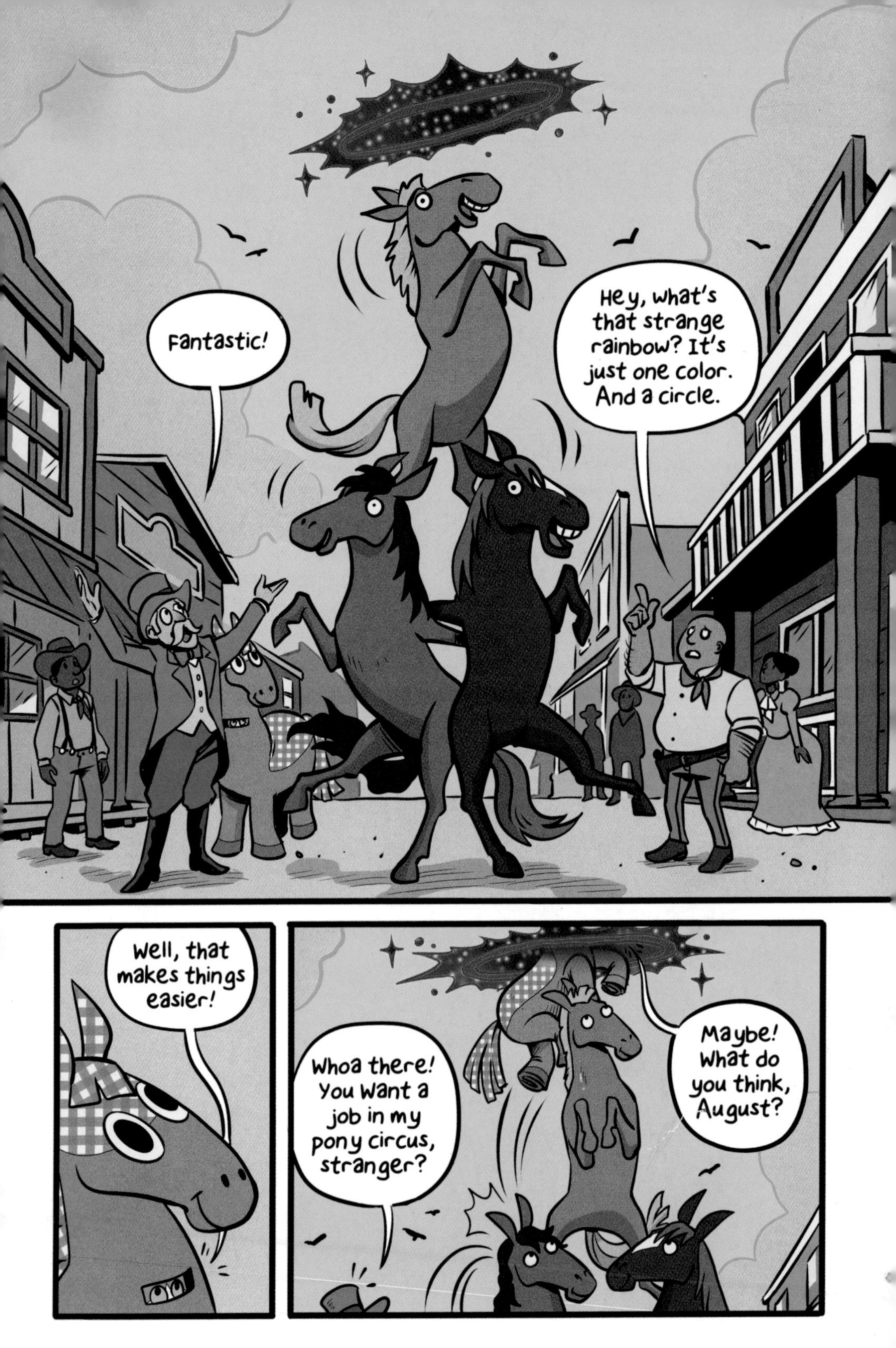
Fantastic!
Hey, what's that strange rainbow? It's just one color. And a circle.
Well, that makes things easier!
Whoa there! You want a job in my pony circus, stranger?
Maybe! What do you think, August?

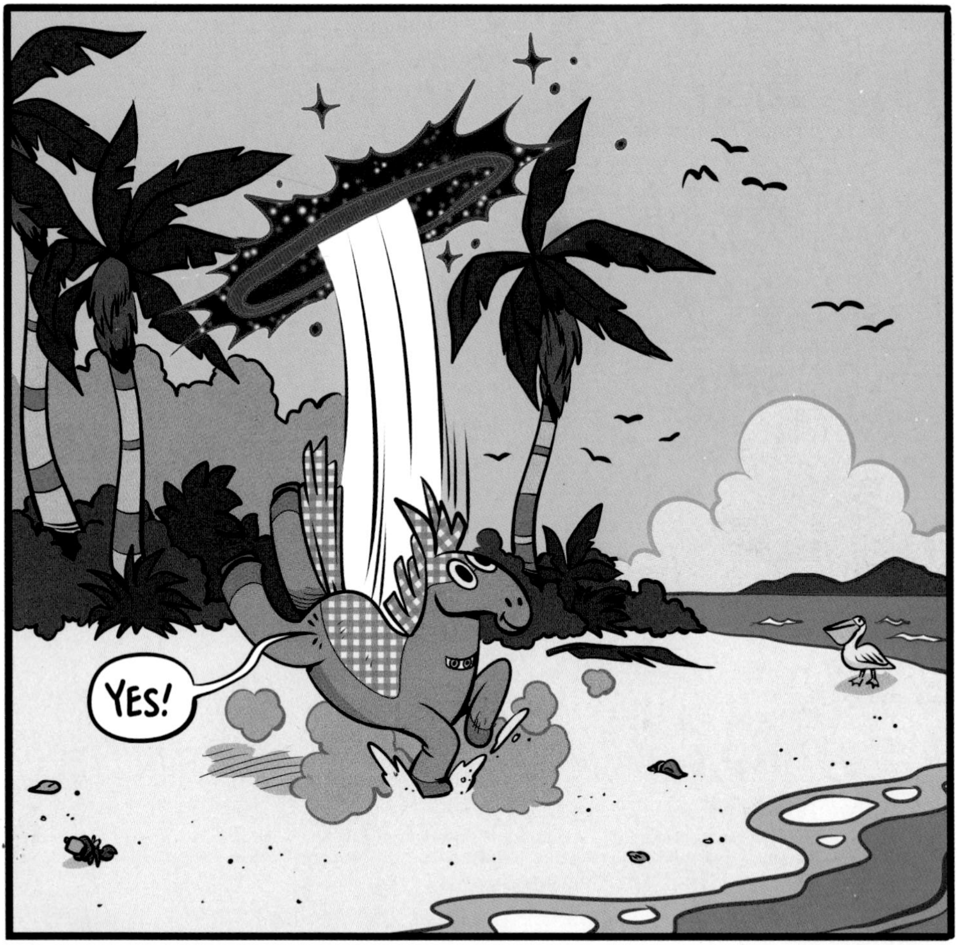
YES!

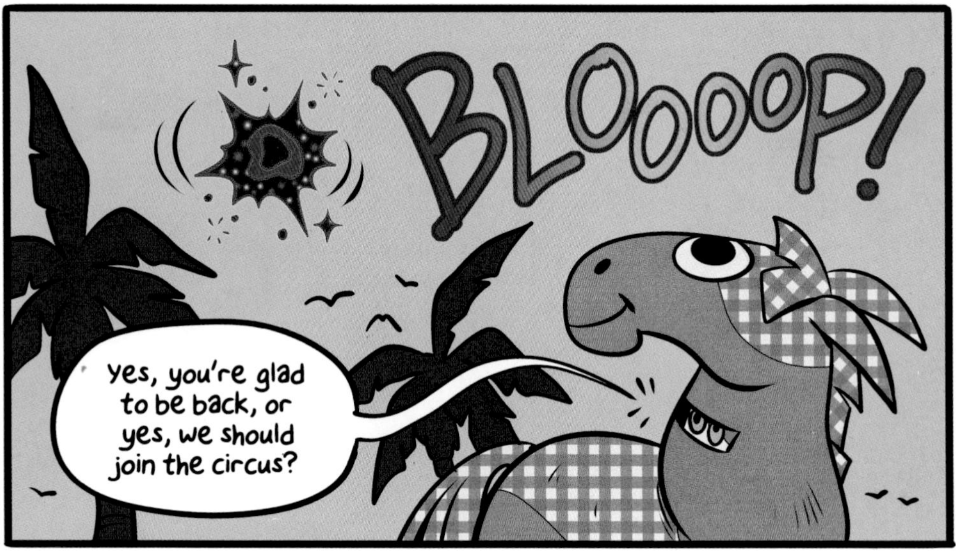
BLOOOOP!
yes, you're glad to be back, or yes, we should join the circus?

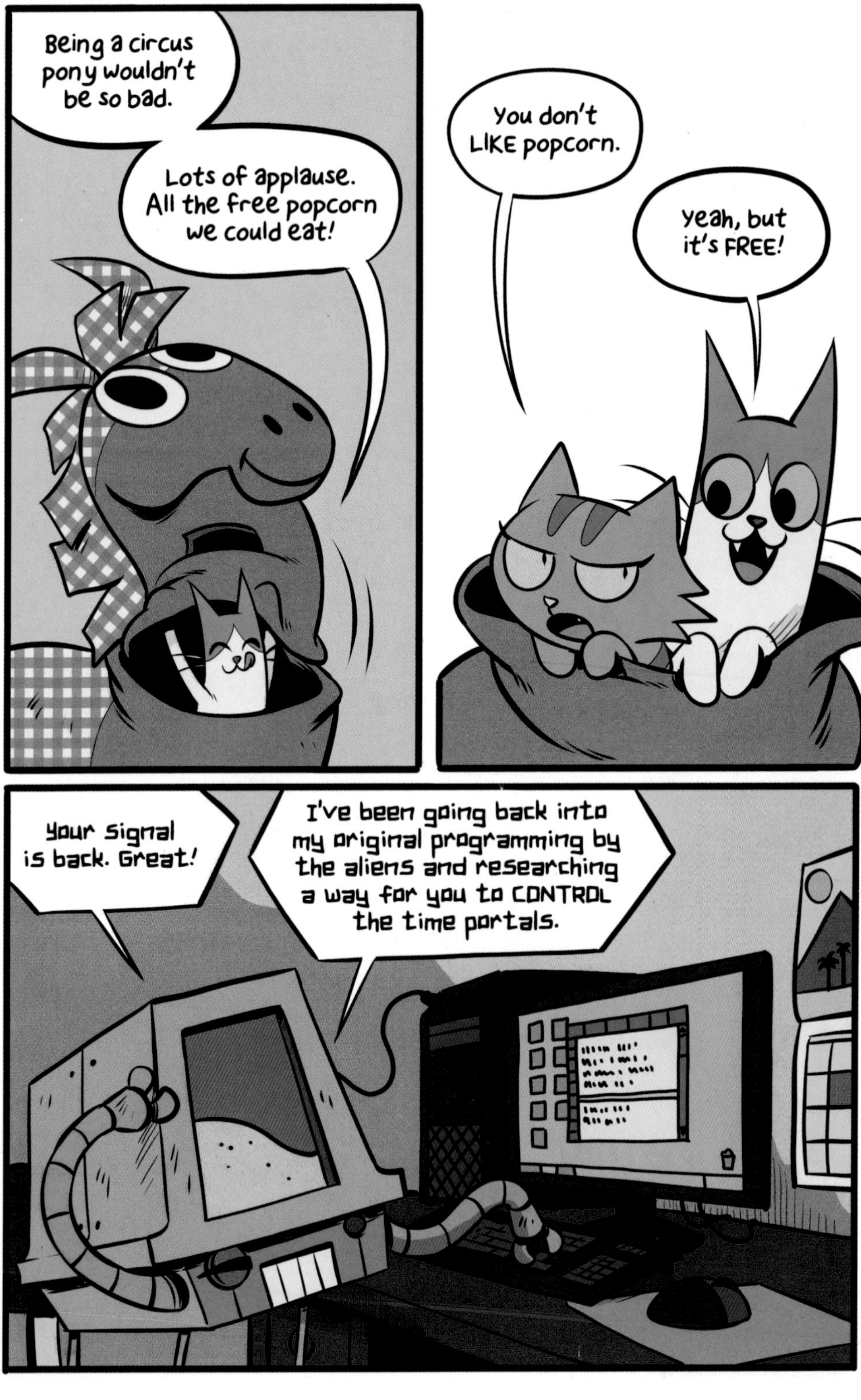
Being a circus pony wouldn't be so bad.
Lots of applause. All the free popcorn we could eat!
You don't LIKE popcorn.
yeah, but it's FREE!
your signal is back. Great!
I've been going back into my original programming by the aliens and researching a way for you to CONTROL the time portals.

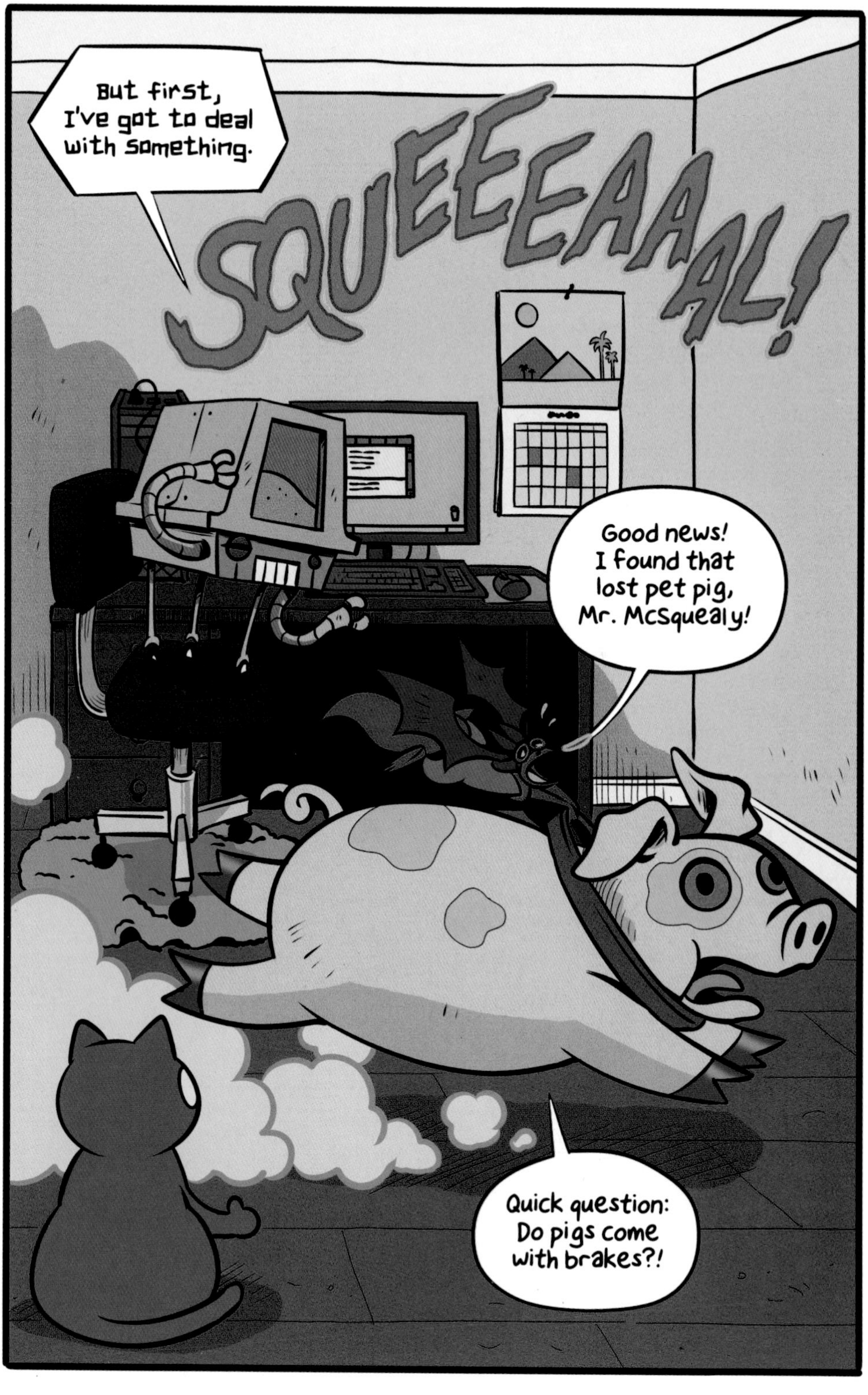
But first, I've got to deal with something.
SQUEEEAAAL!
Good news! I found that lost pet pig, Mr. McSquealy!
Quick question: Do pigs come with brakes?!

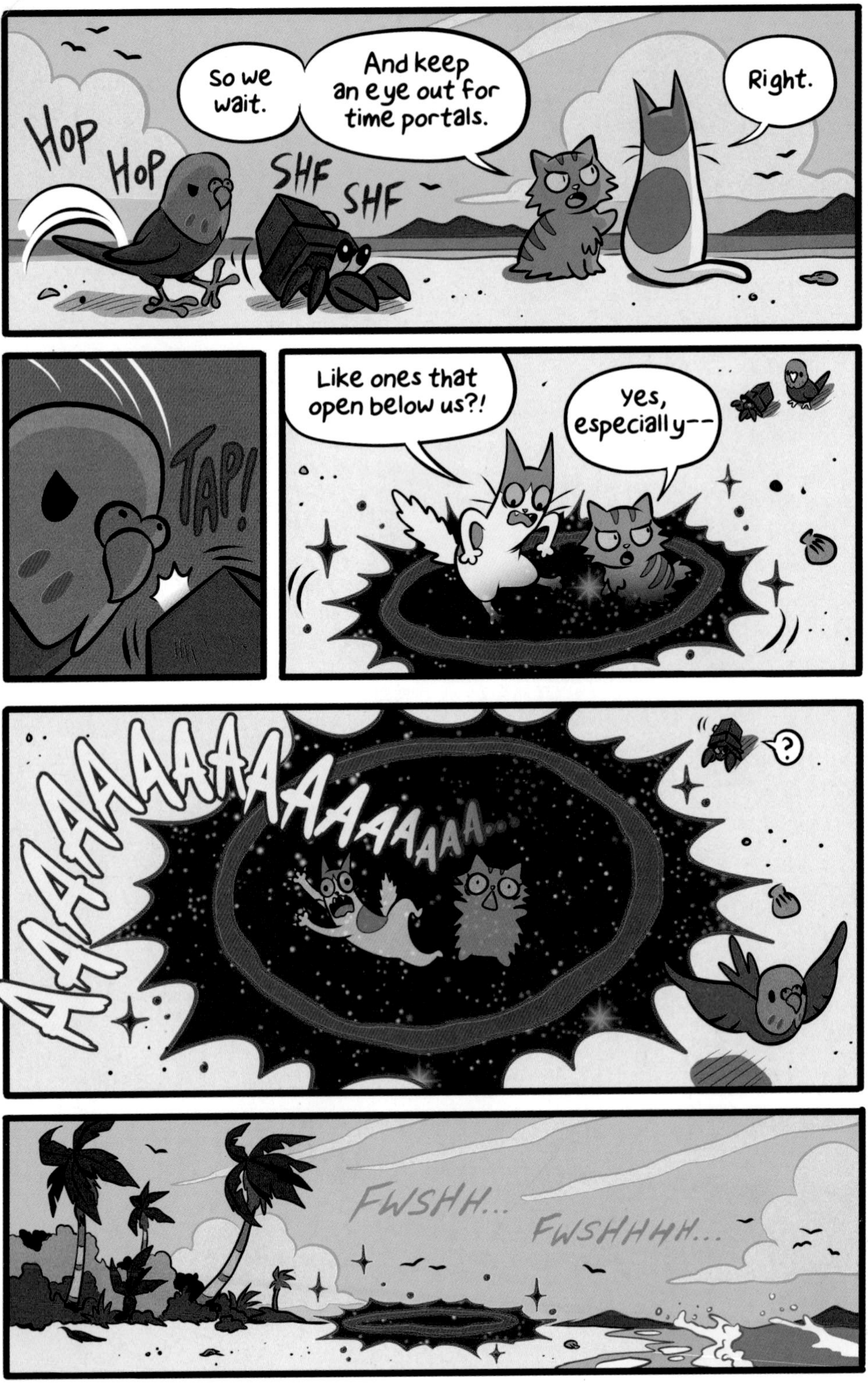
So we wait.
And keep an eye out for time portals.
Right.
HOP HOP
SHF SHF
TAP!
Like ones that open below us?!
yes, especially--
?
AAAAAAAAAAAAAAAAA...
FWSHH...
FWSHHHH...

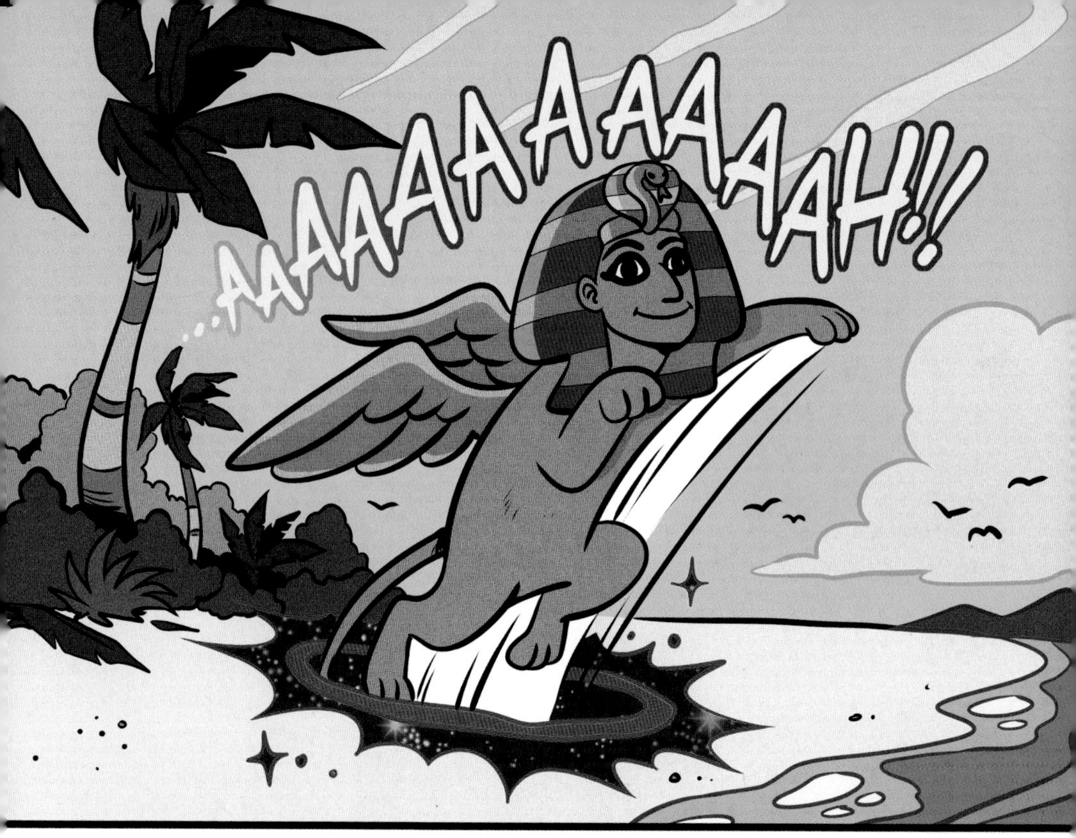
...AAAAAAAAAAAAH!!

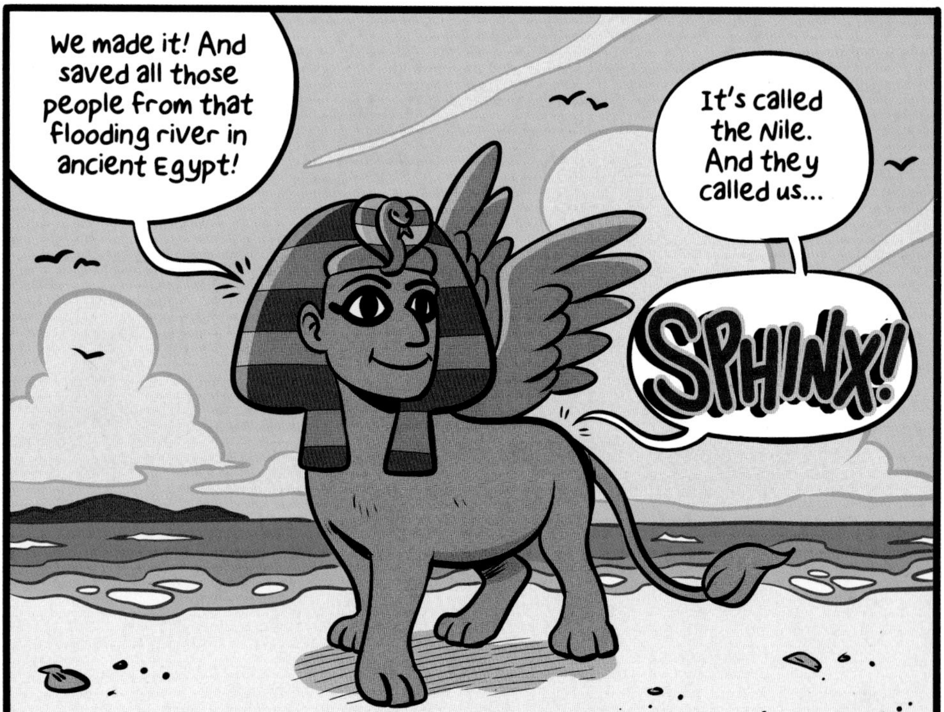
We made it! And saved all those people from that flooding river in ancient Egypt!
It's called the Nile. And they called us...
SPHINX!

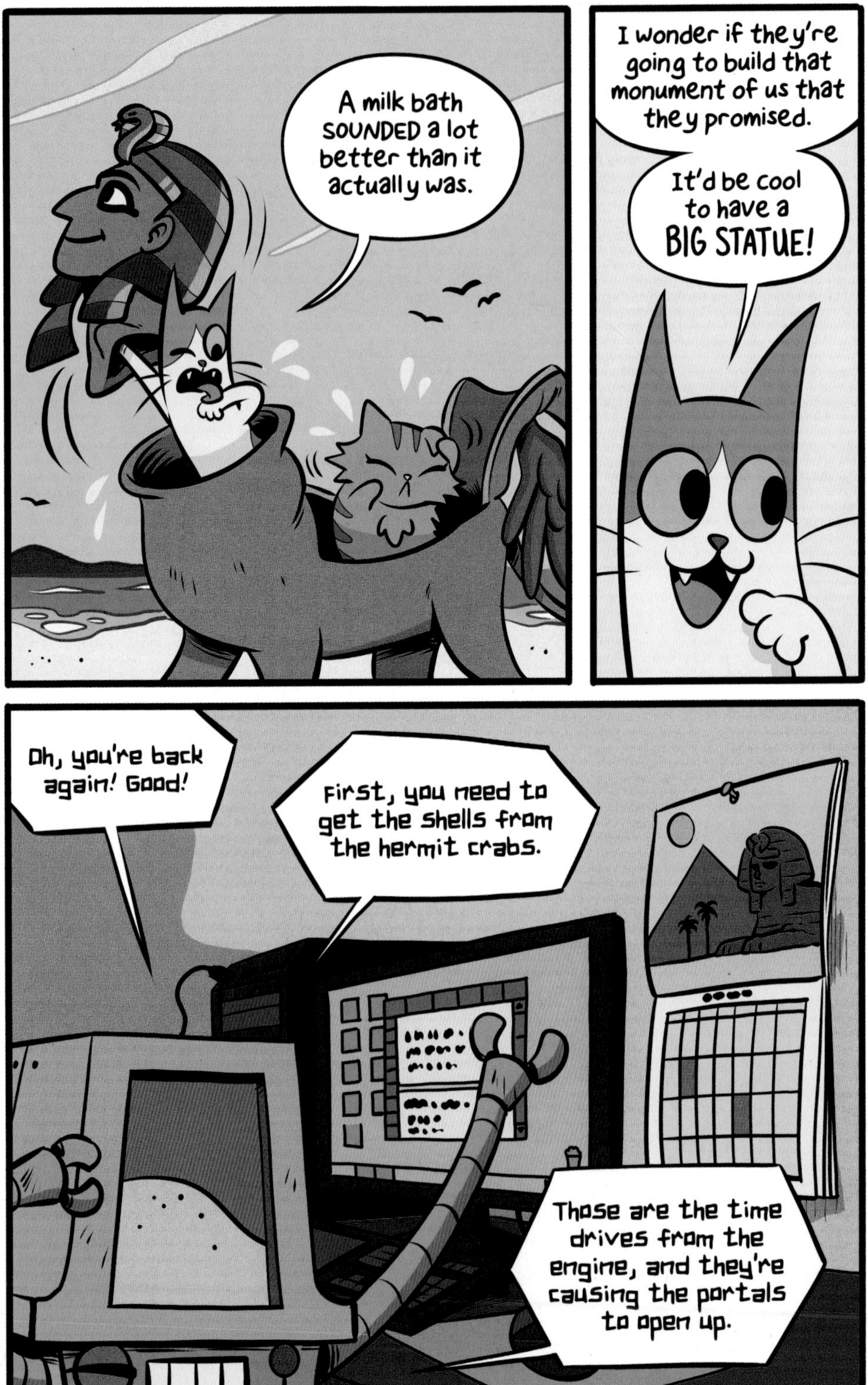
A milk bath SOUNDED a lot better than it actually was.
I wonder if they're going to build that monument of us that they promised.
It'd be cool to have a BIG STATUE!
Oh, you're back again! Good!
First, you need to get the shells from the hermit crabs.
Those are the time drives from the engine, and they're causing the portals to open up.

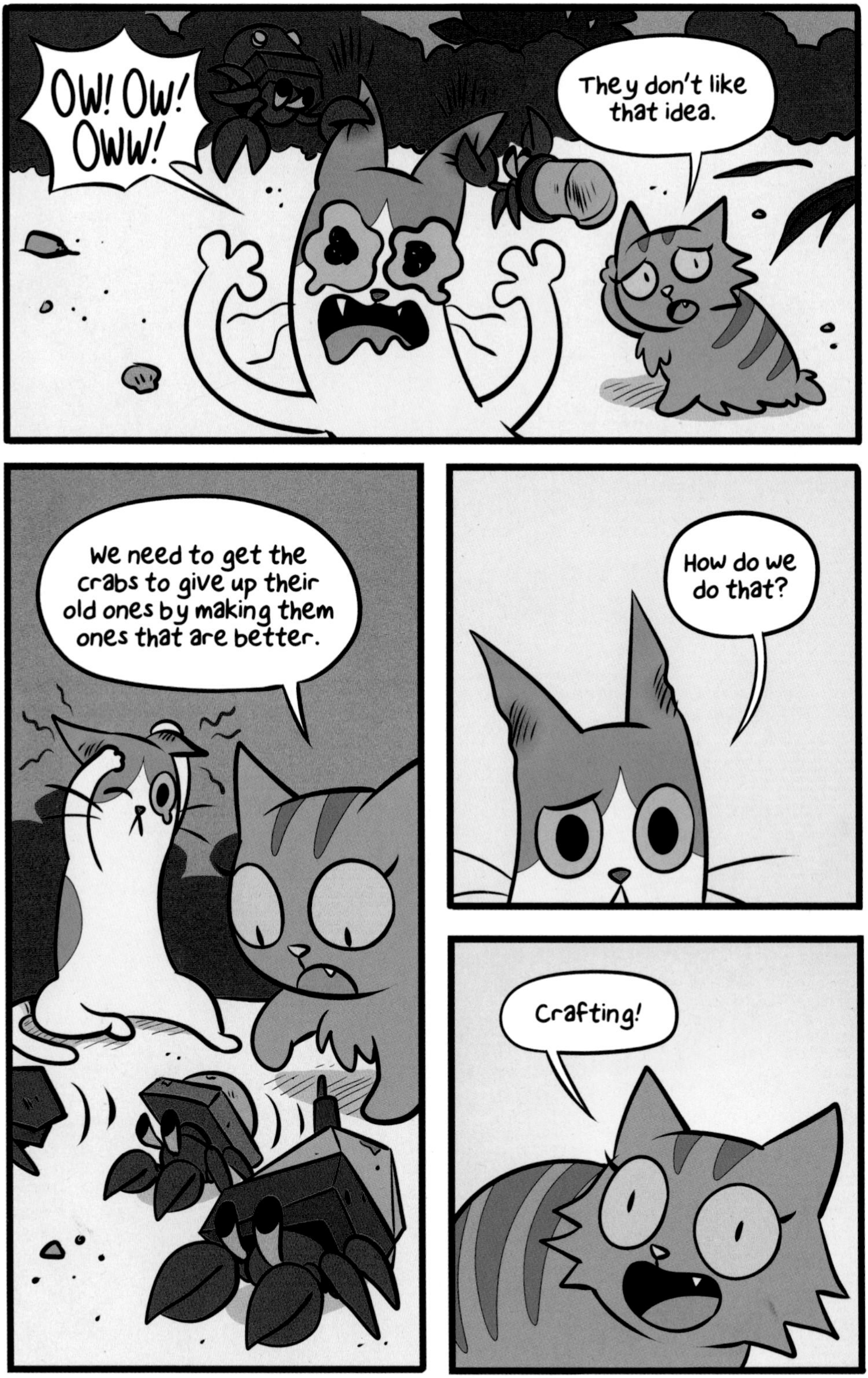
OW! OW! OWW!
They don't like that idea.
We need to get the crabs to give up their old ones by making them ones that are better.
How do we do that?
Crafting!

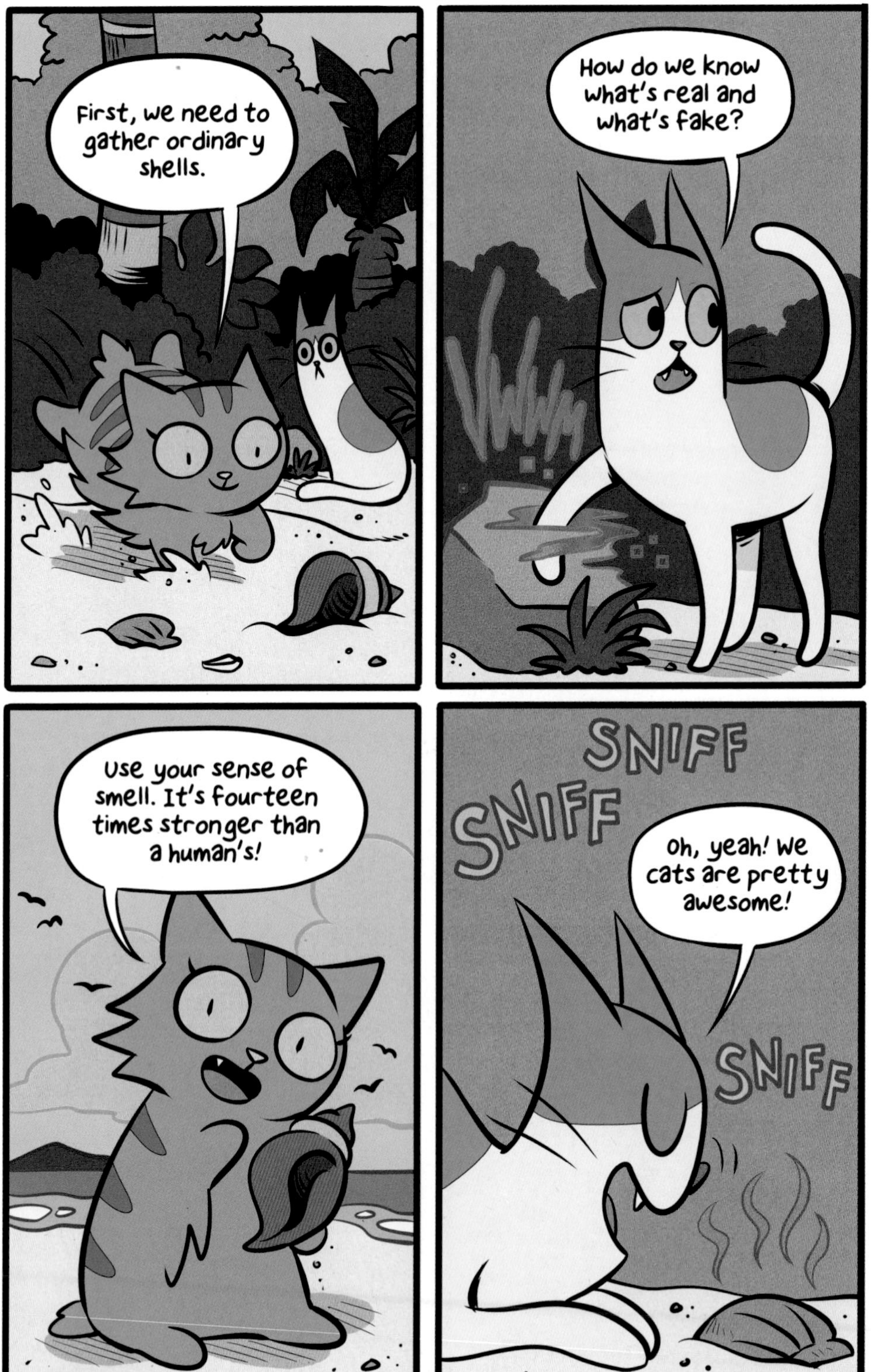
First, we need to gather ordinary shells.
How do we know what's real and what's fake?
Use your sense of smell. It's fourteen times stronger than a human's!
SNIFF
SNIFF
Oh, yeah! We cats are pretty awesome!
SNIFF

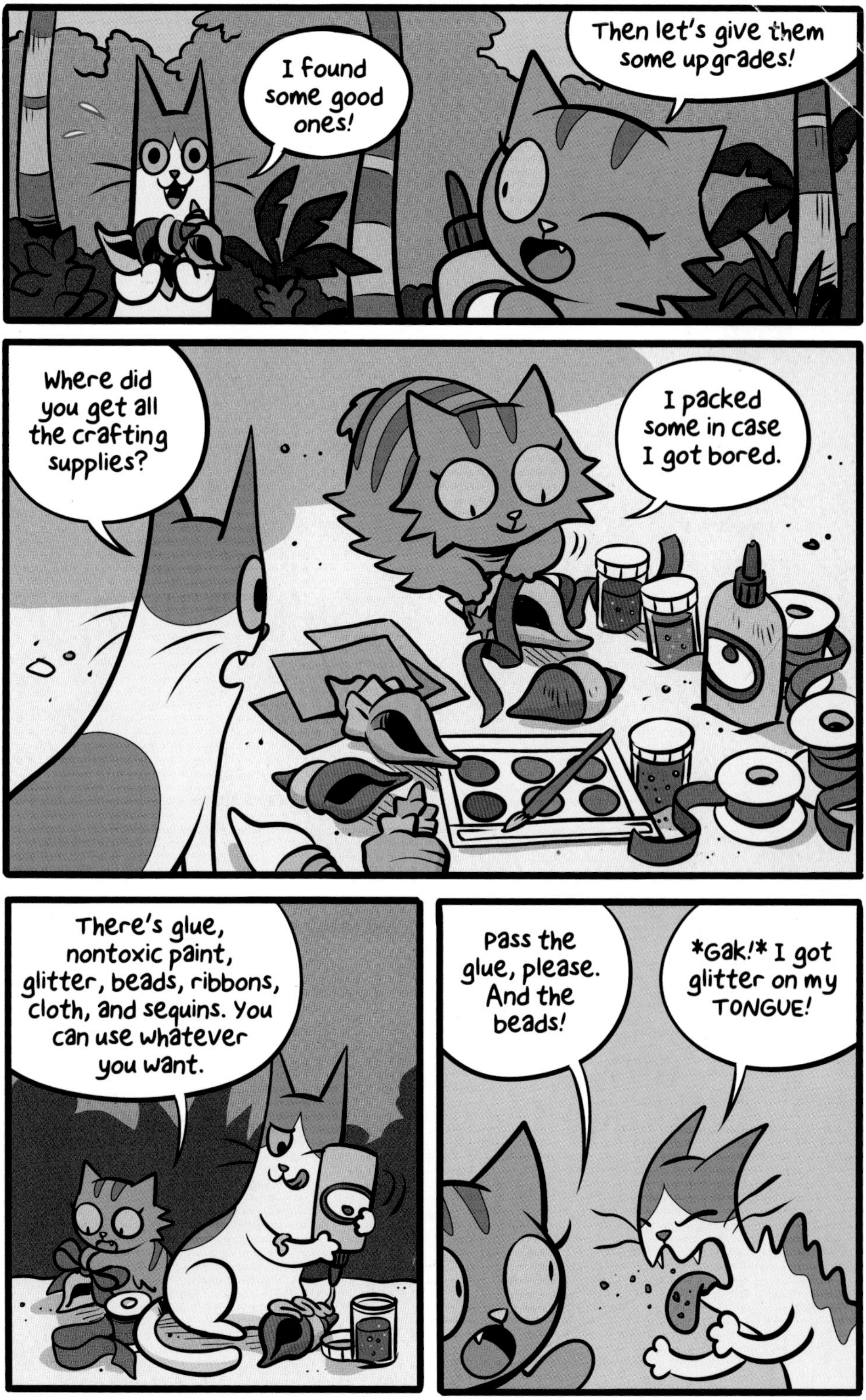

I found some good ones!
Then let's give them some upgrades!
Where did you get all the crafting supplies?
I packed some in case I got bored.
There's glue, nontoxic paint, glitter, beads, ribbons, cloth, and sequins. You can use whatever you want.
Pass the glue, please. And the beads!
Gak! I got glitter on my TONGUE!

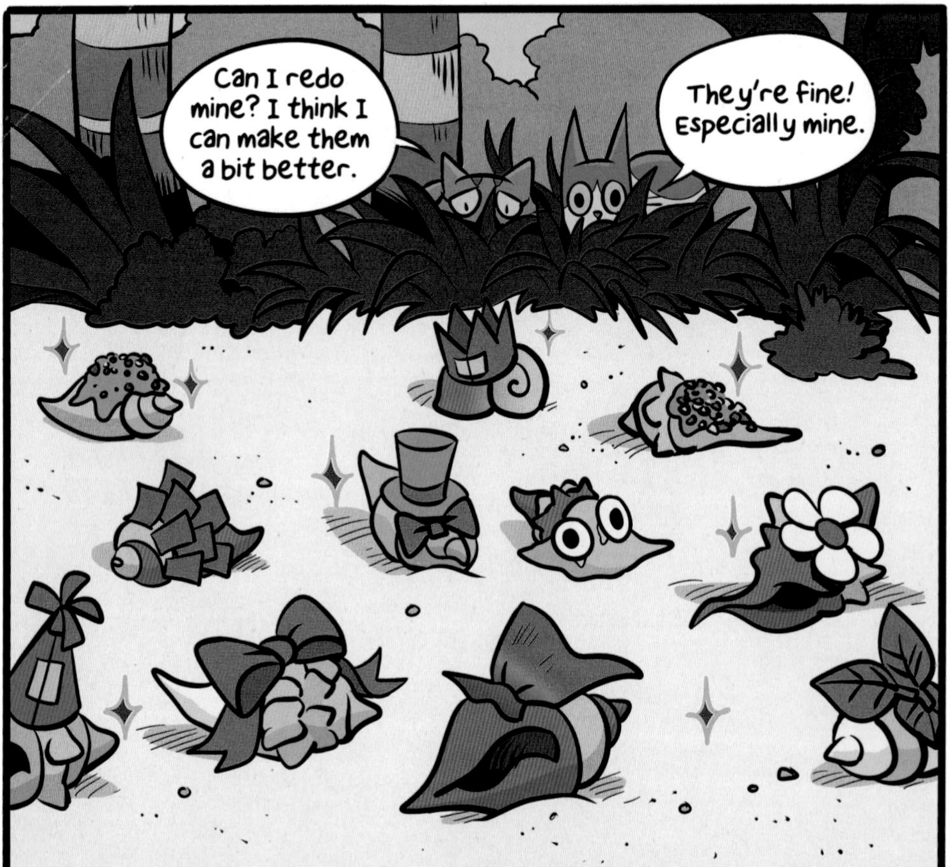
Can I redo mine? I think I can make them a bit better.
They're fine! Especially mine.

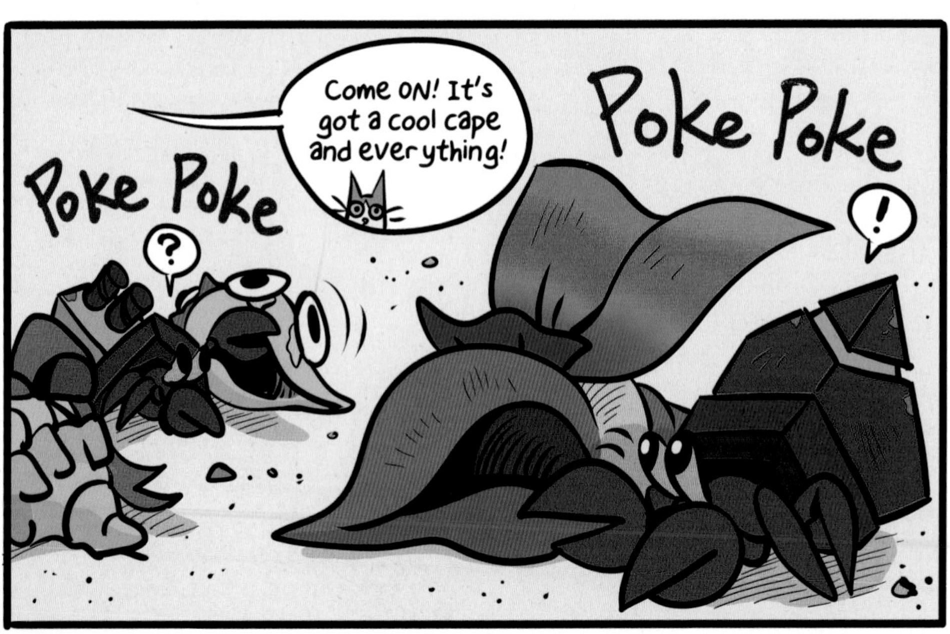
Poke Poke
Come ON! It's got a cool cape and everything!
Poke Poke
?
!

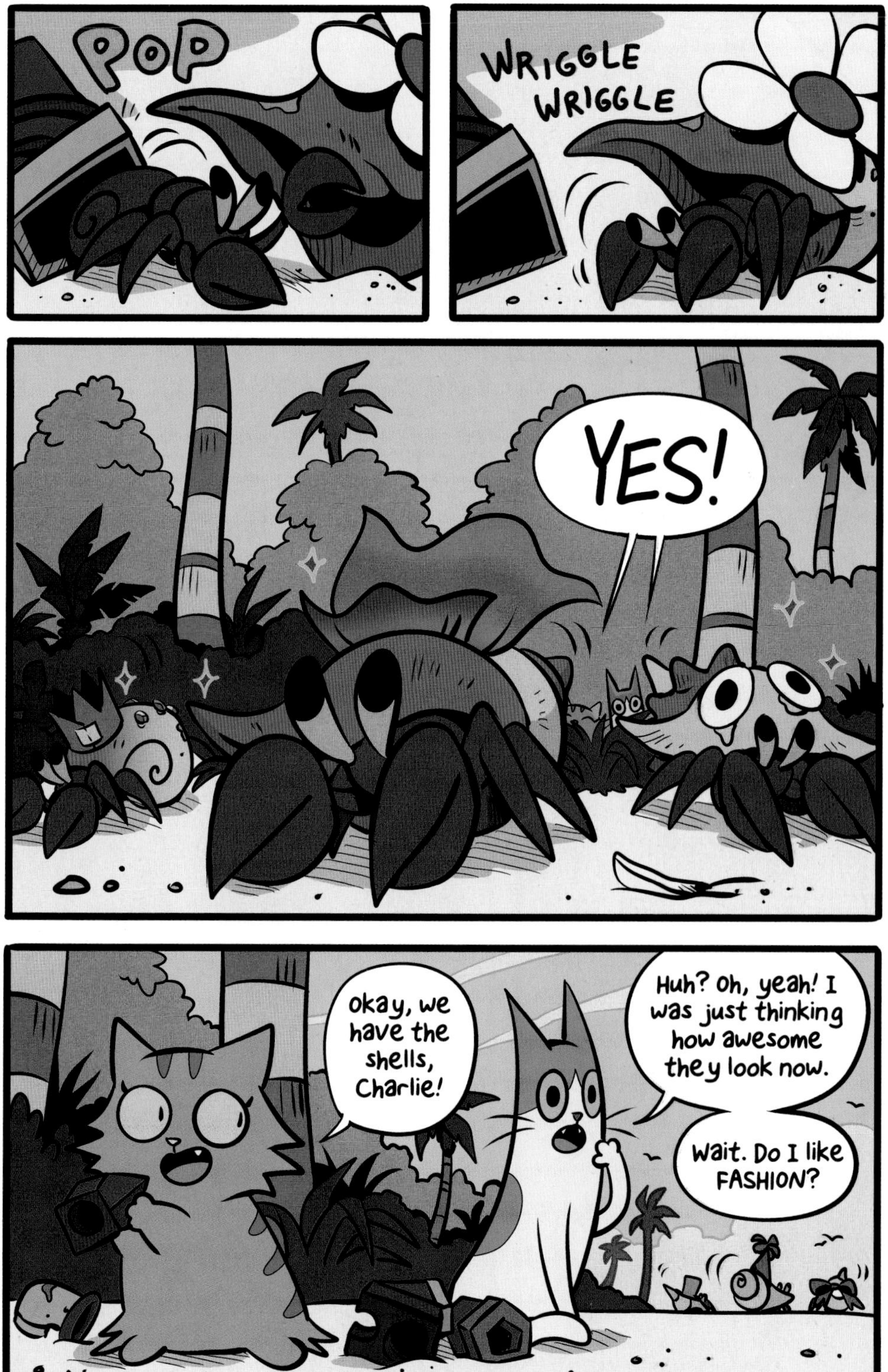
POP
WRIGGLE WRIGGLE
YES!
Okay, we have the shells, Charlie!
Huh? Oh, yeah! I was just thinking how awesome they look now.
Wait. Do I like FASHION?

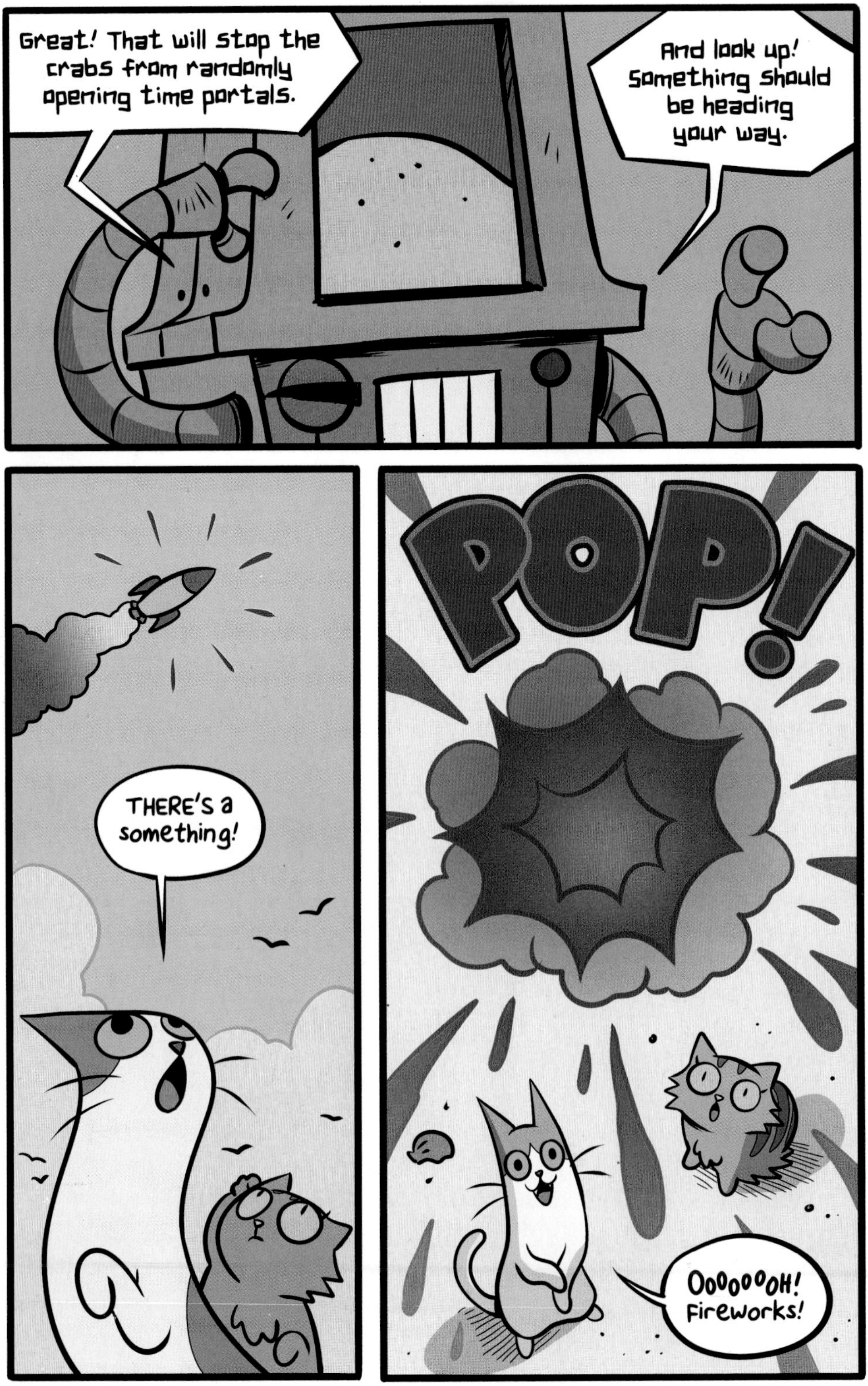
Great! That will stop the crabs from randomly opening time portals.
And look up! Something should be heading your way.
THERE'S a something!
POP!
OOoooooH! Fireworks!

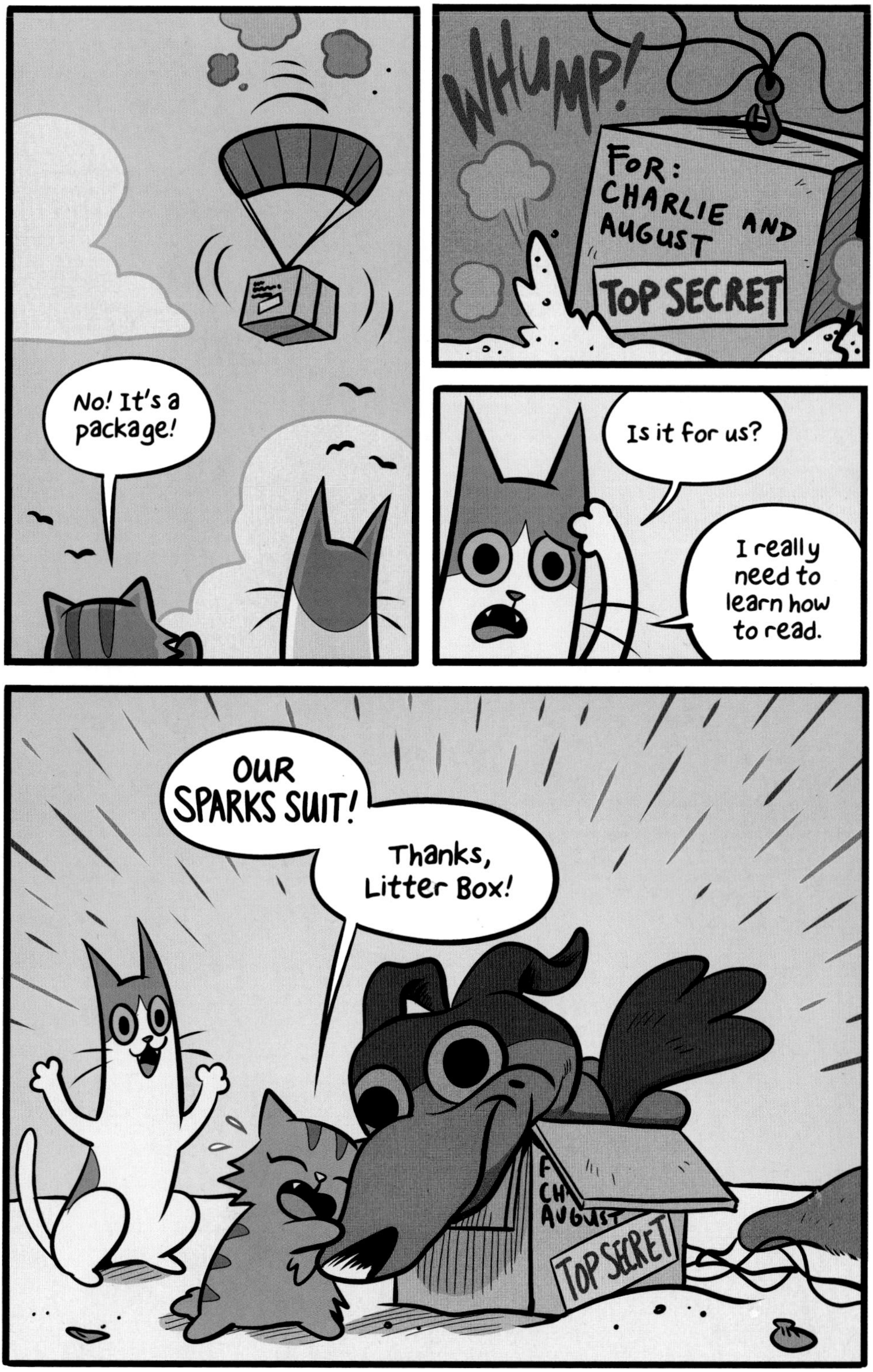
No! It's a package!
WHUMP!
FOR: CHARLIE AND AUGUST
TOP SECRET
Is it for us?
I really need to learn how to read.
OUR SPARKS SUIT!
Thanks, Litter Box!
TOP SECRET

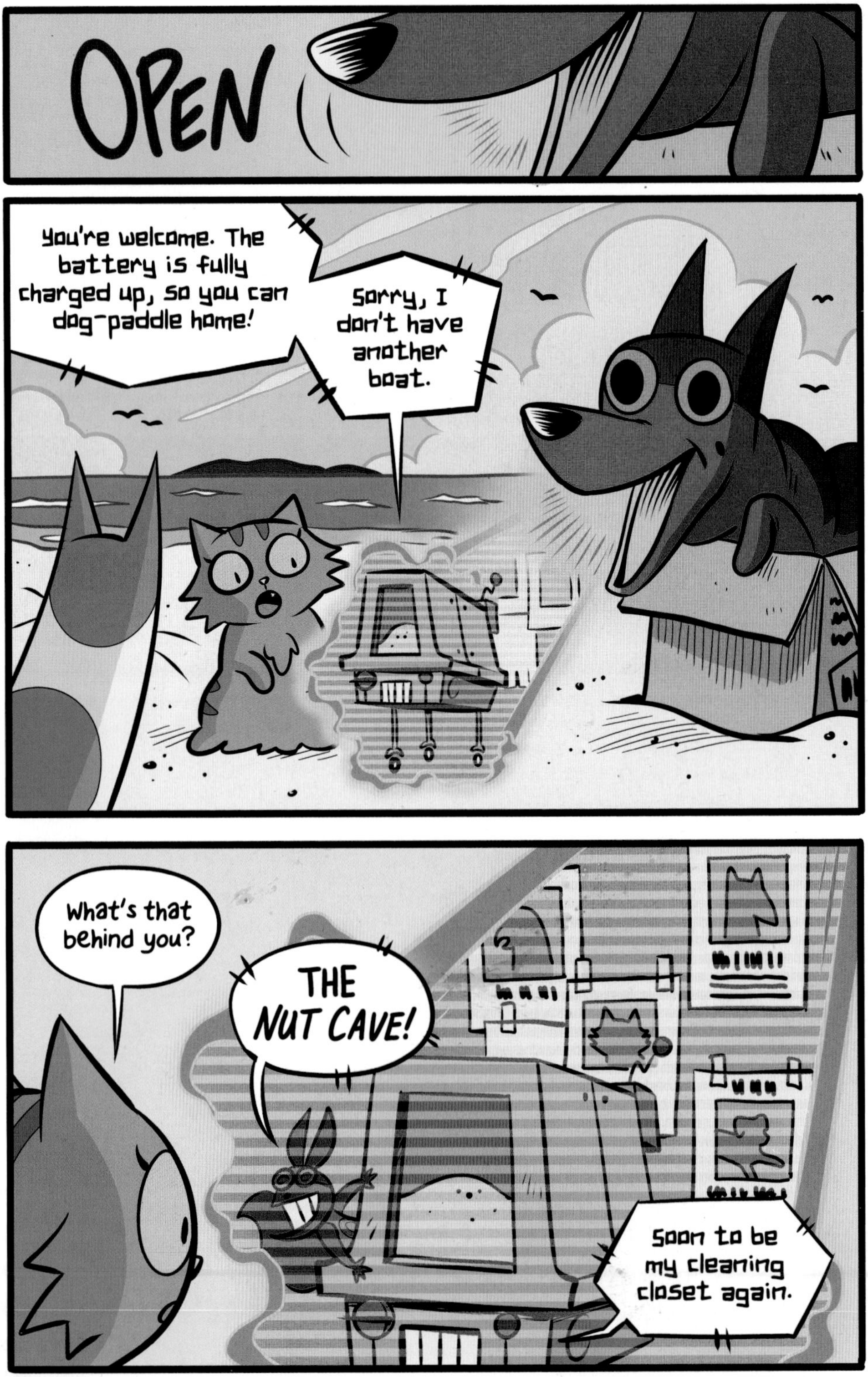
OPEN
You're welcome. The battery is fully charged up, so you can dog-paddle home!
Sorry, I don't have another boat.
What's that behind you?
THE NUT CAVE!
Soon to be my cleaning closet again.

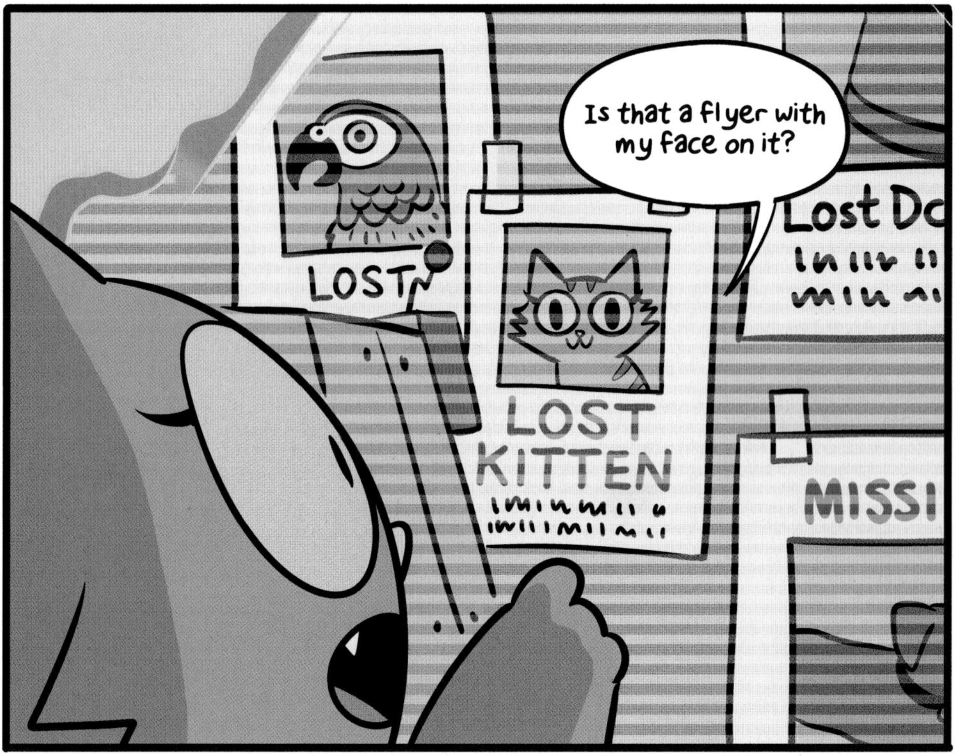
Is that a flyer with my face on it?
LOST
LOST KITTEN
Lost Do
MISSI

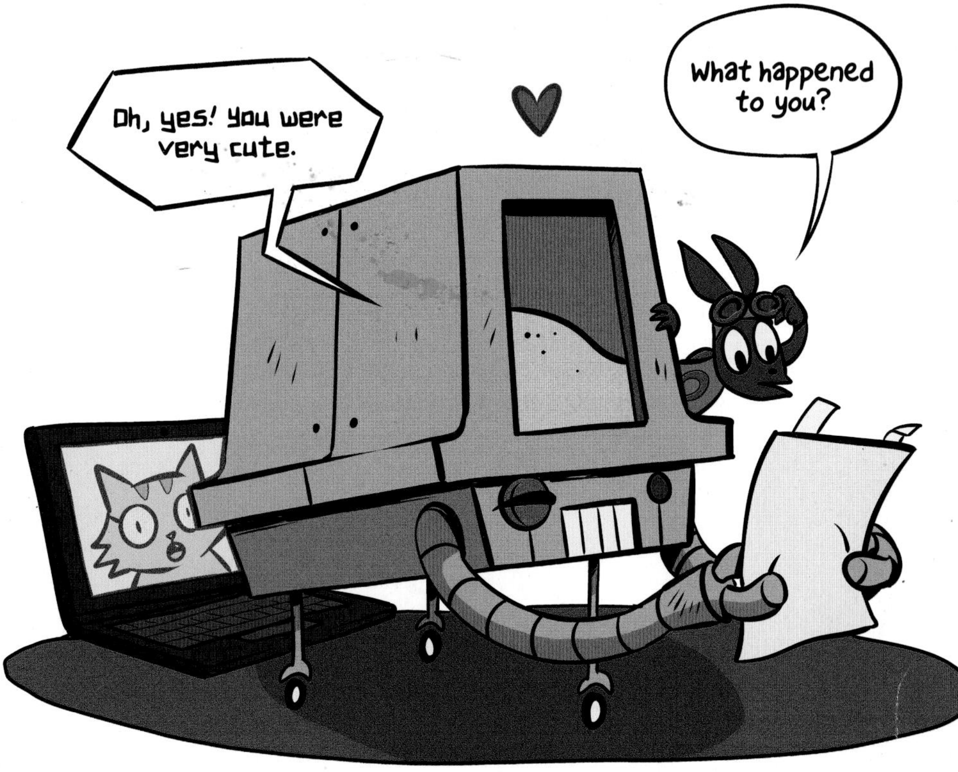
Oh, yes! You were very cute.
What happened to you?

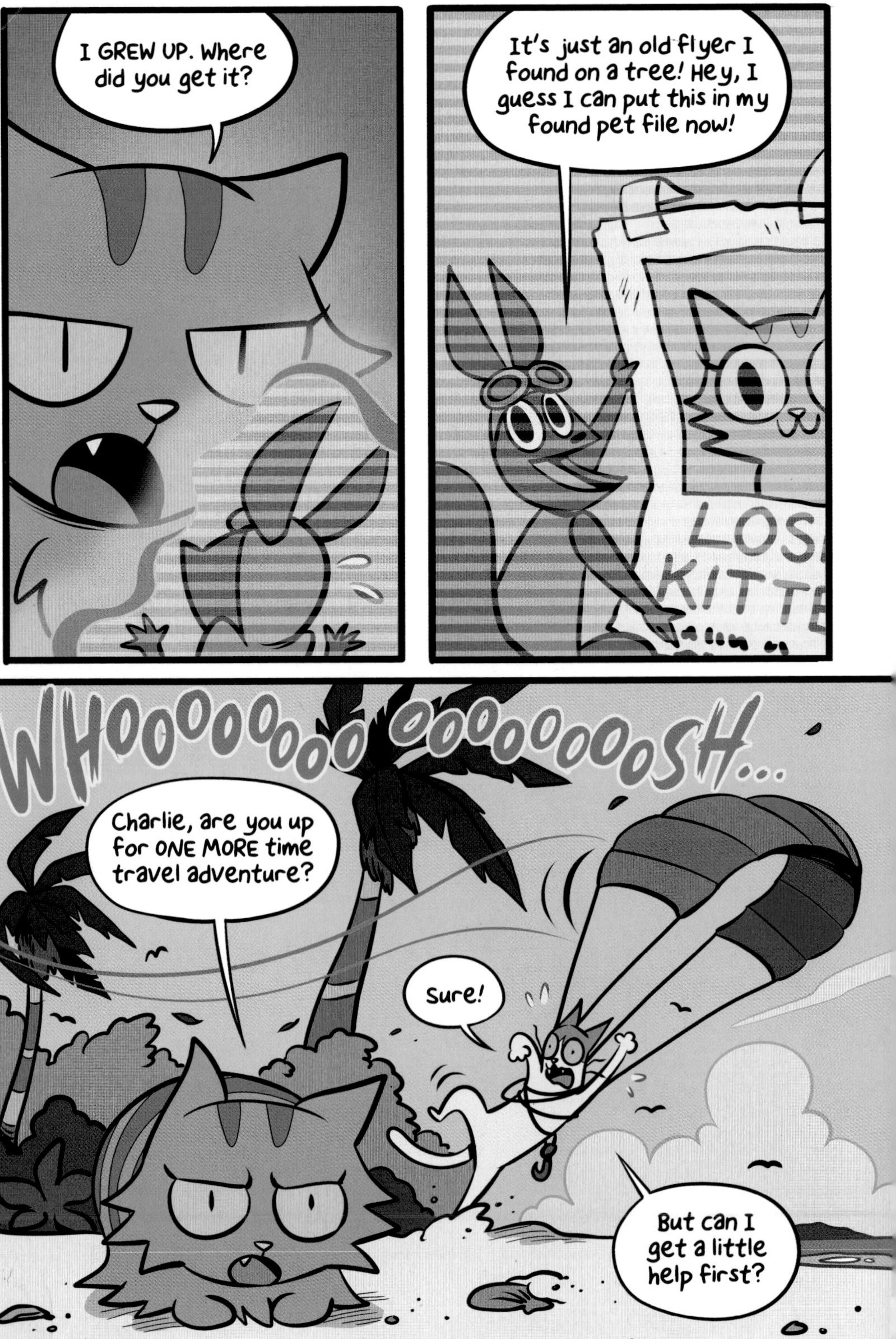
I GREW UP. Where did you get it?
It's just an old flyer I found on a tree! Hey, I guess I can put this in my found pet file now!
LOS
KITTE
WHOOOOOOOO OOOOOOOOOSH...
Charlie, are you up for ONE MORE time travel adventure?
Sure!
But can I get a little help first?

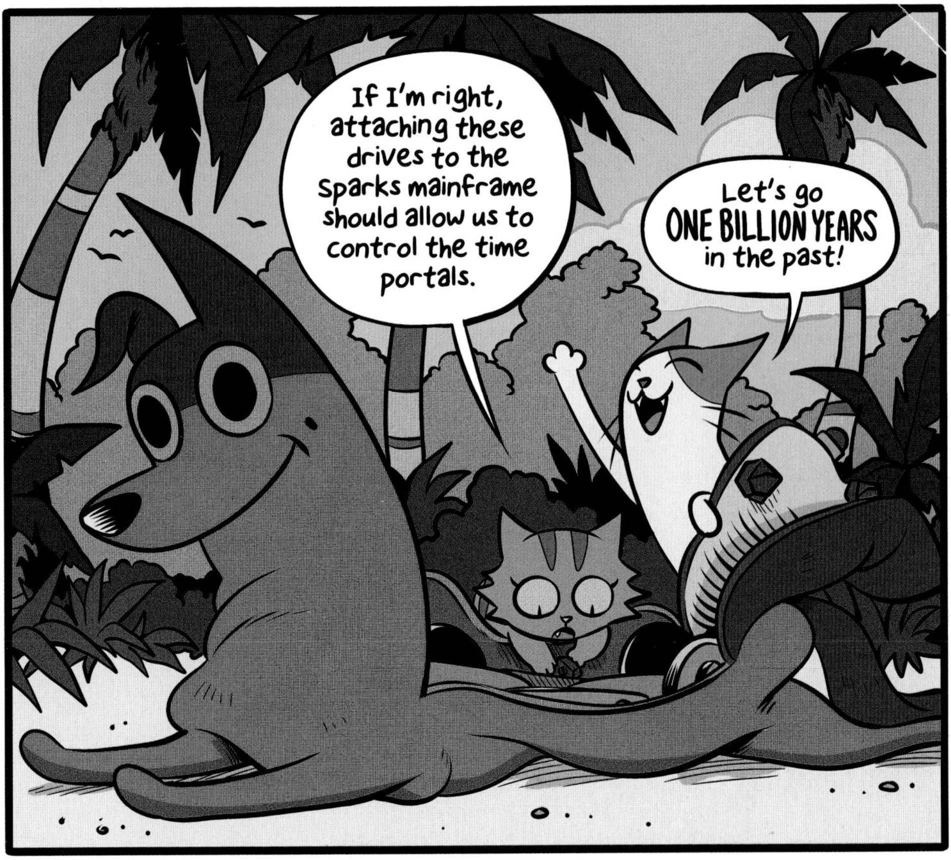
If I'm right, attaching these drives to the Sparks mainframe should allow us to control the time portals.
Let's go ONE BILLION YEARS in the past!

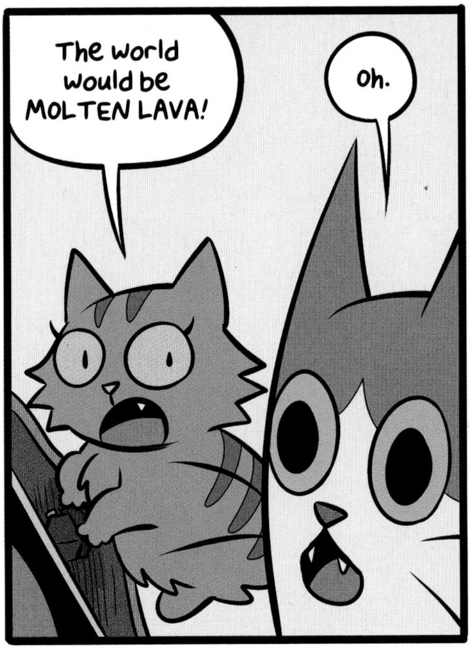
The world would be MOLTEN LAVA!
Oh.

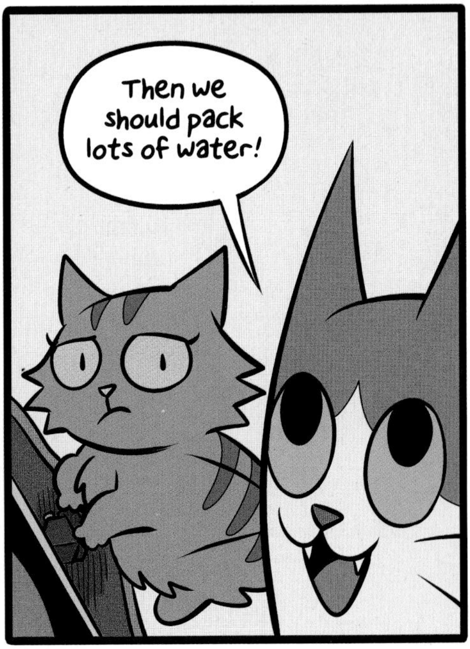
Then we should pack lots of water!

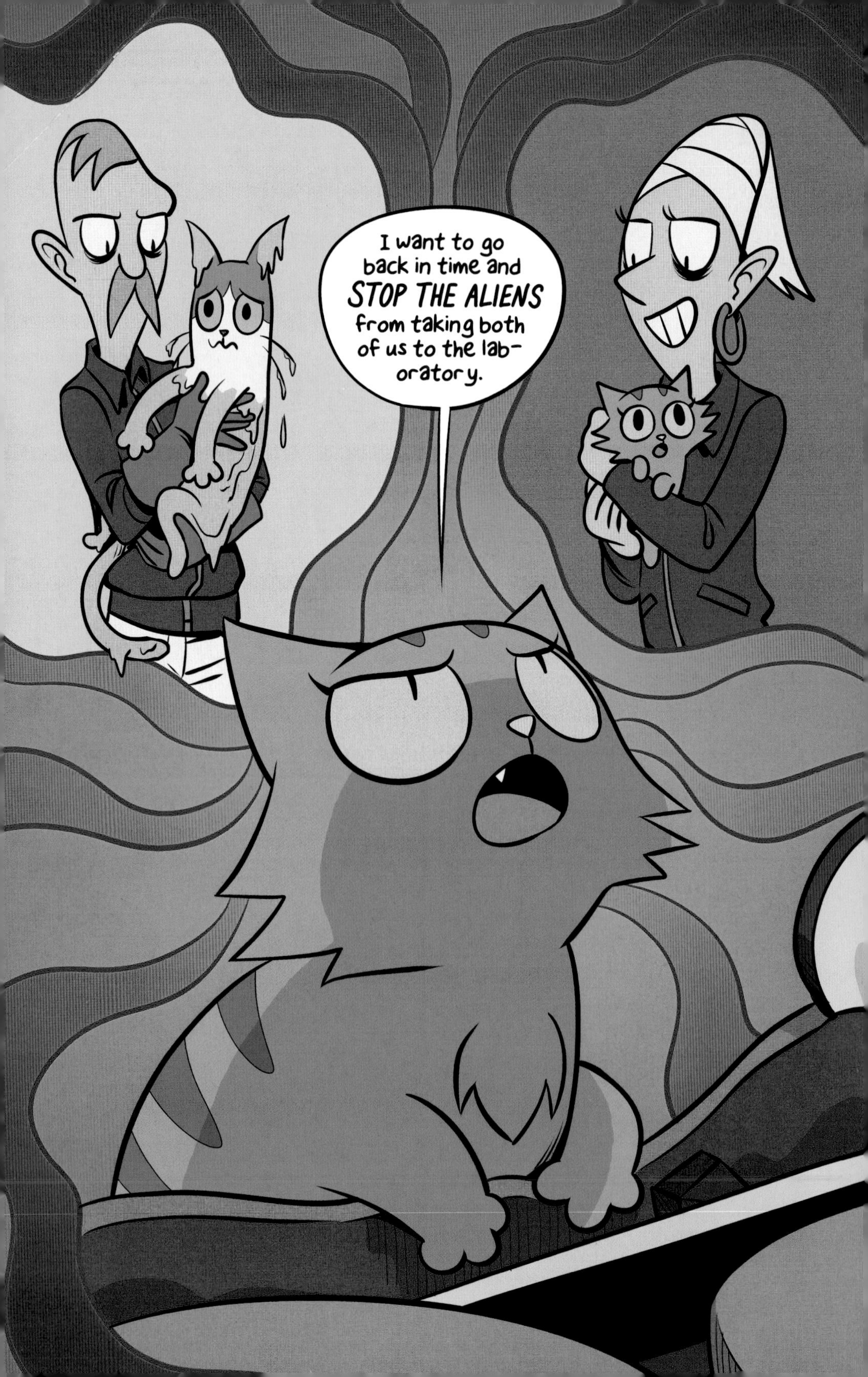
I want to go back in time and STOP THE ALIENS from taking both of us to the lab-oratory.

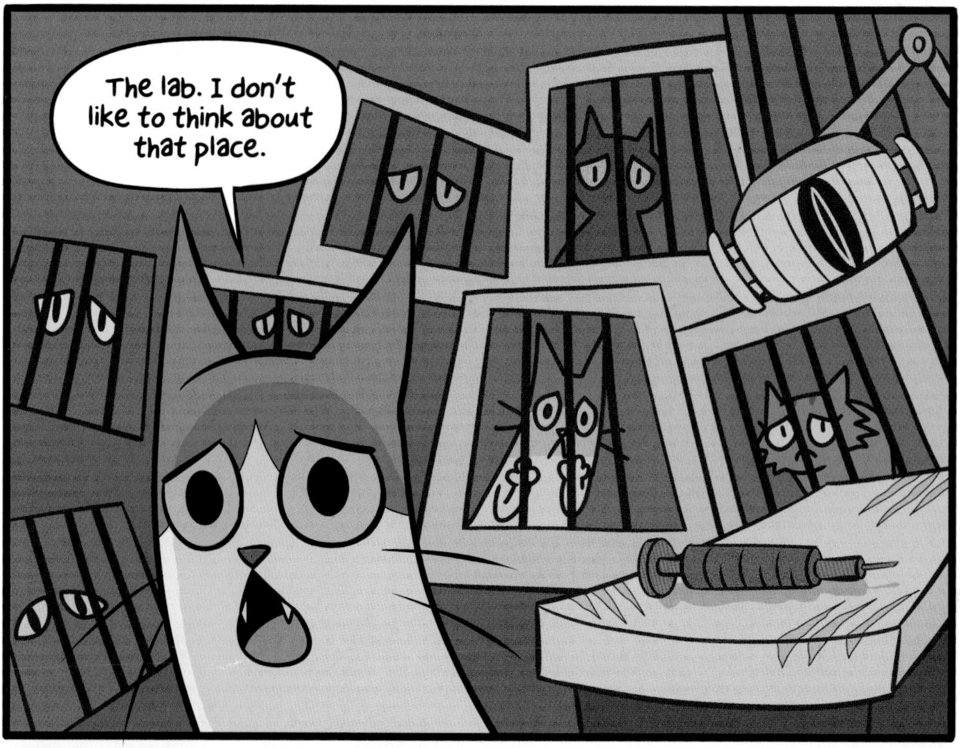
The lab. I don't like to think about that place.

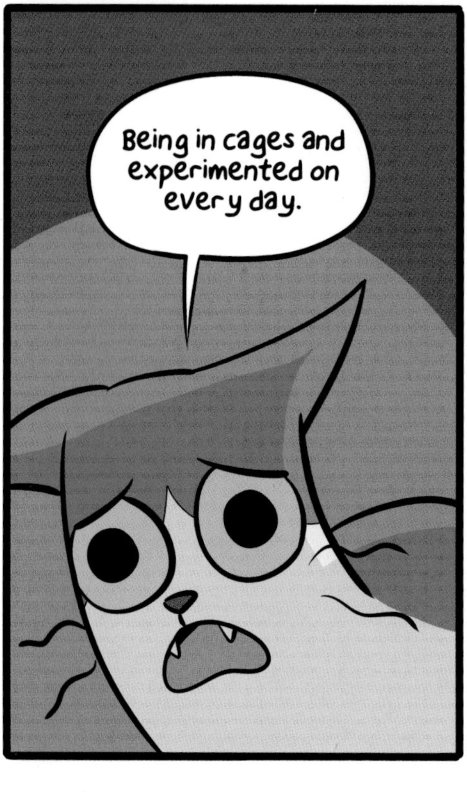
Being in cages and experimented on every day.

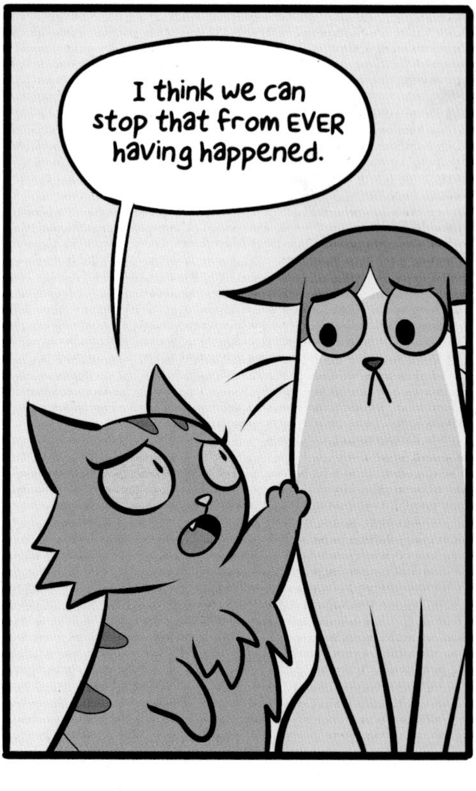
I think we can stop that from EVER having happened.

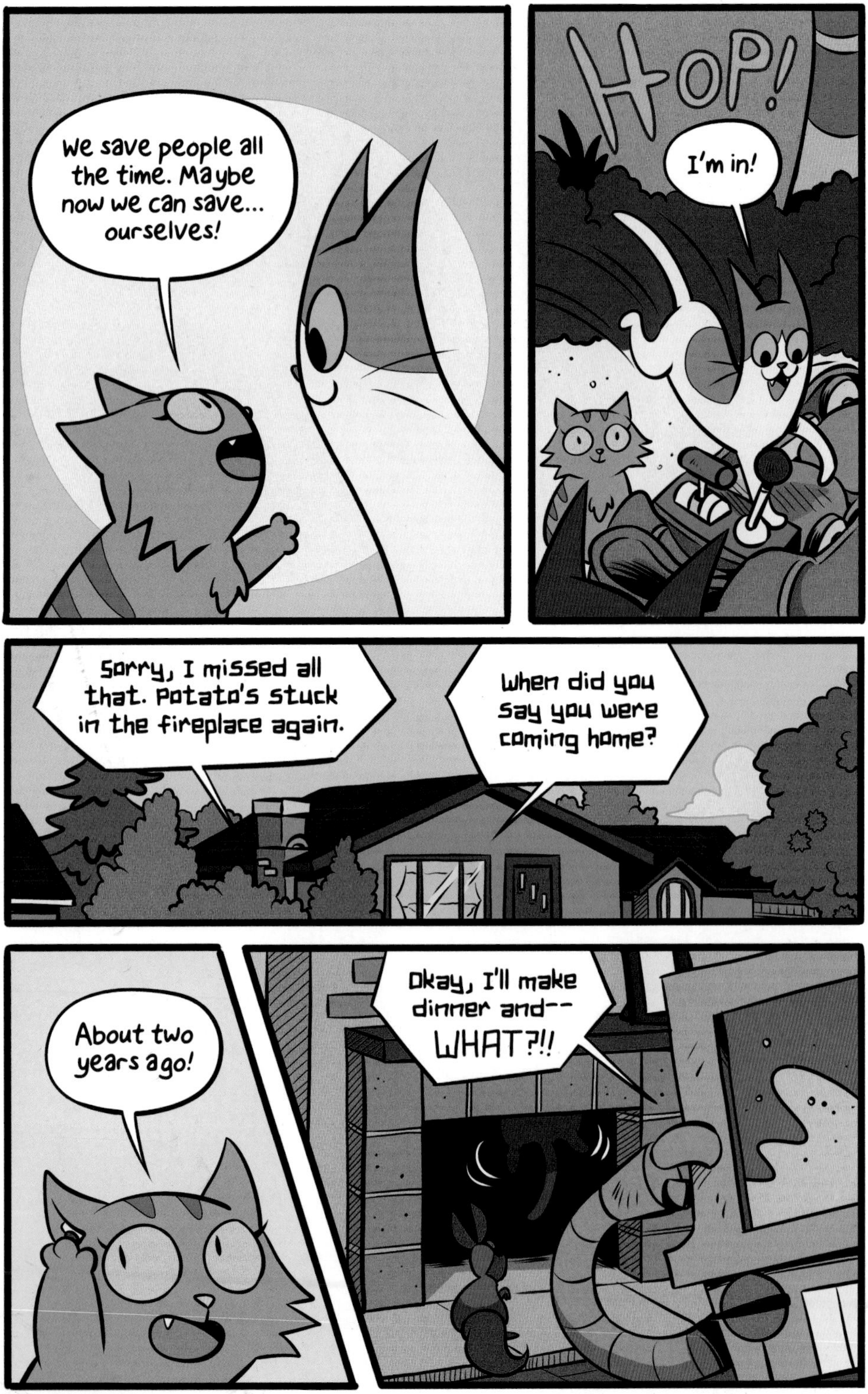
We save people all the time. Maybe now we can save... ourselves!
HOP!
I'm in!
Sorry, I missed all that. Potato's stuck in the fireplace again.
When did you say you were coming home?
About two years ago!
Okay, I'll make dinner and-- WHAT?!!

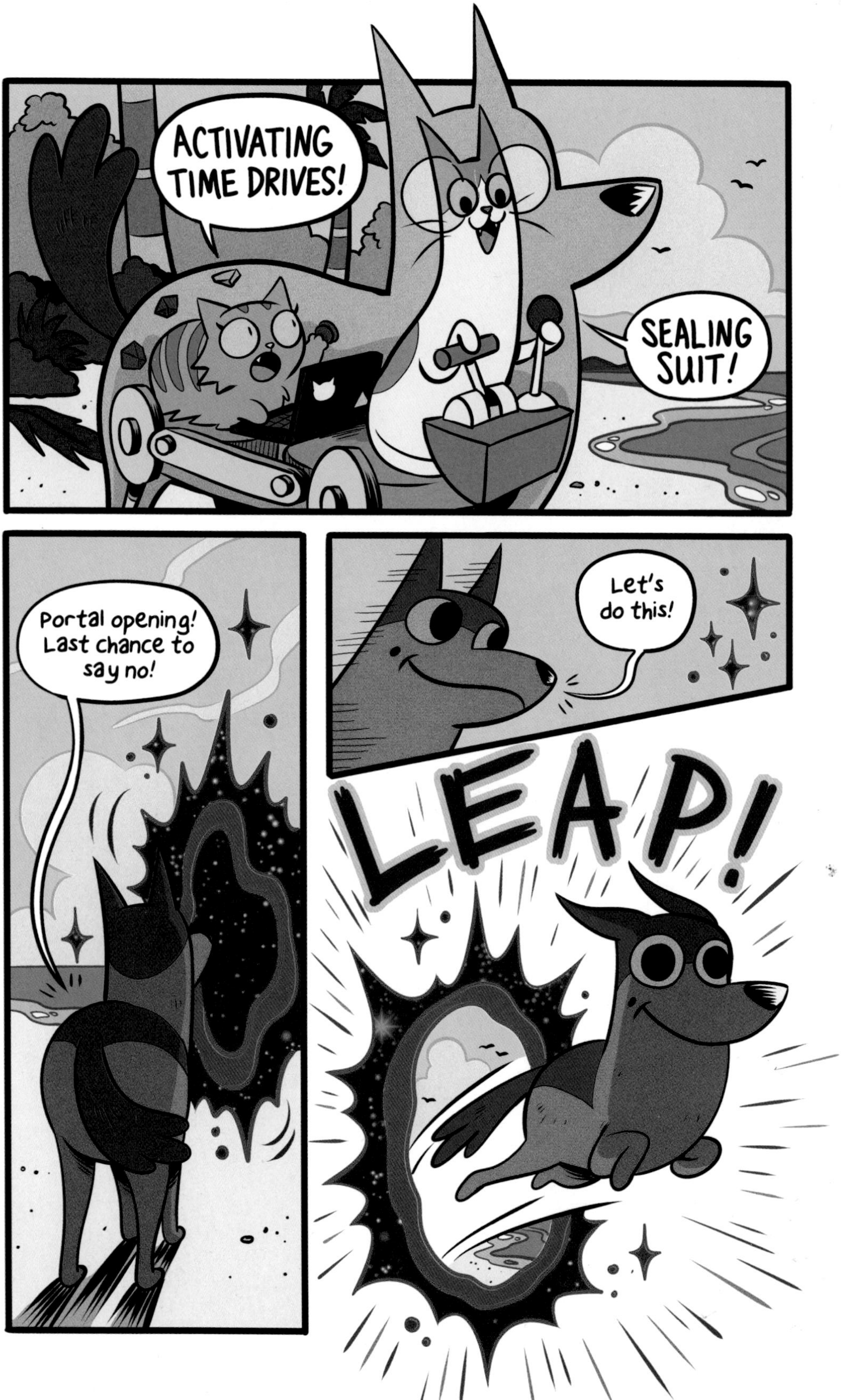
ACTIVATING TIME DRIVES!
SEALING SUIT!
Portal opening! Last chance to say no!
Let's do this!
LEAP!

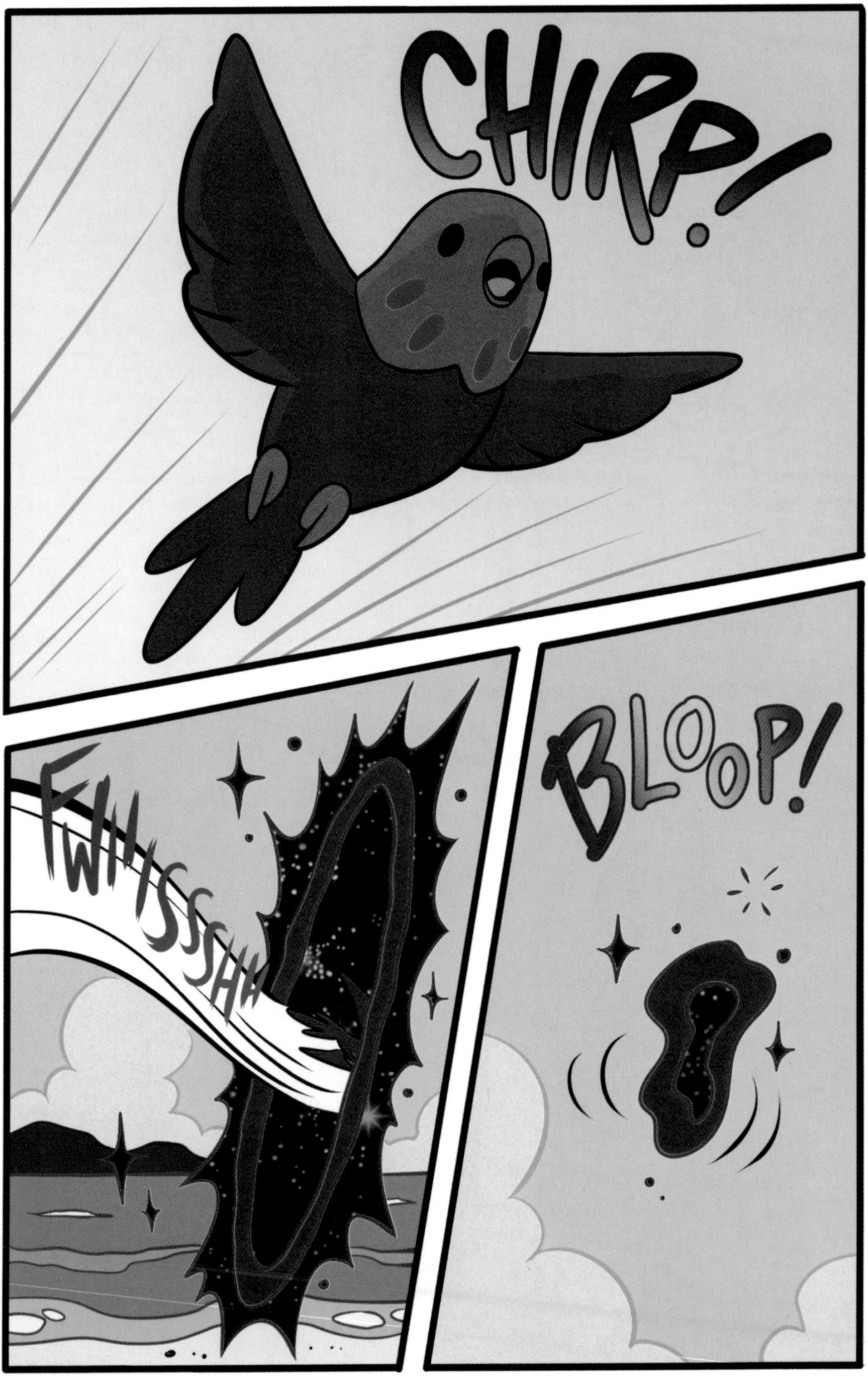
CHIRP!
FWIISSSHH
BLOOP!

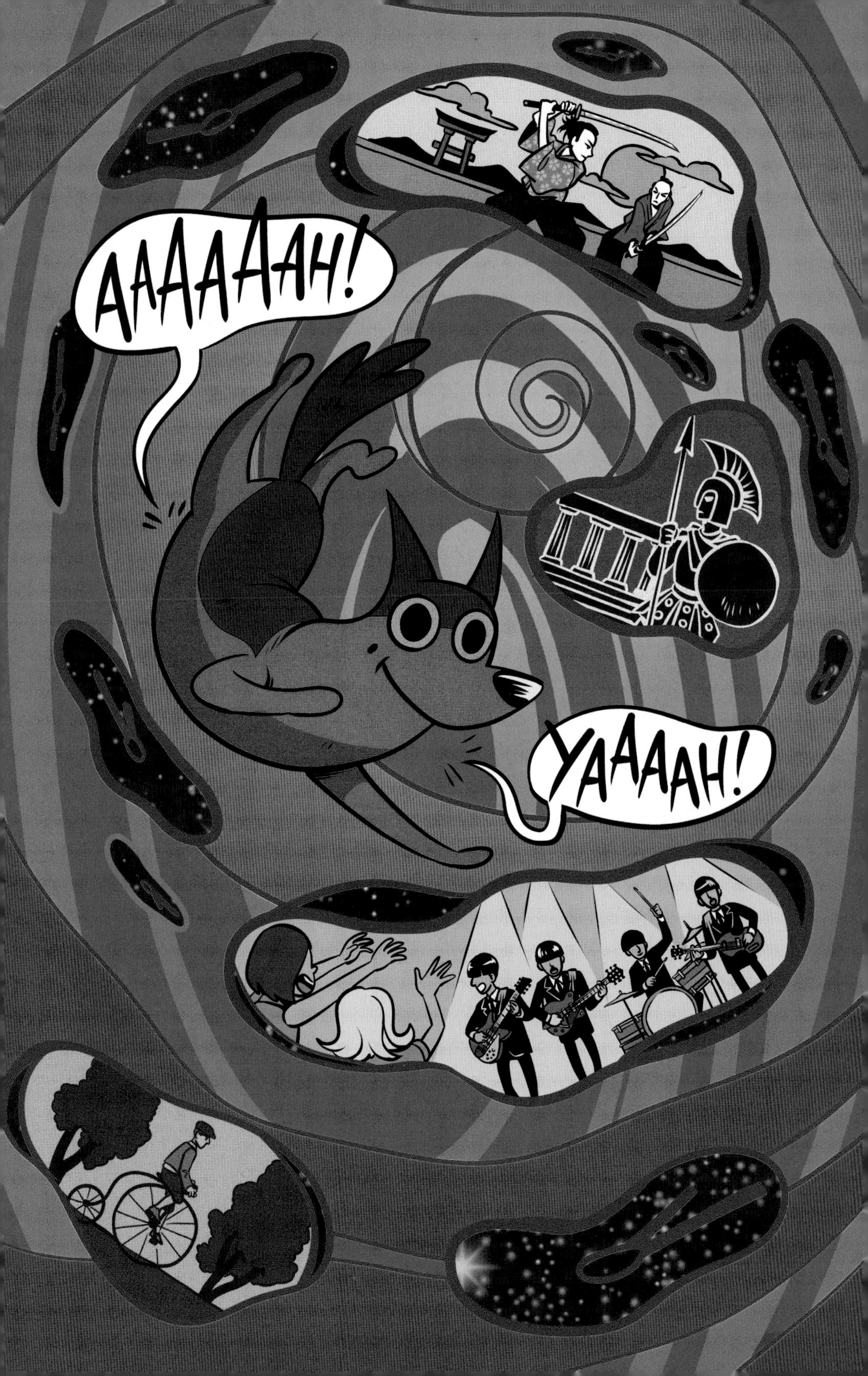
AAAAAAAH!
YAAAAH!

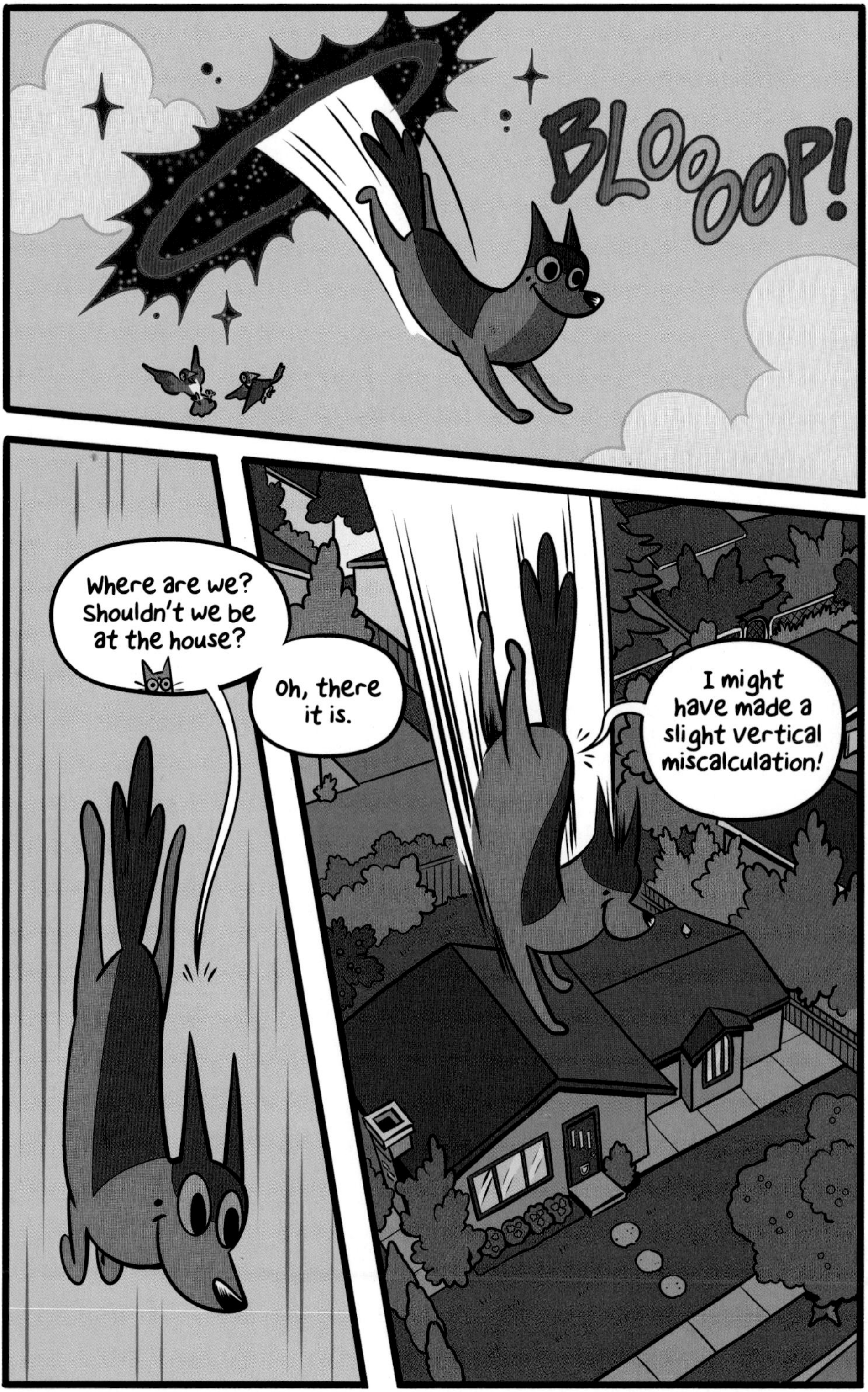
BLOOOOP!
Where are we? Shouldn't we be at the house?
Oh, there it is.
I might have made a slight vertical miscalculation!

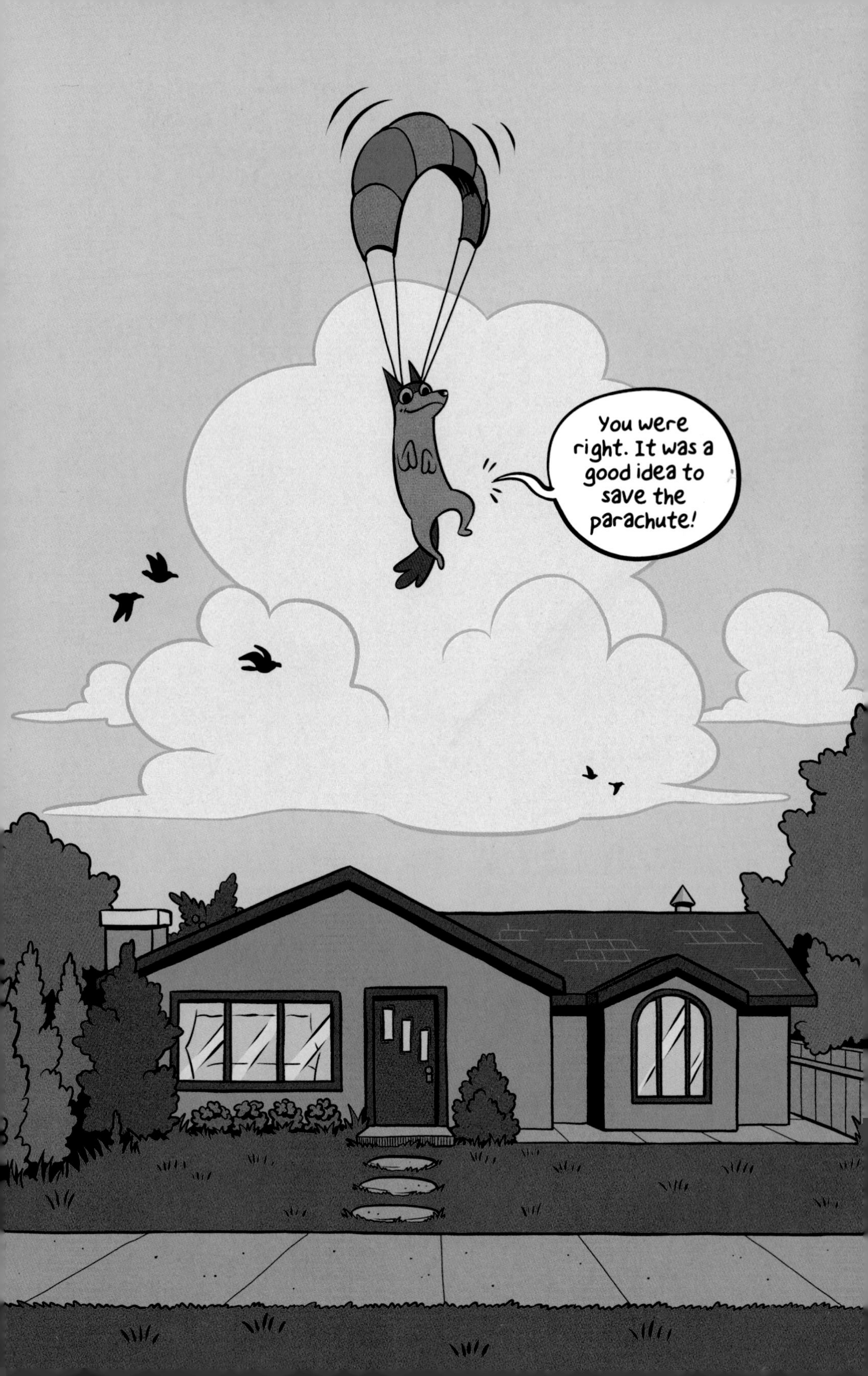
You were right. It was a good idea to save the parachute!

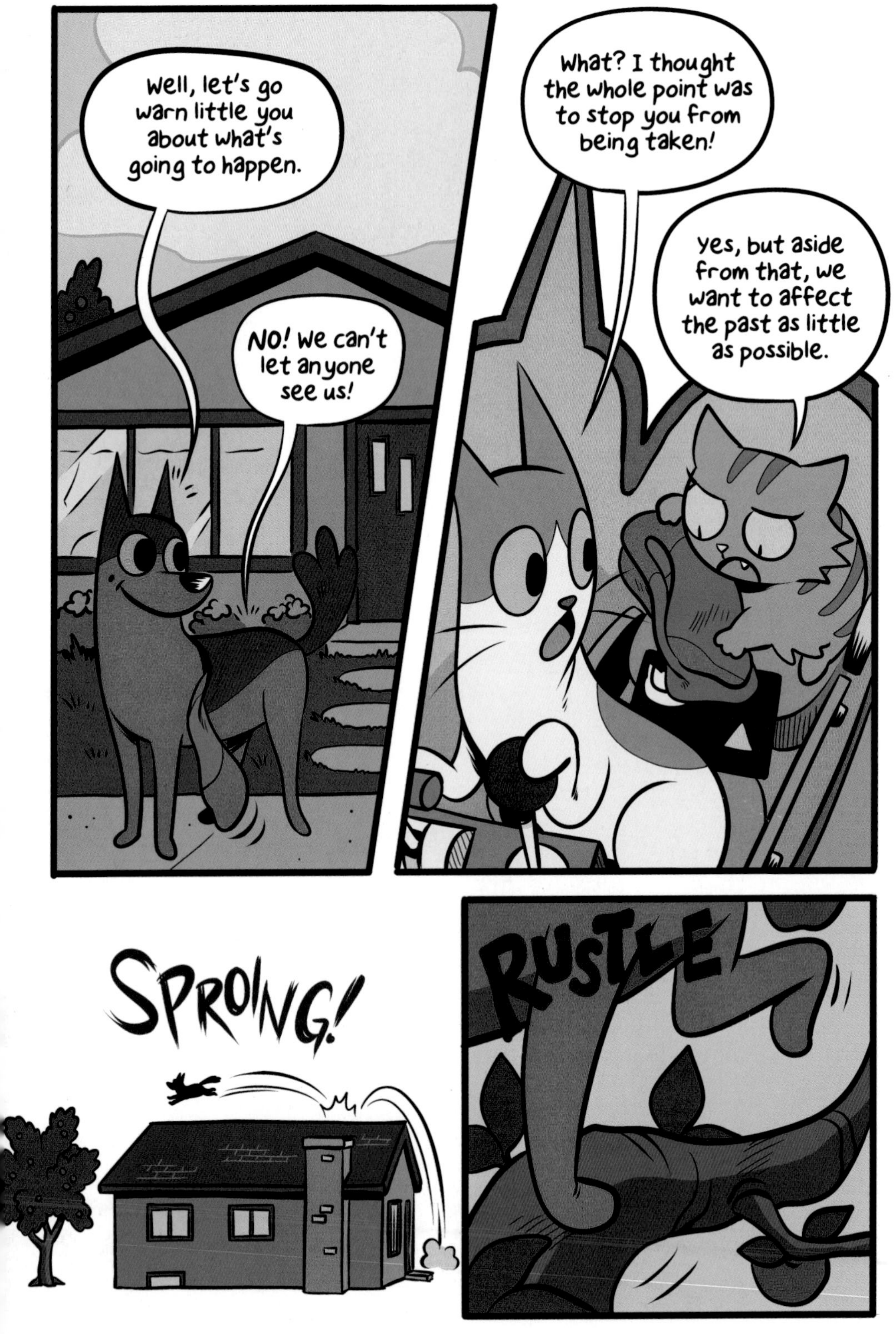
Well, let's go warn little you about what's going to happen.
NO! We can't let anyone see us!
What? I thought the whole point was to stop you from being taken!
Yes, but aside from that, we want to affect the past as little as possible.
SPROING!
RUSTLE

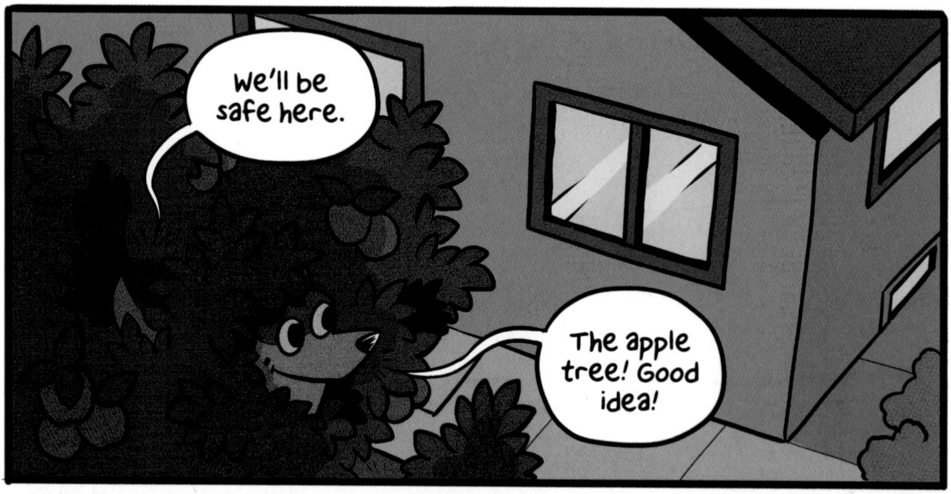
We'll be safe here.
The apple tree! Good idea!

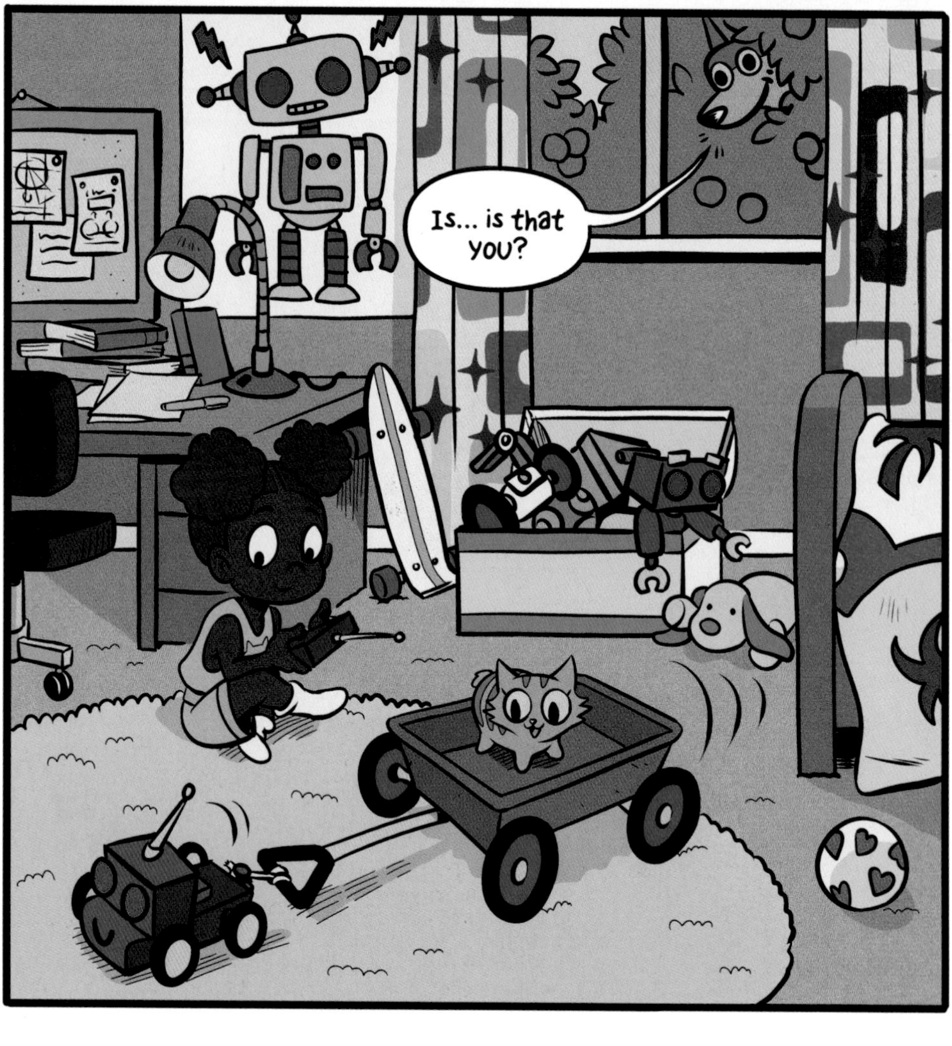
Is... is that you?

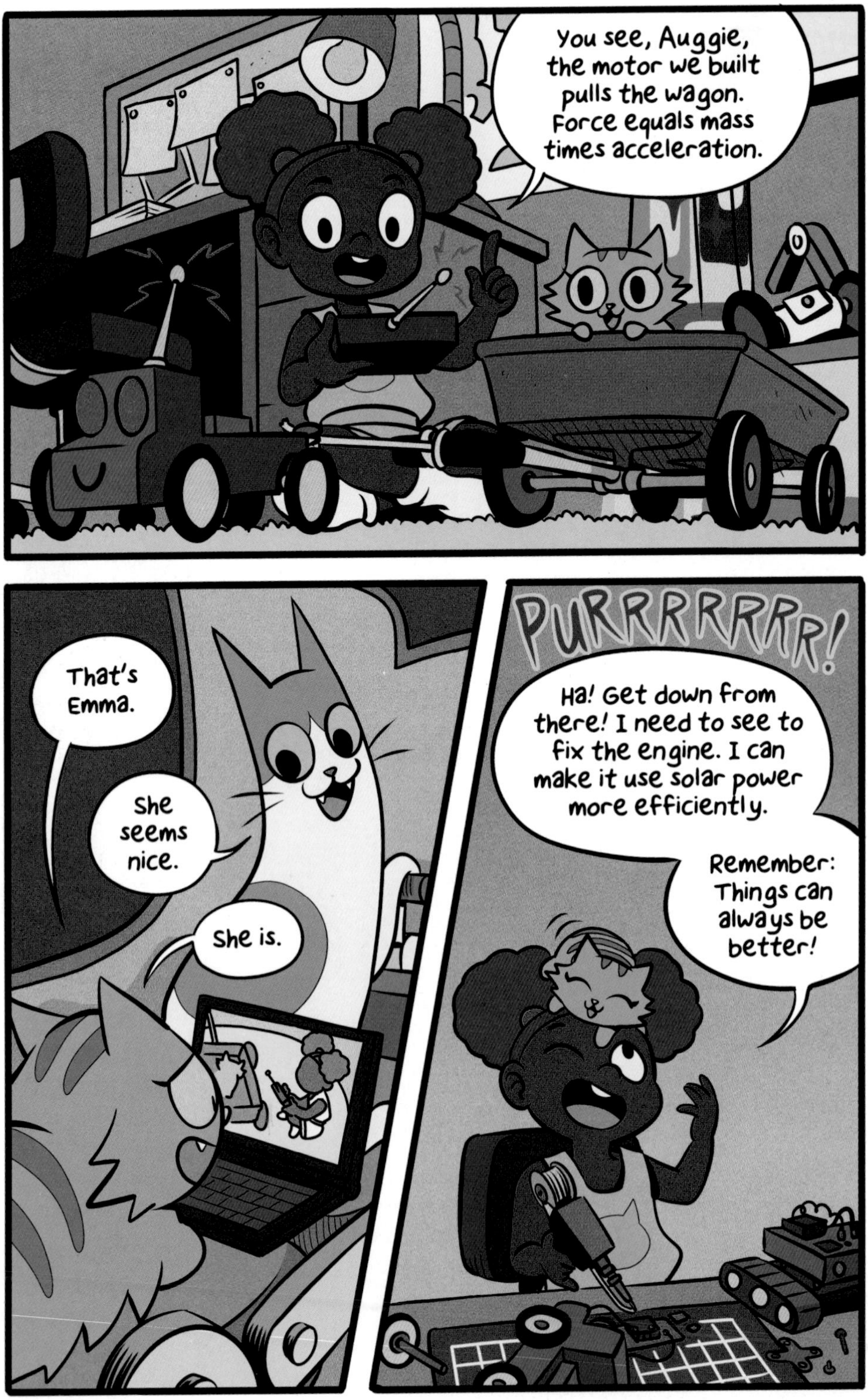

You see, Auggie, the motor we built pulls the wagon. Force equals mass times acceleration.
That's Emma.
She seems nice.
She is.
PURRRRRRR!
Ha! Get down from there! I need to see to fix the engine. I can make it use solar power more efficiently.
Remember: Things can always be better!

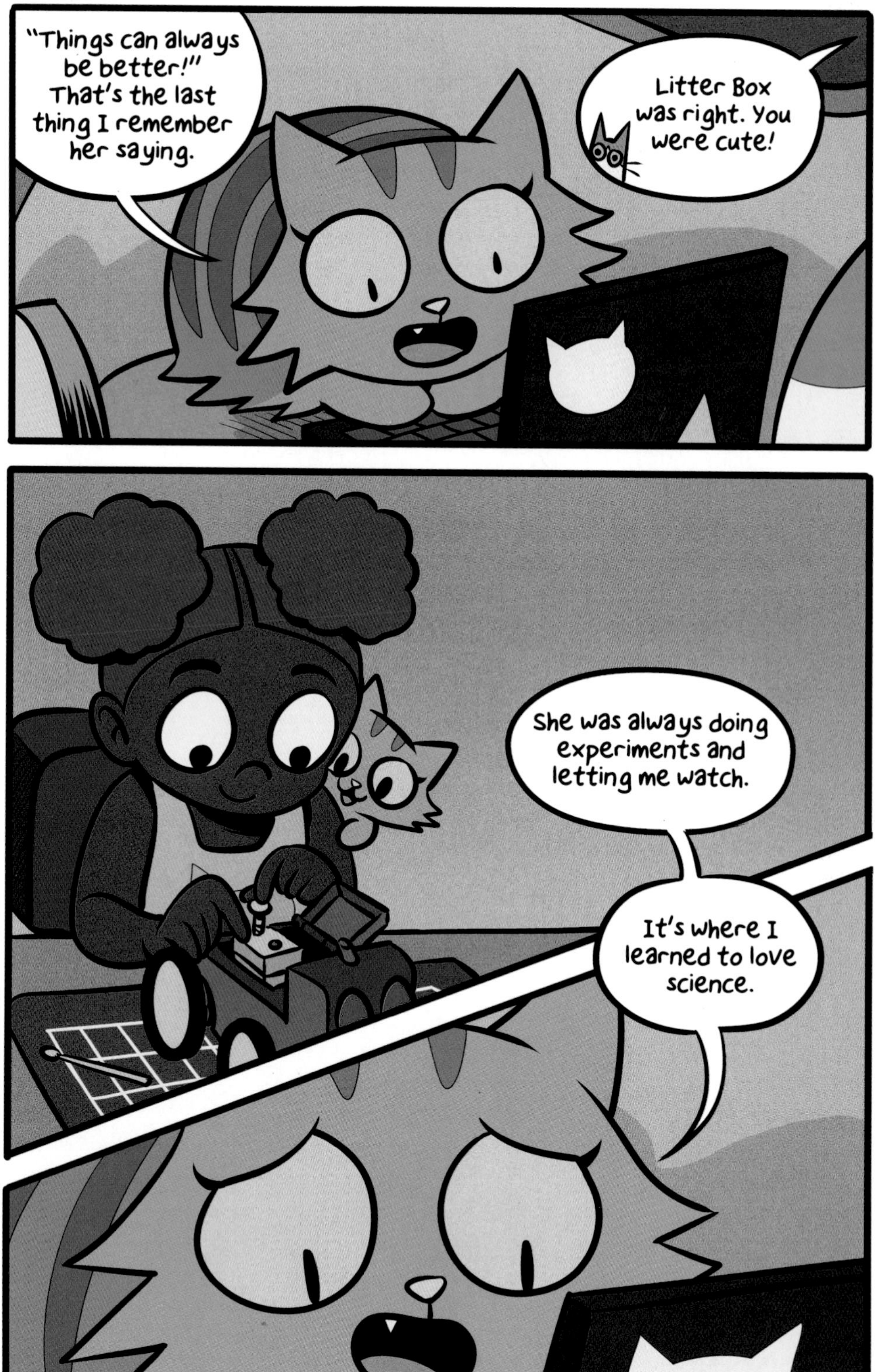
"Things can always be better!" That's the last thing I remember her saying.
Litter Box was right. You were cute!
She was always doing experiments and letting me watch.
It's where I learned to love science.

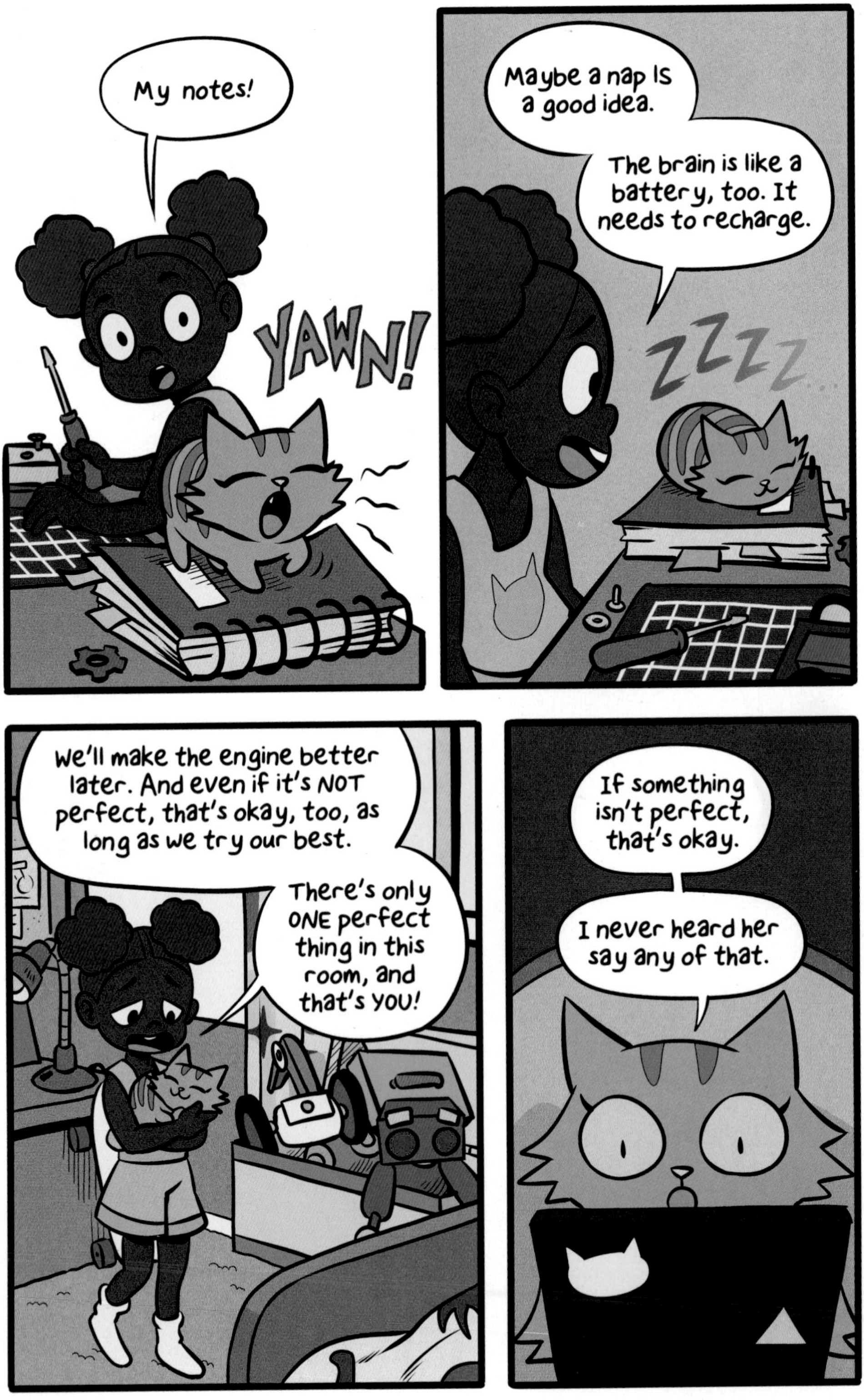
My notes!
YAWN!
Maybe a nap is a good idea.
The brain is like a battery, too. It needs to recharge.
ZZZZ
We'll make the engine better later. And even if it's NOT perfect, that's okay, too, as long as we try our best.
There's only ONE perfect thing in this room, and that's YOU!
If something isn't perfect, that's okay.
I never heard her say any of that.

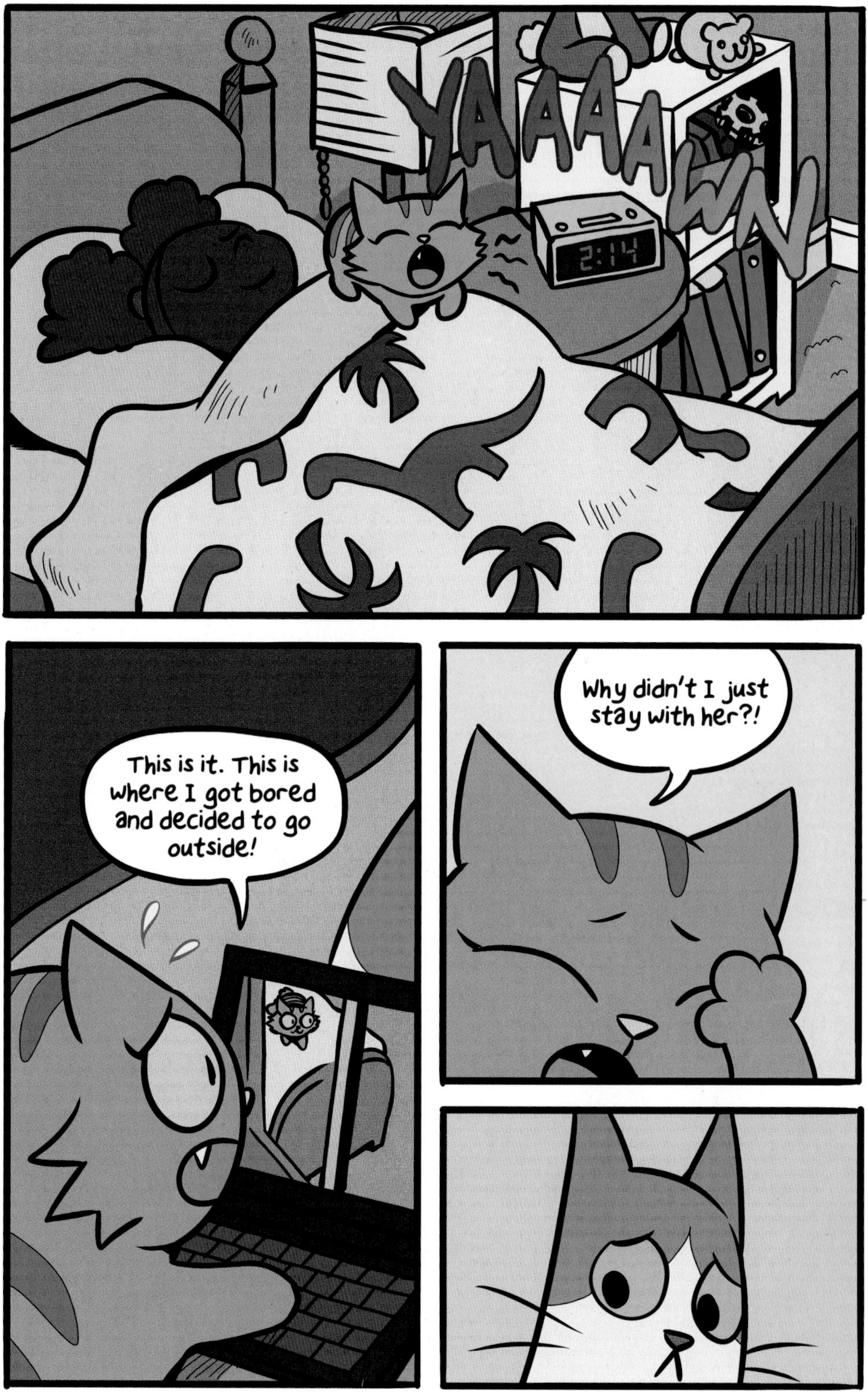

YAAAAWN
2:14
This is it. This is where I got bored and decided to go outside!
Why didn't I just stay with her?!

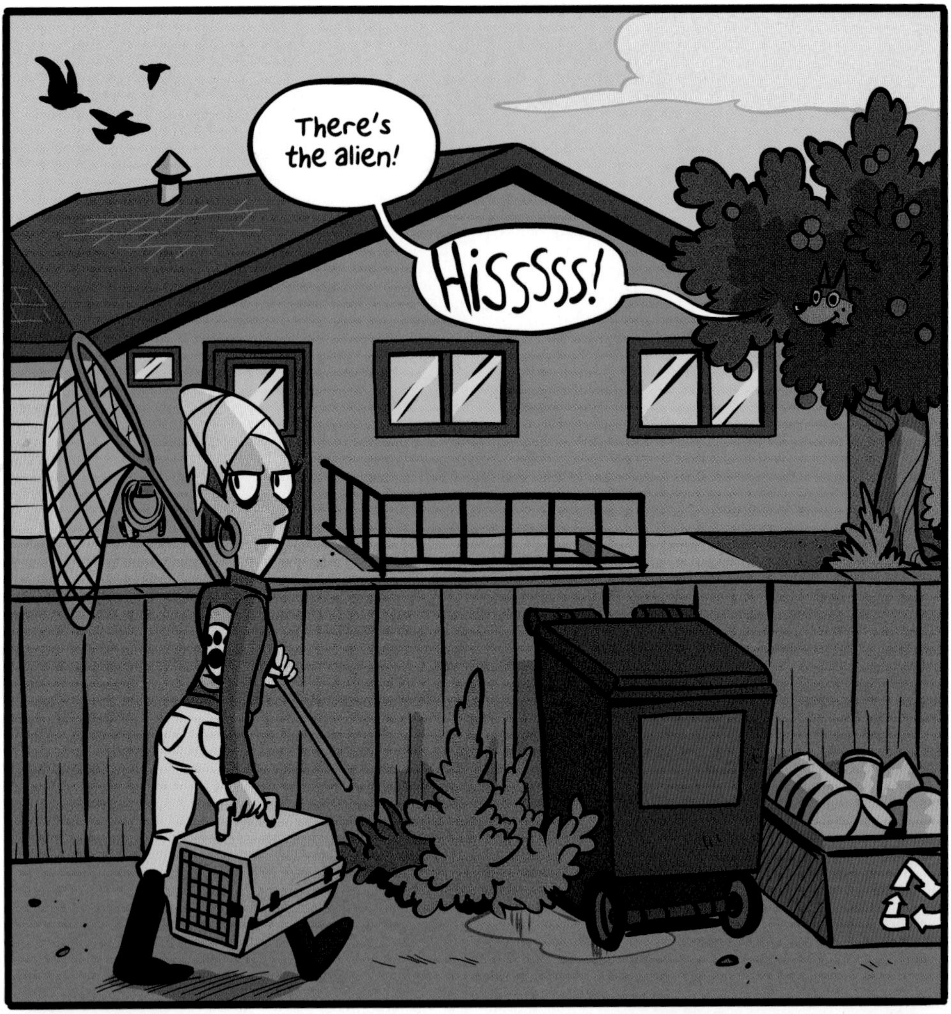
There's the alien!
Hisssss!

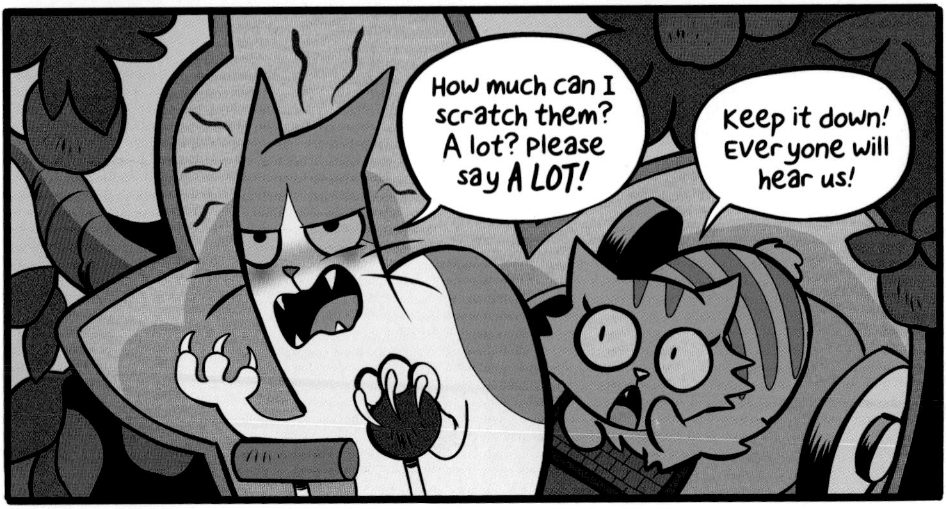
How much can I scratch them? A lot? Please say A LOT!
Keep it down! Everyone will hear us!

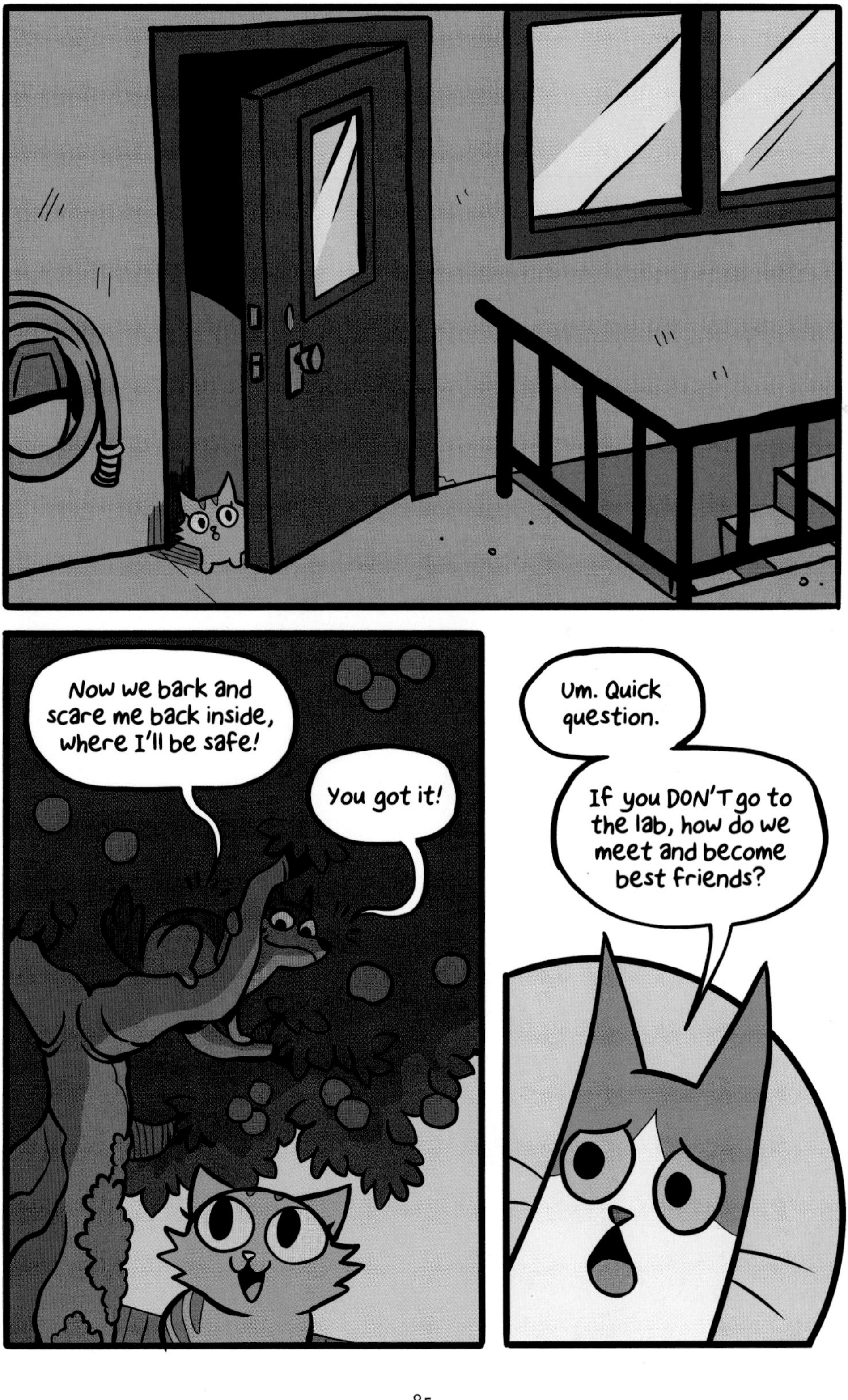
Now we bark and scare me back inside, where I'll be safe!
You got it!
Um. Quick question.
If you DON'T go to the lab, how do we meet and become best friends?

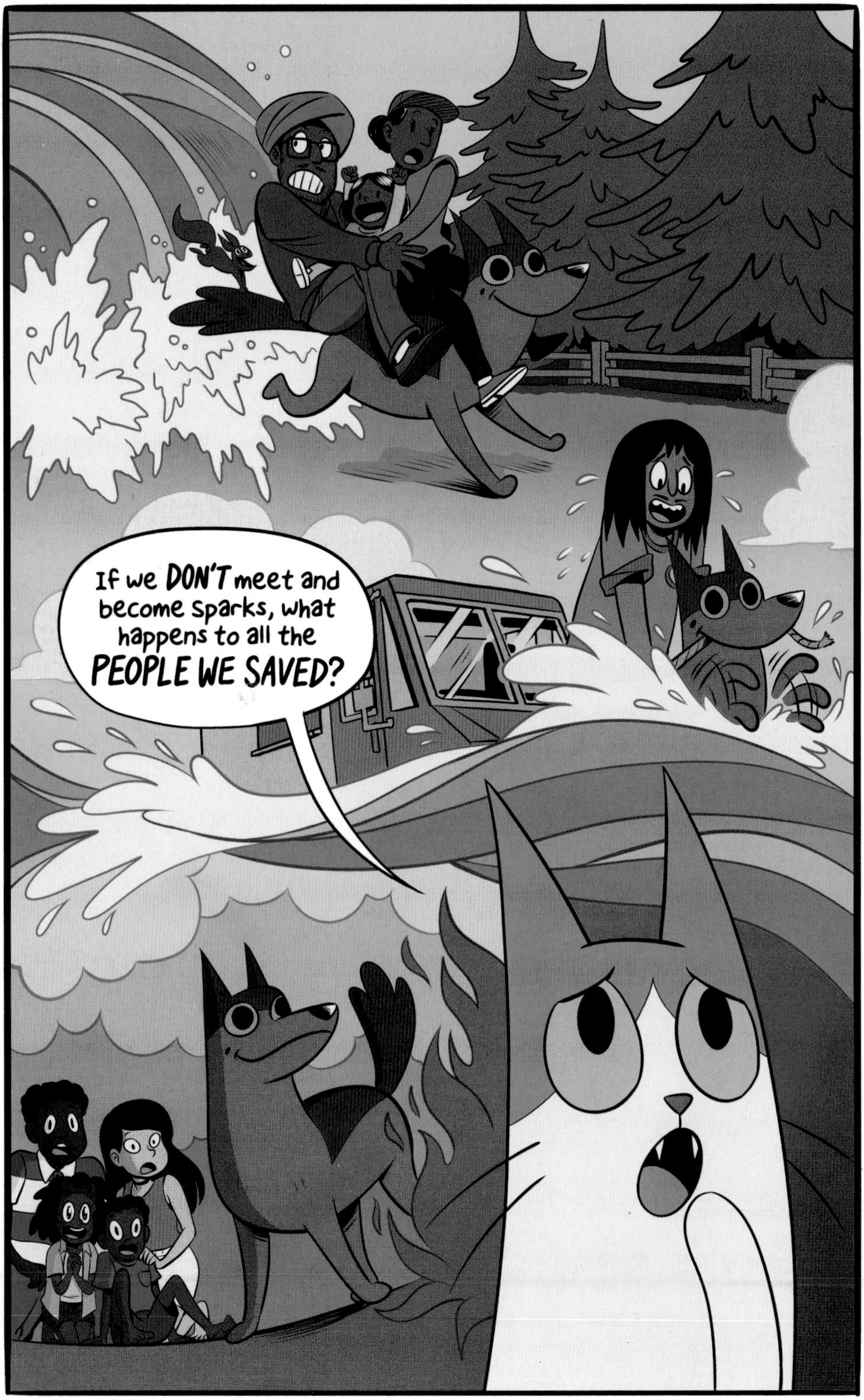
If we DON'T meet and become sparks, what happens to all the PEOPLE WE SAVED?

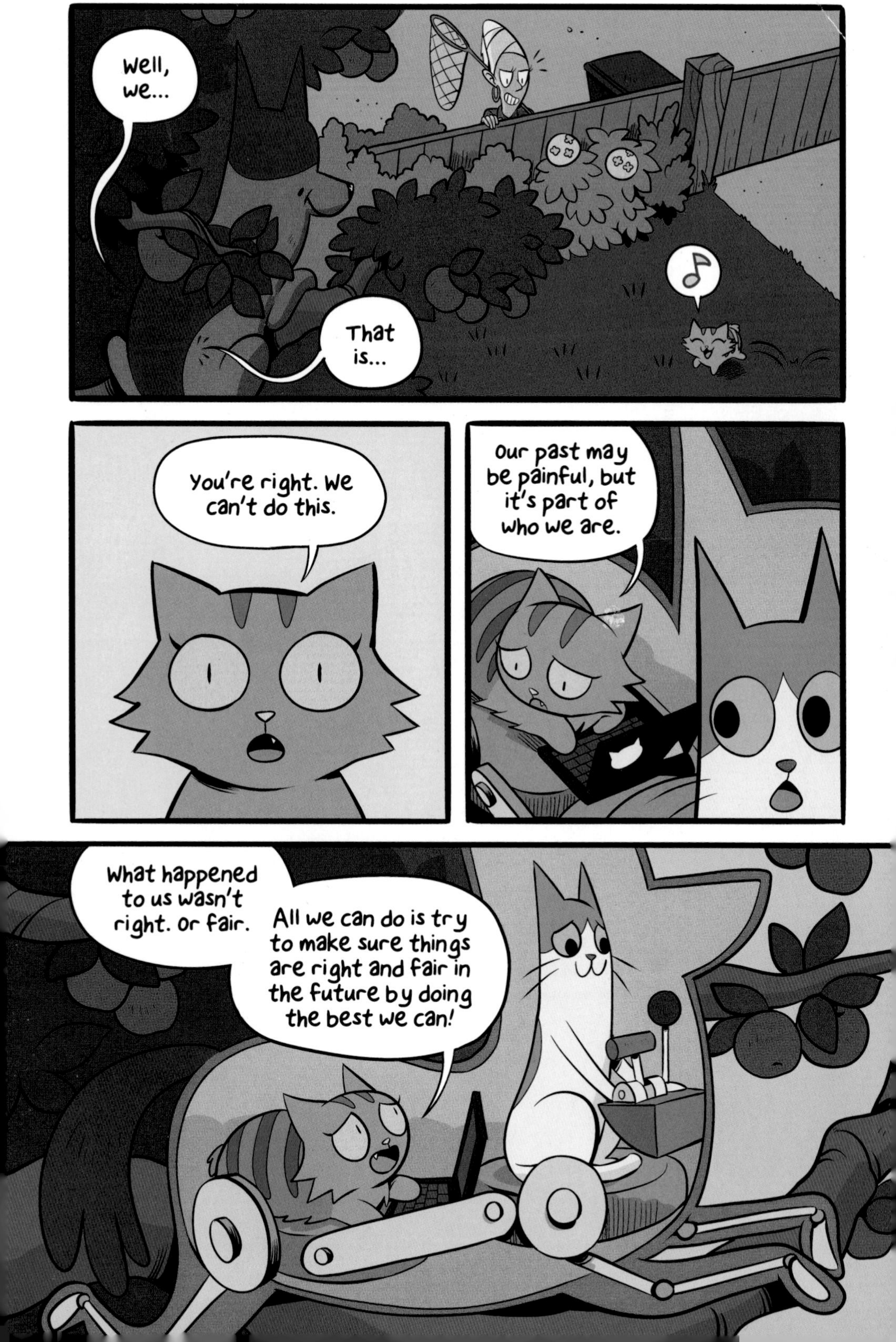
Well, we...
That is...
♪
You're right. We can't do this.
Our past may be painful, but it's part of who we are.
What happened to us wasn't right. Or fair.
All we can do is try to make sure things are right and fair in the future by doing the best we can!

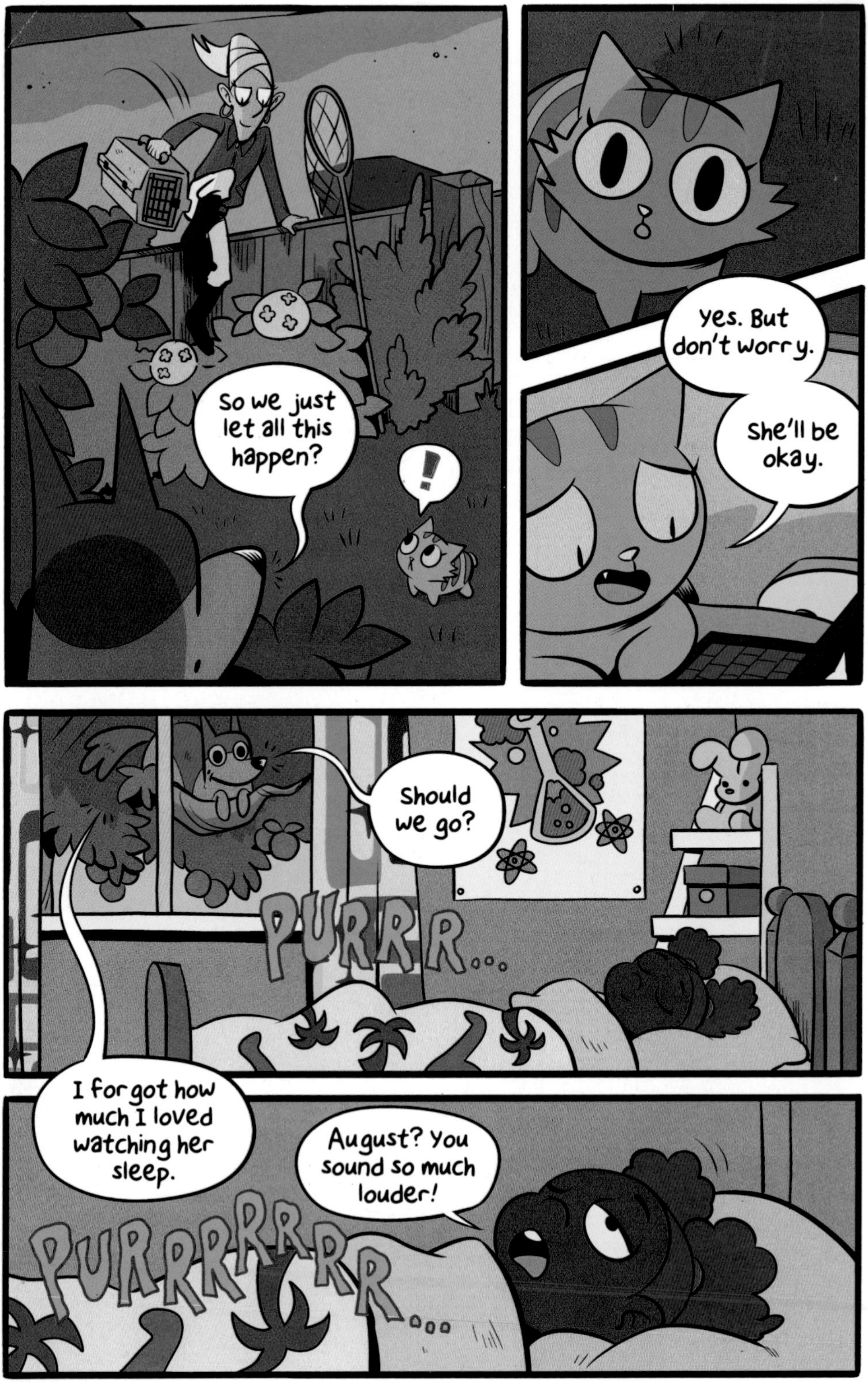
So we just let all this happen?
!
Yes. But don't worry.
She'll be okay.
Should we go?
PURRR...
I forgot how much I loved watching her sleep.
August? You sound so much louder!
PURRRRRRR...

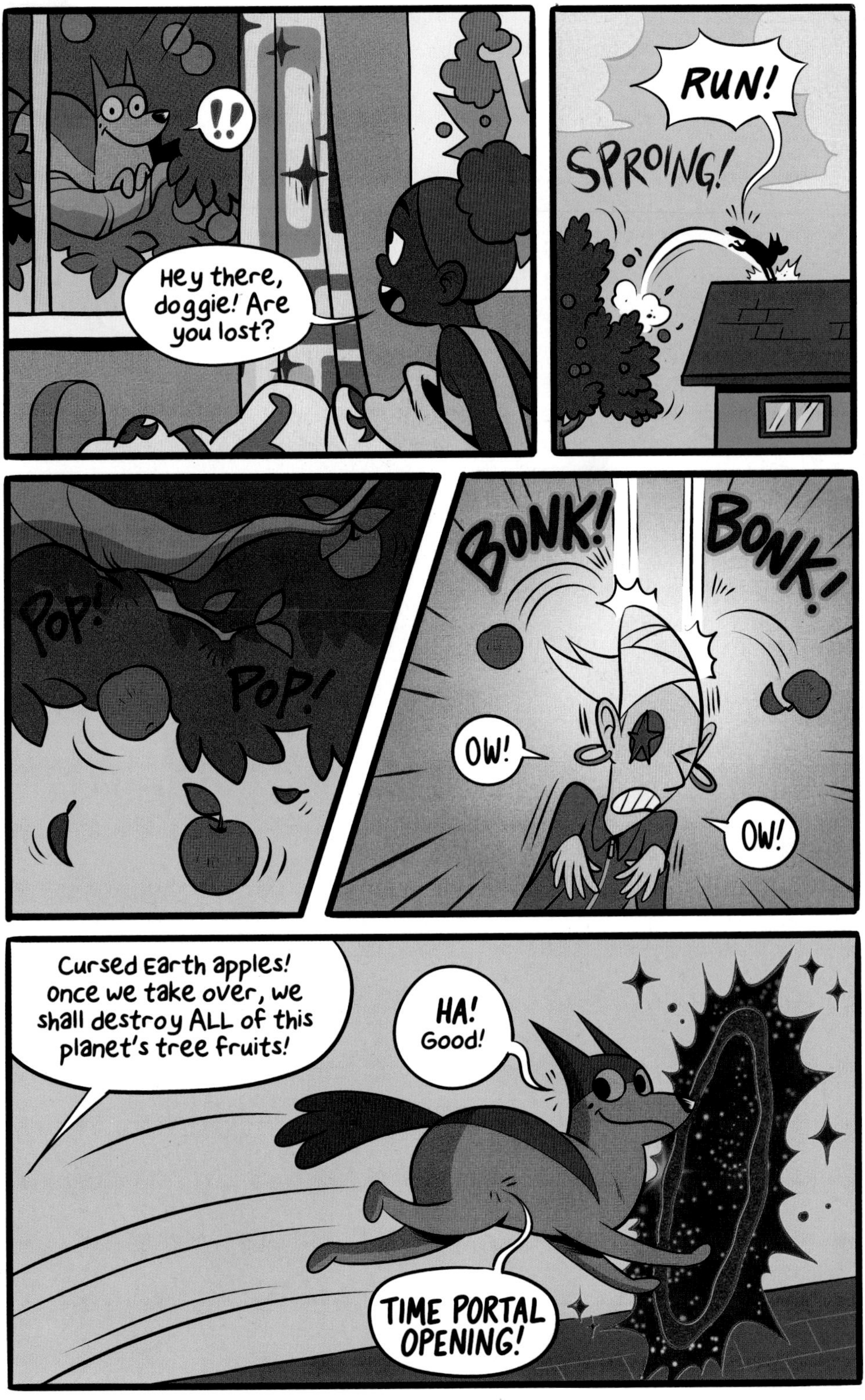
!!
Hey there, doggie! Are you lost?
RUN!
SPROING!
POP!
POP!
BONK!
BONK!
OW!
OW!
Cursed Earth apples! once we take over, we shall destroy ALL of this planet's tree fruits!
HA! Good!
TIME PORTAL OPENING!

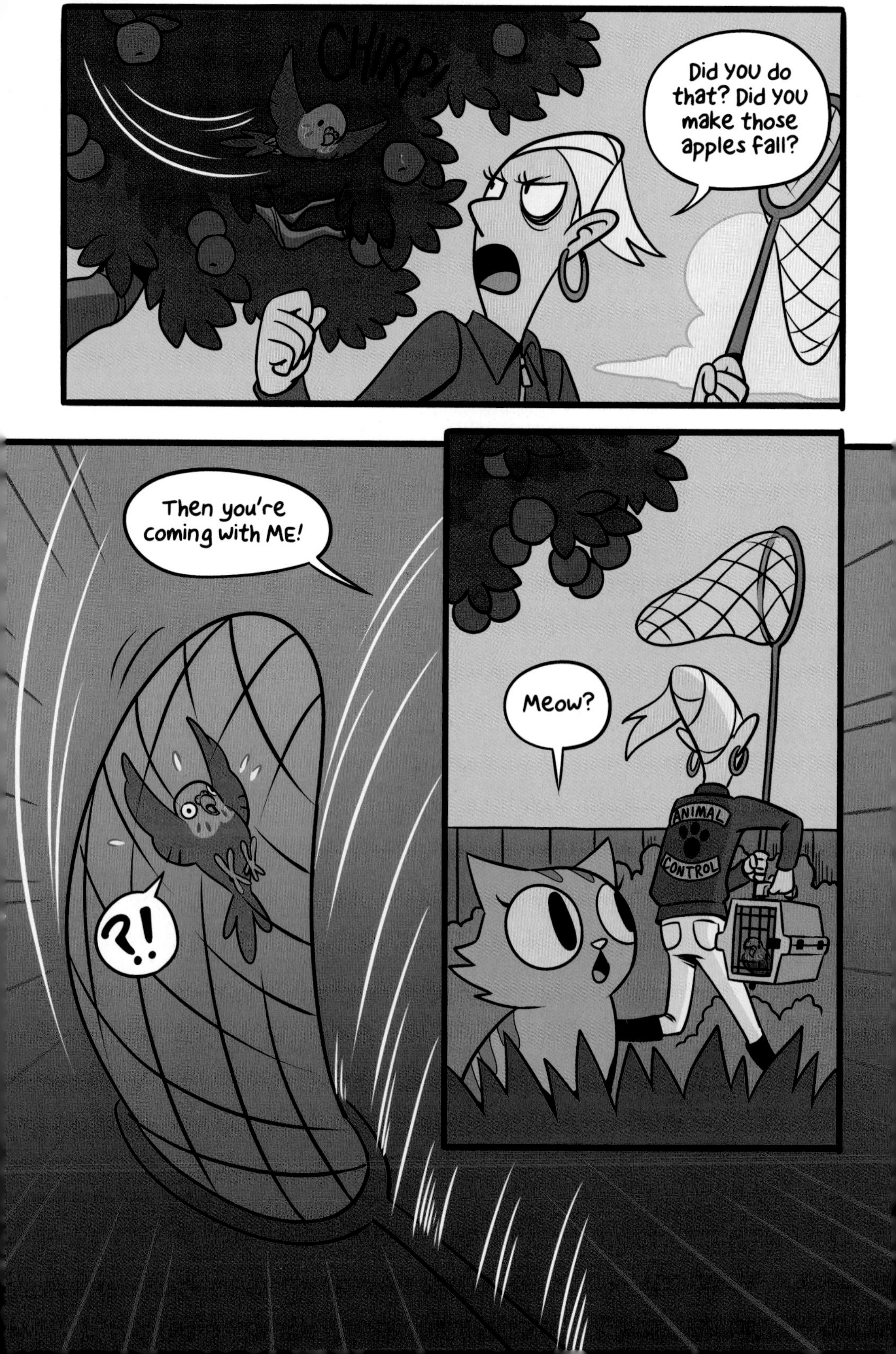
CHIRP!
Did YOU do that? Did YOU make those apples fall?
Then you're coming with ME!
?!
Meow?
ANIMAL CONTROL

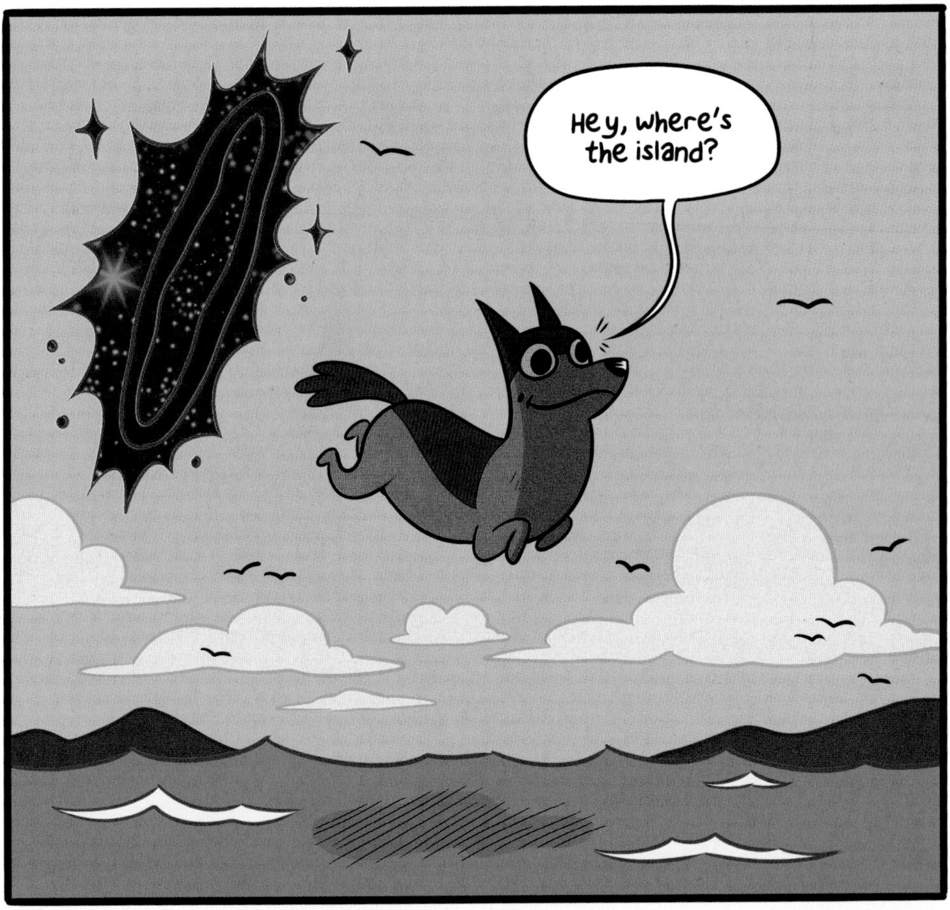
Hey, where's the island?

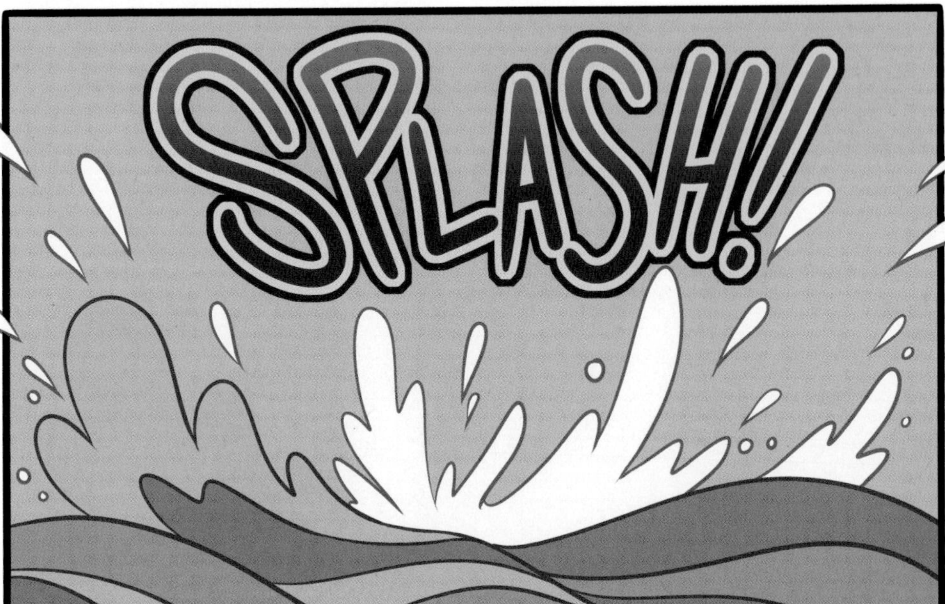
SPLASH!

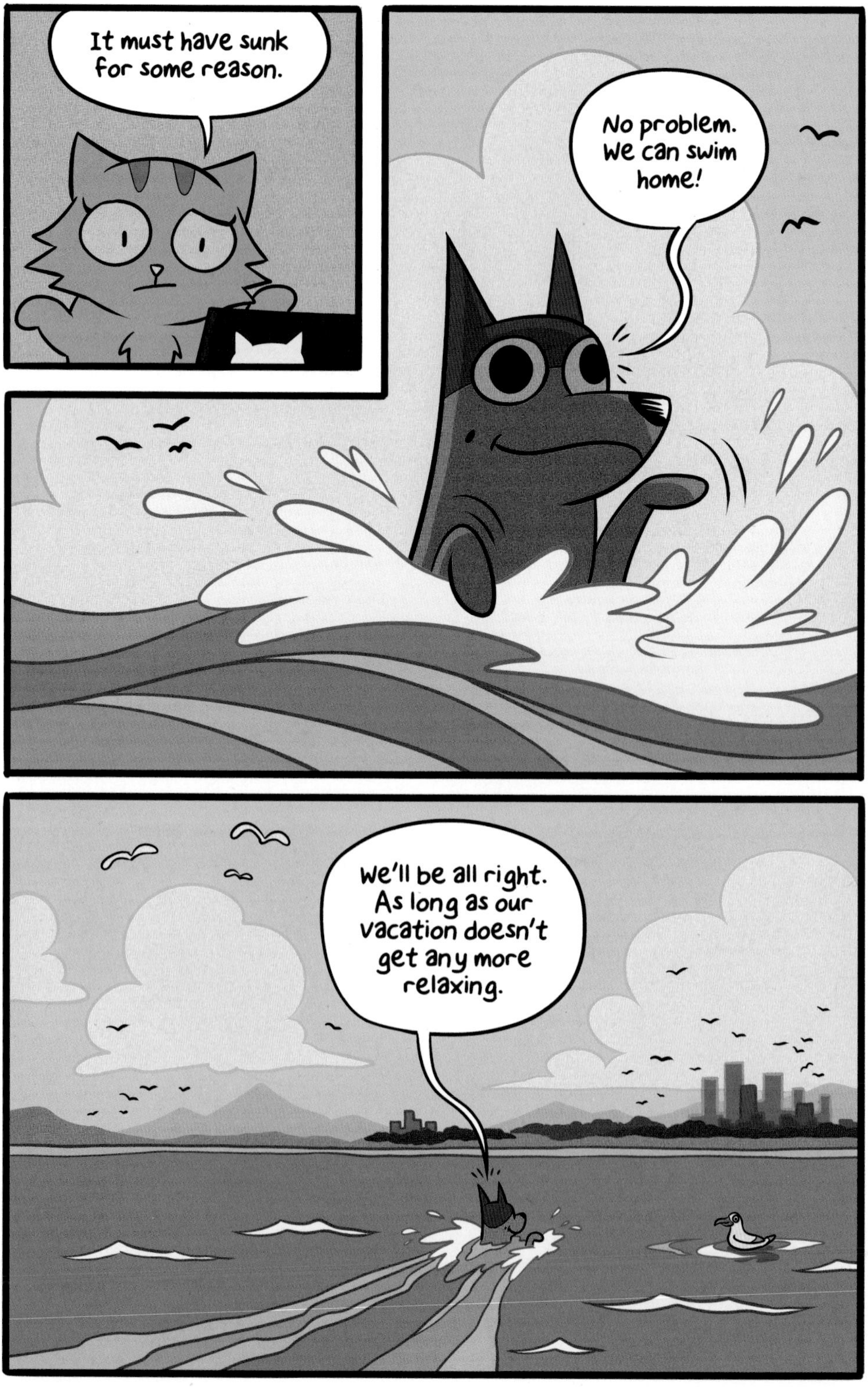
It must have sunk for some reason.
No problem. We can swim home!
We'll be all right. As long as our vacation doesn't get any more relaxing.

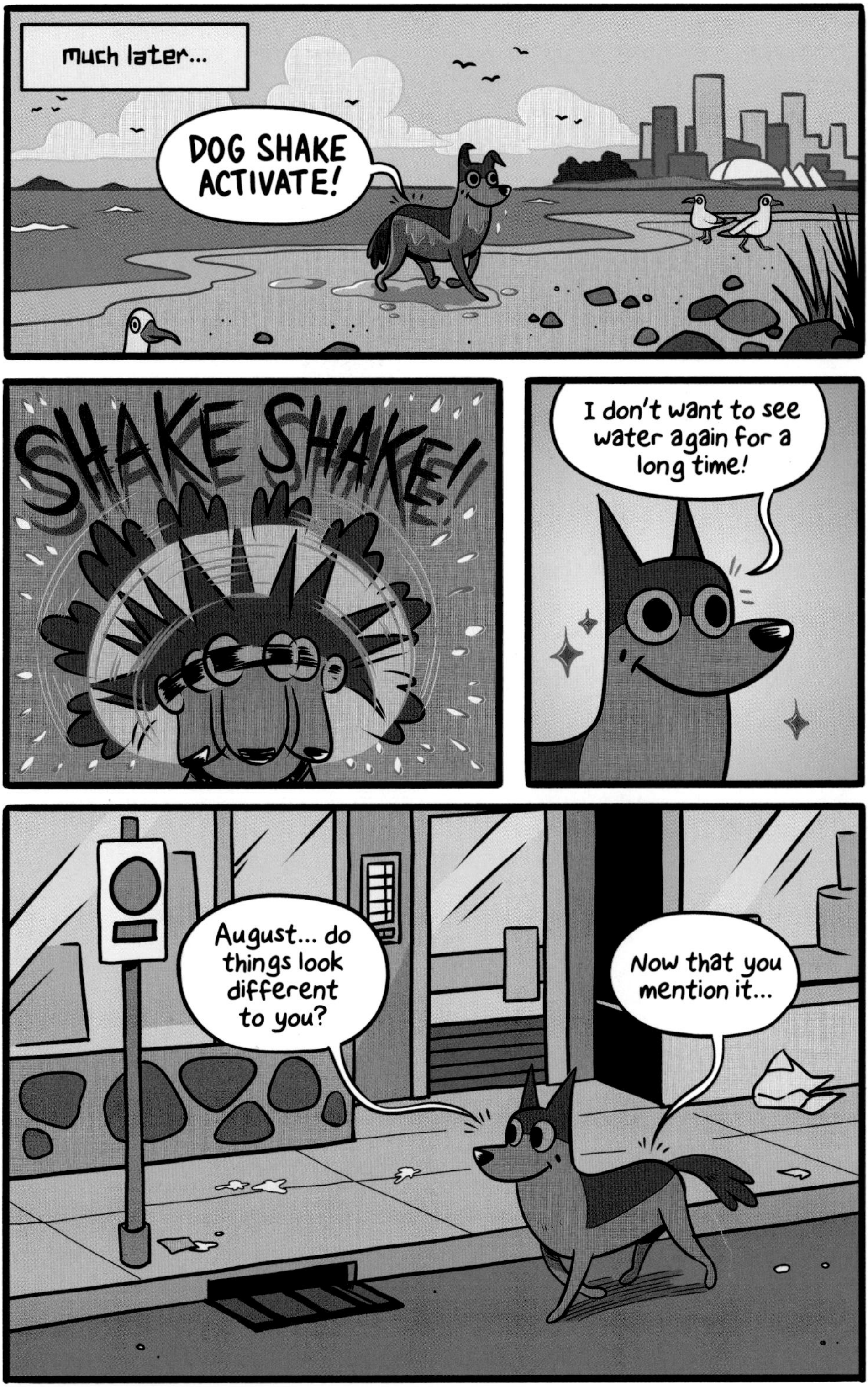
much later...
DOG SHAKE ACTIVATE!
SHAKE SHAKE!
I don't want to see water again for a long time!
August... do things look different to you?
Now that you mention it...

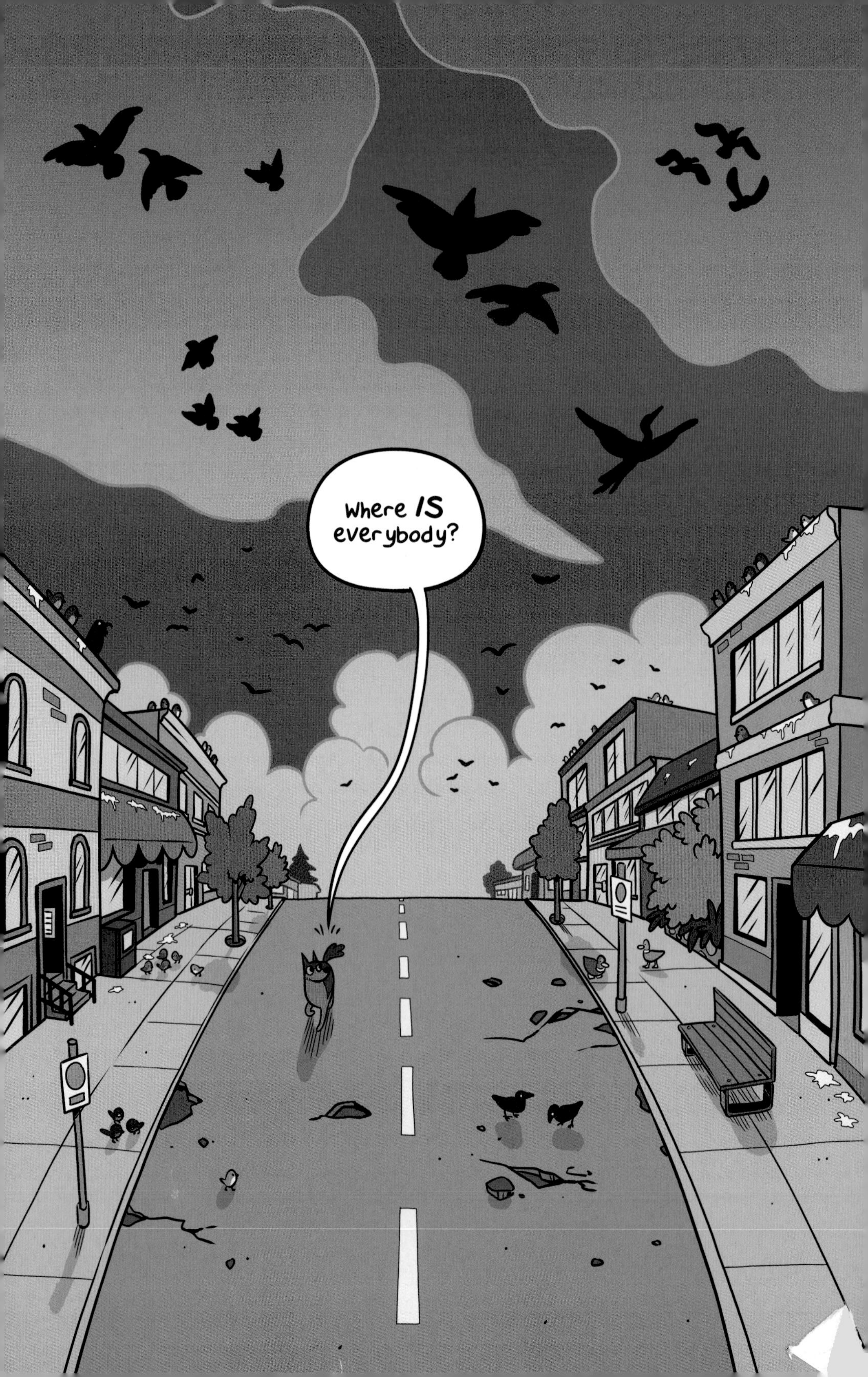
Where IS everybody?

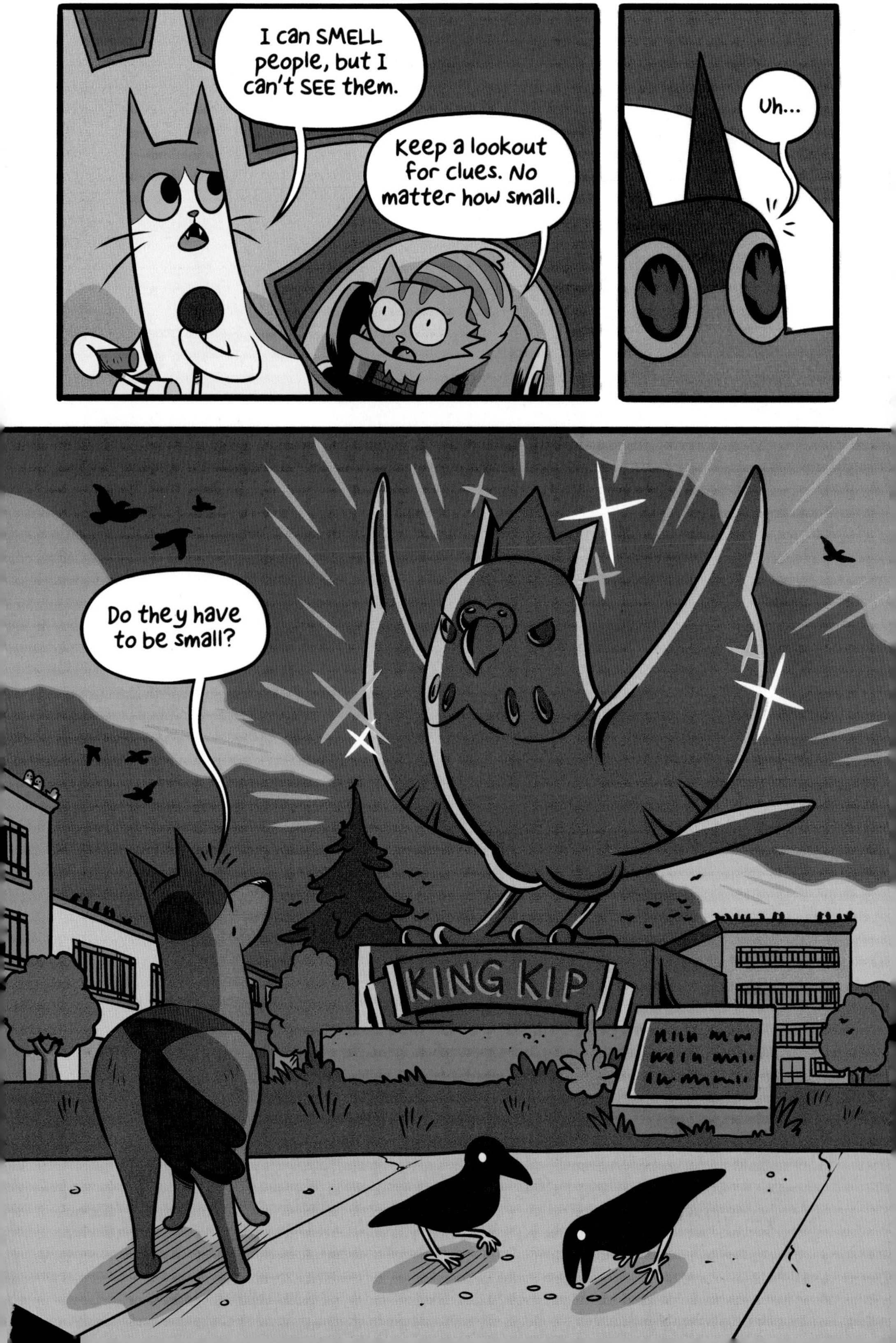
I can SMELL people, but I can't SEE them.
Keep a lookout for clues. No matter how small.
Uh...
Do they have to be small?
KING KIP

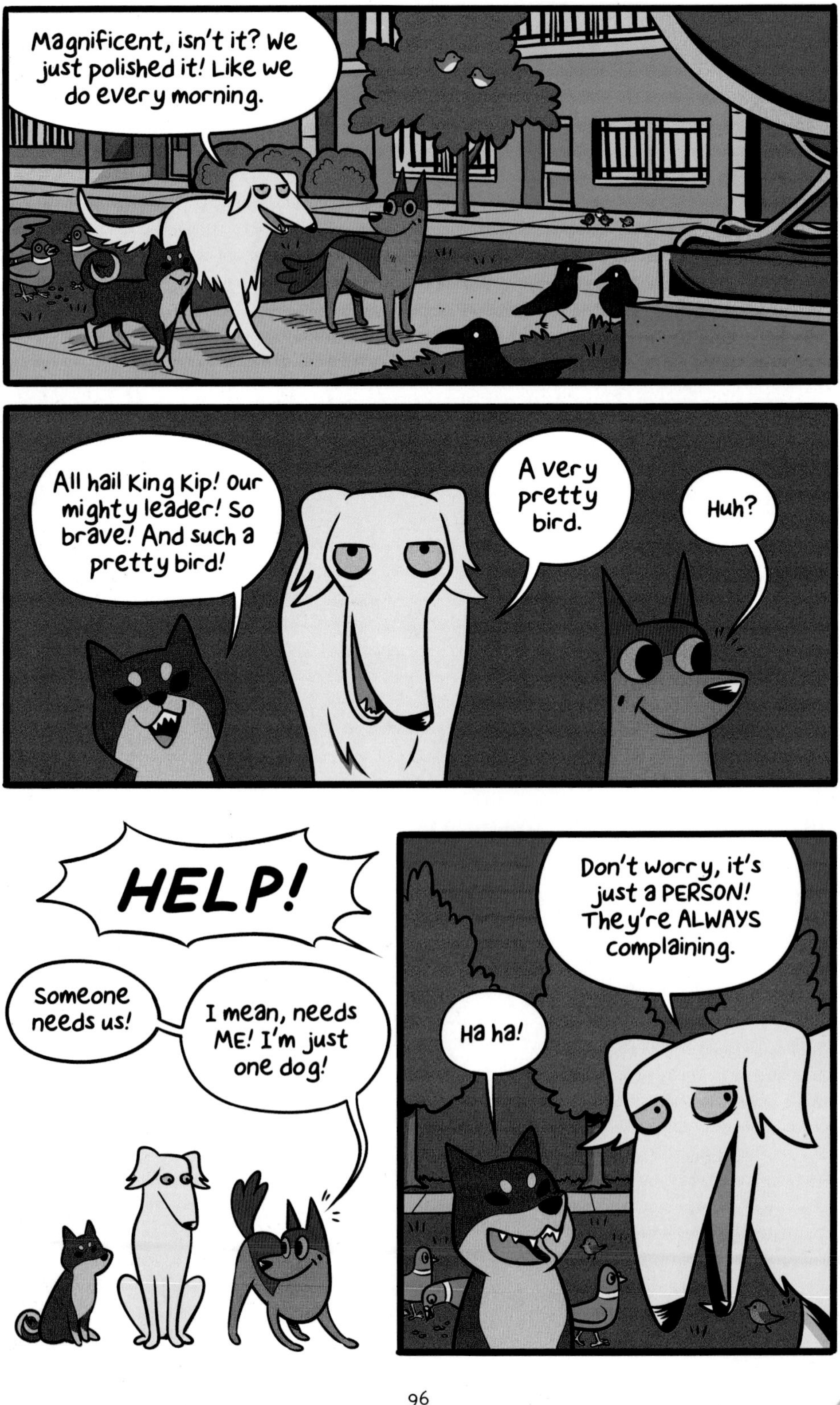
Magnificent, isn't it? We just polished it! Like we do every morning.
All hail King Kip! Our mighty leader! So brave! And such a pretty bird!
A very pretty bird.
Huh?
HELP!
Someone needs us!
I mean, needs ME! I'm just one dog!
Don't worry, it's just a PERSON! They're ALWAYS complaining.
Ha ha!

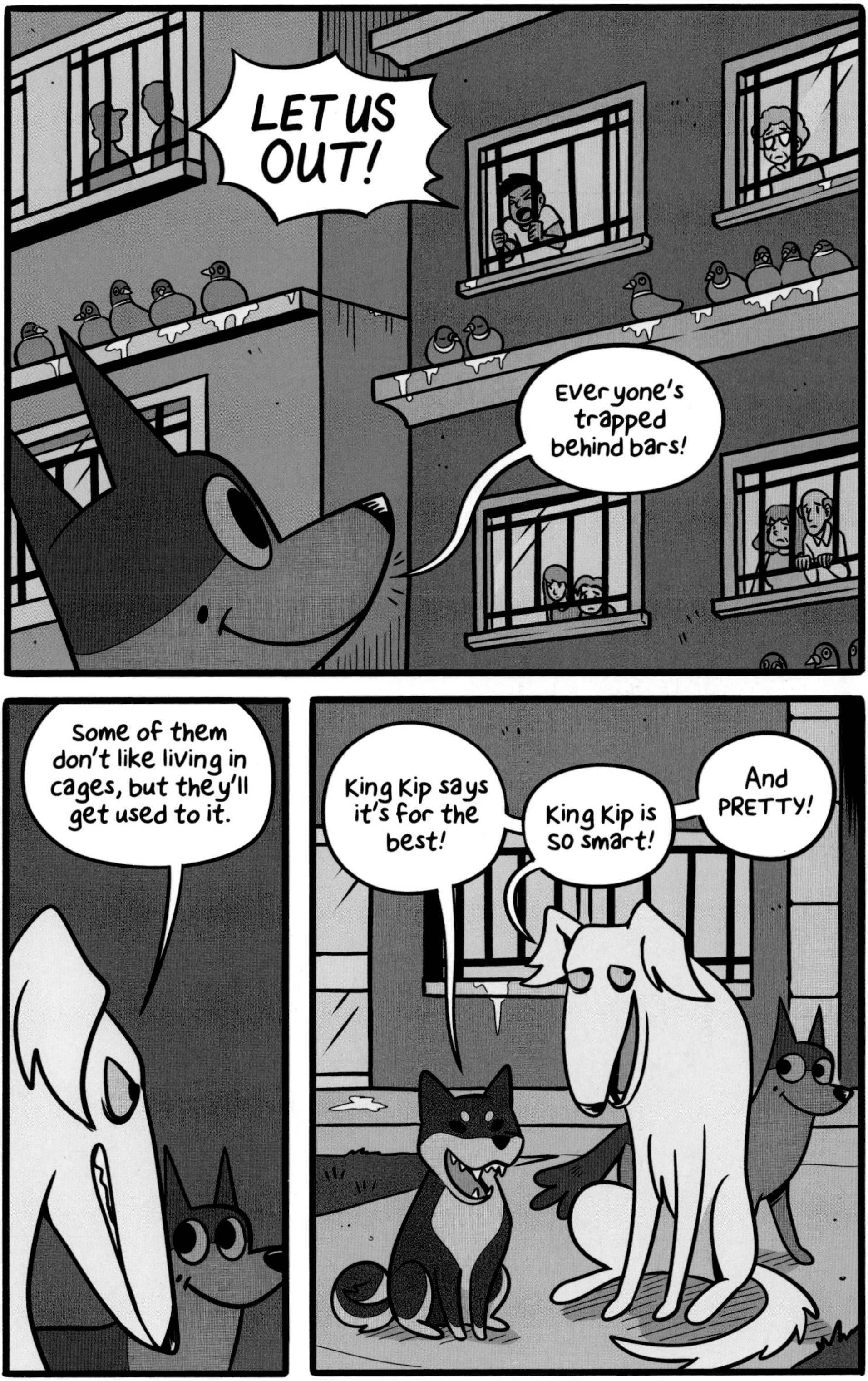
LET US OUT!
Everyone's trapped behind bars!
Some of them don't like living in cages, but they'll get used to it.
King Kip says it's for the best!
King Kip is so smart!
And PRETTY!

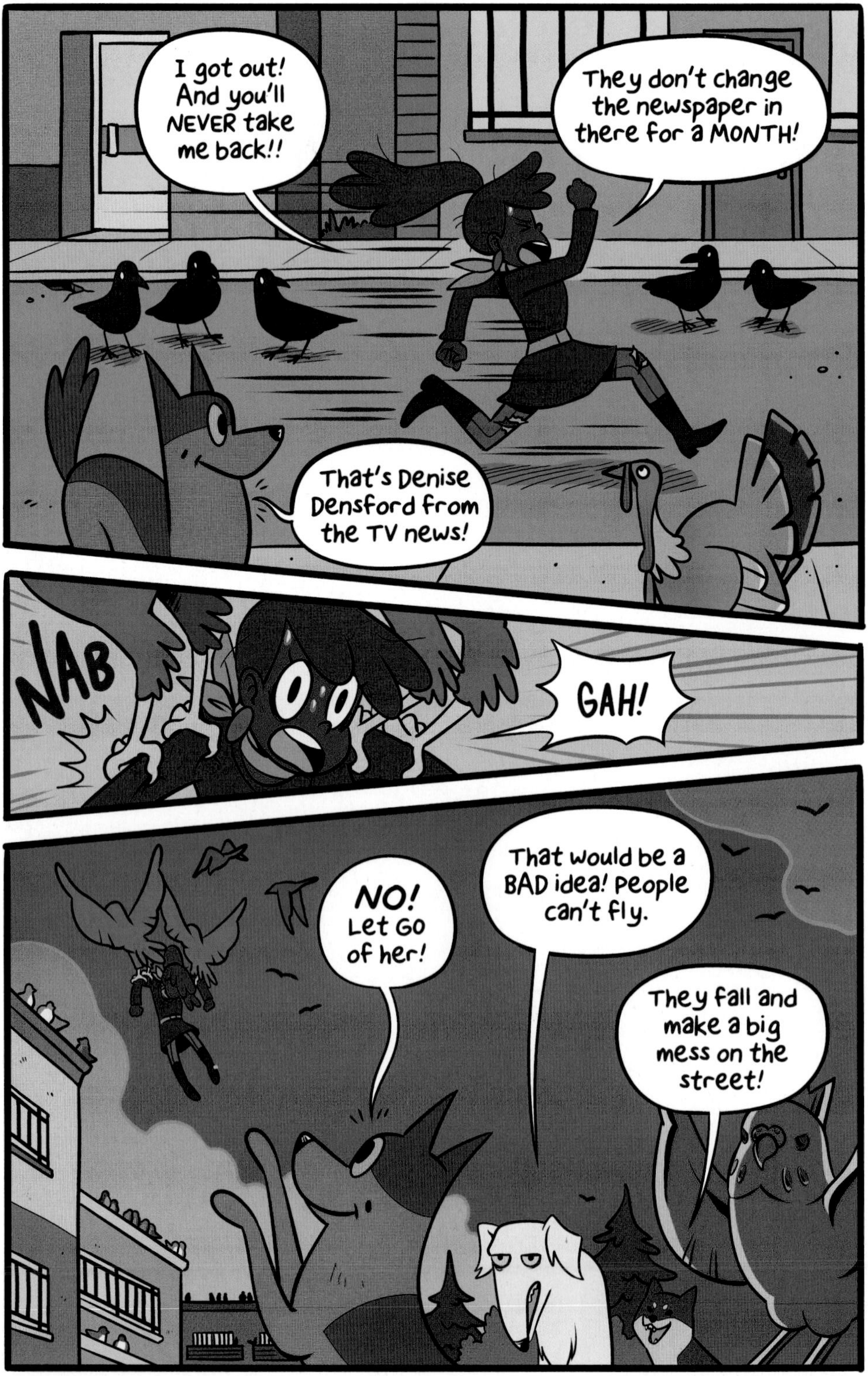
I got out! And you'll NEVER take me back!!
They don't change the newspaper in there for a MONTH!
That's Denise Densford from the TV news!
NAB
GAH!
NO! Let GO of her!
That would be a BAD idea! People can't fly.
They fall and make a big mess on the street!

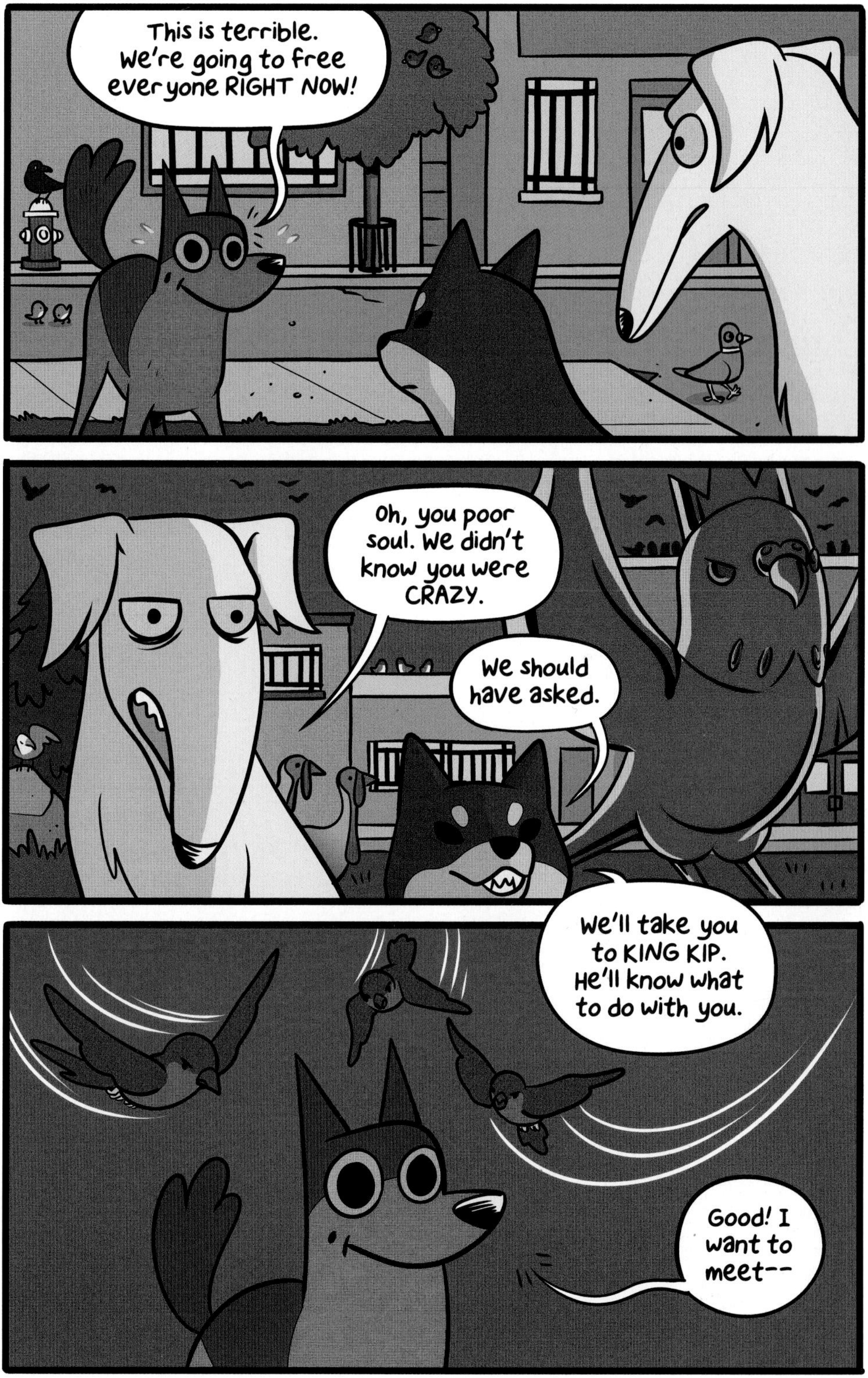
This is terrible. We're going to free everyone RIGHT NOW!
Oh, you poor soul. We didn't know you were CRAZY.
We should have asked.
We'll take you to KING KIP. He'll know what to do with you.
Good! I want to meet--

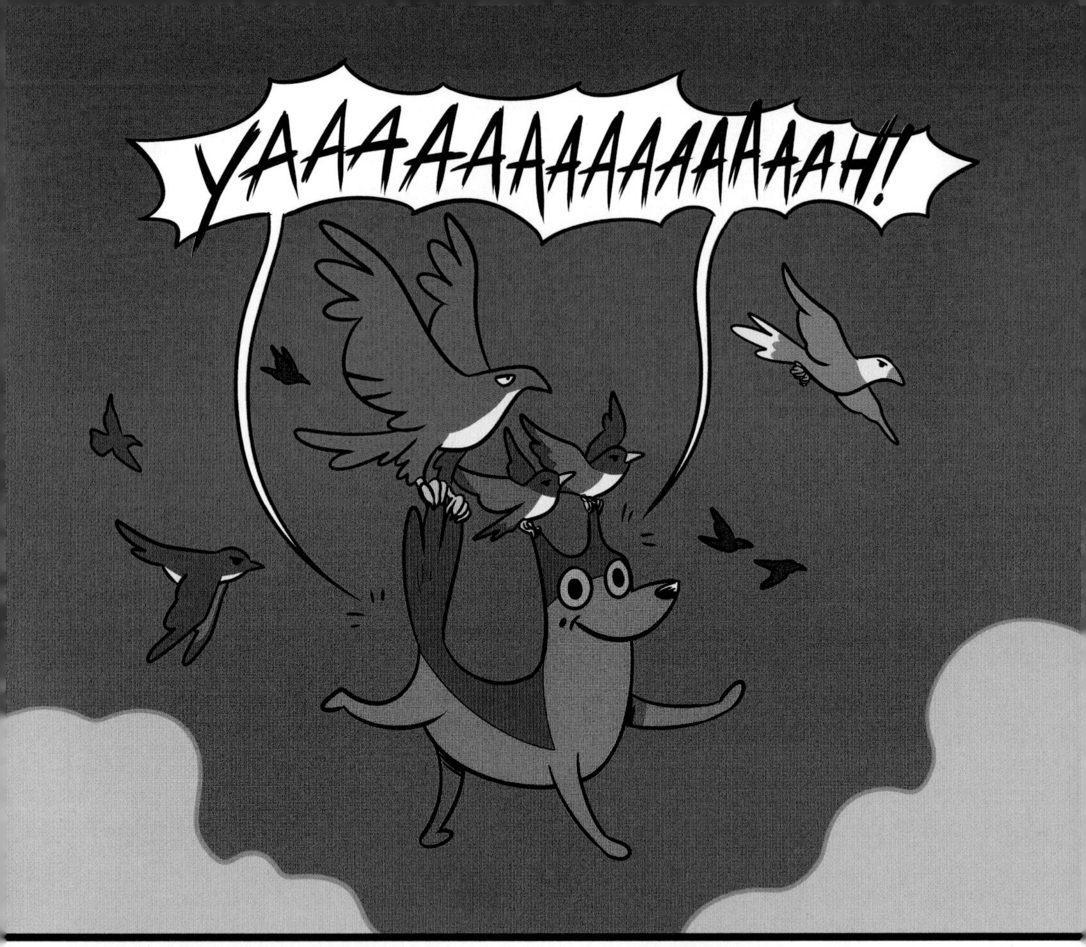
YAAAAAAAAAAAAAAH!

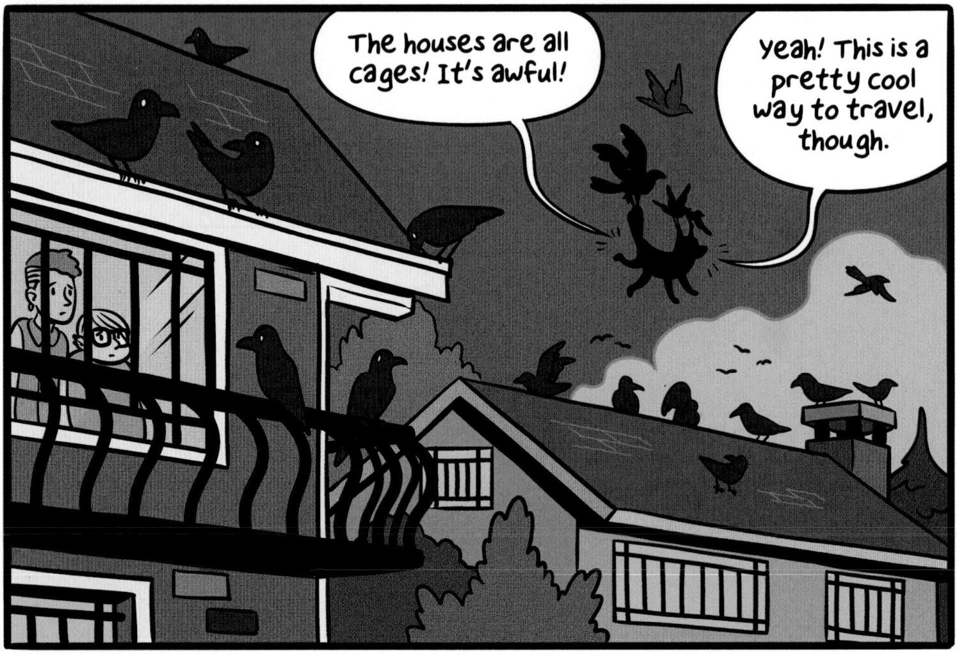
The houses are all cages! It's awful!
Yeah! This is a pretty cool way to travel, though.

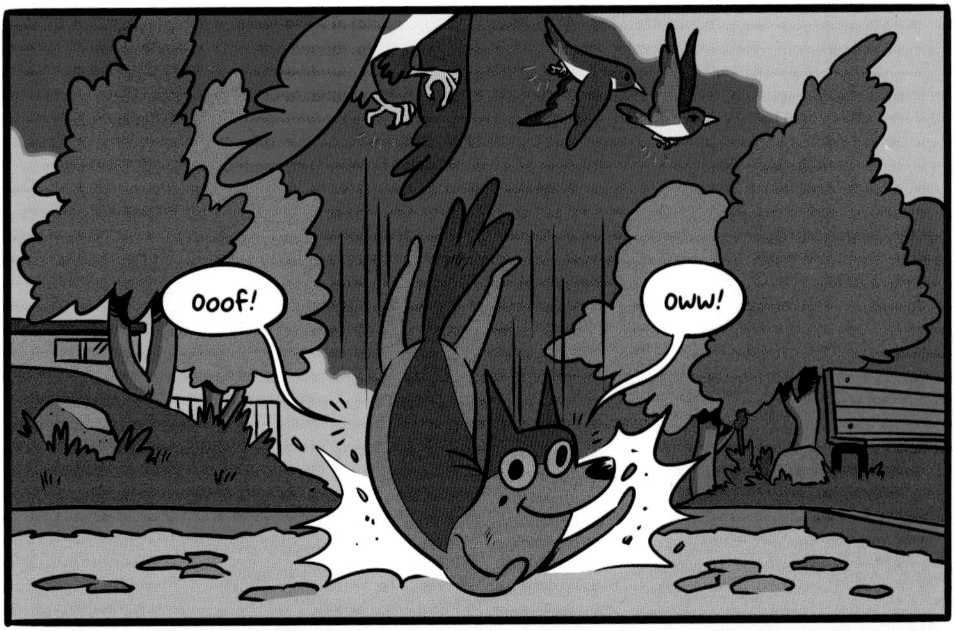
Ooof!
OWW!

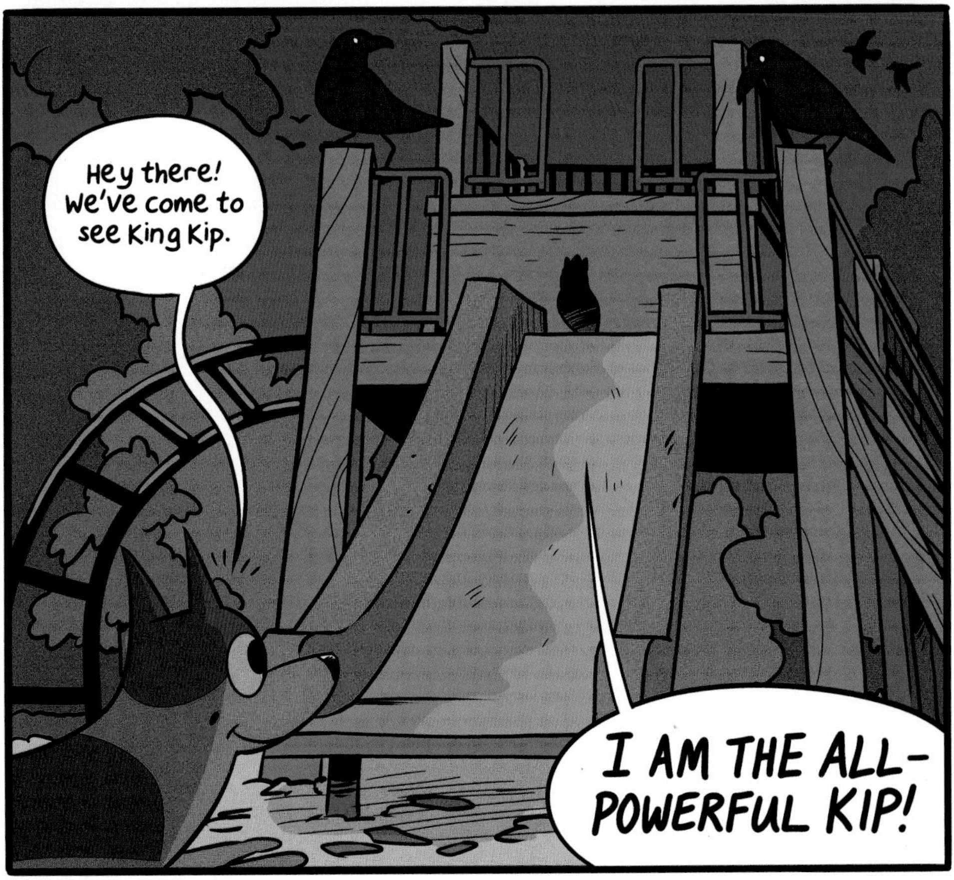
Hey there! We've come to see King Kip.
I AM THE ALL-POWERFUL KIP!

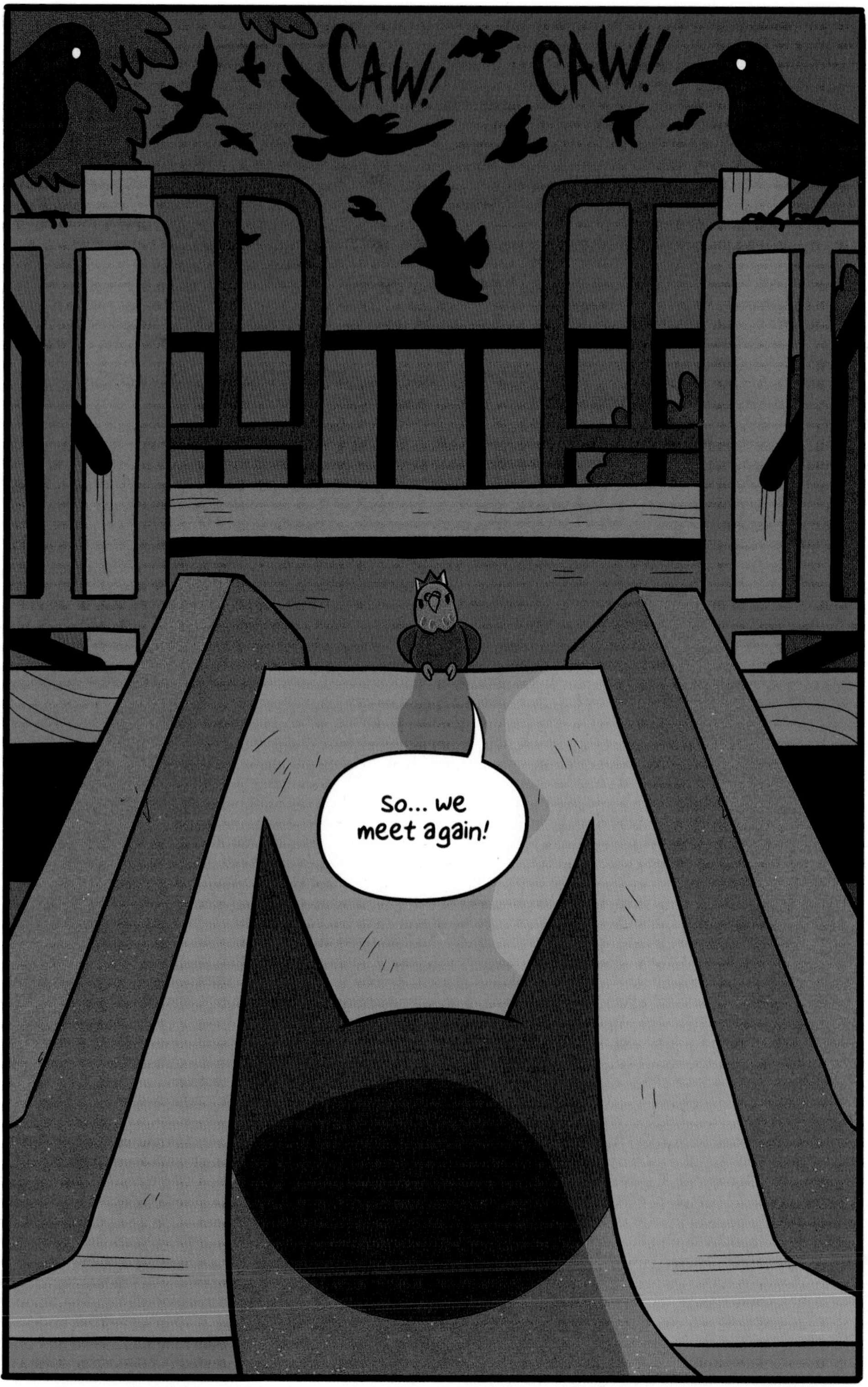
CAW! CAW!
So... we meet again!

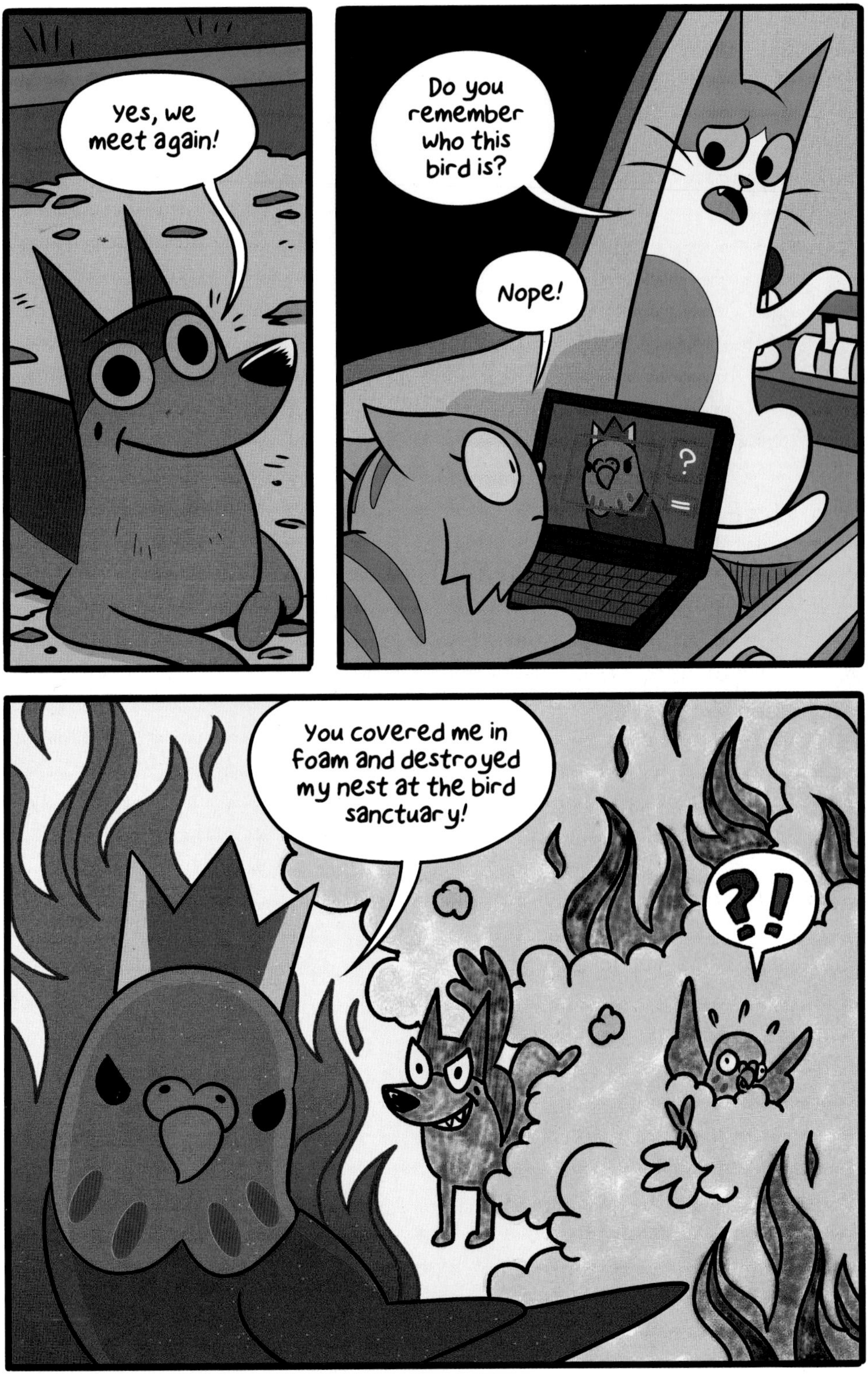
yes, we meet again!
Do you remember who this bird is?
Nope!
?
=
You covered me in foam and destroyed my nest at the bird sanctuary!
?!

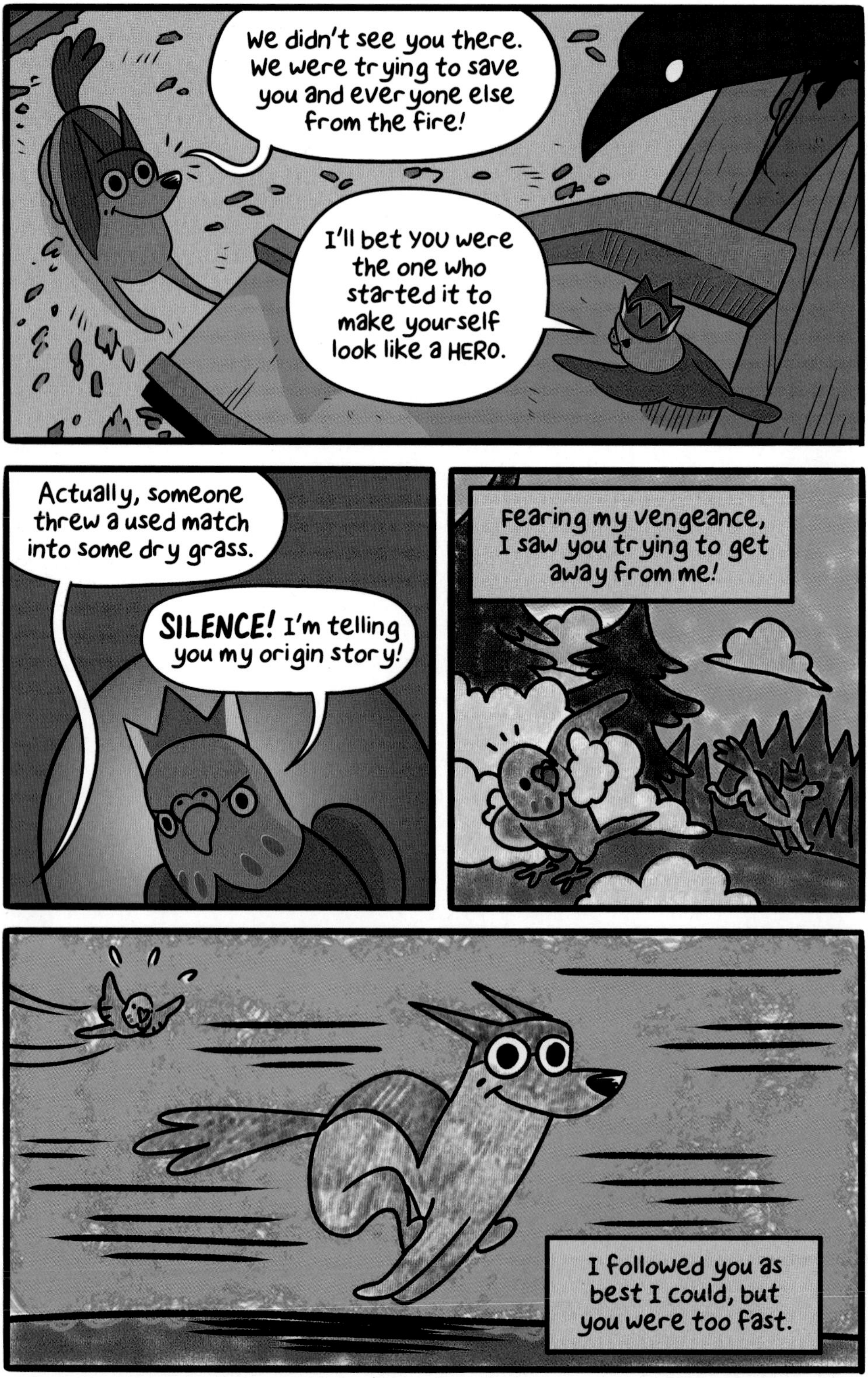

We didn't see you there. We were trying to save you and everyone else from the fire!
I'll bet you were the one who started it to make yourself look like a HERO.
Actually, someone threw a used match into some dry grass.
SILENCE! I'm telling you my origin story!
Fearing my vengeance, I saw you trying to get away from me!
I followed you as best I could, but you were too fast.

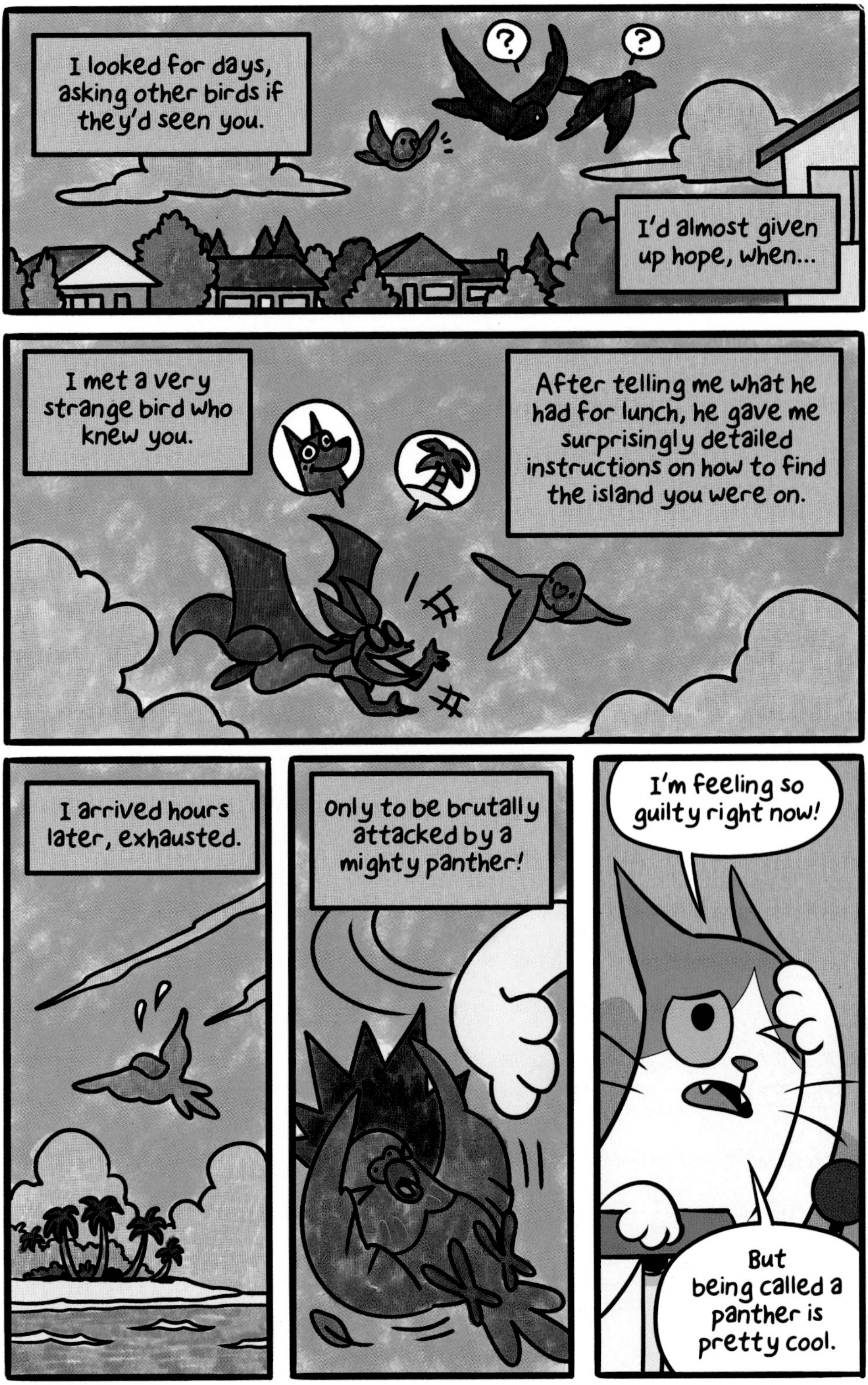
I looked for days, asking other birds if they'd seen you.
?
?
I'd almost given up hope, when...
I met a very strange bird who knew you.
After telling me what he had for lunch, he gave me surprisingly detailed instructions on how to find the island you were on.
I arrived hours later, exhausted.
Only to be brutally attacked by a mighty panther!
I'm feeling so guilty right now!
But being called a panther is pretty cool.

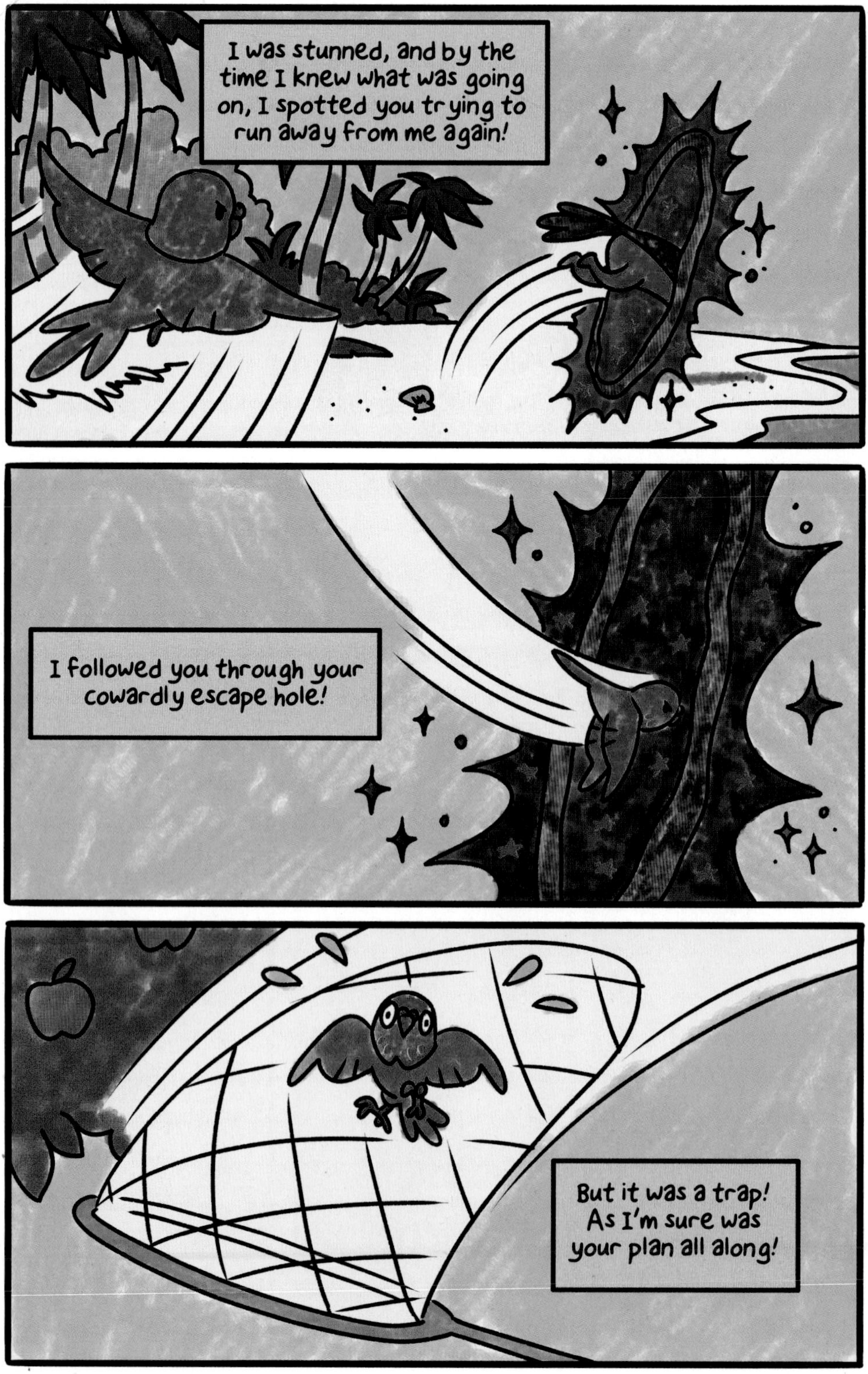
I was stunned, and by the time I knew what was going on, I spotted you trying to run away from me again!
I followed you through your cowardly escape hole!
But it was a trap! As I'm sure was your plan all along!

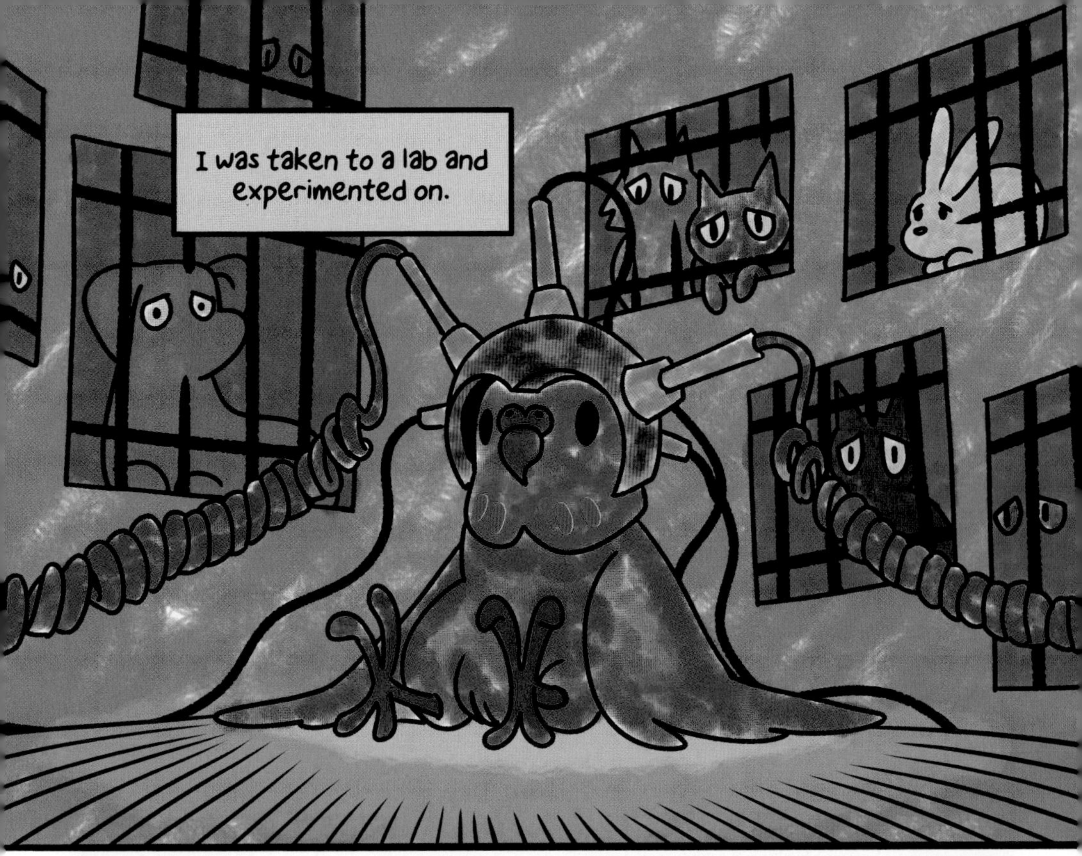
I was taken to a lab and experimented on.

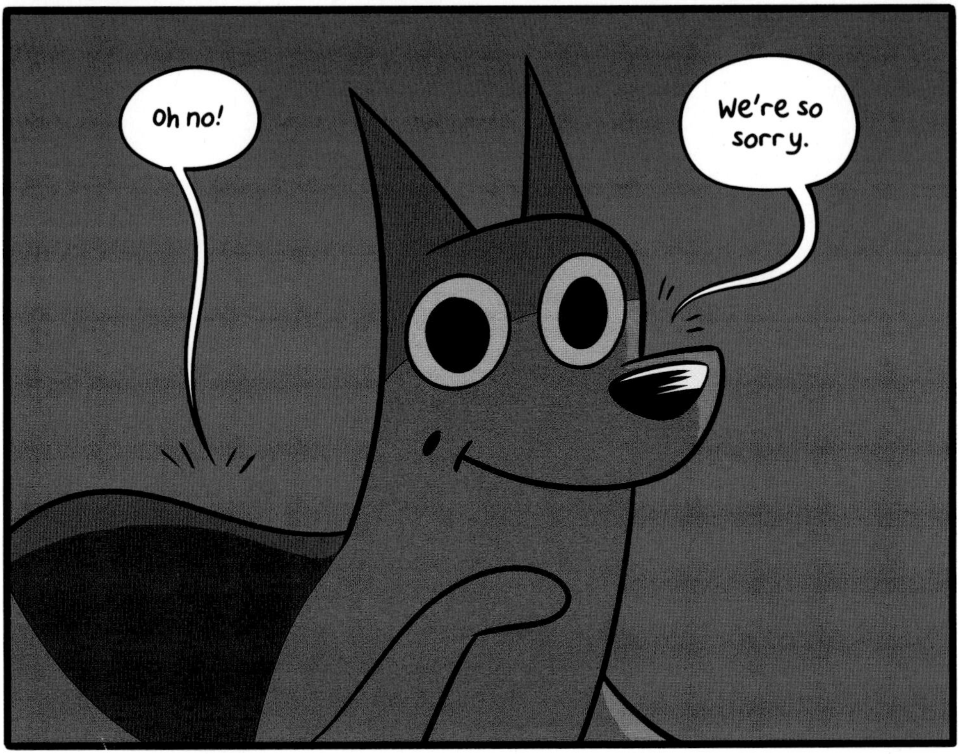
Oh no!
We're so sorry.

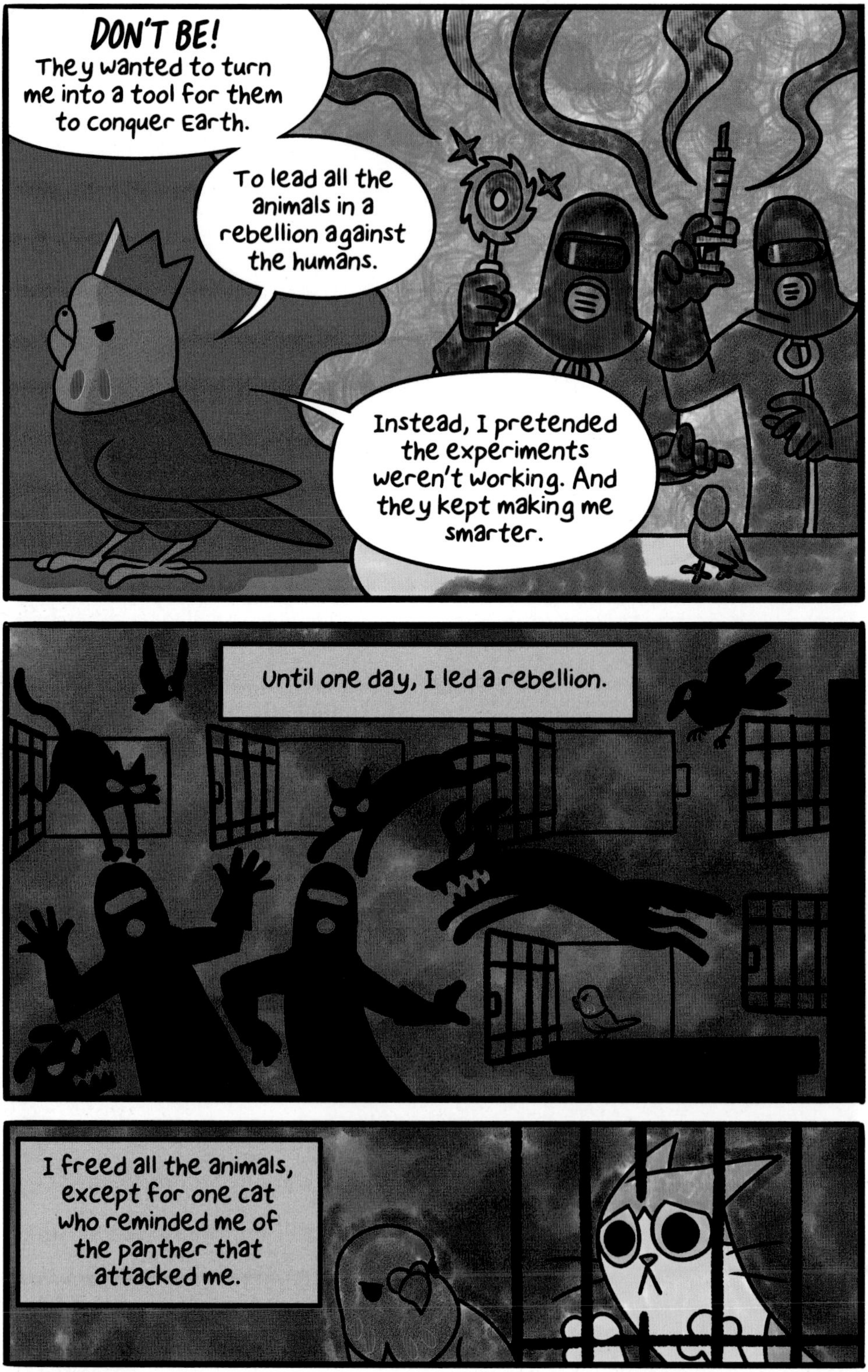
DON'T BE! They wanted to turn me into a tool for them to conquer Earth.
To lead all the animals in a rebellion against the humans.
Instead, I pretended the experiments weren't working. And they kept making me smarter.
Until one day, I led a rebellion.
I freed all the animals, except for one cat who reminded me of the panther that attacked me.

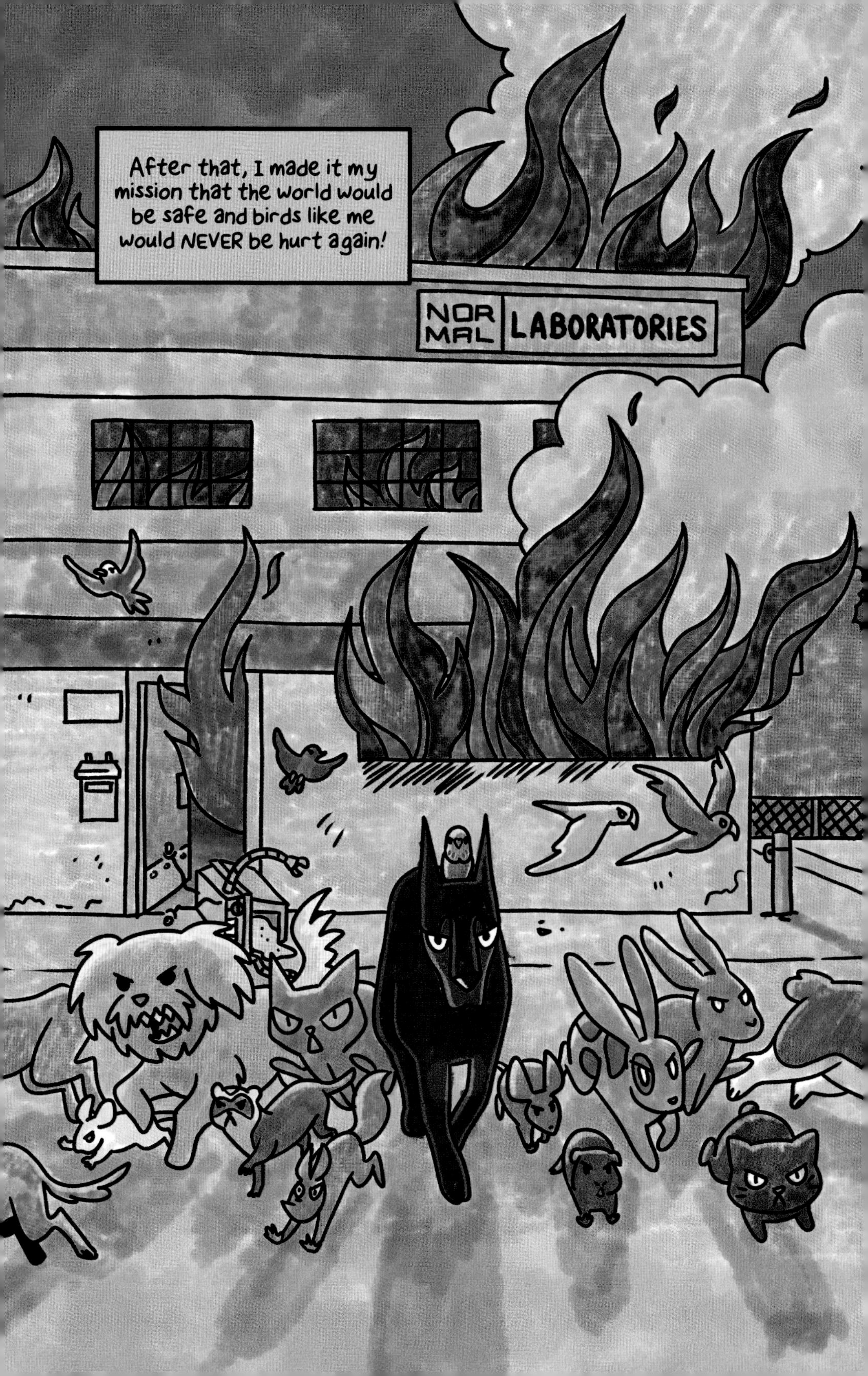
After that, I made it my mission that the world would be safe and birds like me would NEVER be hurt again!
NOR MAL
LABORATORIES

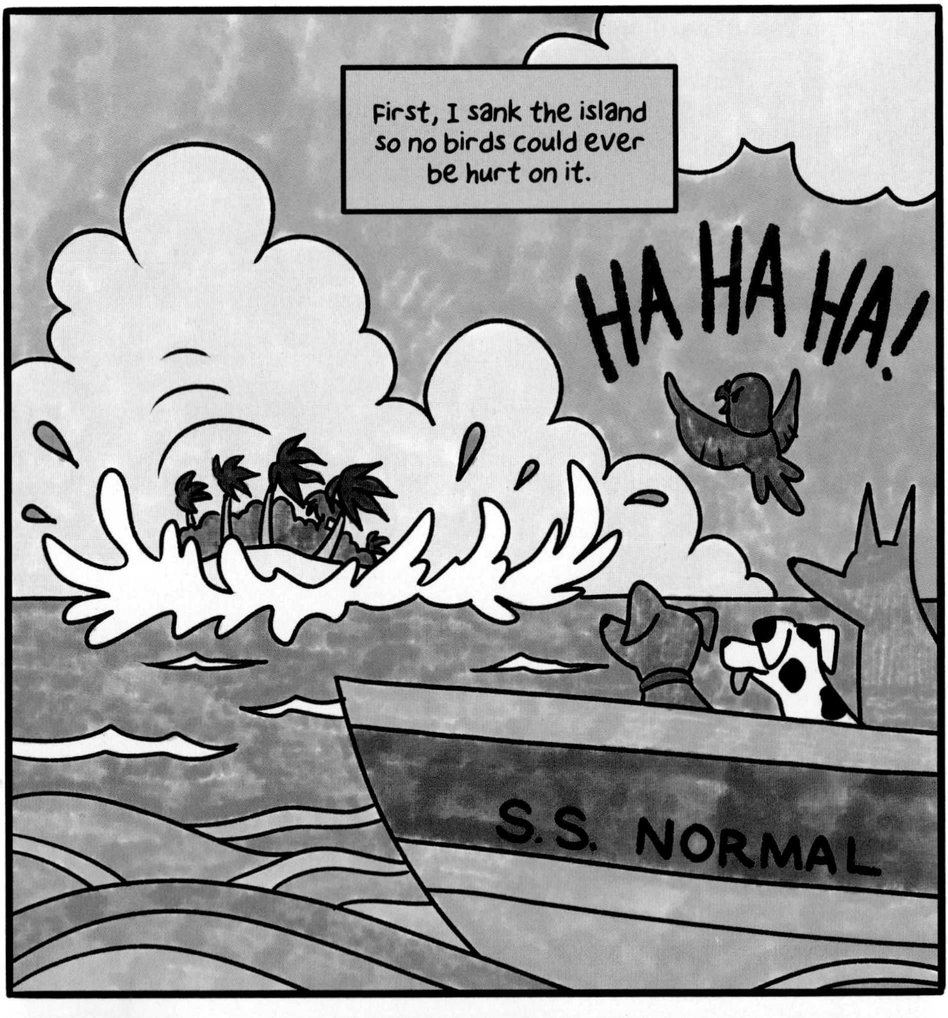
First, I sank the island so no birds could ever be hurt on it.
HA HA HA!
S.S. NORMAL

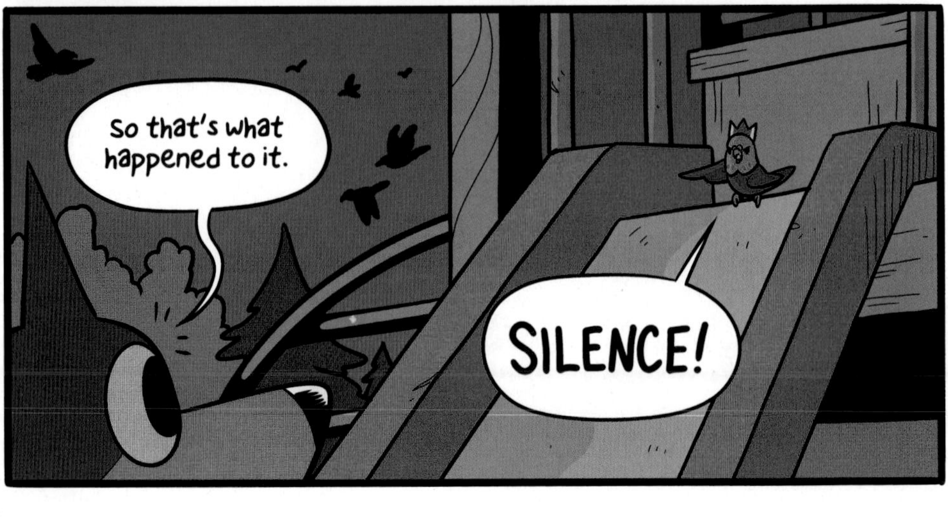
So that's what happened to it.
SILENCE!

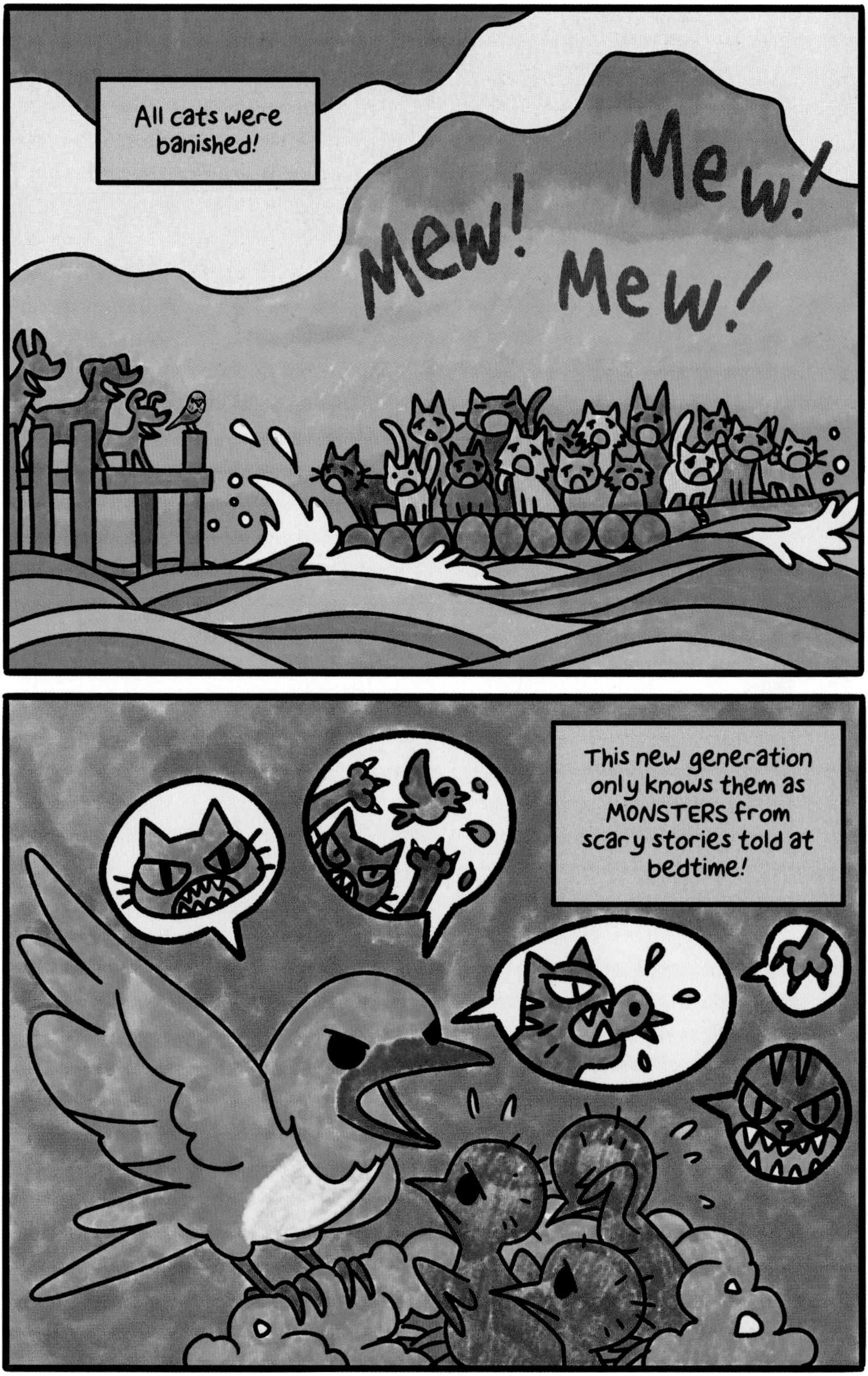
All cats were banished!
Mew!
Mew!
Mew!
This new generation only knows them as MONSTERS from scary stories told at bedtime!

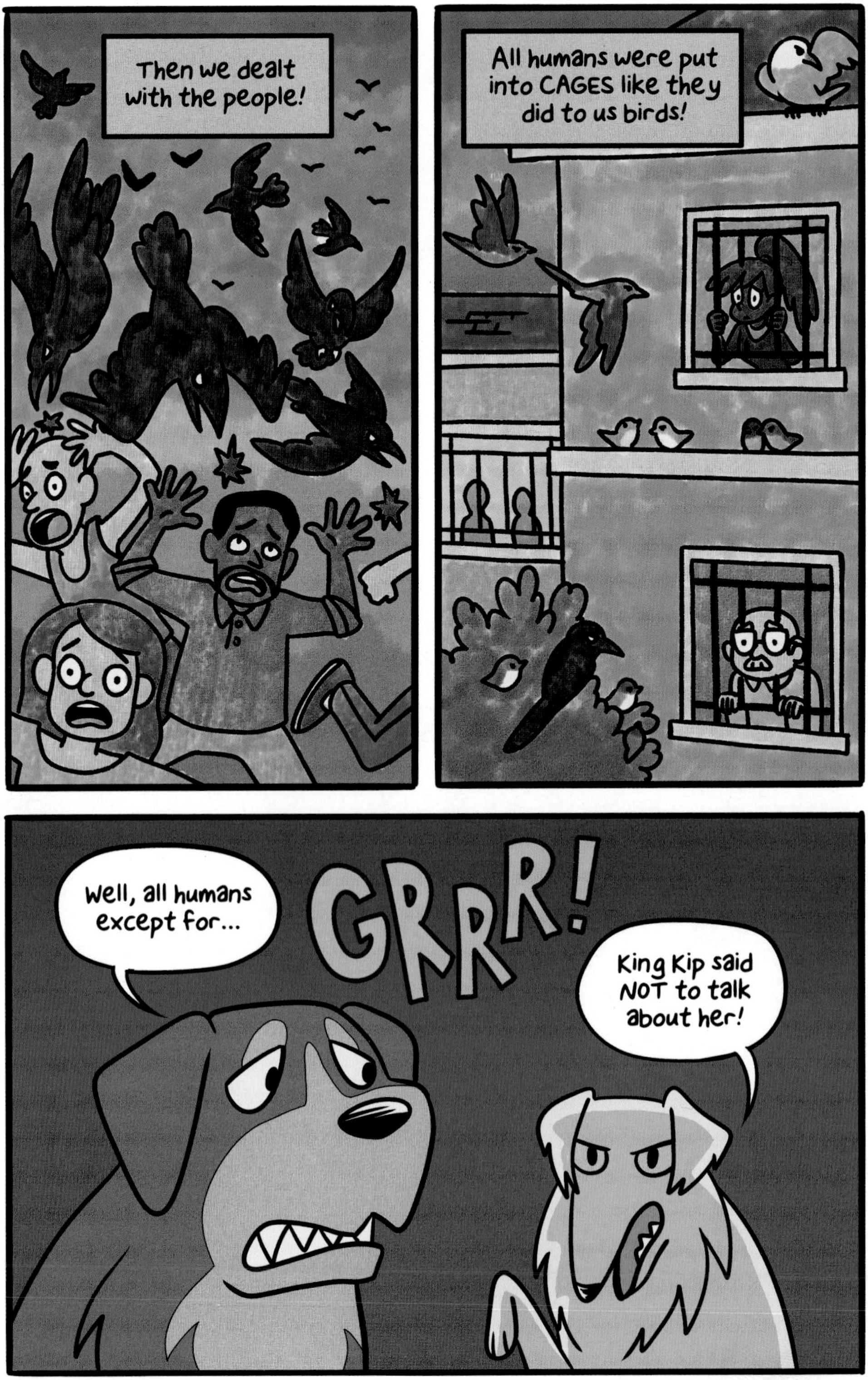
Then we dealt with the people!
All humans were put into CAGES like they did to us birds!
Well, all humans except for...
GRRR!
King Kip said NOT to talk about her!

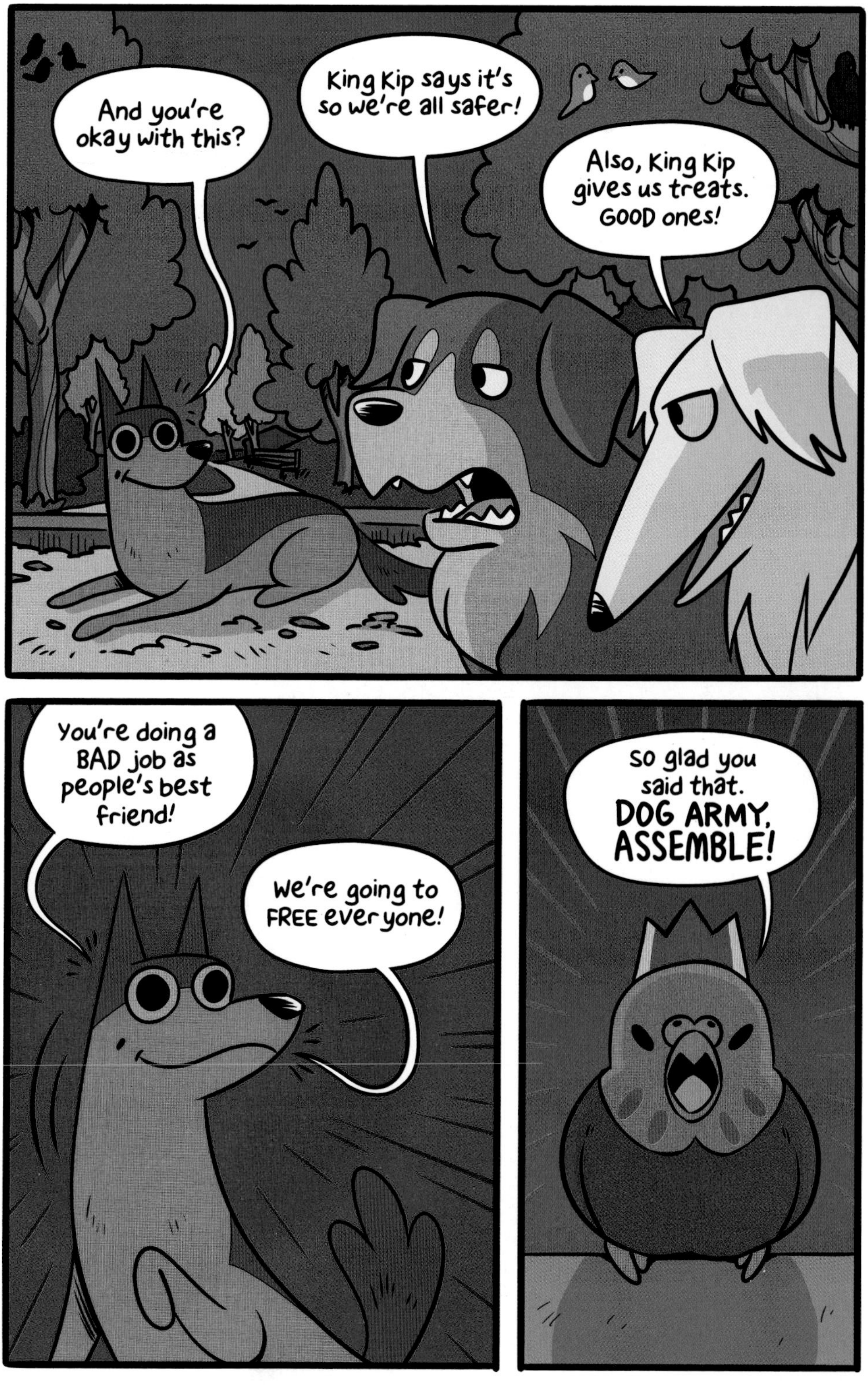
And you're okay with this?
King Kip says it's so we're all safer!
Also, King Kip gives us treats. GOOD ones!
You're doing a BAD job as people's best friend!
We're going to FREE everyone!
So glad you said that. DOG ARMY, ASSEMBLE!

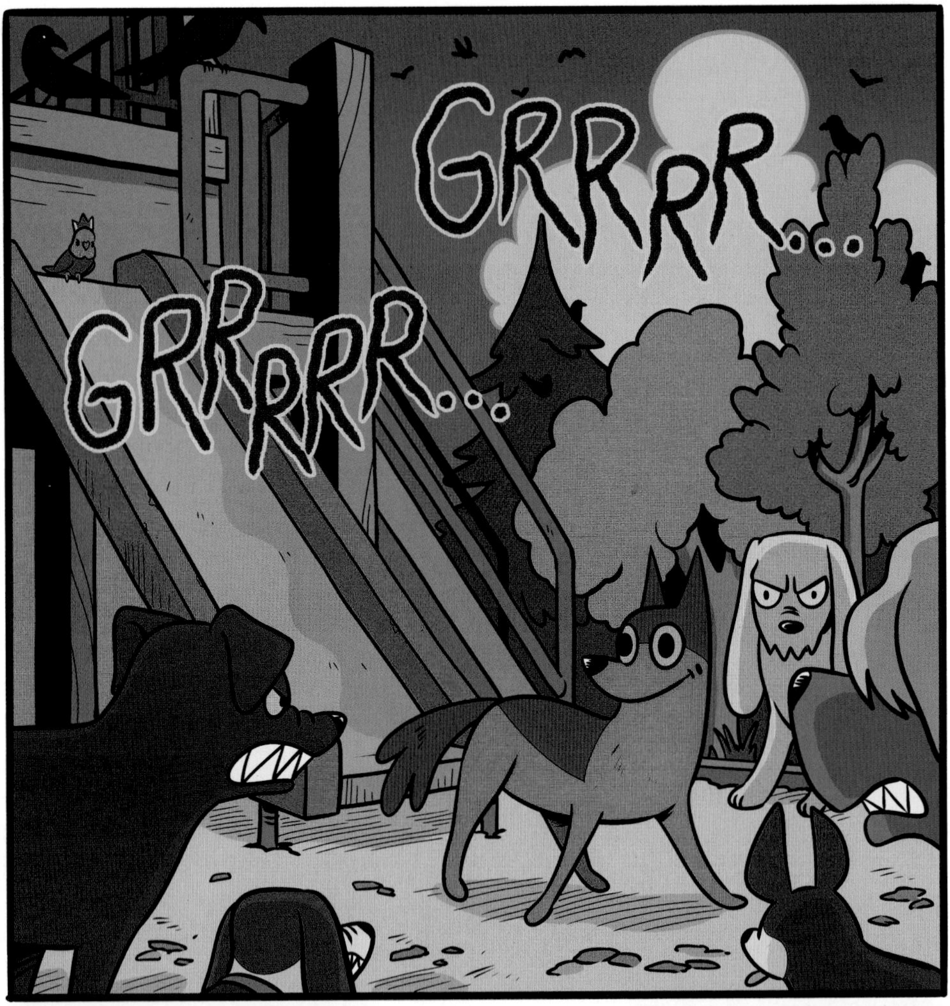
GRRRR...
GRRRRR...

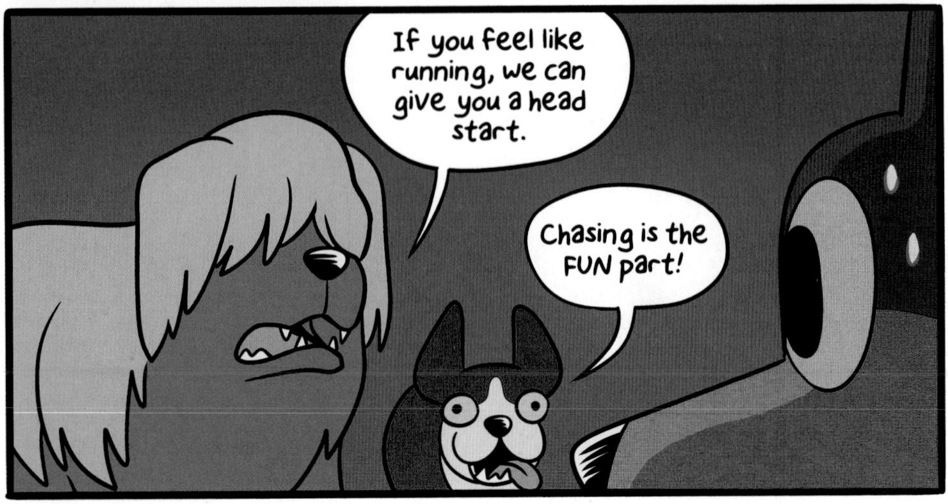
If you feel like running, we can give you a head start.
Chasing is the FUN part!

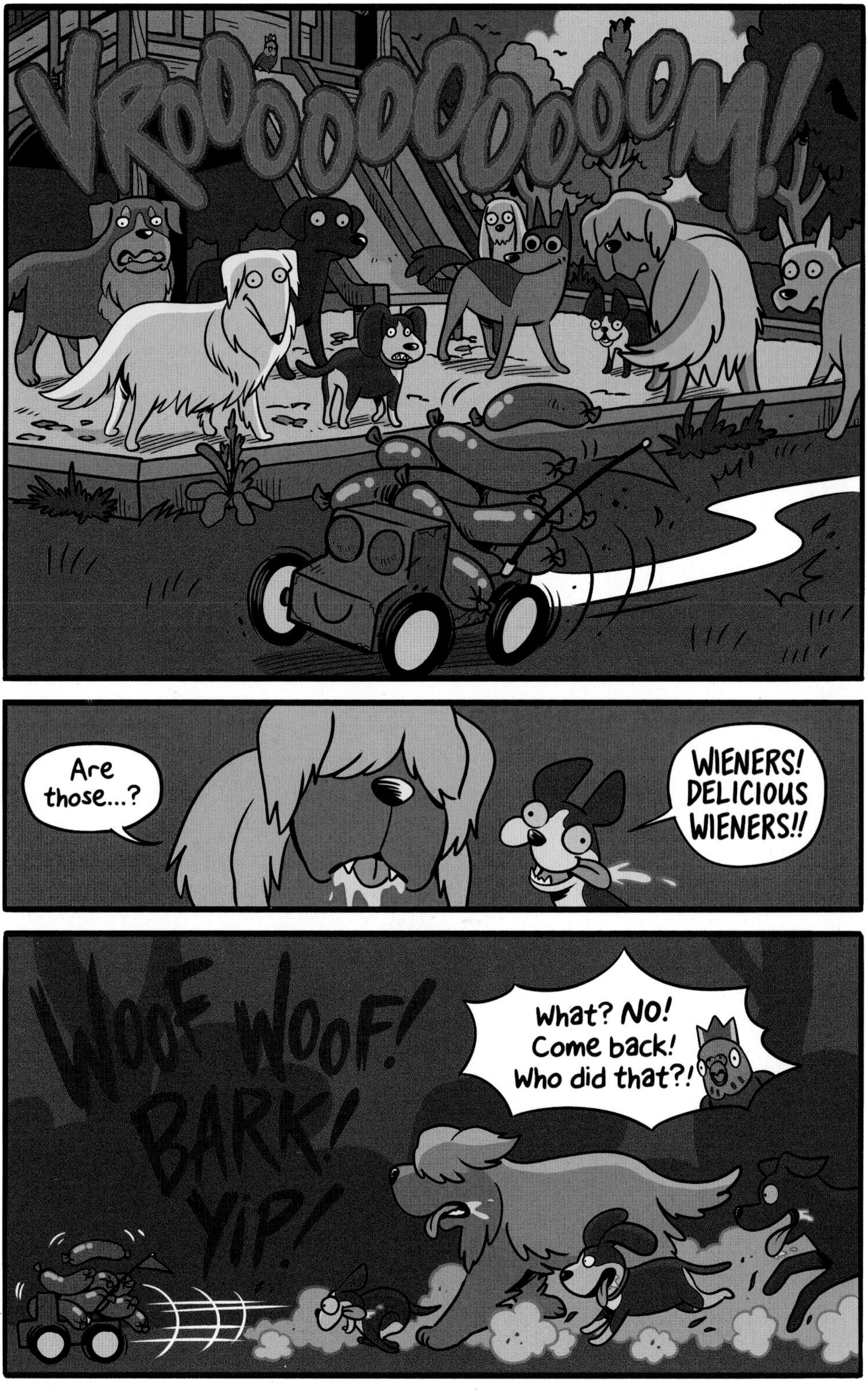
VROOOOOOOOOM!
Are those...?
WIENERS! DELICIOUS WIENERS!!
WOOF WOOF! BARK! YIP!
What? NO! Come back! Who did that?!

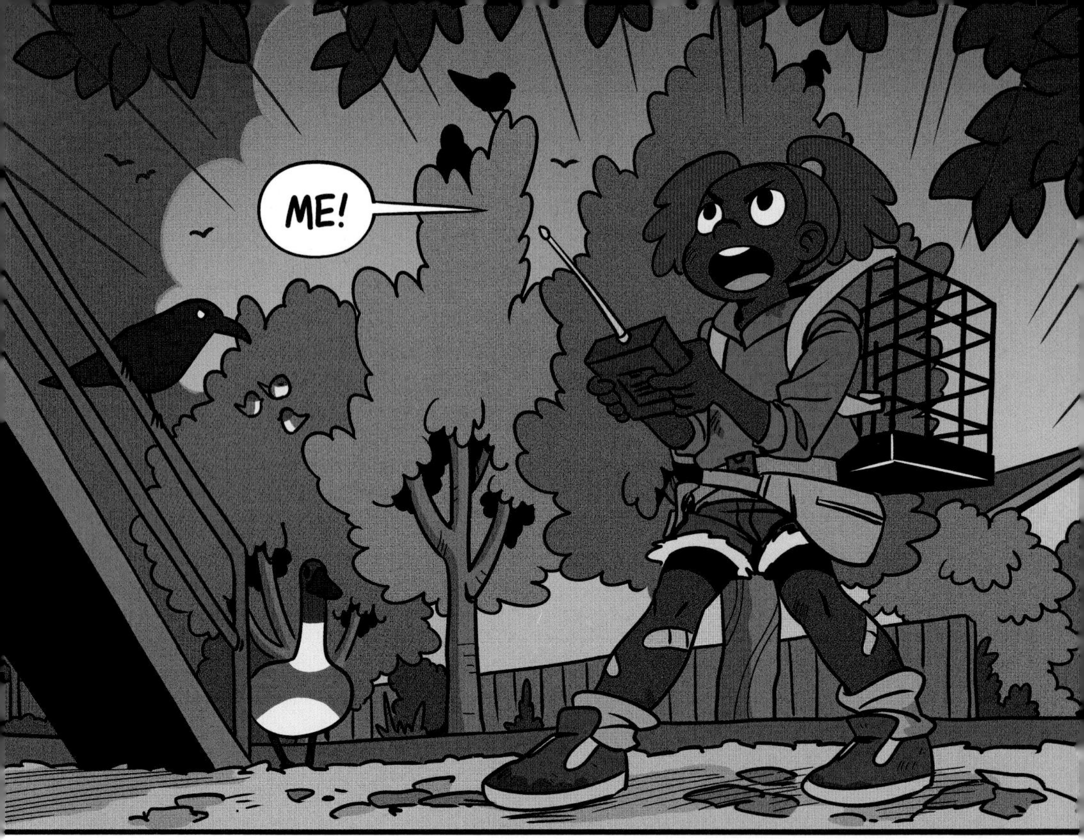
ME!

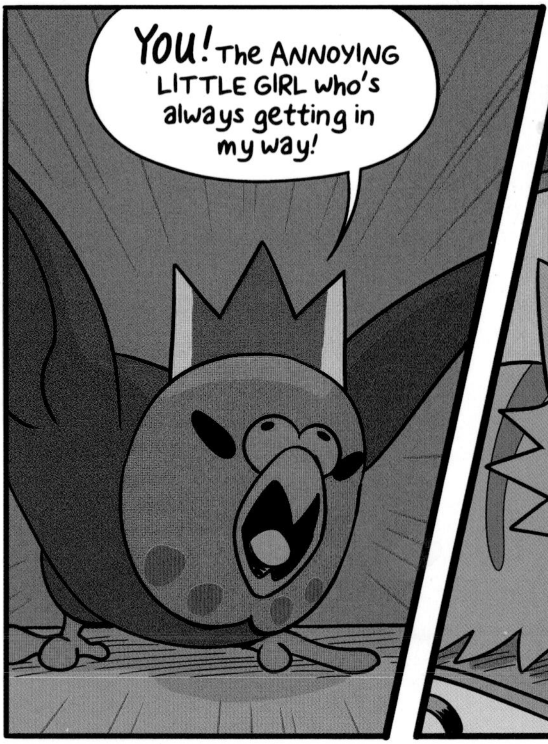
YOU! The ANNOYING LITTLE GIRL who's always getting in my way!

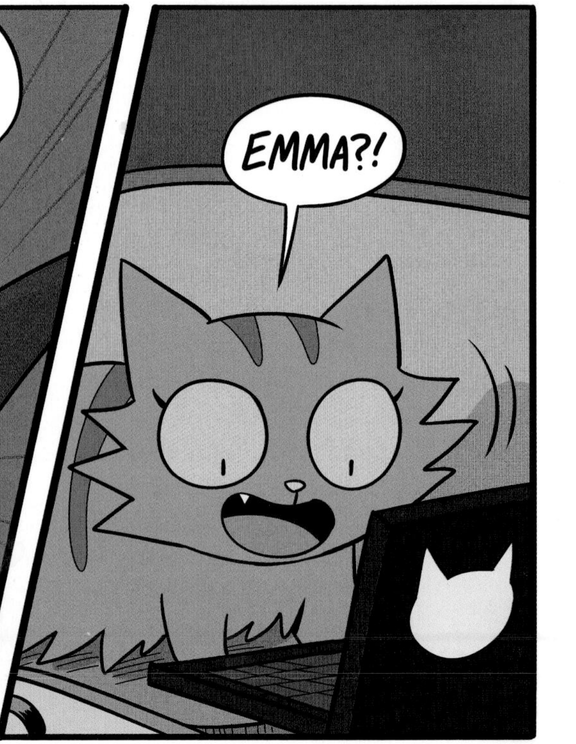
EMMA?!

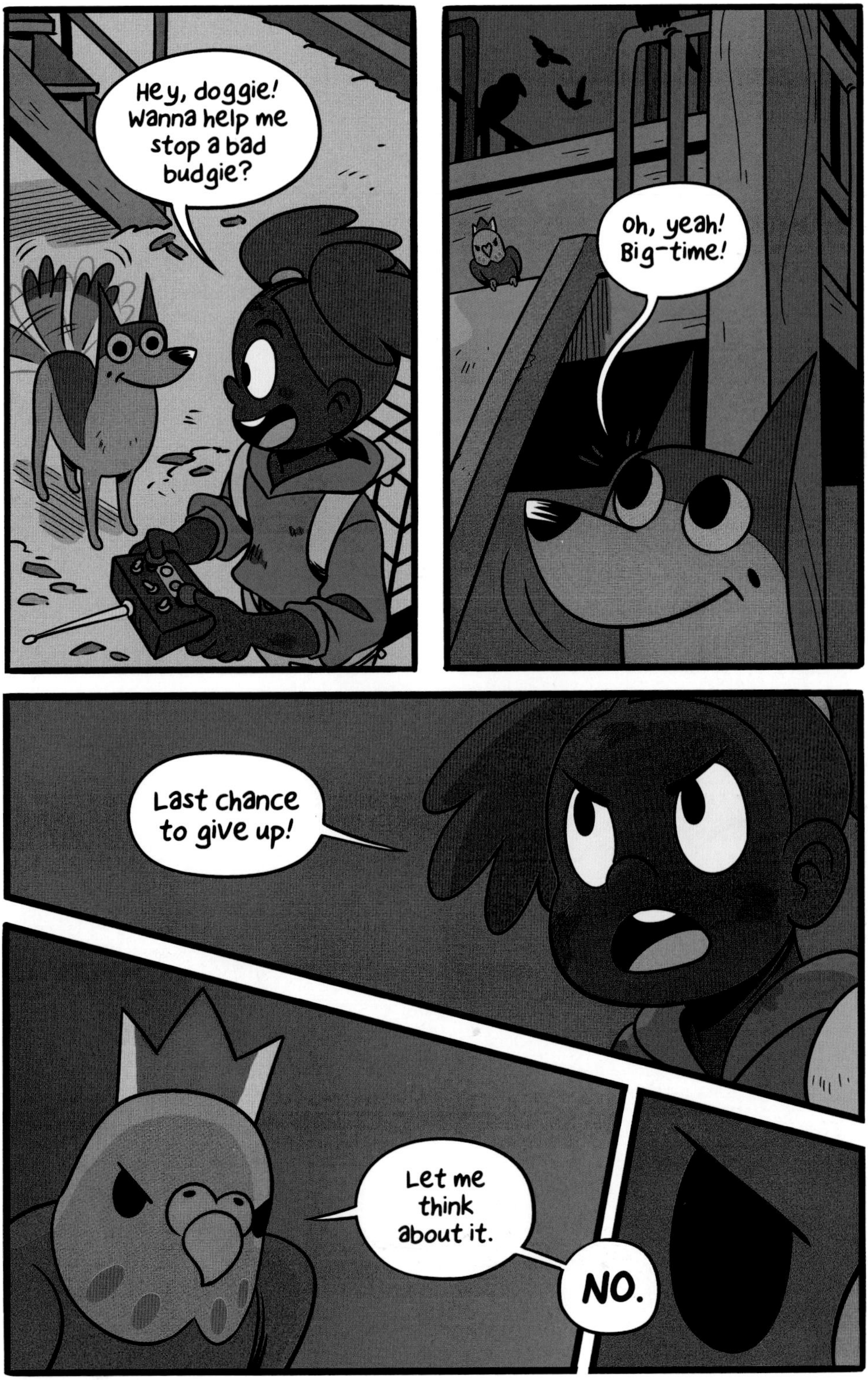
Hey, doggie! Wanna help me stop a bad budgie?
Oh, yeah! Big-time!
Last chance to give up!
Let me think about it.
NO.

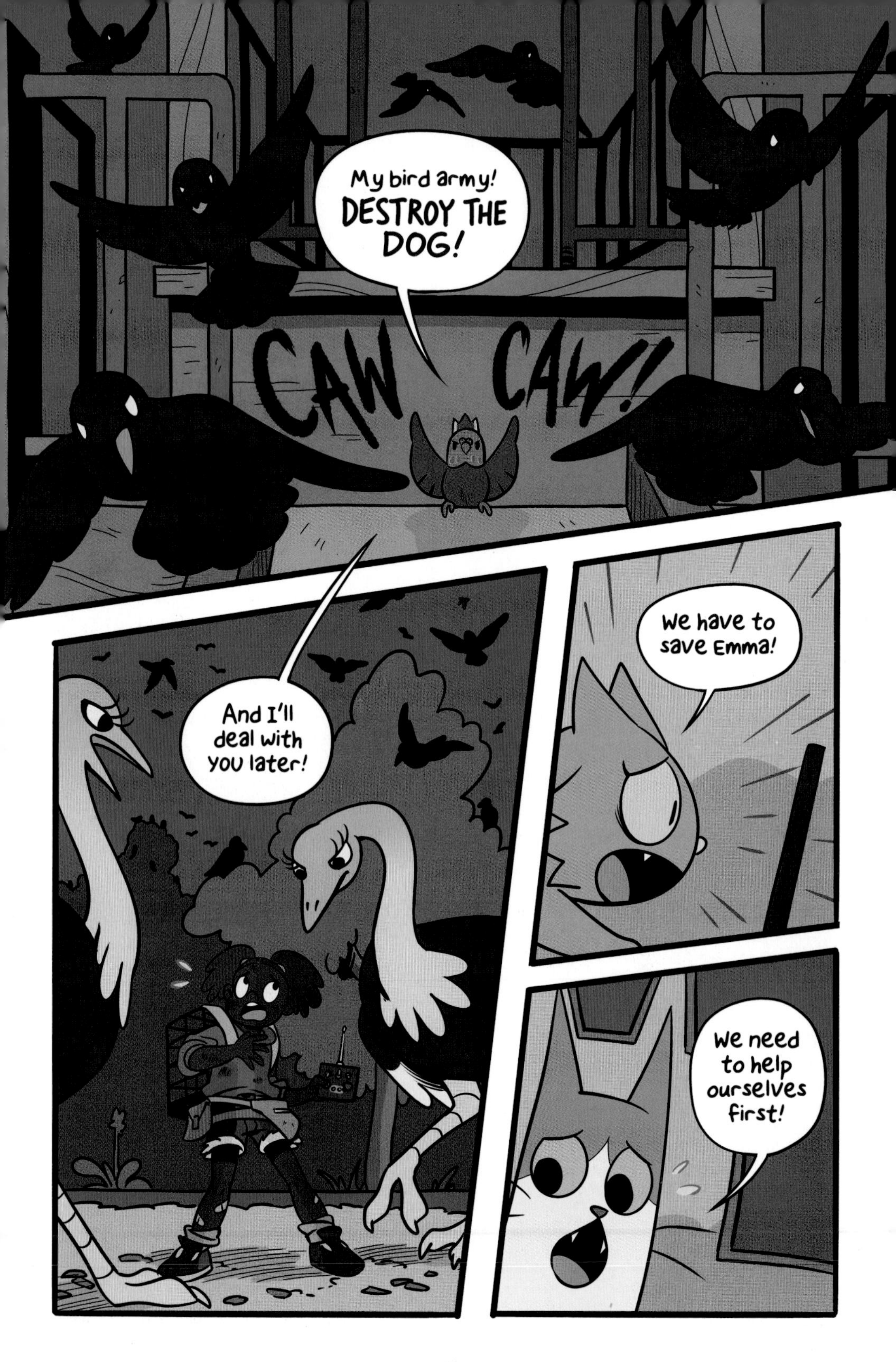

My bird army! DESTROY THE DOG!
CAW CAW!
And I'll deal with you later!
We have to save Emma!
We need to help ourselves first!

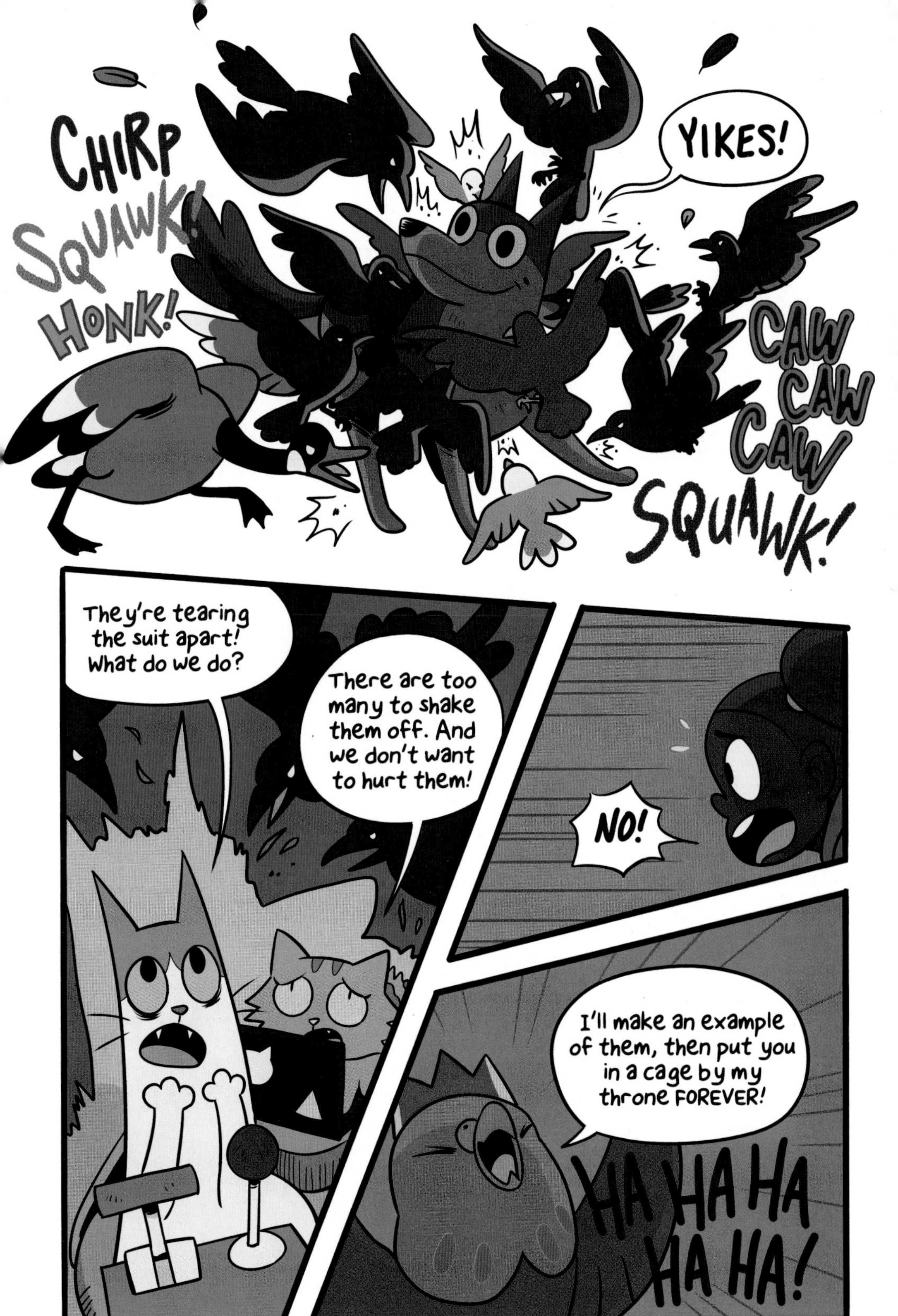
CHIRP
SQUAWK!
HONK!
YIKES!
CAW CAW CAW
SQUAWK!
They're tearing the suit apart! What do we do?
There are too many to shake them off. And we don't want to hurt them!
NO!
I'll make an example of them, then put you in a cage by my throne FOREVER!
HA HA HA HA HA HA!

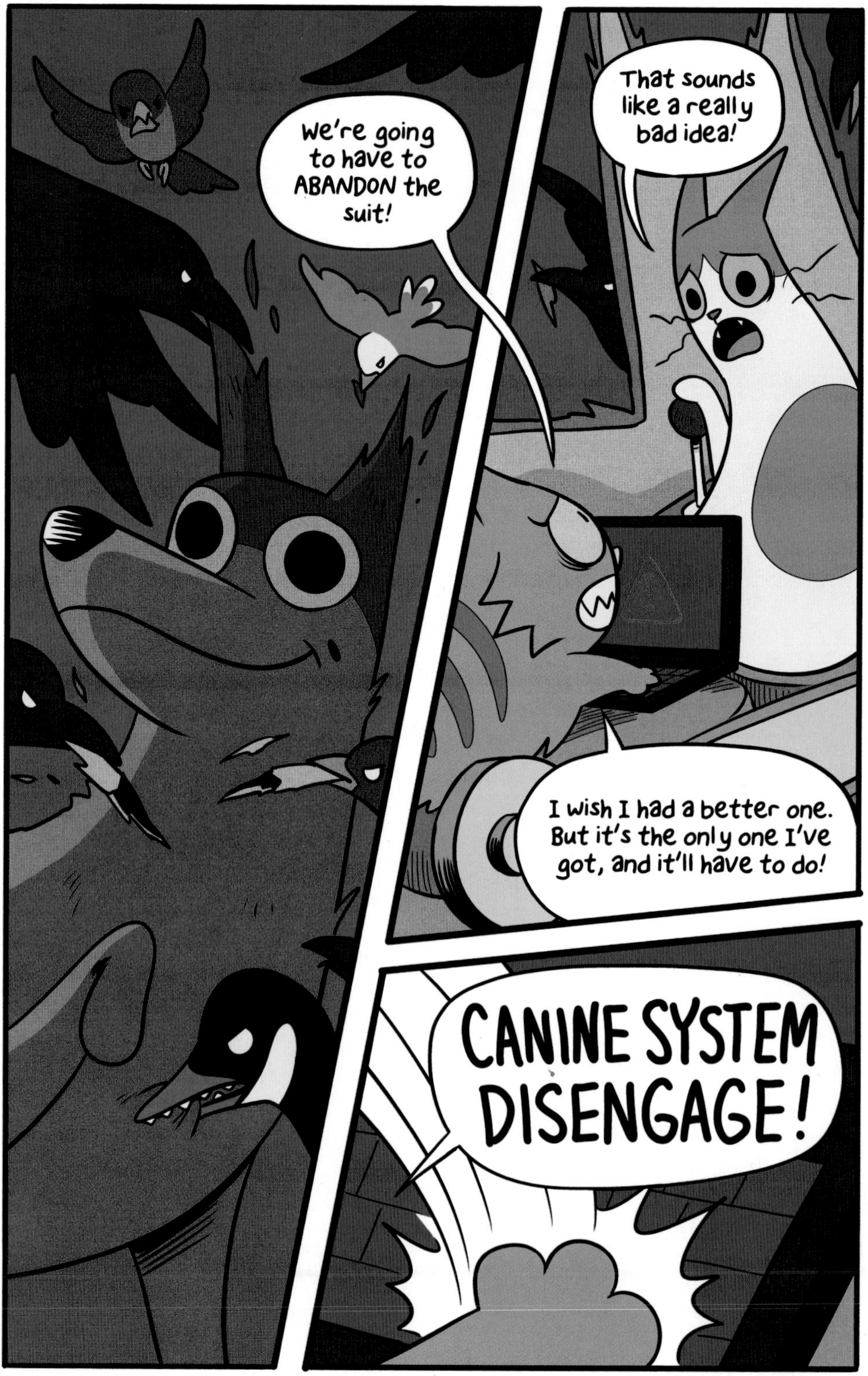
We're going to have to ABANDON the suit!
That sounds like a really bad idea!
I wish I had a better one. But it's the only one I've got, and it'll have to do!
CANINE SYSTEM DISENGAGE!

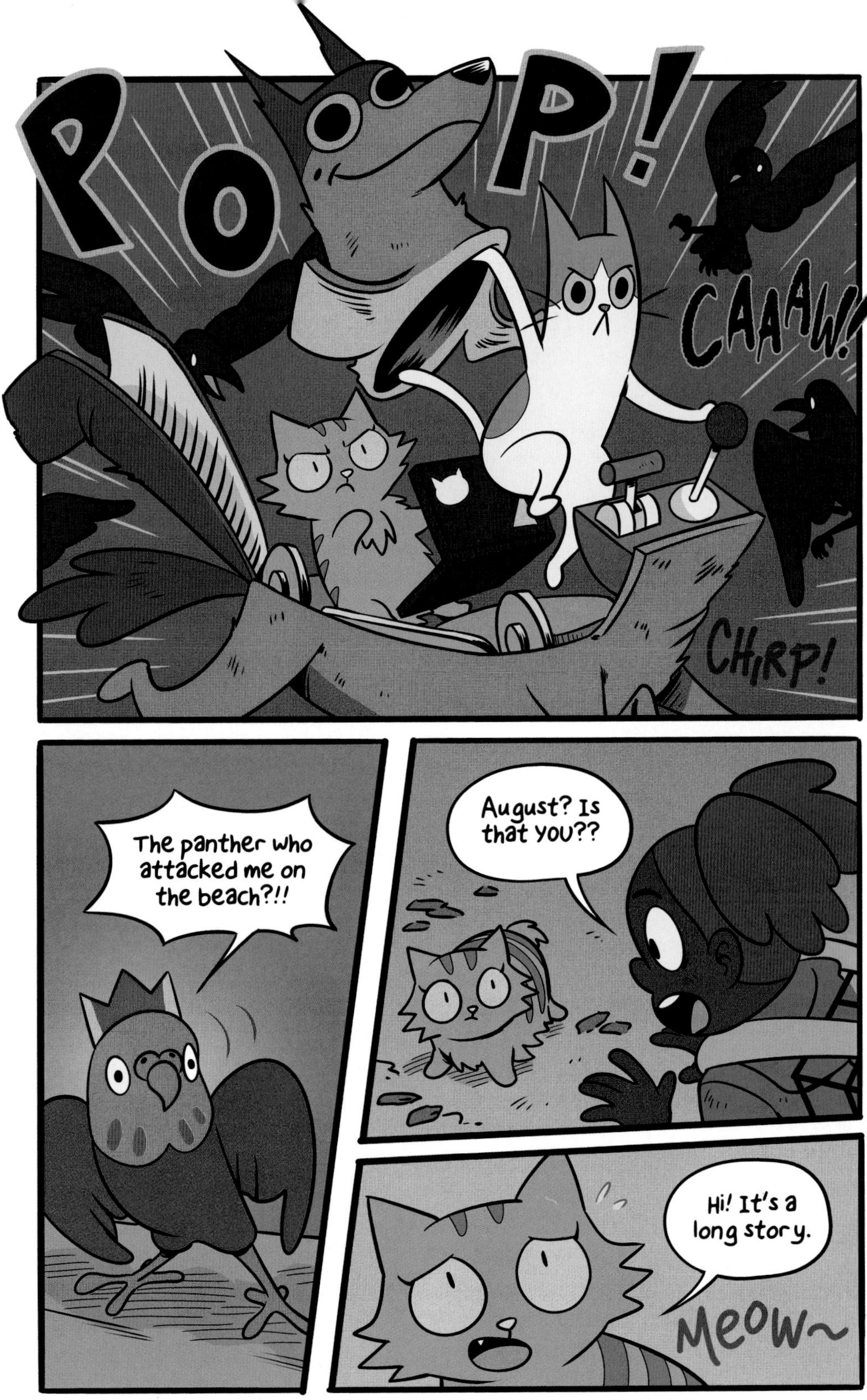
POP!
CAAAW!
CHIRP!
The panther who attacked me on the beach?!!
August? Is that you??
Hi! It's a long story.
Meow~

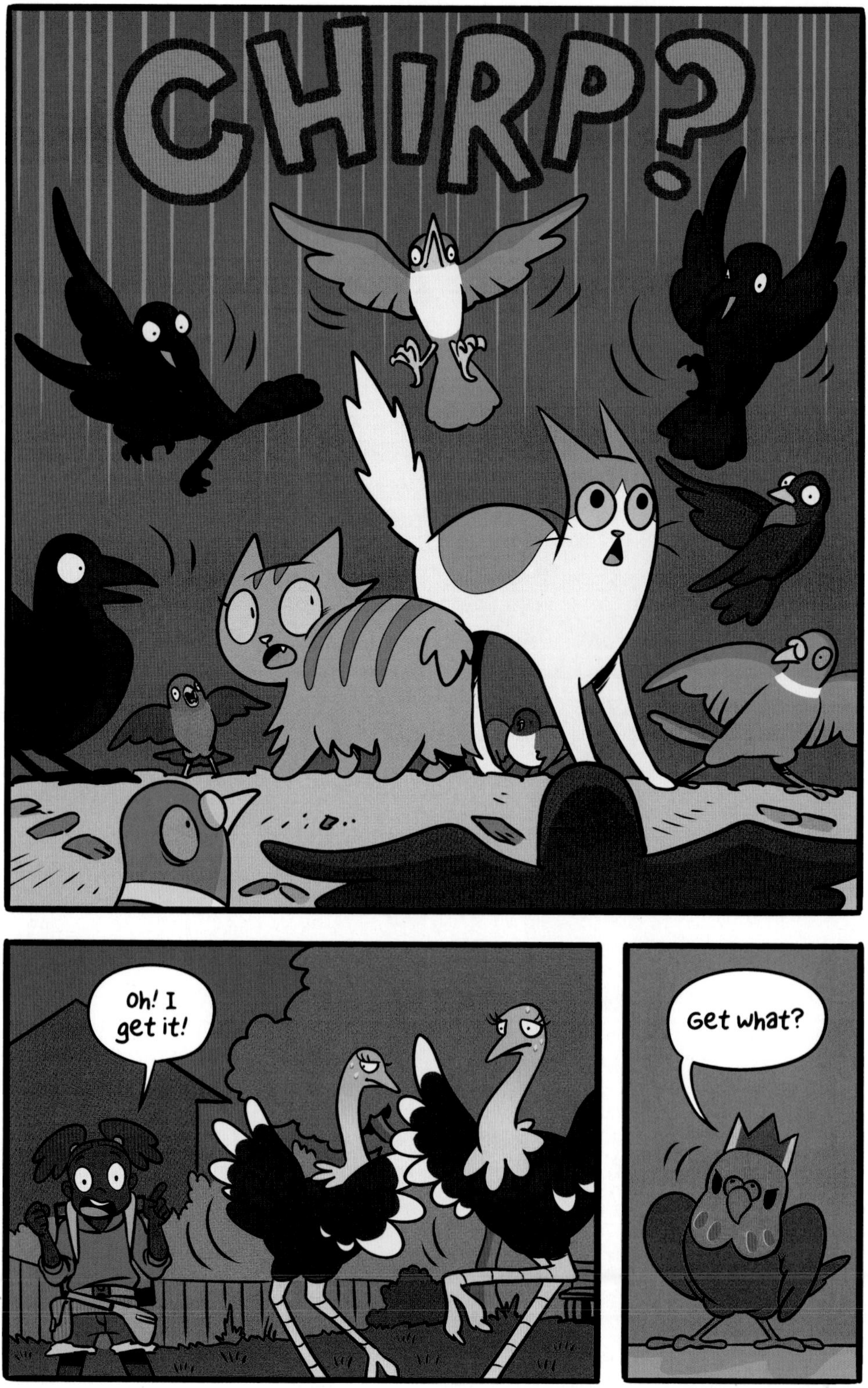
CHIRP?
Oh! I get it!
Get what?

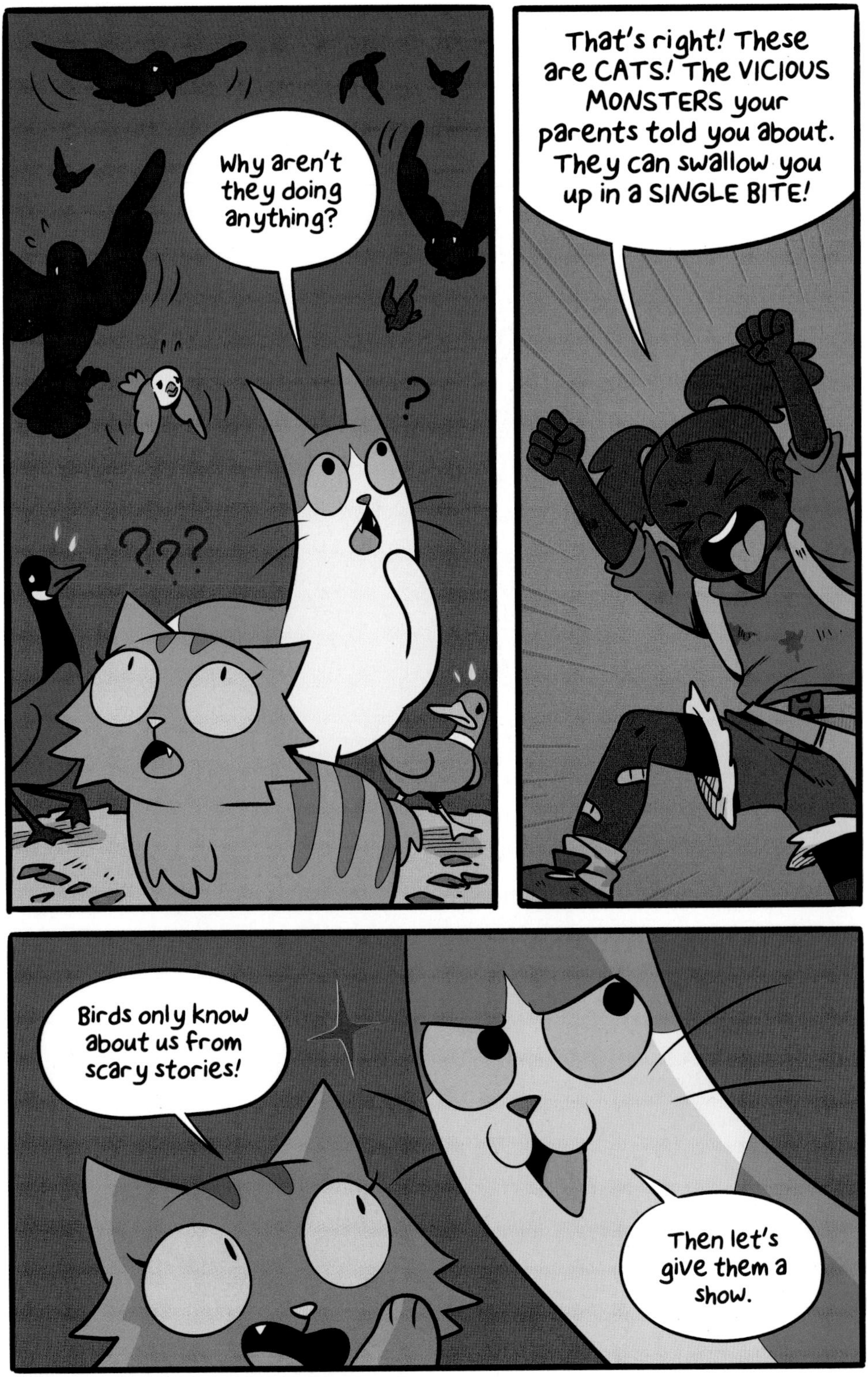
???
Why aren't they doing anything?
?
That's right! These are CATS! The VICIOUS MONSTERS your parents told you about. They can swallow you up in a SINGLE BITE!
Birds only know about us from scary stories!
Then let's give them a show.

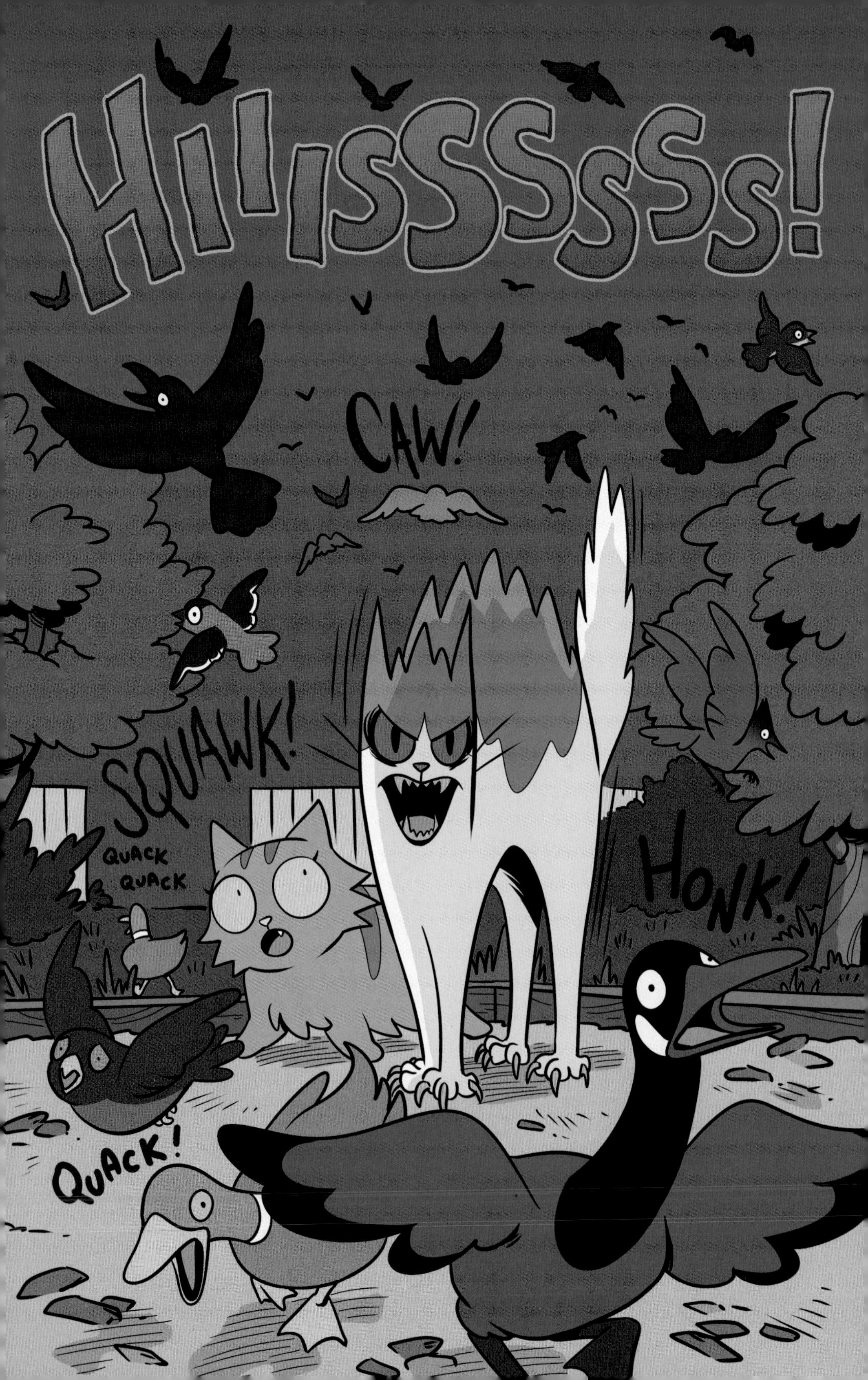
HIIISSSSSSS!
CAW!
SQUAWK!
QUACK
QUACK
HONK!
QUACK!

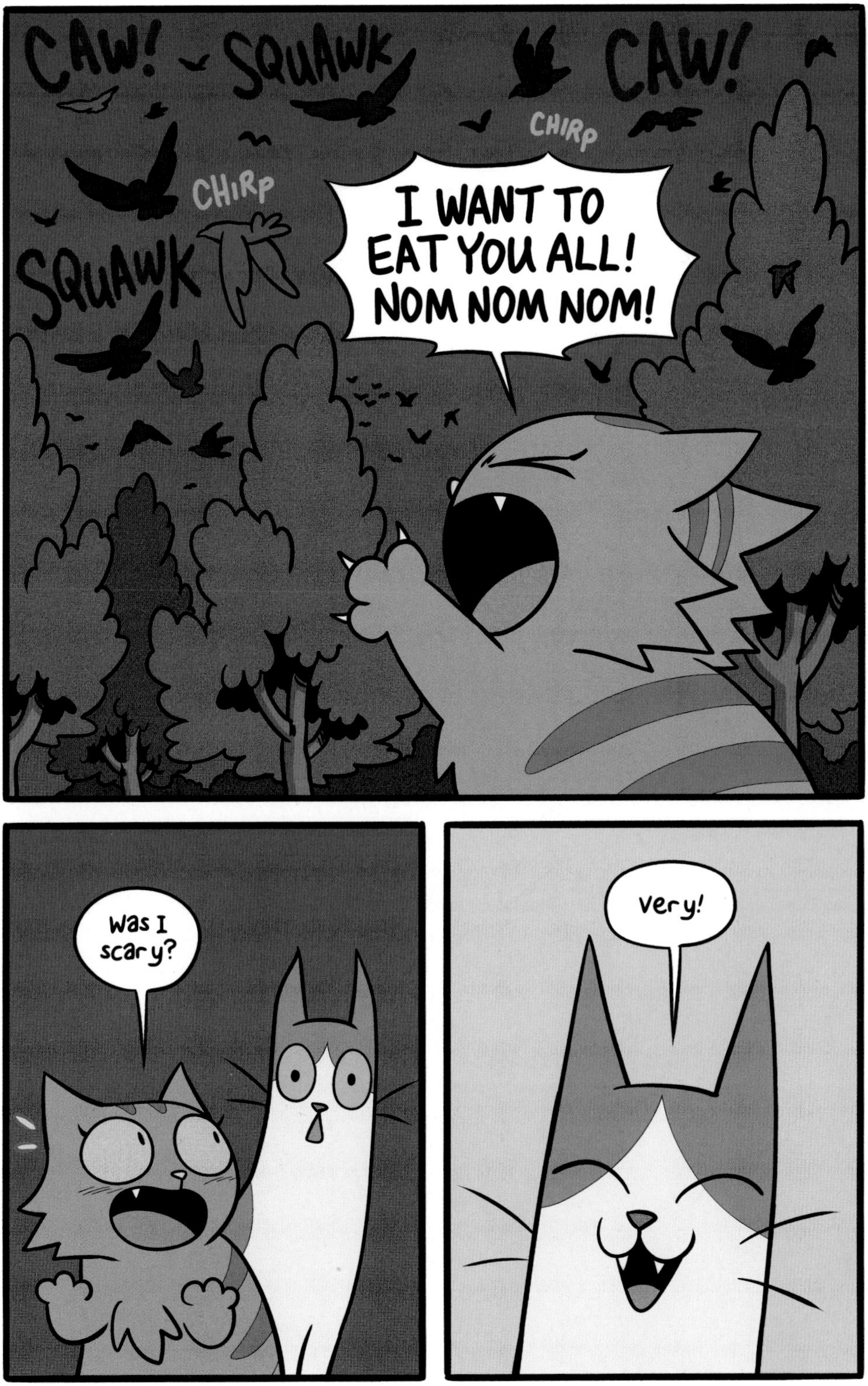
CAW!
SQUAWK
CAW!
CHIRP
CHIRP
SQUAWK
I WANT TO EAT YOU ALL! NOM NOM NOM!
Was I scary?
very!

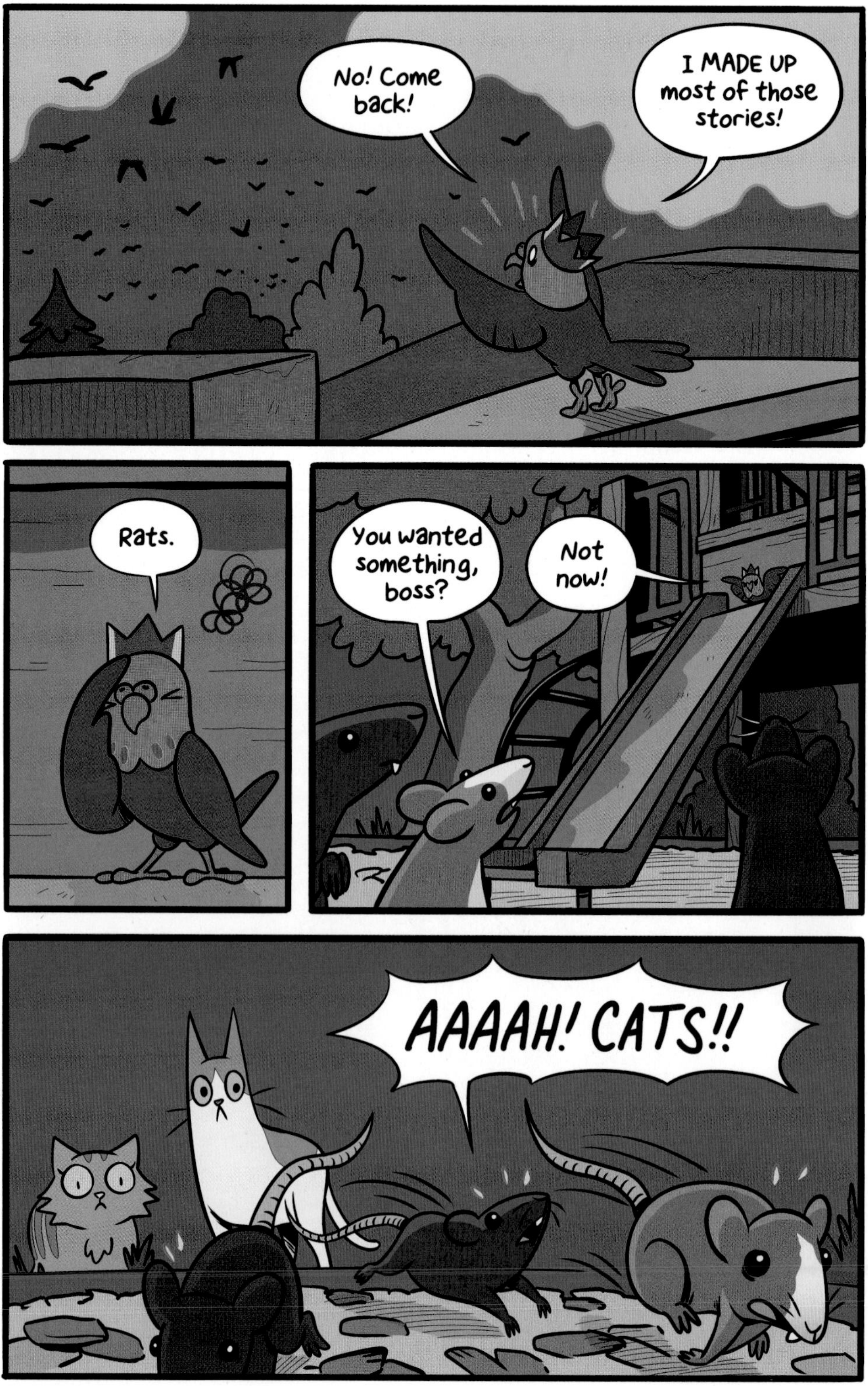
No! Come back!
I MADE UP most of those stories!
Rats.
You wanted something, boss?
Not now!
AAAAH! CATS!!

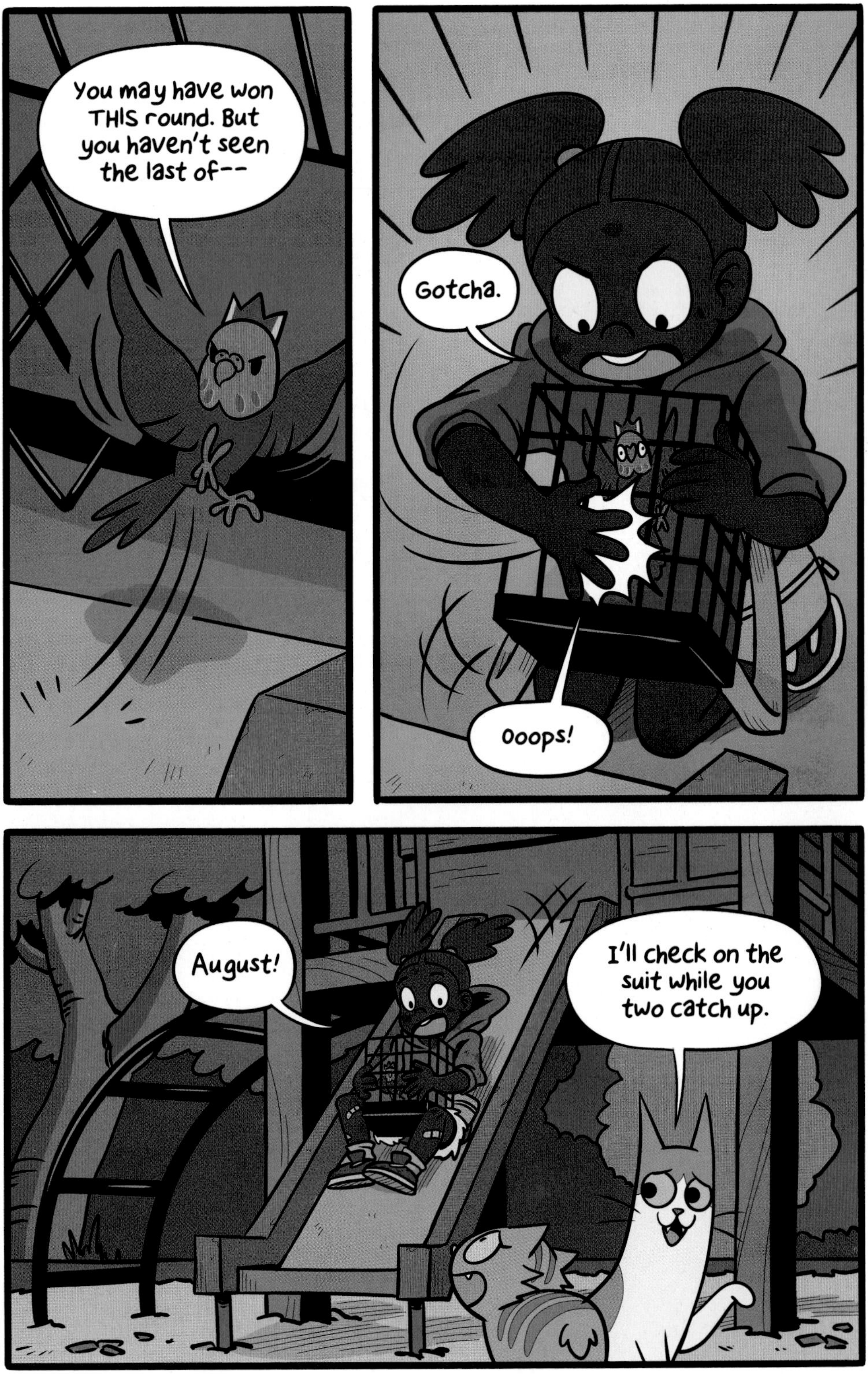
You may have won THIS round. But you haven't seen the last of--
Gotcha.
Ooops!
August!
I'll check on the suit while you two catch up.

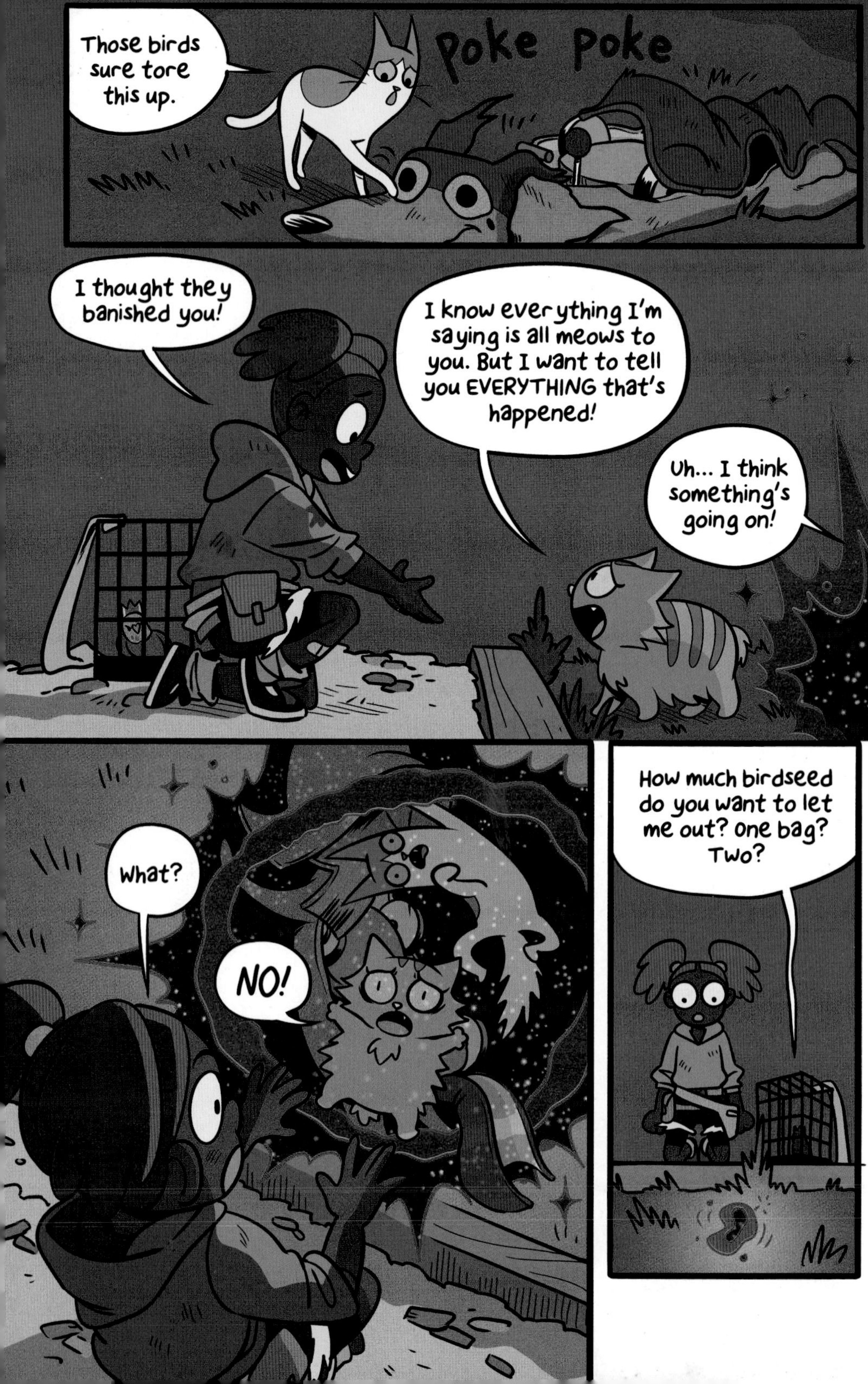
Those birds sure tore this up.
Poke Poke
I thought they banished you!
I know everything I'm saying is all meows to you. But I want to tell you EVERYTHING that's happened!
Uh... I think something's going on!
What?
NO!
How much birdseed do you want to let me out? One bag? Two?

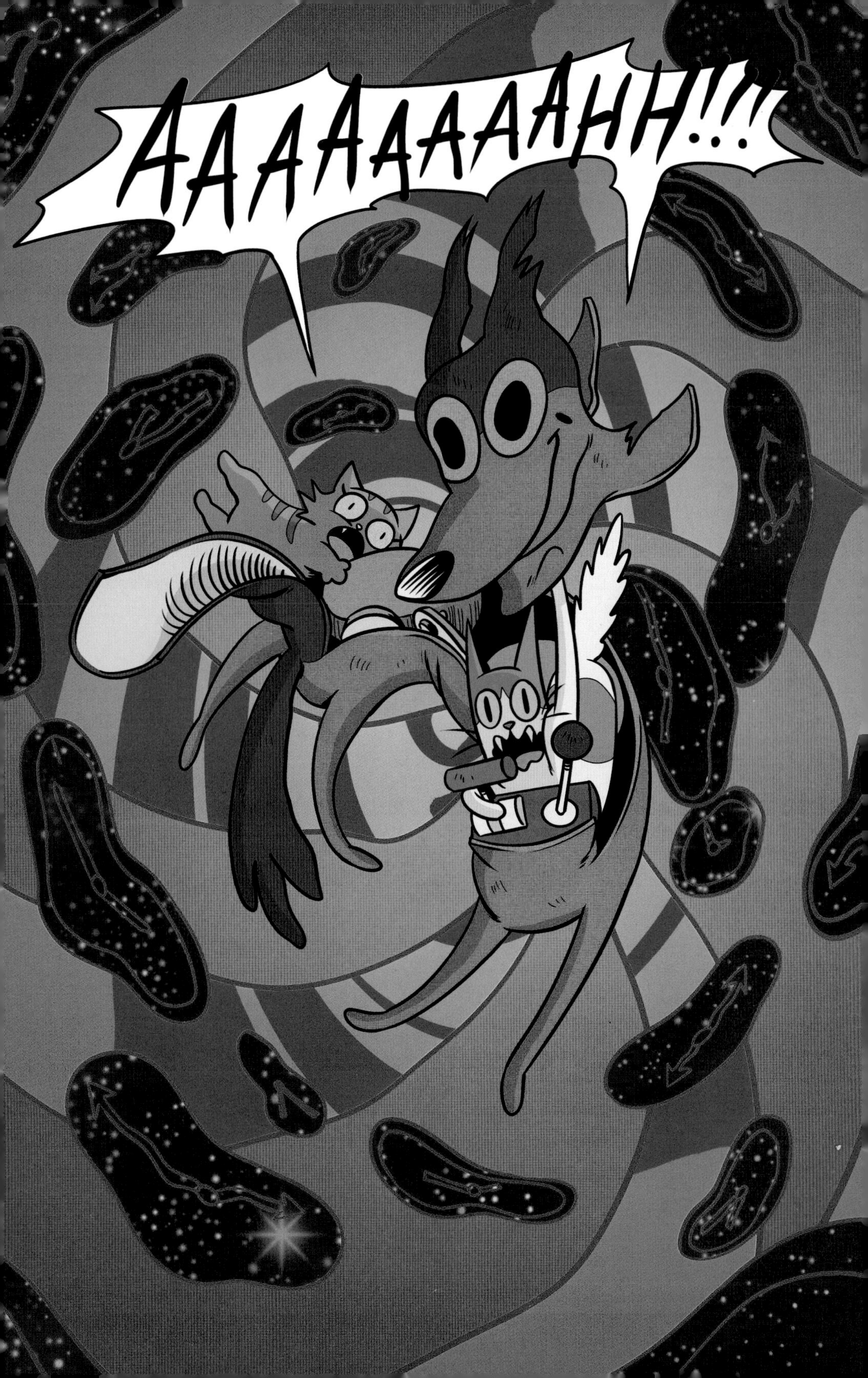
AAAAAAAAHH!!!

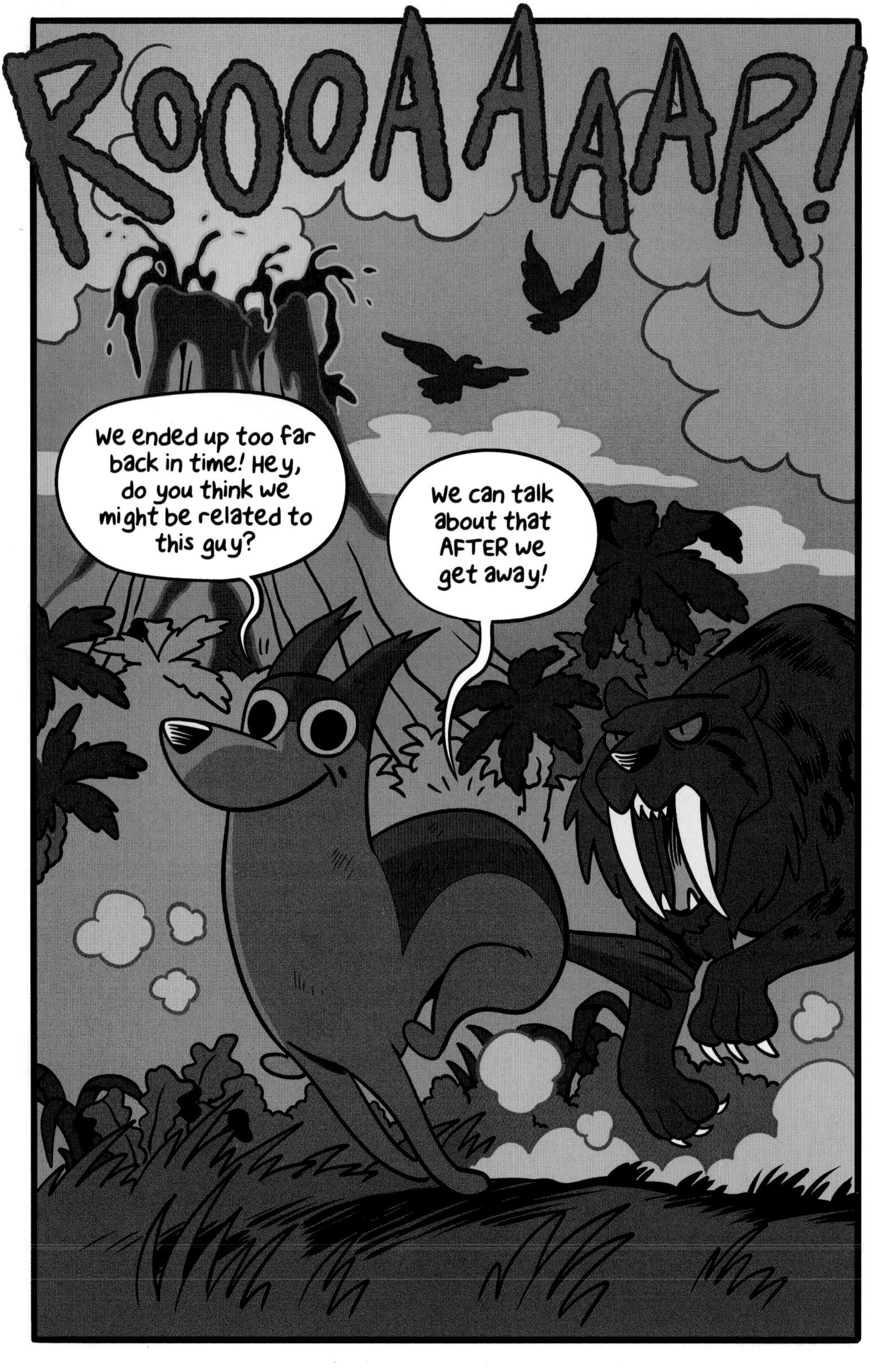
ROOOAAAAR!
We ended up too far back in time! Hey, do you think we might be related to this guy?
We can talk about that AFTER we get away!

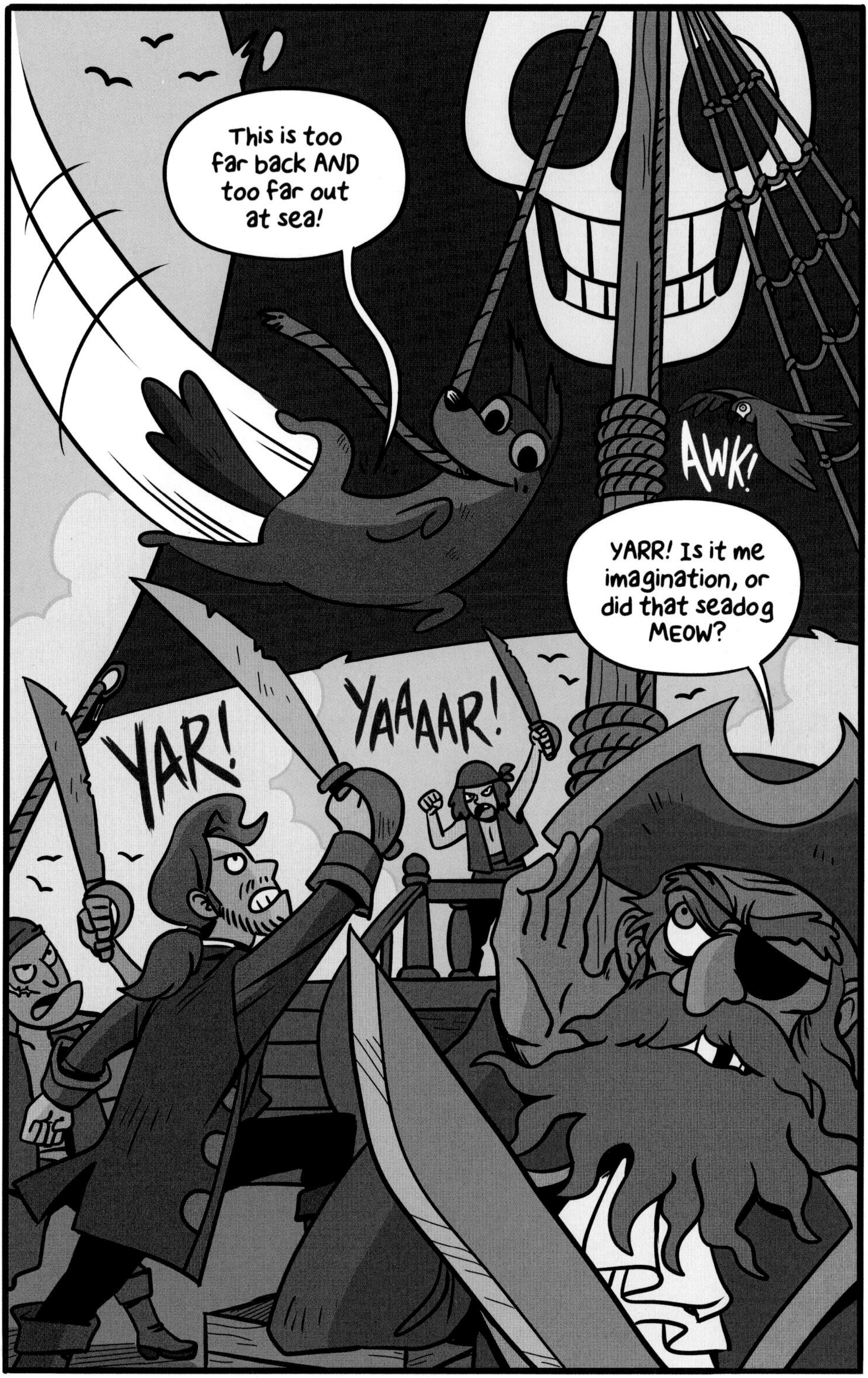
This is too far back AND too far out at sea!
AWK!
YARR! Is it me imagination, or did that seadog MEOW?
YAR!
YAAAAR!

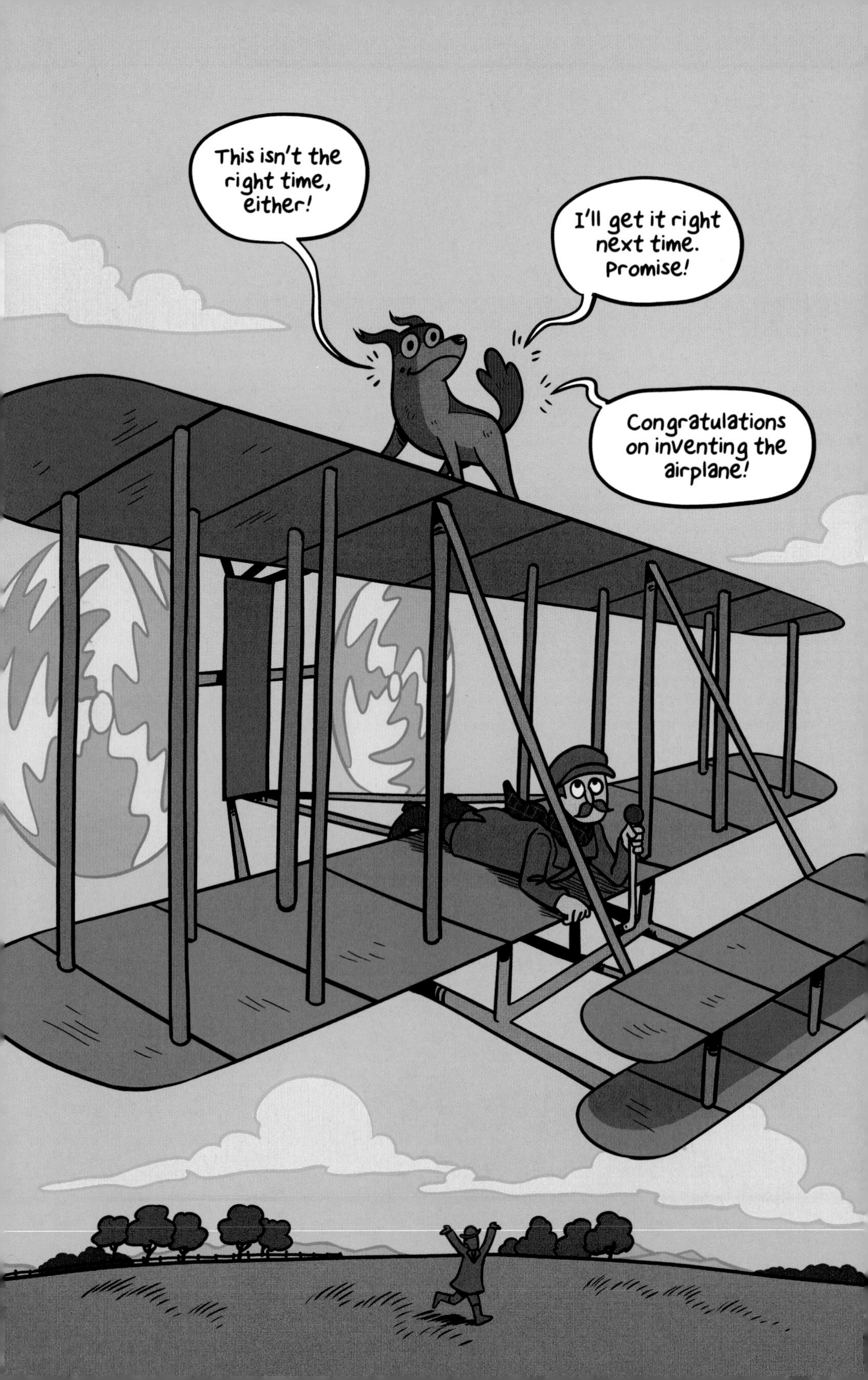
This isn't the right time, either!
I'll get it right next time. Promise!
Congratulations on inventing the airplane!

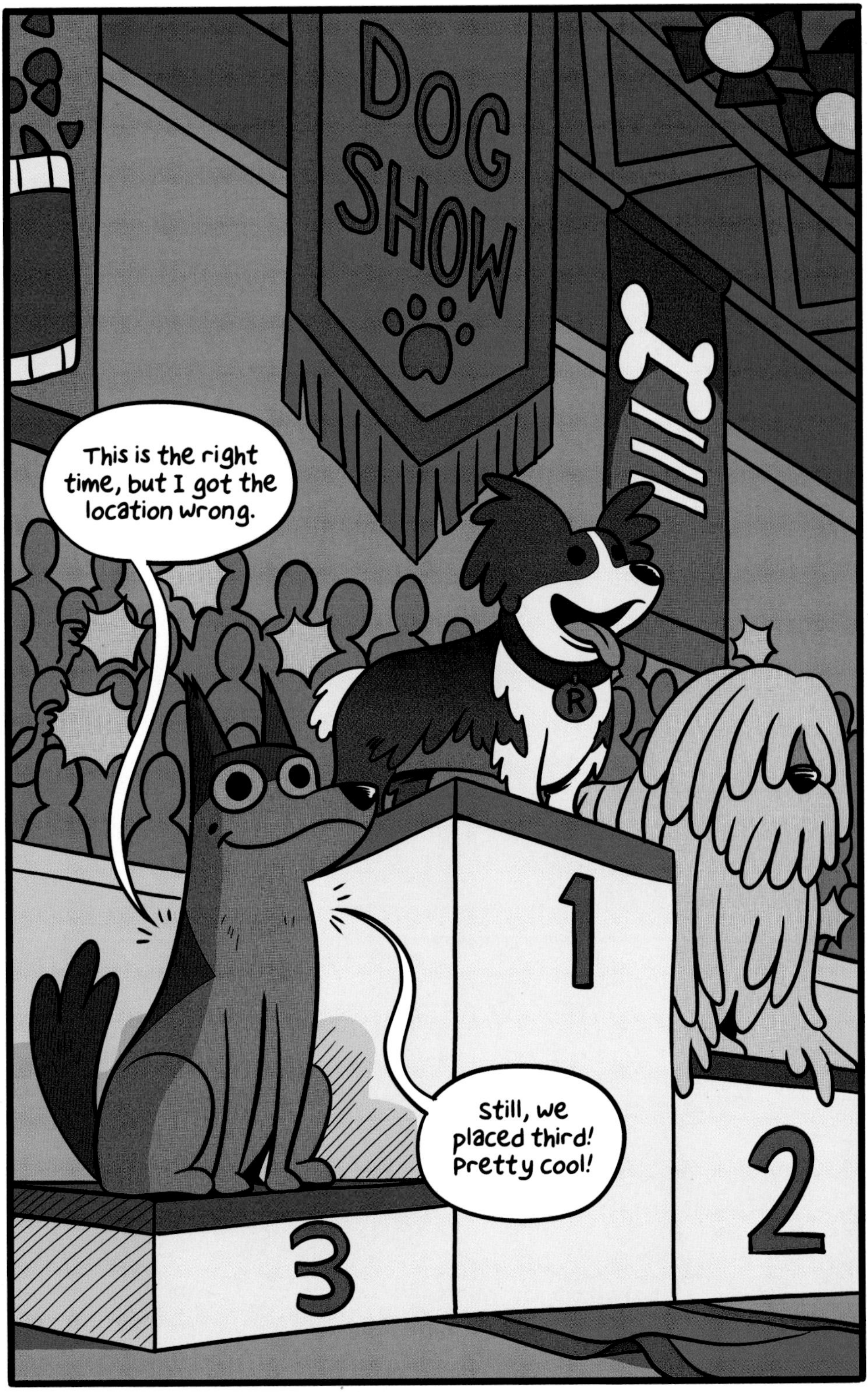
DOG SHOW
This is the right time, but I got the location wrong.
1
Still, we placed third! Pretty cool!
3
2

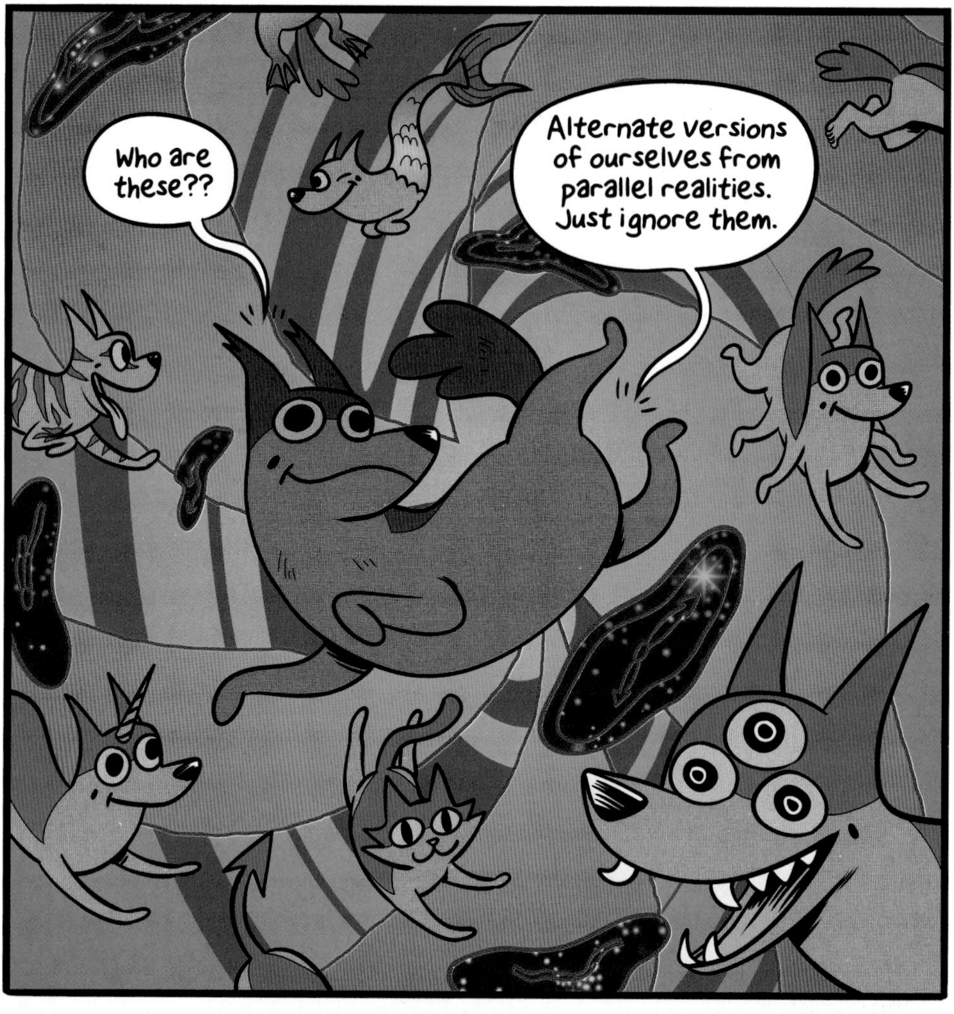
Who are these??
Alternate versions of ourselves from parallel realities. Just ignore them.

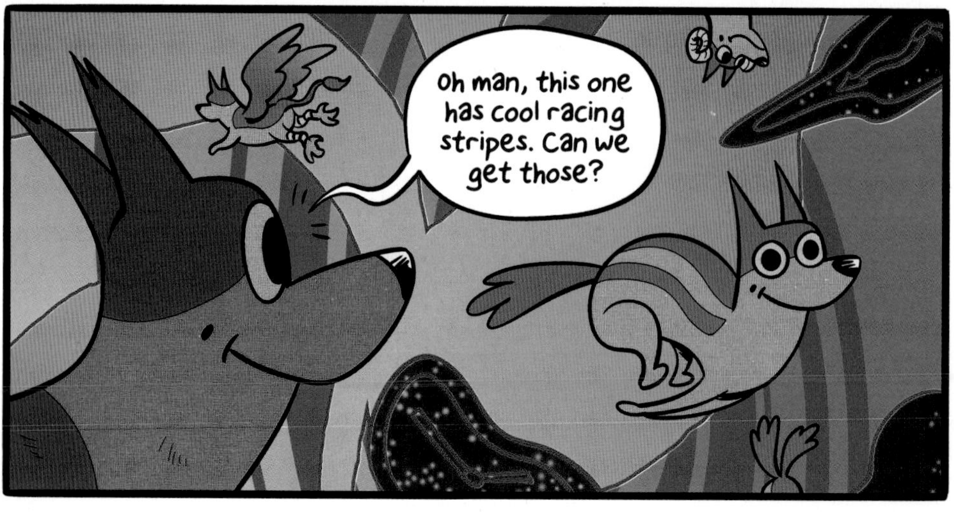
Oh man, this one has cool racing stripes. Can we get those?

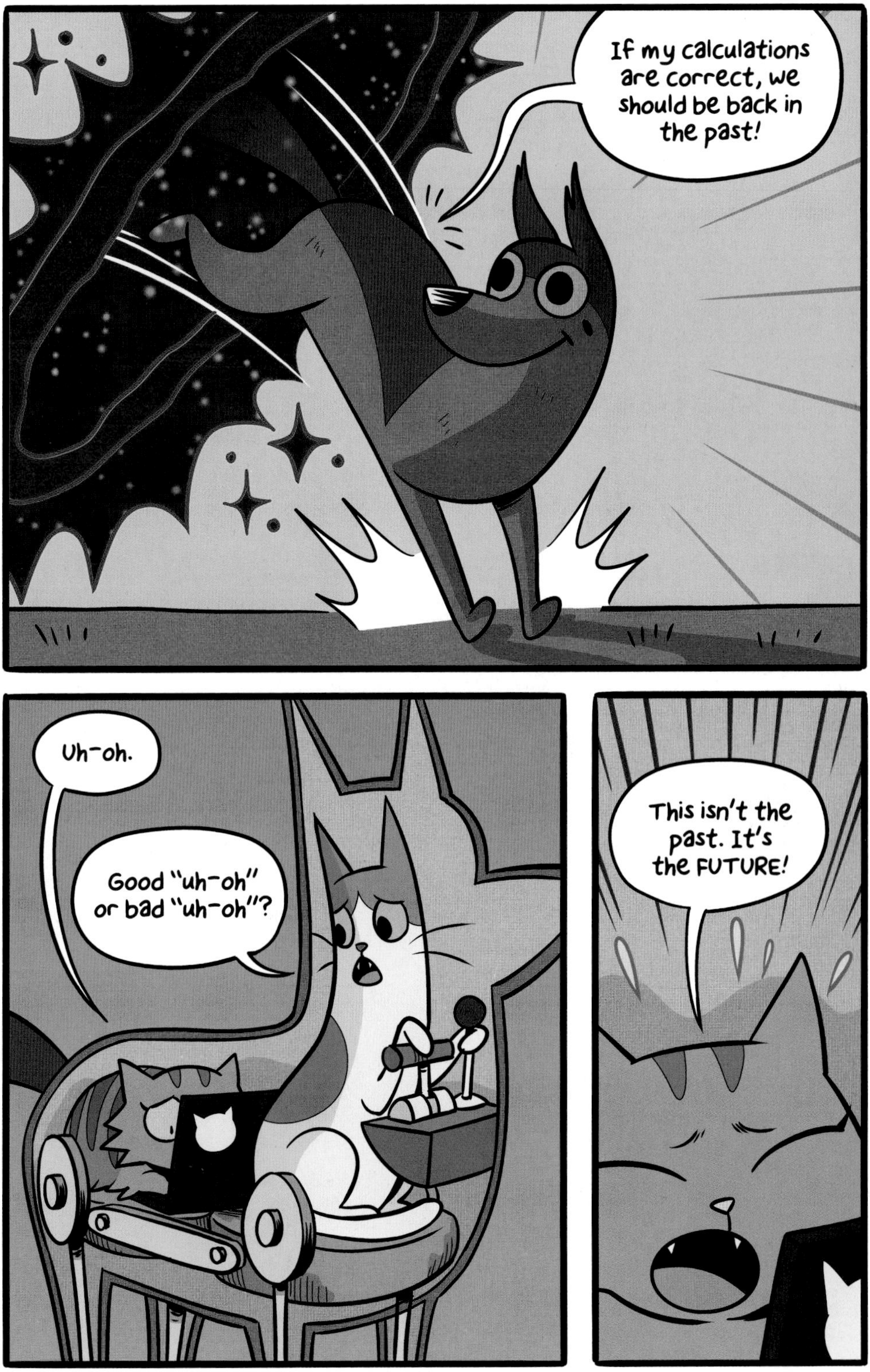
If my calculations are correct, we should be back in the past!
Uh-oh.
Good "uh-oh" or bad "uh-oh"?
This isn't the past. It's the FUTURE!

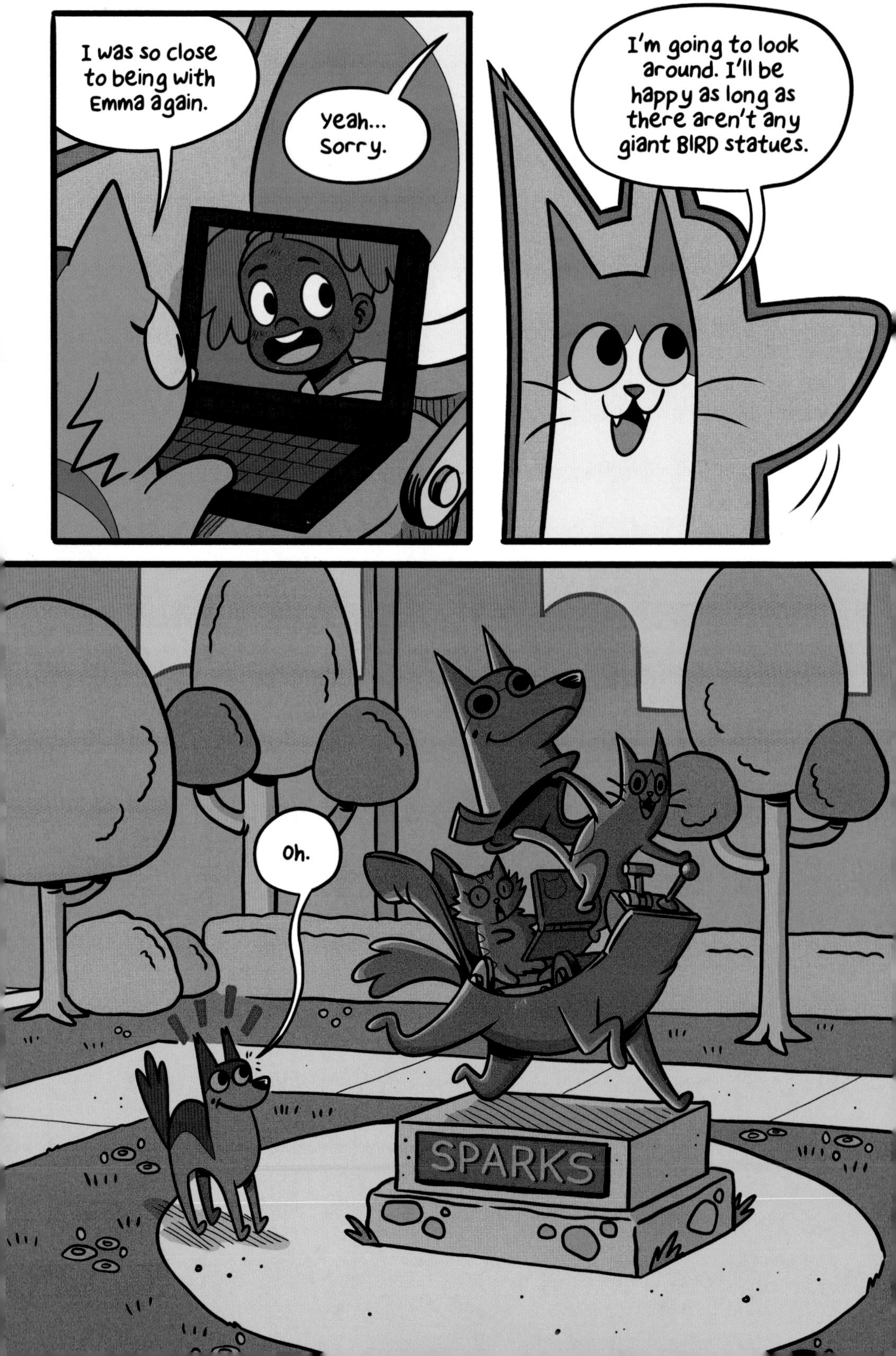
I was so close to being with Emma again.
yeah... Sorry.
I'm going to look around. I'll be happy as long as there aren't any giant BIRD statues.
Oh.
SPARKS

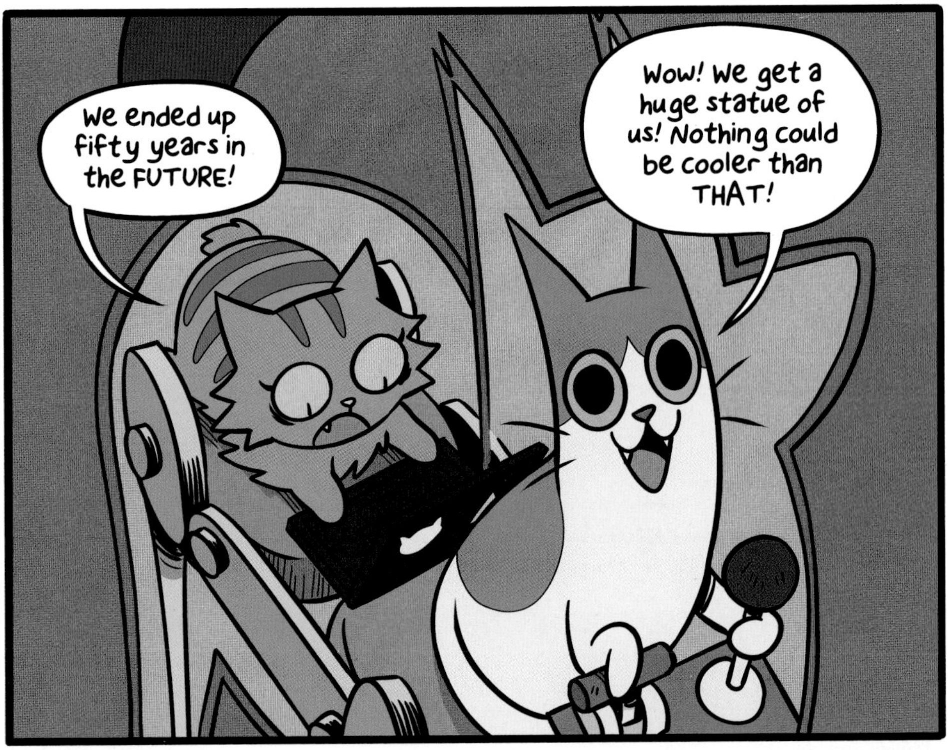
We ended up fifty years in the FUTURE!
Wow! We get a huge statue of us! Nothing could be cooler than THAT!

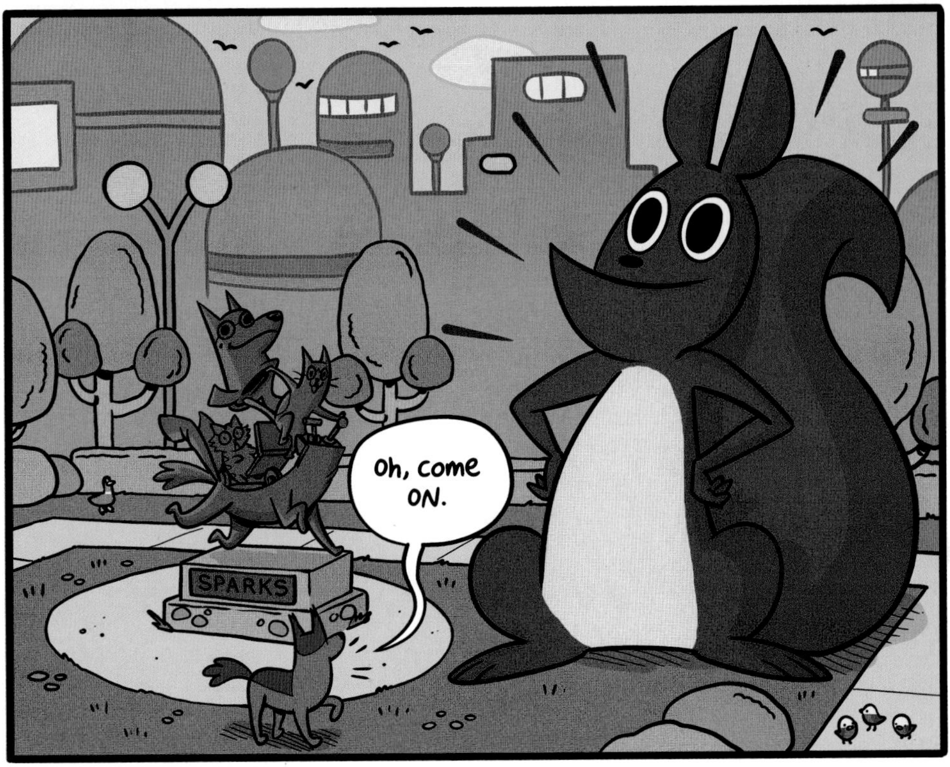
SPARKS
Oh, come ON.

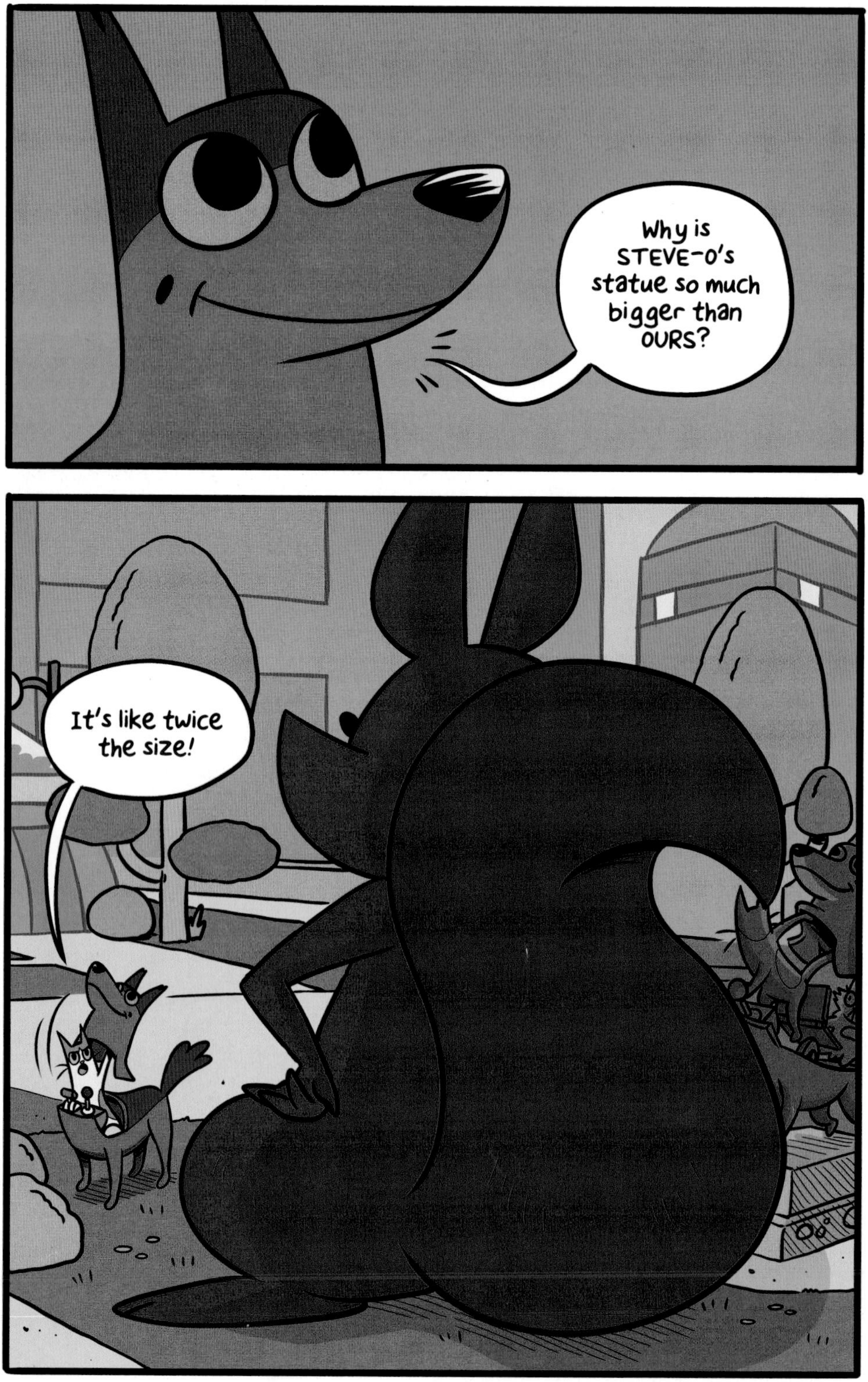
Why is STEVE-O's statue so much bigger than OURS?
It's like twice the size!

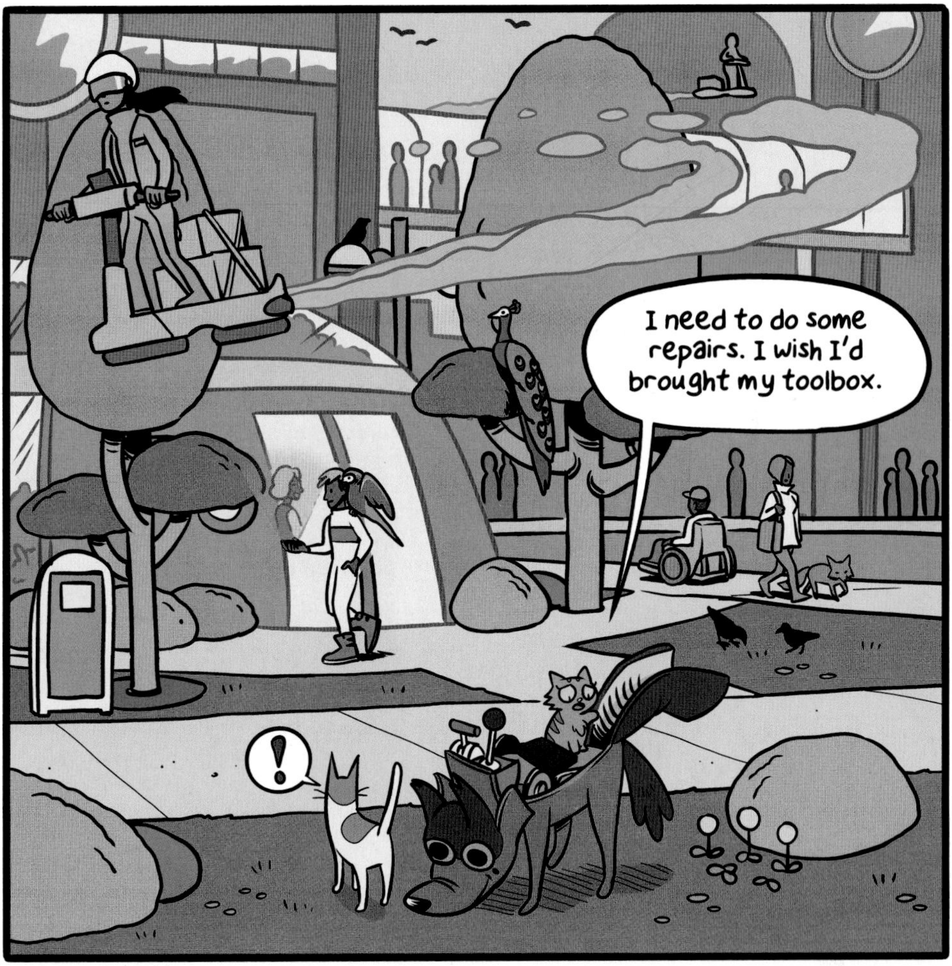
I need to do some repairs. I wish I'd brought my toolbox.
!

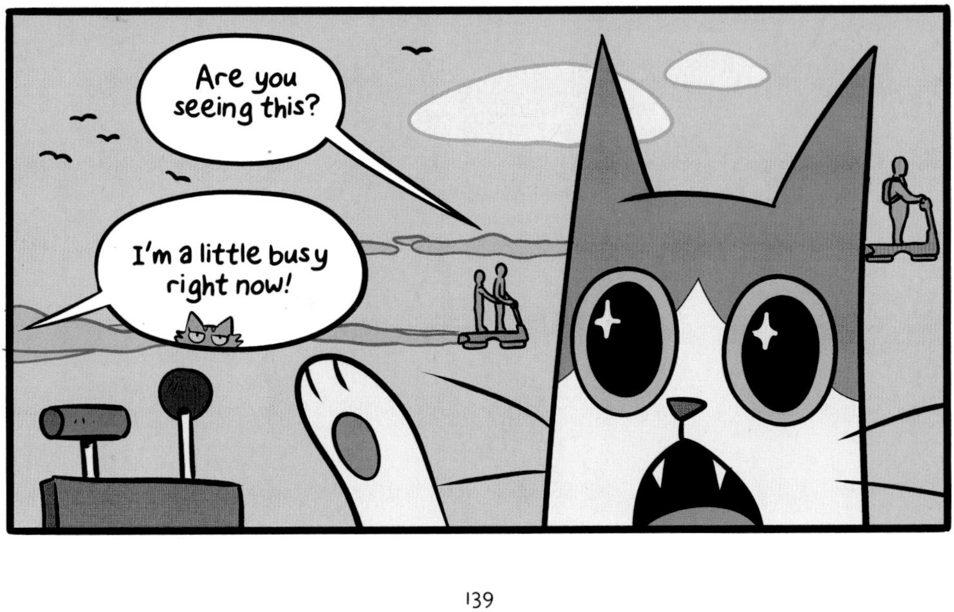
Are you seeing this?
I'm a little busy right now!

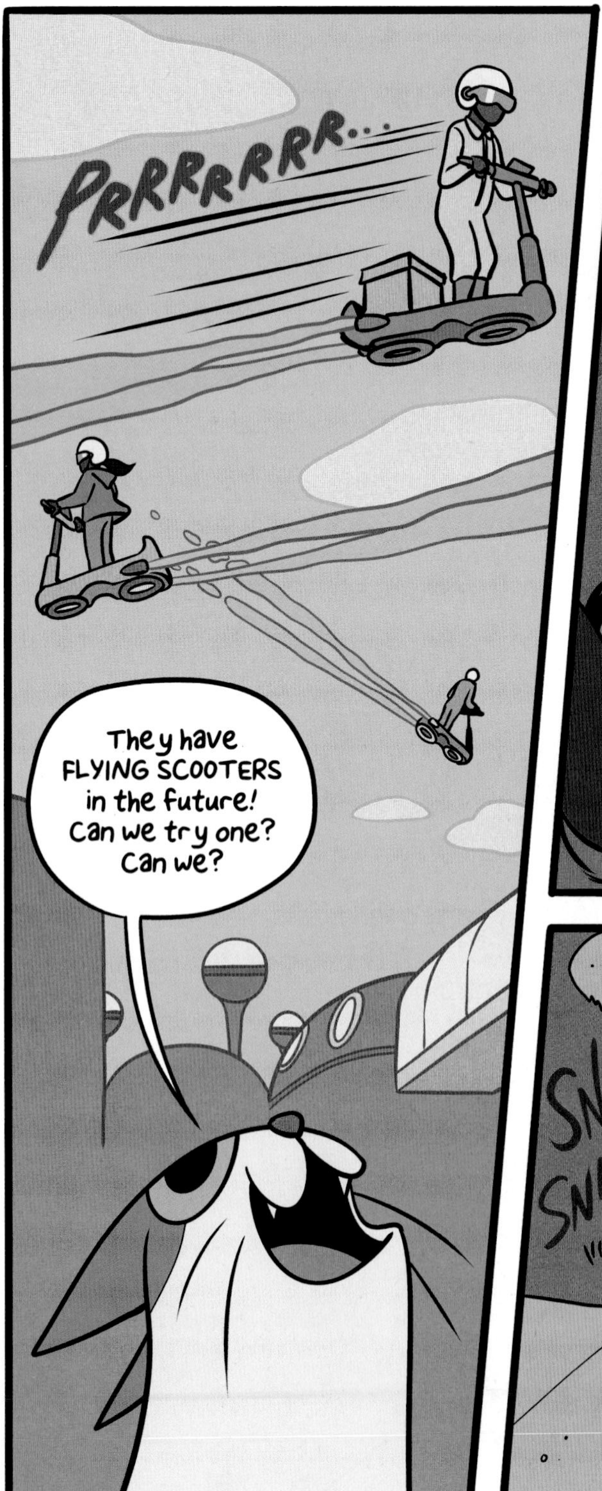
PRRRRRRR...
They have FLYING SCOOTERS in the future! Can we try one? Can we?

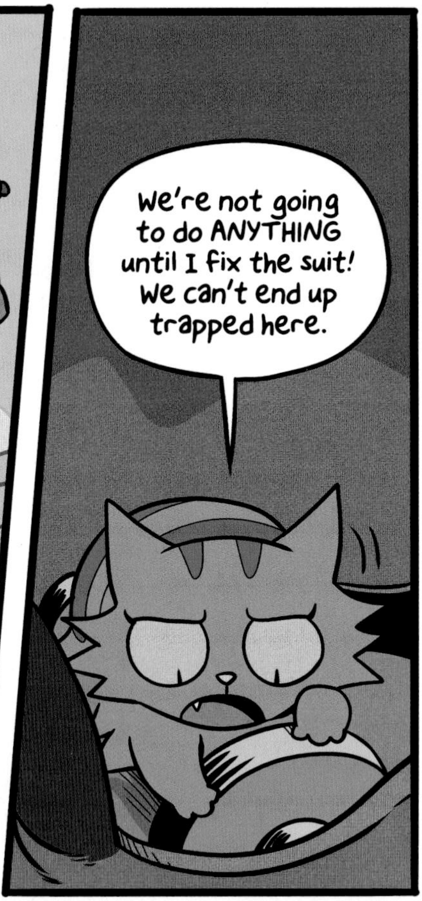
We're not going to do ANYTHING until I fix the suit! We can't end up trapped here.

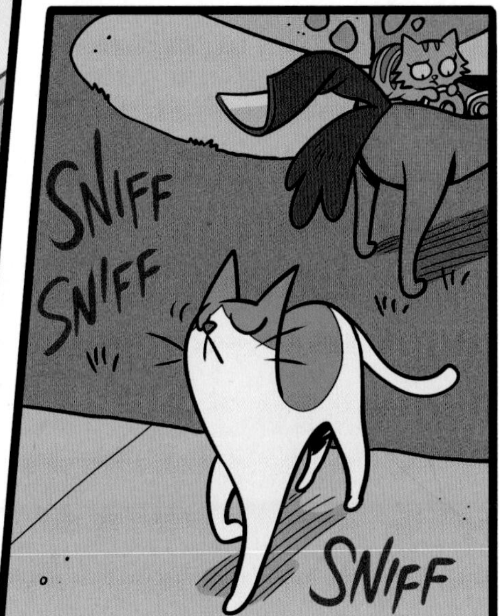
SNIFF
SNIFF
SNIFF

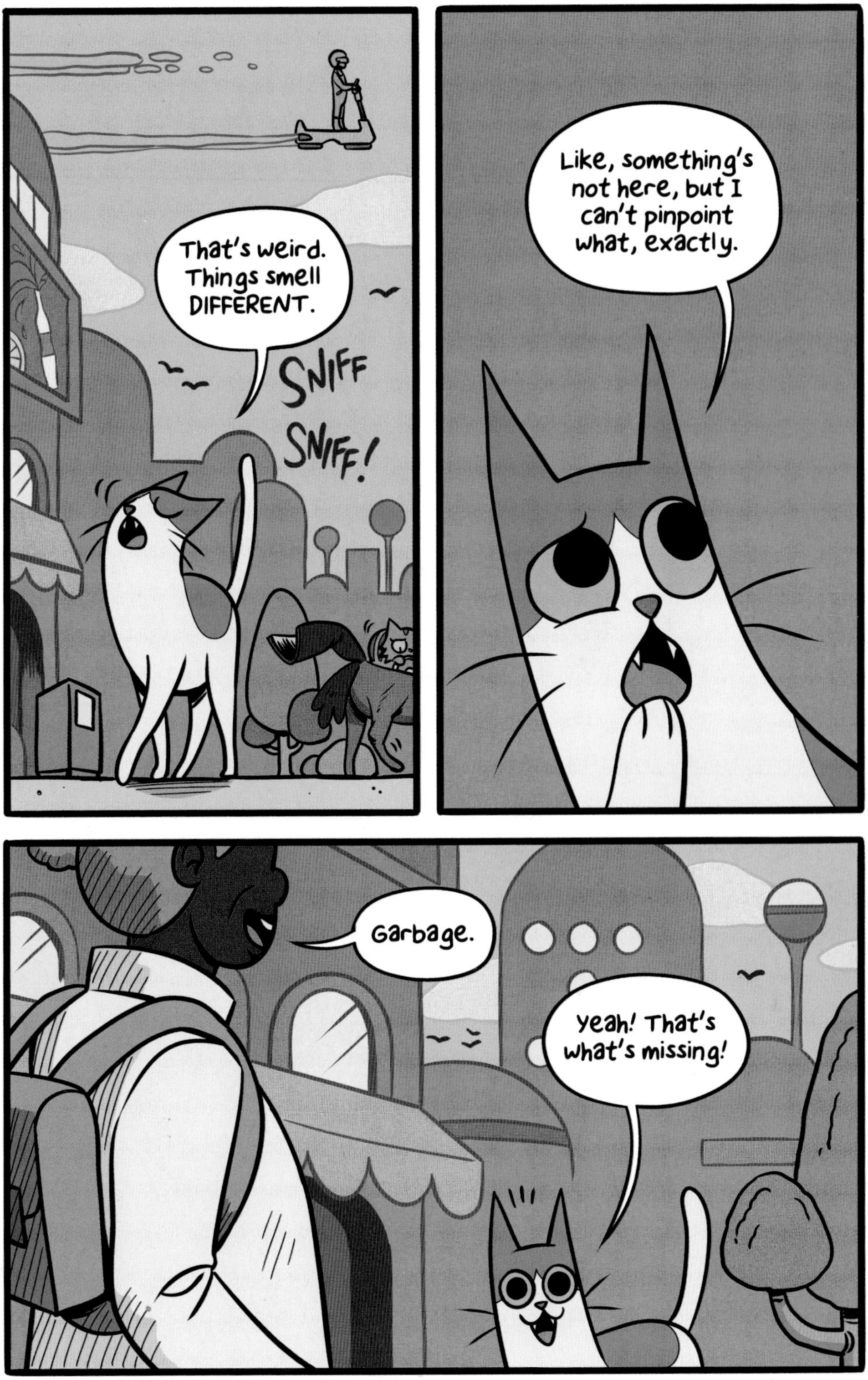
That's weird. Things smell DIFFERENT.
SNIFF
SNIFF!
Like, something's not here, but I can't pinpoint what, exactly.
Garbage.
Yeah! That's what's missing!

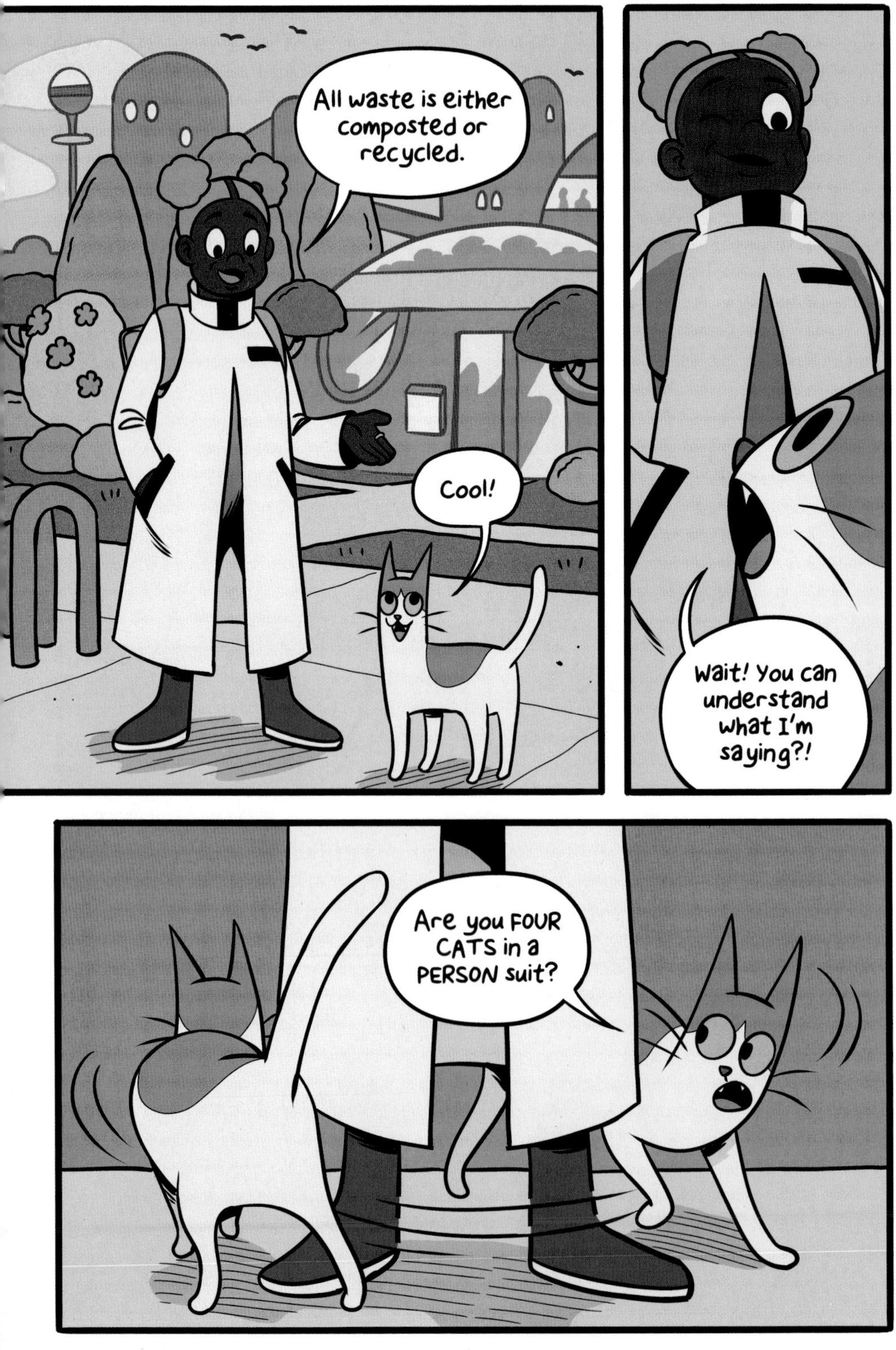
All waste is either composted or recycled.
Cool!
Wait! You can understand what I'm saying?!
Are you FOUR CATS in a PERSON suit?

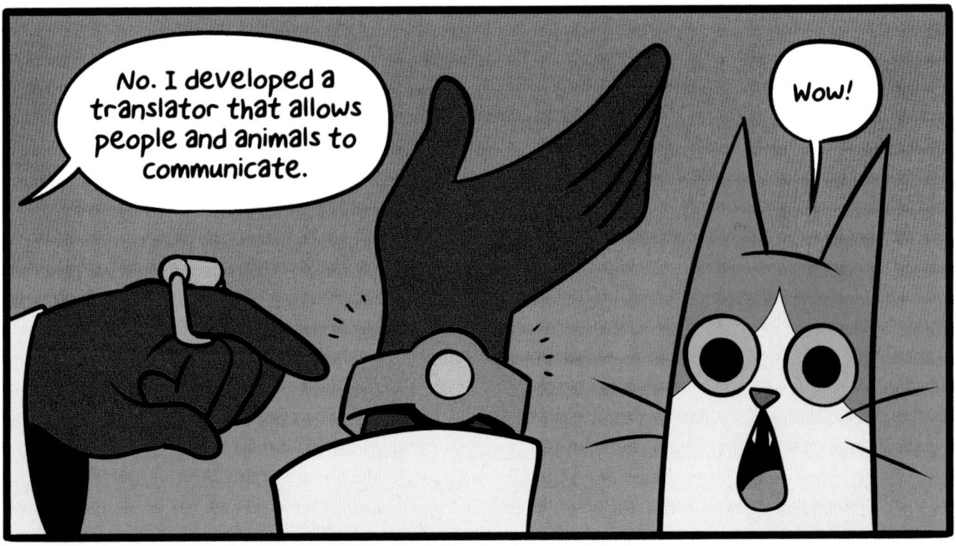
No. I developed a translator that allows people and animals to communicate.
Wow!

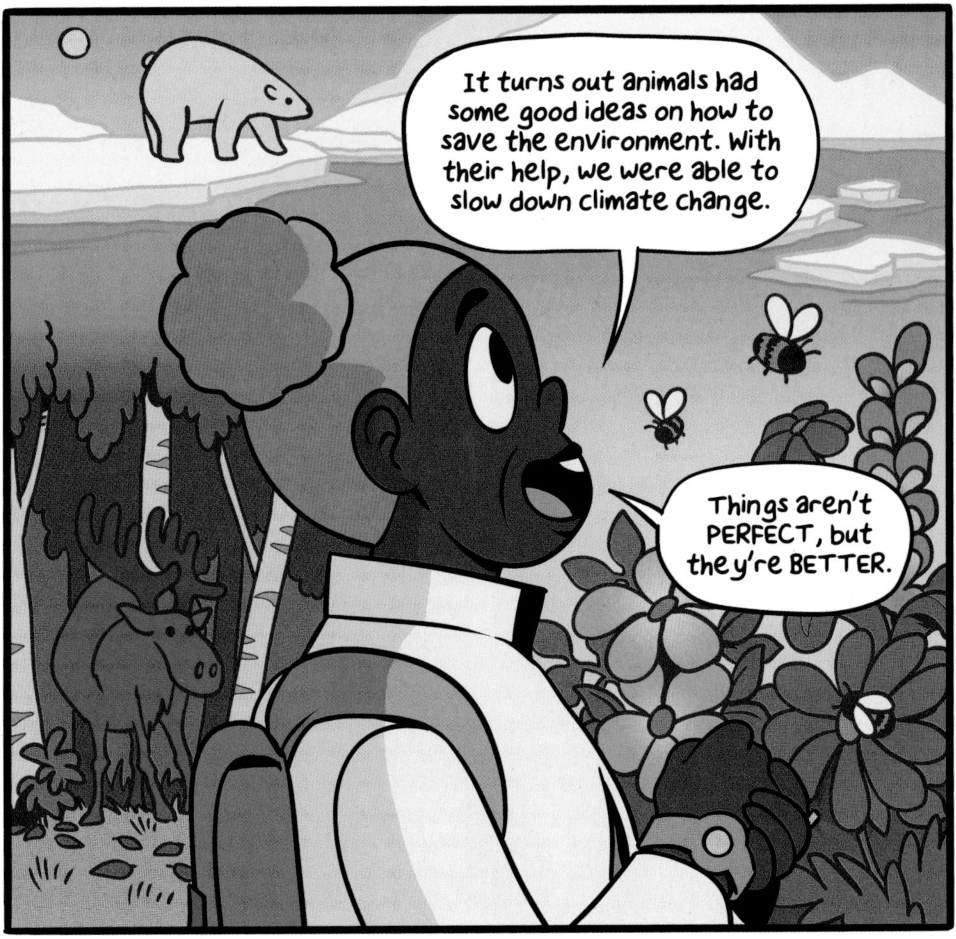
It turns out animals had some good ideas on how to save the environment. With their help, we were able to slow down climate change.
Things aren't PERFECT, but they're BETTER.

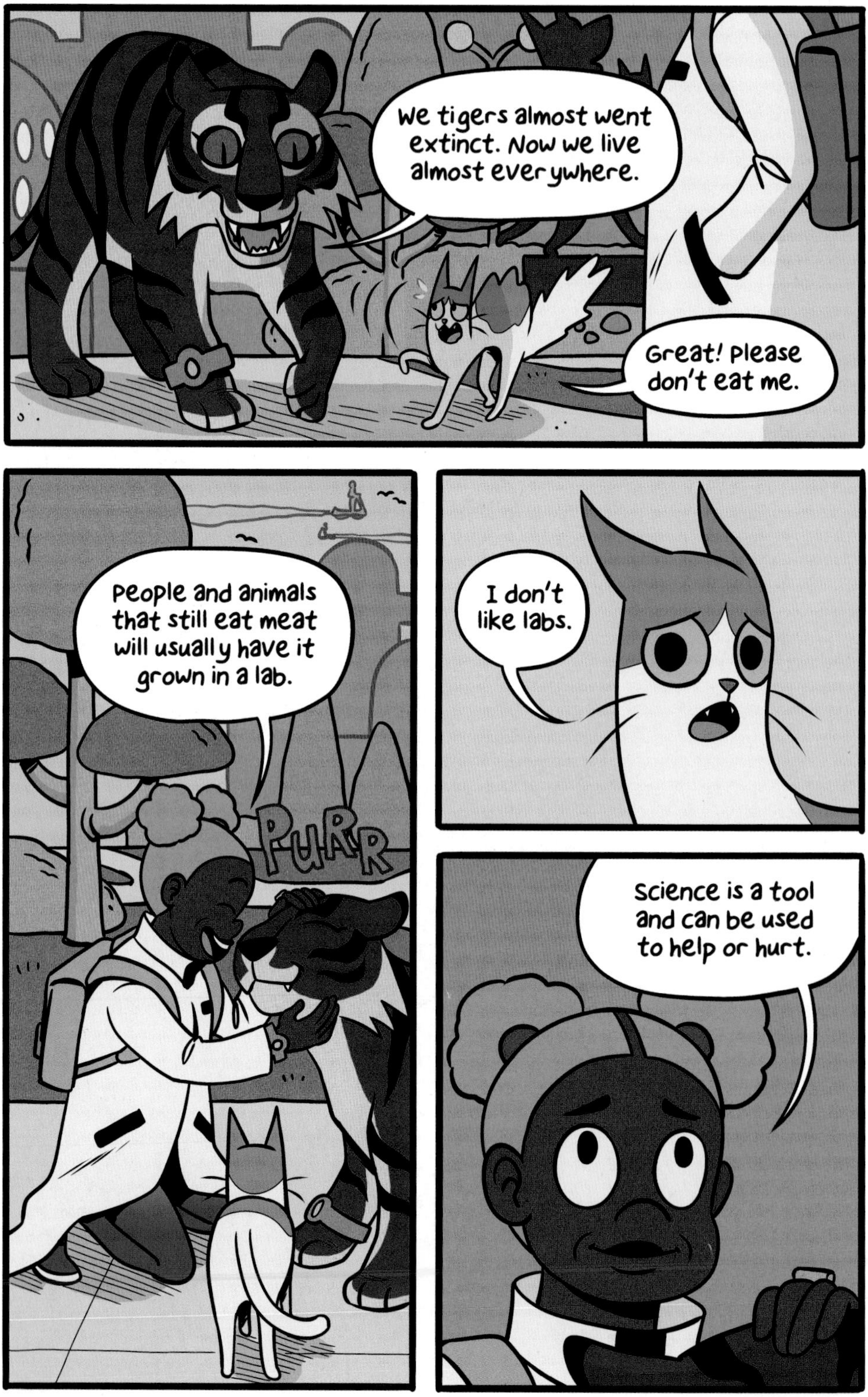
We tigers almost went extinct. Now we live almost everywhere.
Great! Please don't eat me.
People and animals that still eat meat will usually have it grown in a lab.
PURR
I don't like labs.
Science is a tool and can be used to help or hurt.

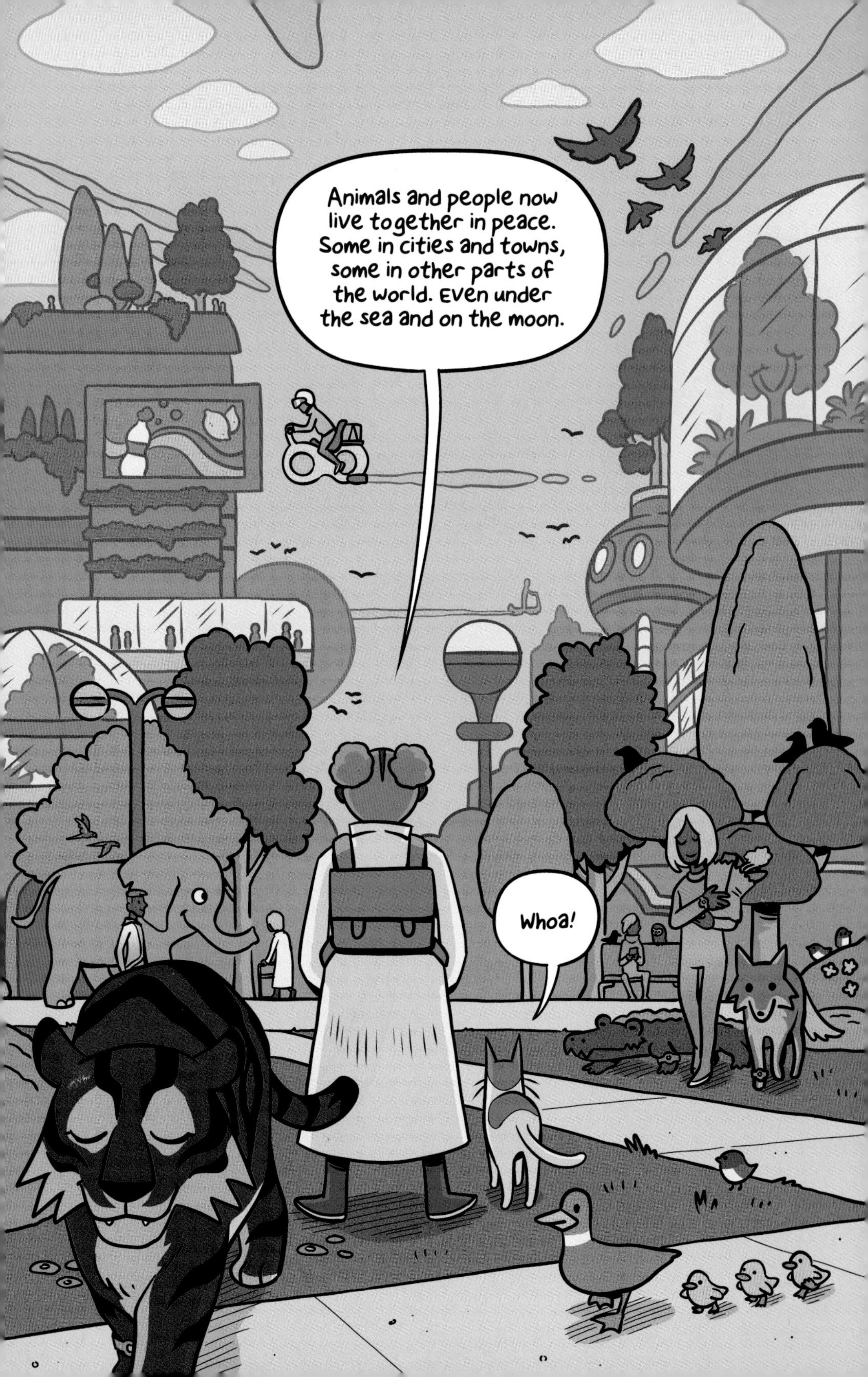
Animals and people now live together in peace. Some in cities and towns, some in other parts of the world. Even under the sea and on the moon.
Whoa!

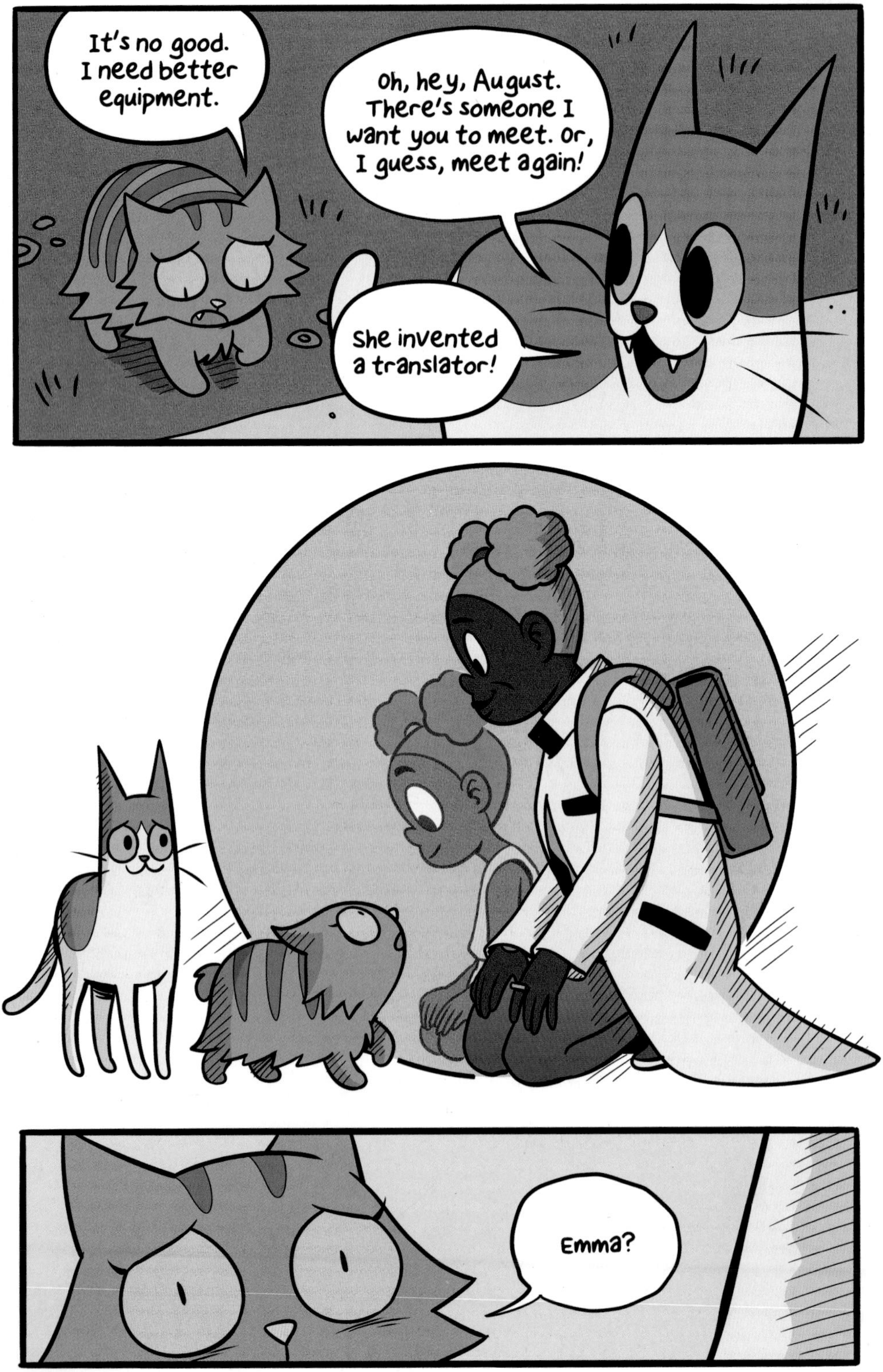
It's no good. I need better equipment.
Oh, hey, August. There's someone I want you to meet. Or, I guess, meet again!
She invented a translator!
Emma?

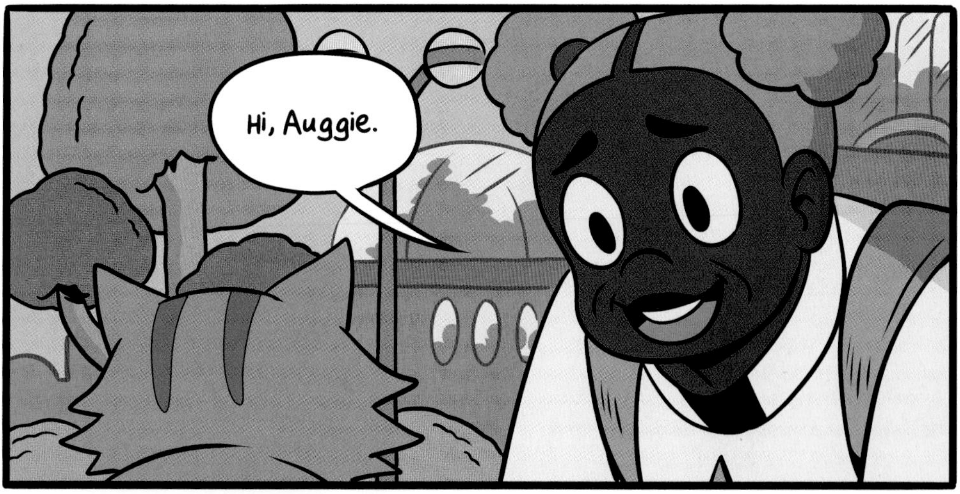
Hi, Auggie.

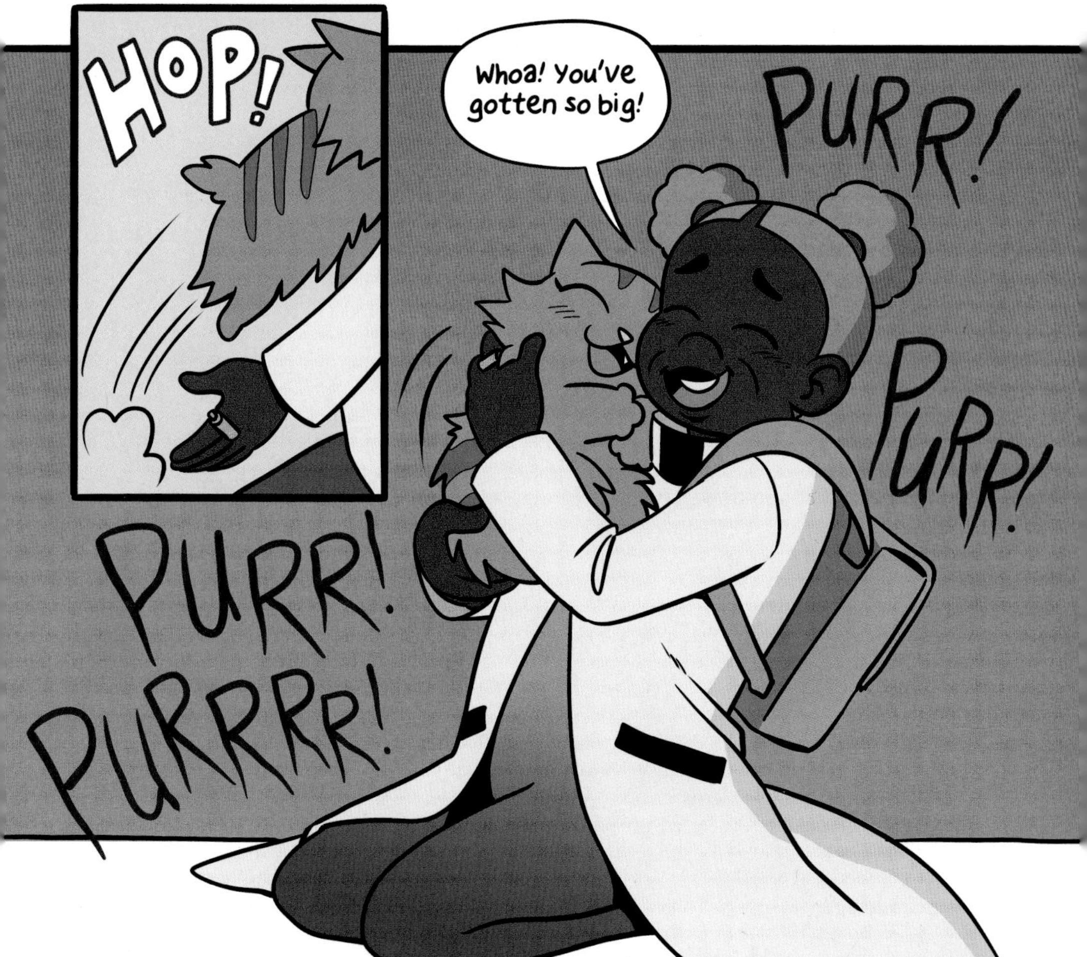
HOP!
Whoa! You've gotten so big!
PURR!
PURR!
PURR!
PURRRR!

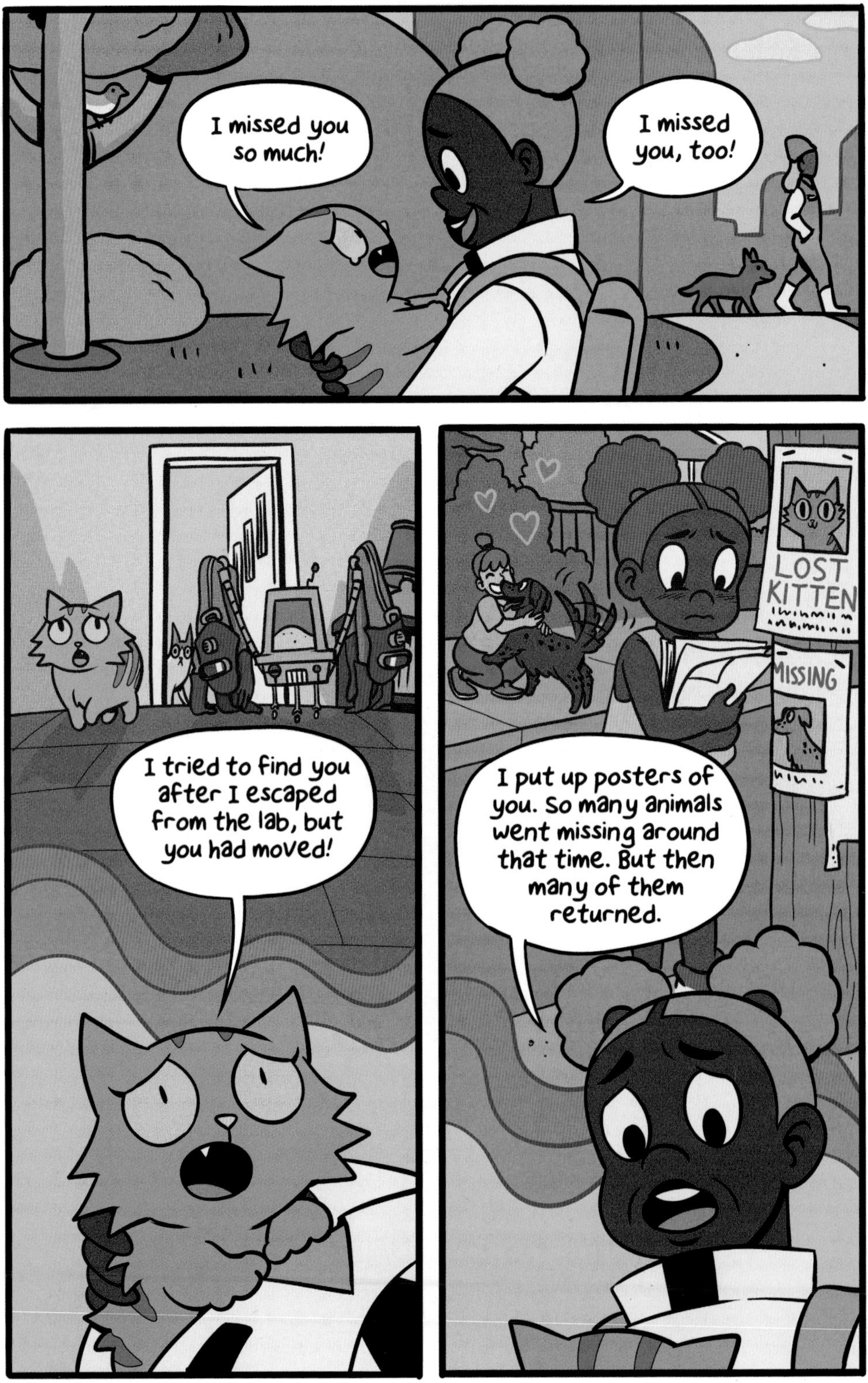
I missed you so much!
I missed you, too!
I tried to find you after I escaped from the lab, but you had moved!
LOST KITTEN
MISSING
I put up posters of you. So many animals went missing around that time. But then many of them returned.

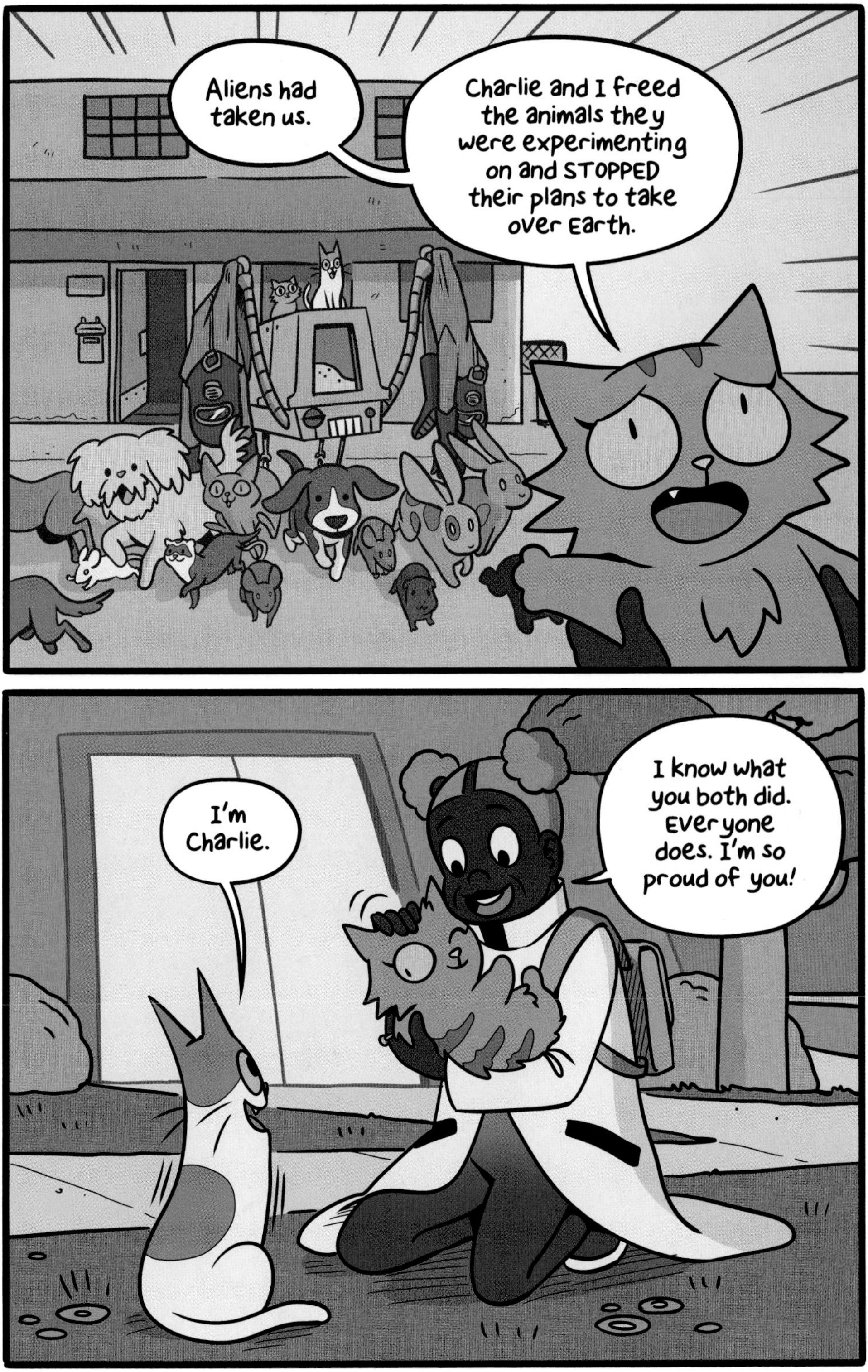
Aliens had taken us.
Charlie and I freed the animals they were experimenting on and STOPPED their plans to take over Earth.
I'm Charlie.
I know what you both did. Everyone does. I'm so proud of you!

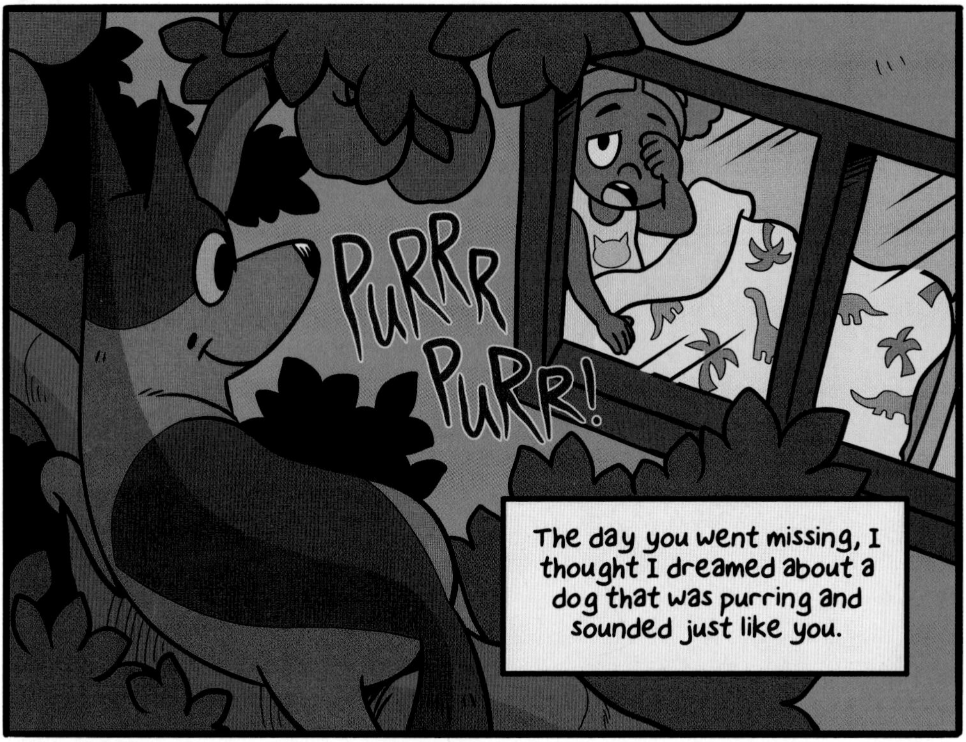
PURRR PURR!
The day you went missing, I thought I dreamed about a dog that was purring and sounded just like you.

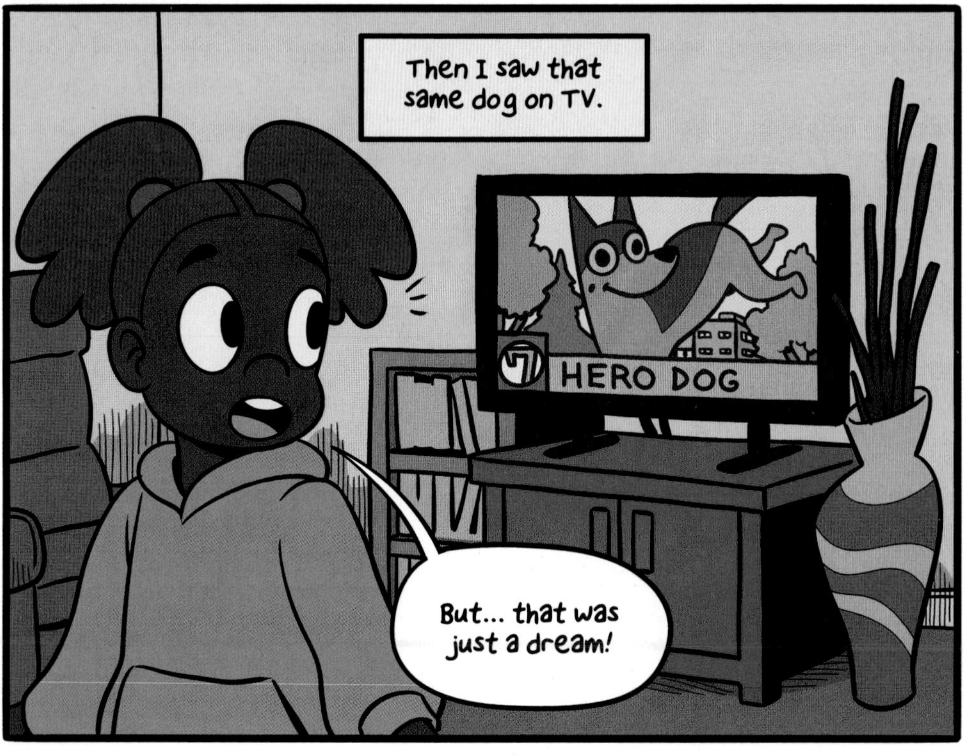
Then I saw that same dog on TV.
HERO DOG
But... that was just a dream!

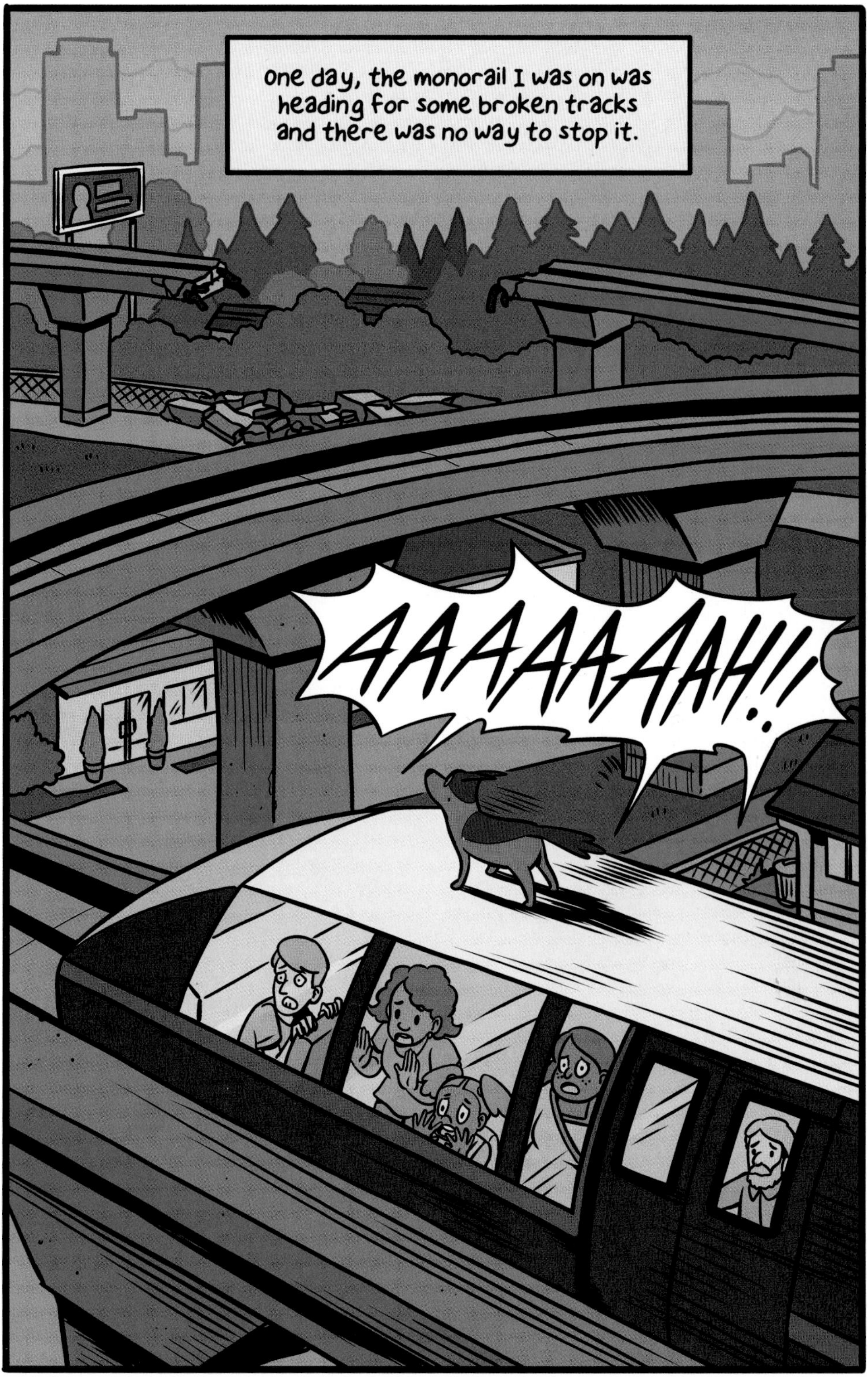
one day, the monorail I was on was heading for some broken tracks and there was no way to stop it.
AAAAAAAAH!!

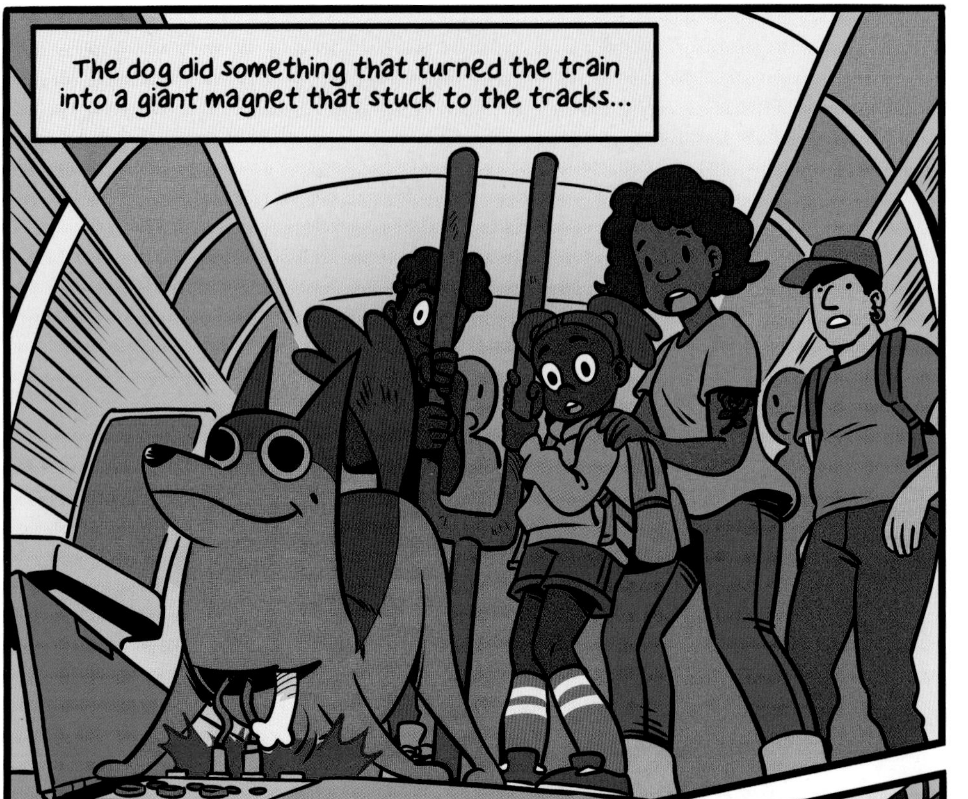
The dog did something that turned the train into a giant magnet that stuck to the tracks...

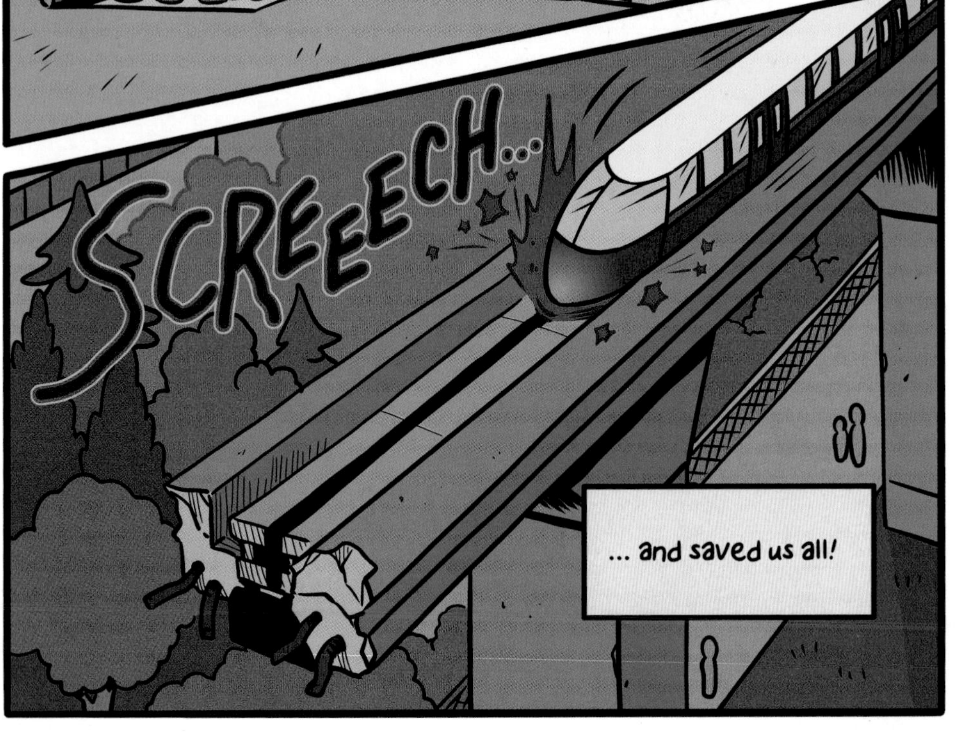
SCREEECH...
... and saved us all!

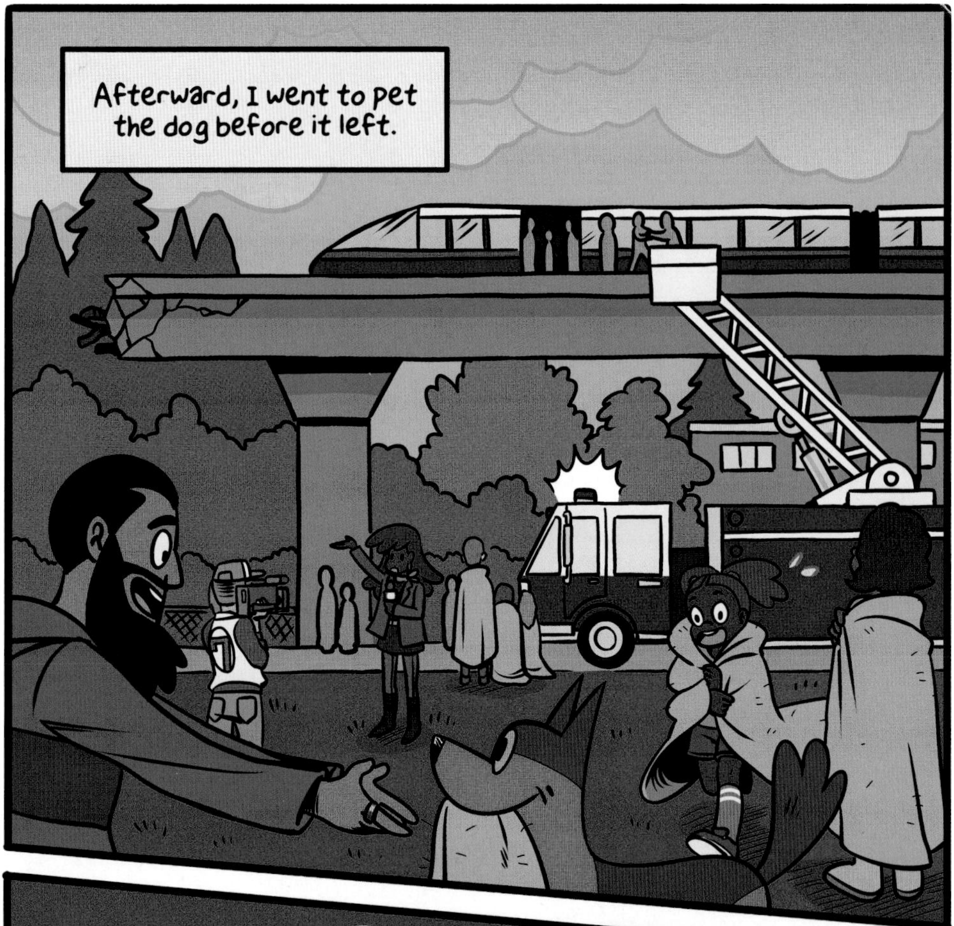
Afterward, I went to pet the dog before it left.

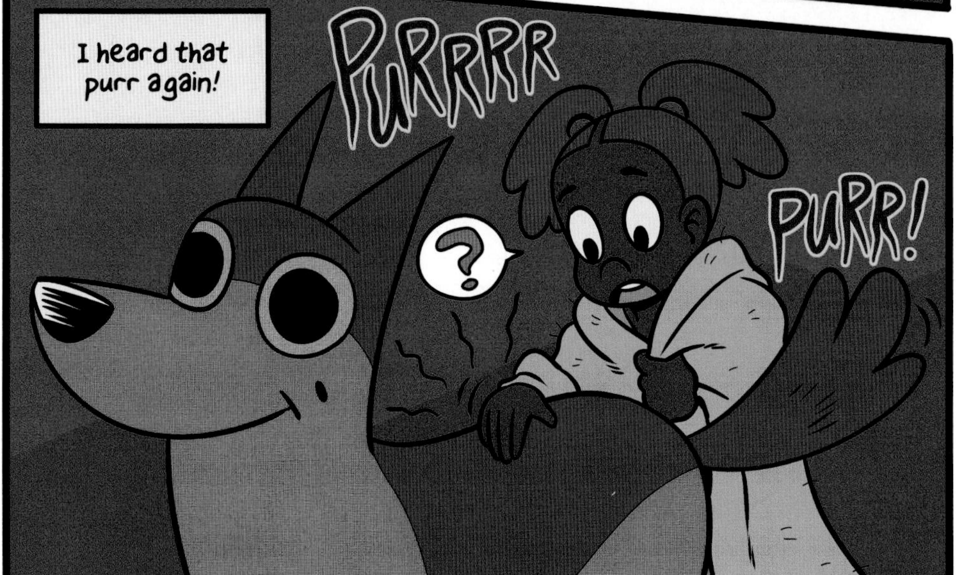
I heard that purr again!
PURRRR
?
PURR!

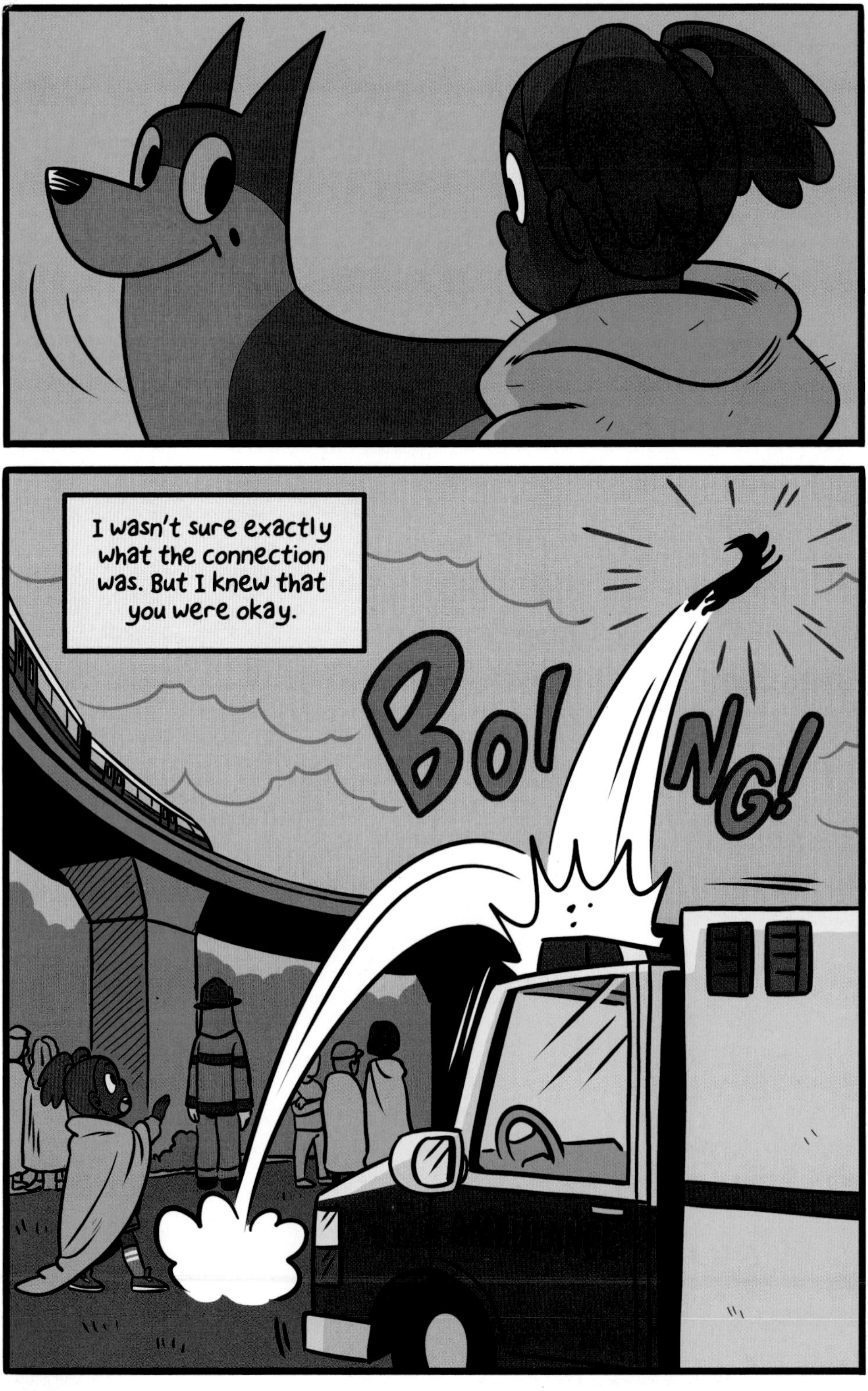
I wasn't sure exactly what the connection was. But I knew that you were okay.
BOING!

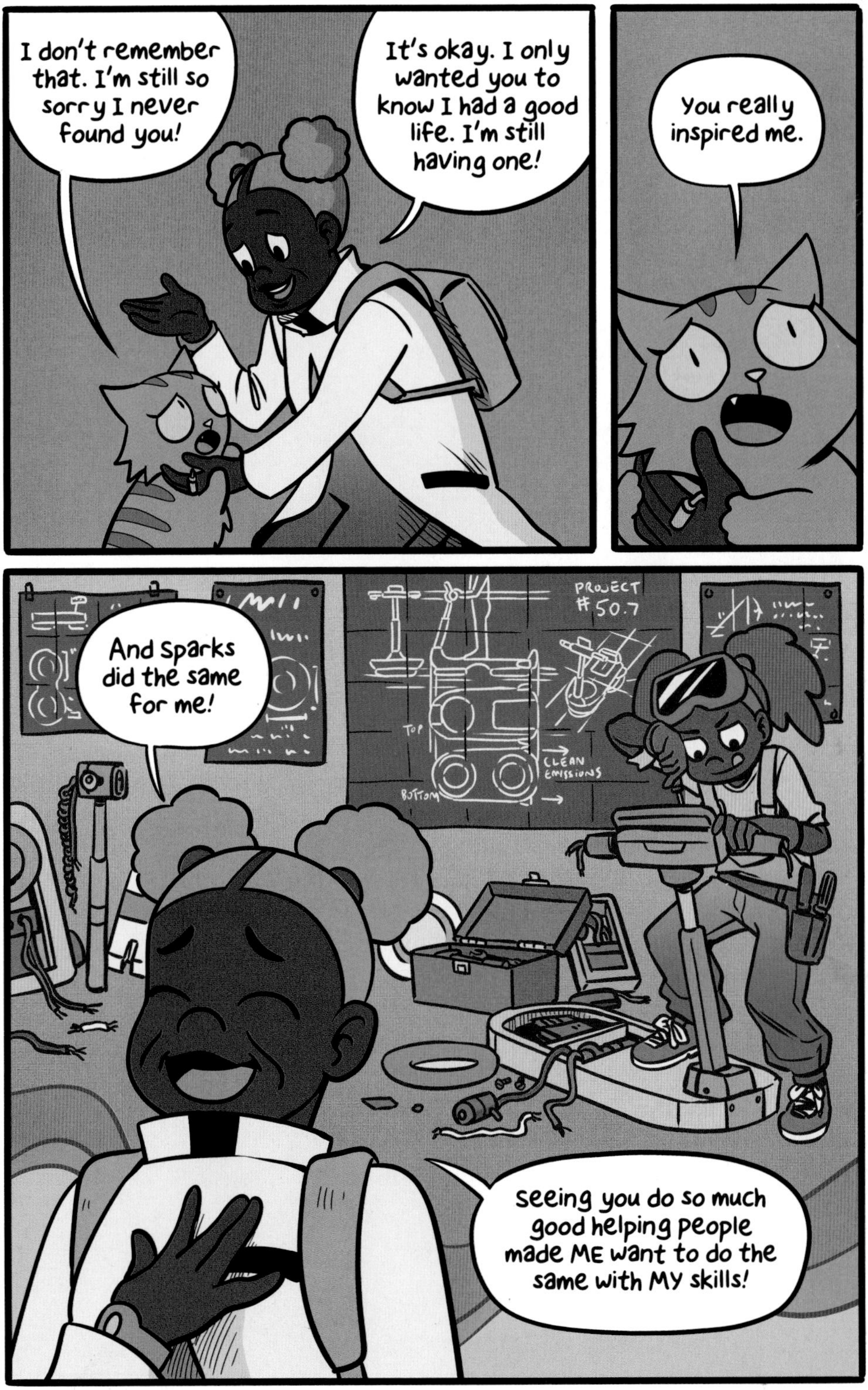
I don't remember that. I'm still so sorry I never found you!
It's okay. I only wanted you to know I had a good life. I'm still having one!
You really inspired me.
PROJECT #50.7
TOP
BOTTOM
CLEAN EMISSIONS
And Sparks did the same for me!
Seeing you do so much good helping people made ME want to do the same with MY skills!

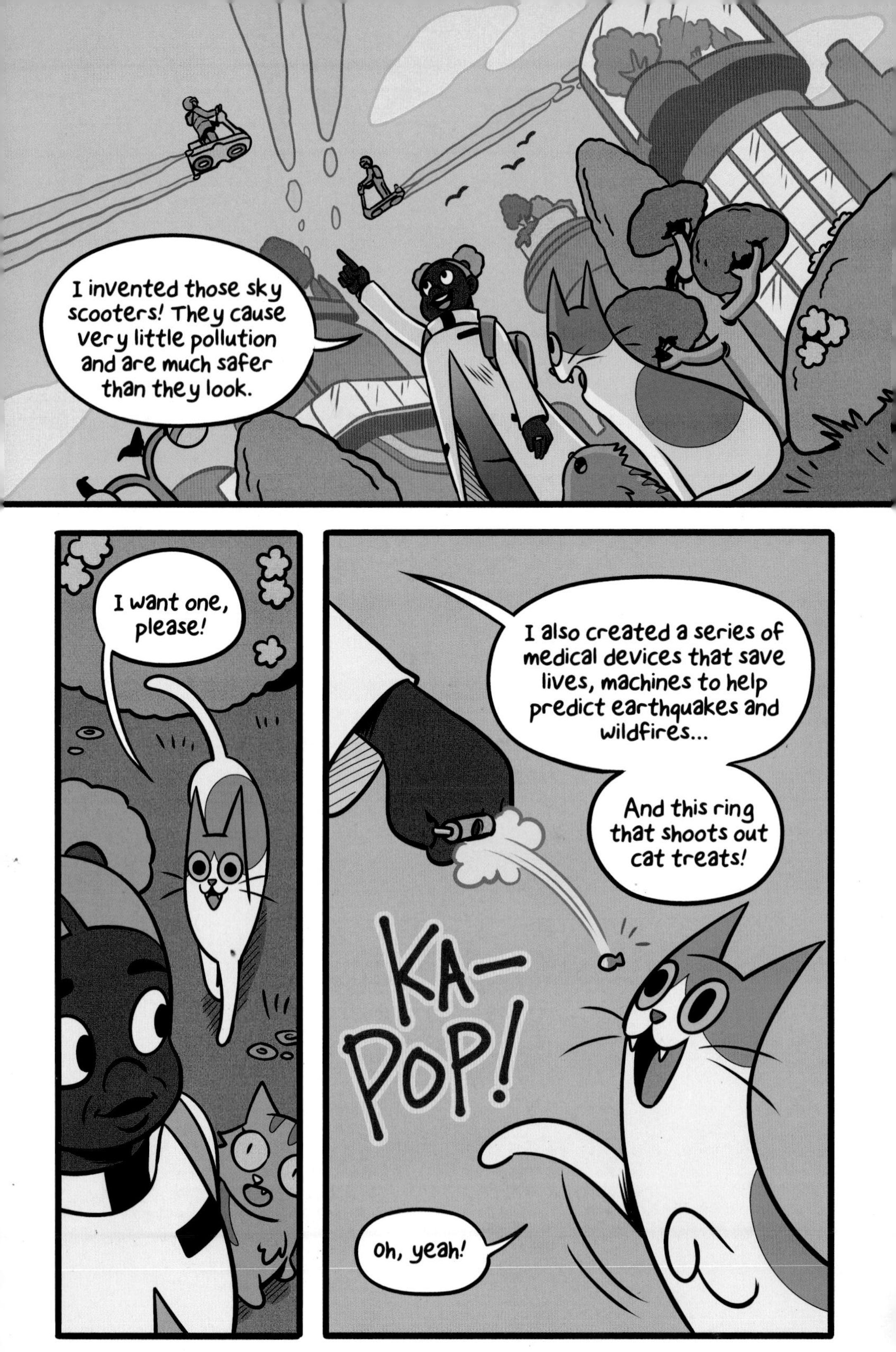
I invented those sky scooters! They cause very little pollution and are much safer than they look.
I want one, please!
I also created a series of medical devices that save lives, machines to help predict earthquakes and wildfires...
And this ring that shoots out cat treats!
KA-POP!
Oh, yeah!

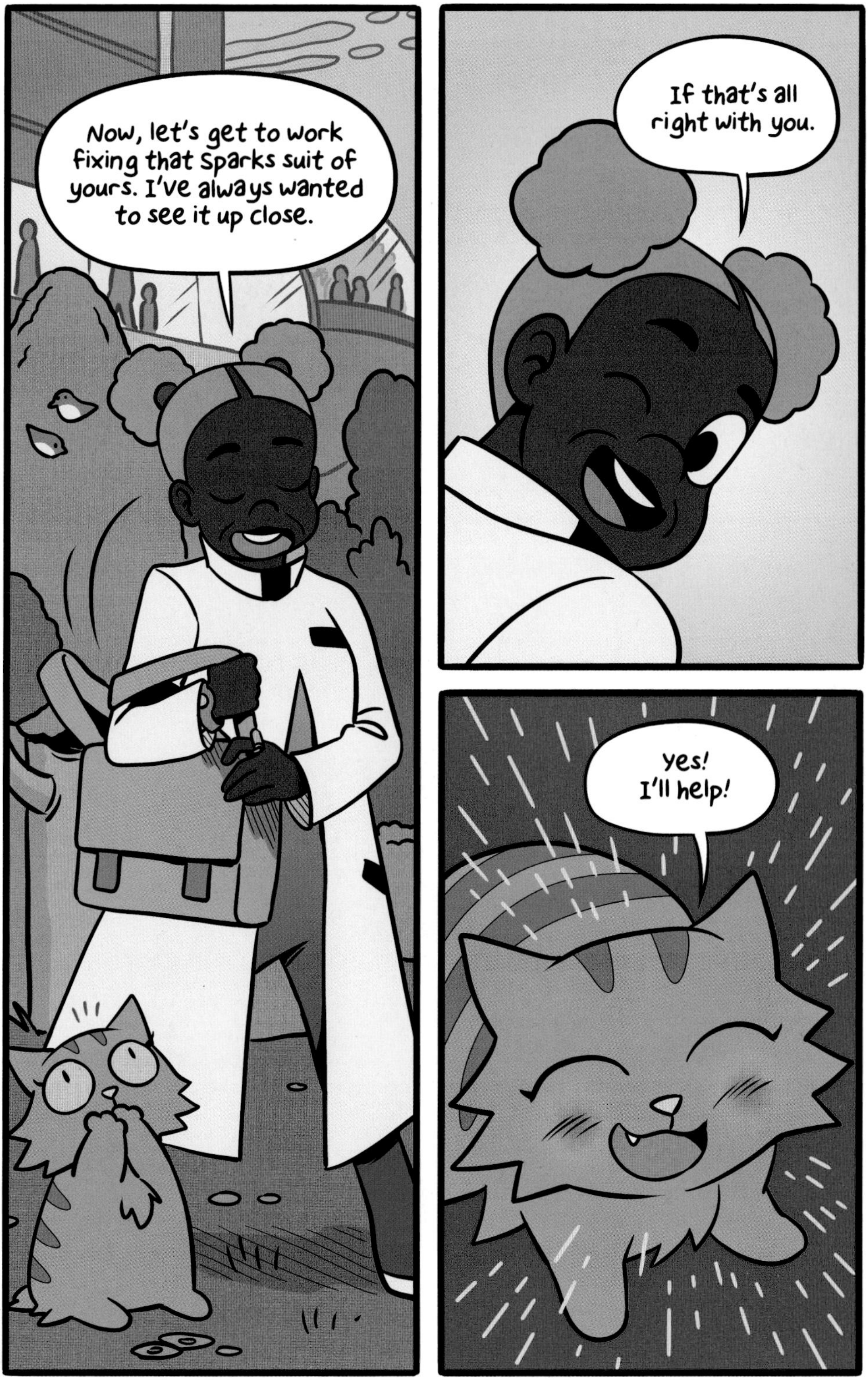
Now, let's get to work fixing that Sparks suit of yours. I've always wanted to see it up close.
If that's all right with you.
yes! I'll help!

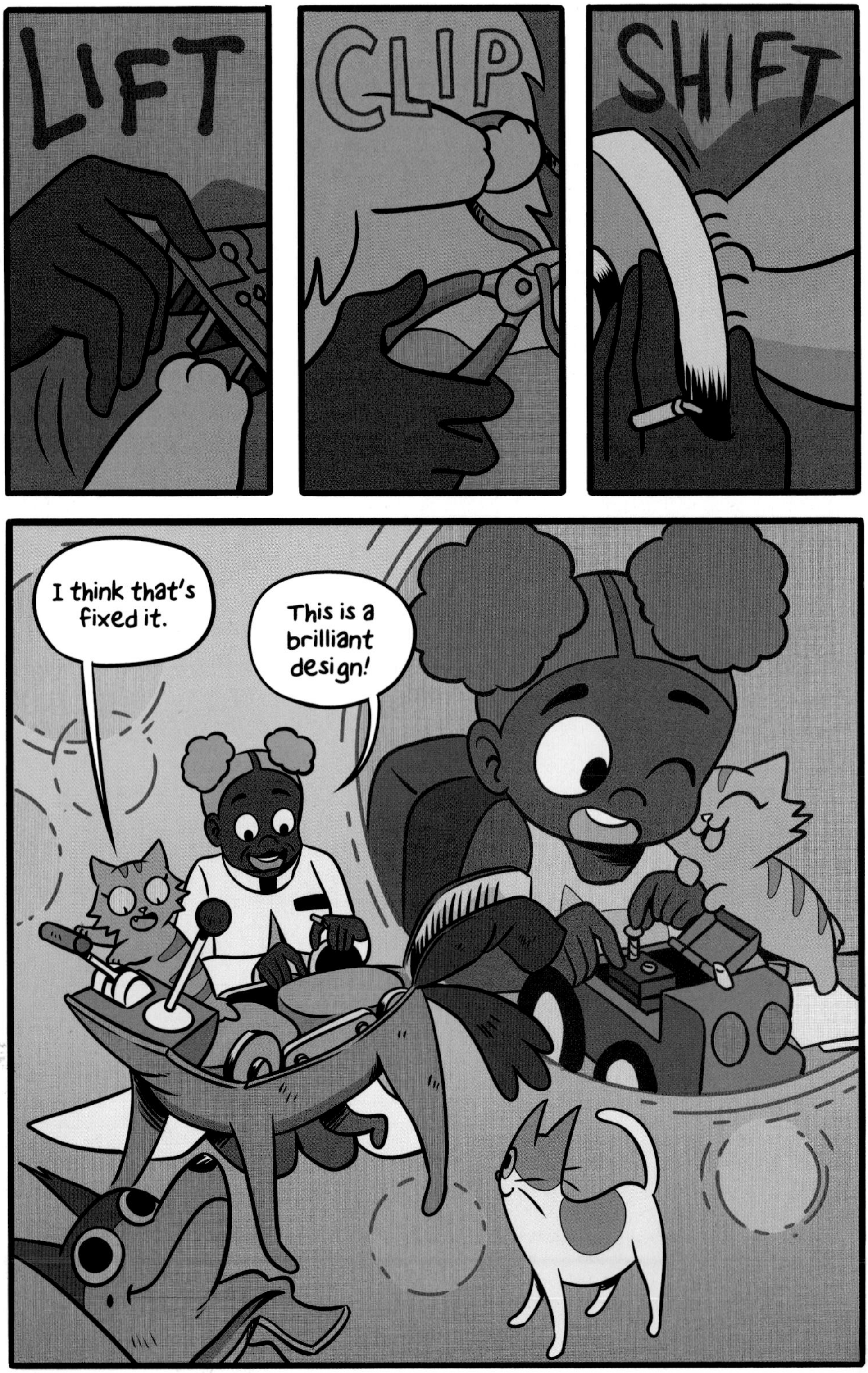
LIFT
CLIP
SHIFT
I think that's fixed it.
This is a brilliant design!

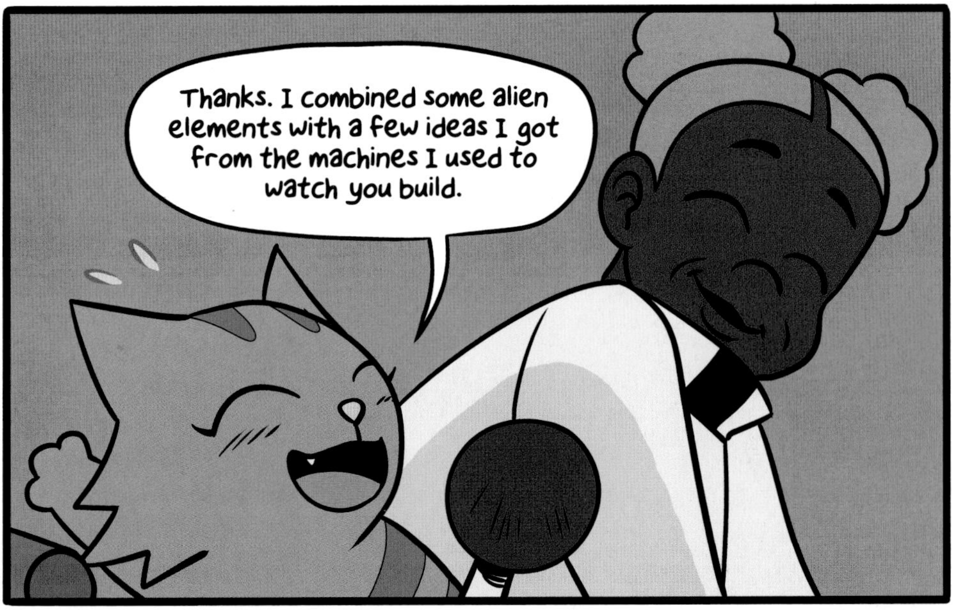
Thanks. I combined some alien elements with a few ideas I got from the machines I used to watch you build.

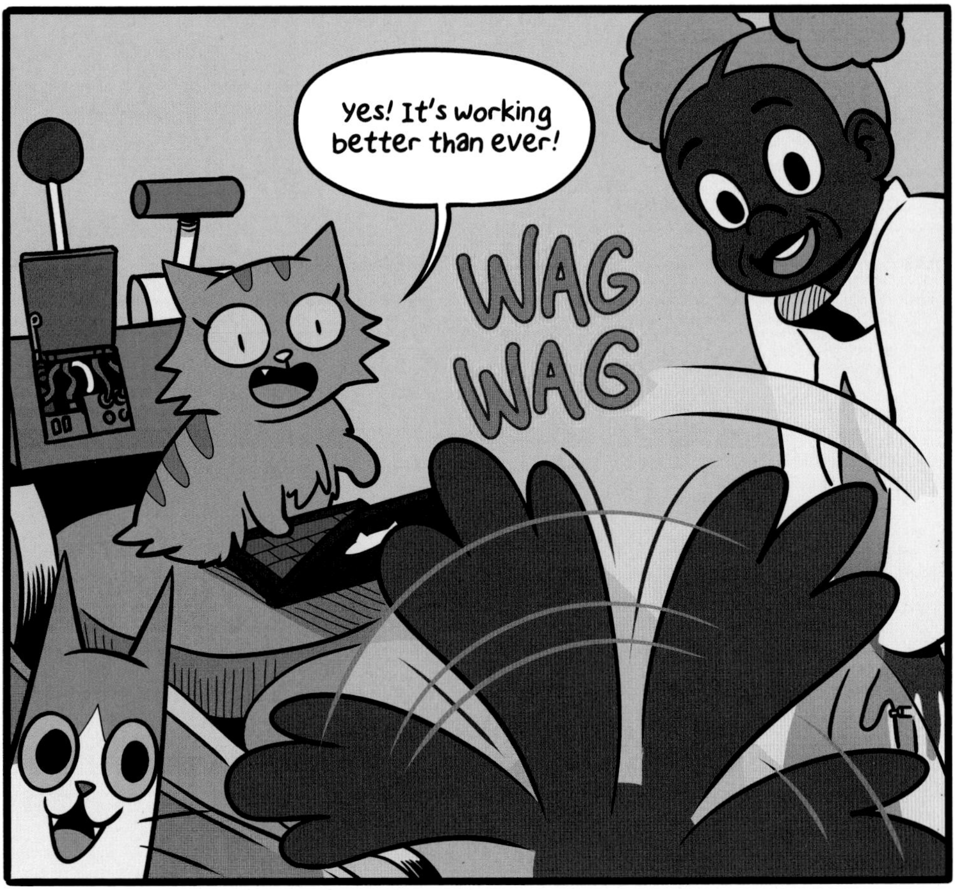
yes! It's working better than ever!
WAG
WAG

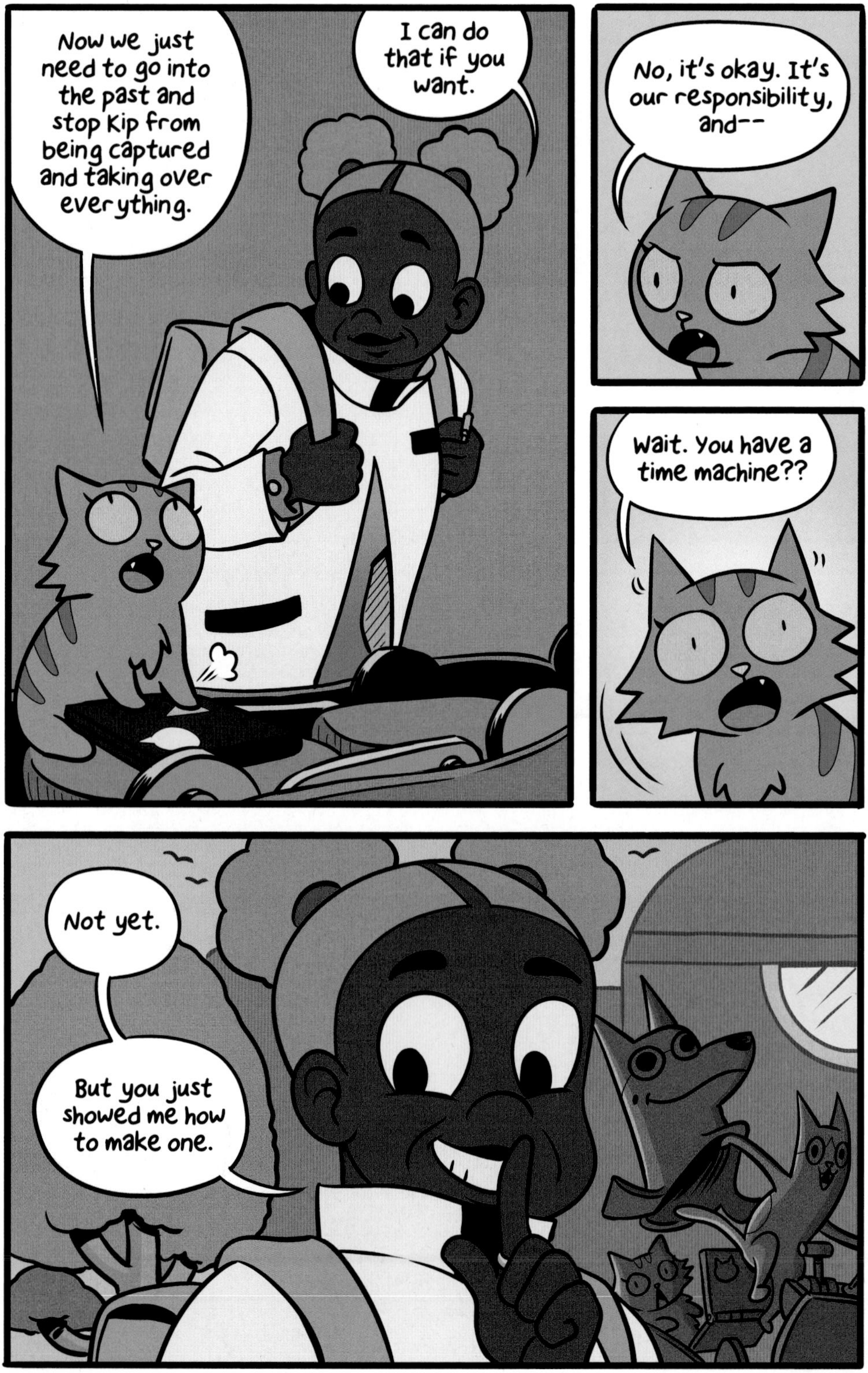
Now we just need to go into the past and stop Kip from being captured and taking over everything.
I can do that if you want.
No, it's okay. It's our responsibility, and--
Wait. You have a time machine??
Not yet.
But you just showed me how to make one.

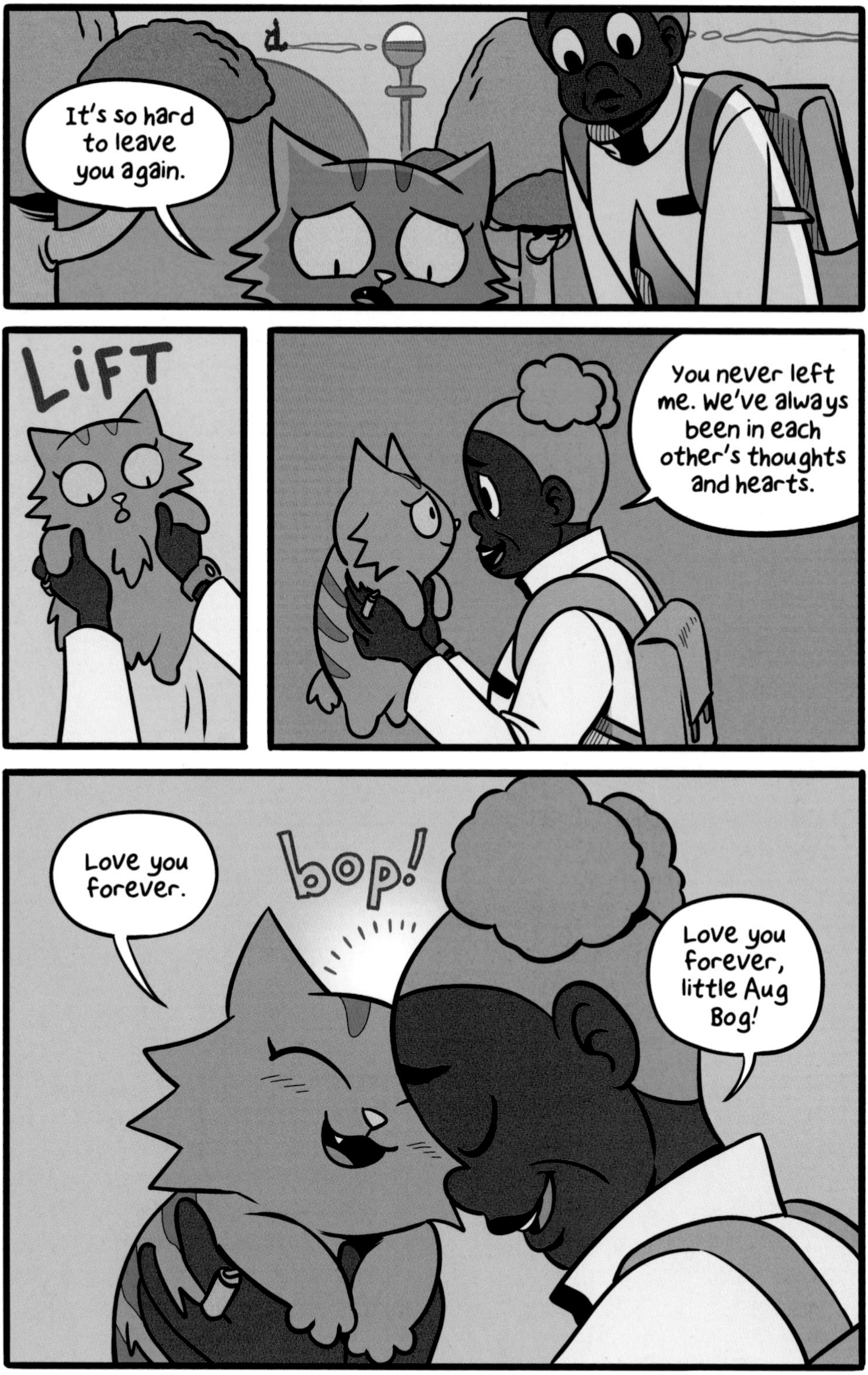

It's so hard to leave you again.
LIFT
You never left me. We've always been in each other's thoughts and hearts.
Love you forever.
bop!
Love you forever, little Aug Bog!

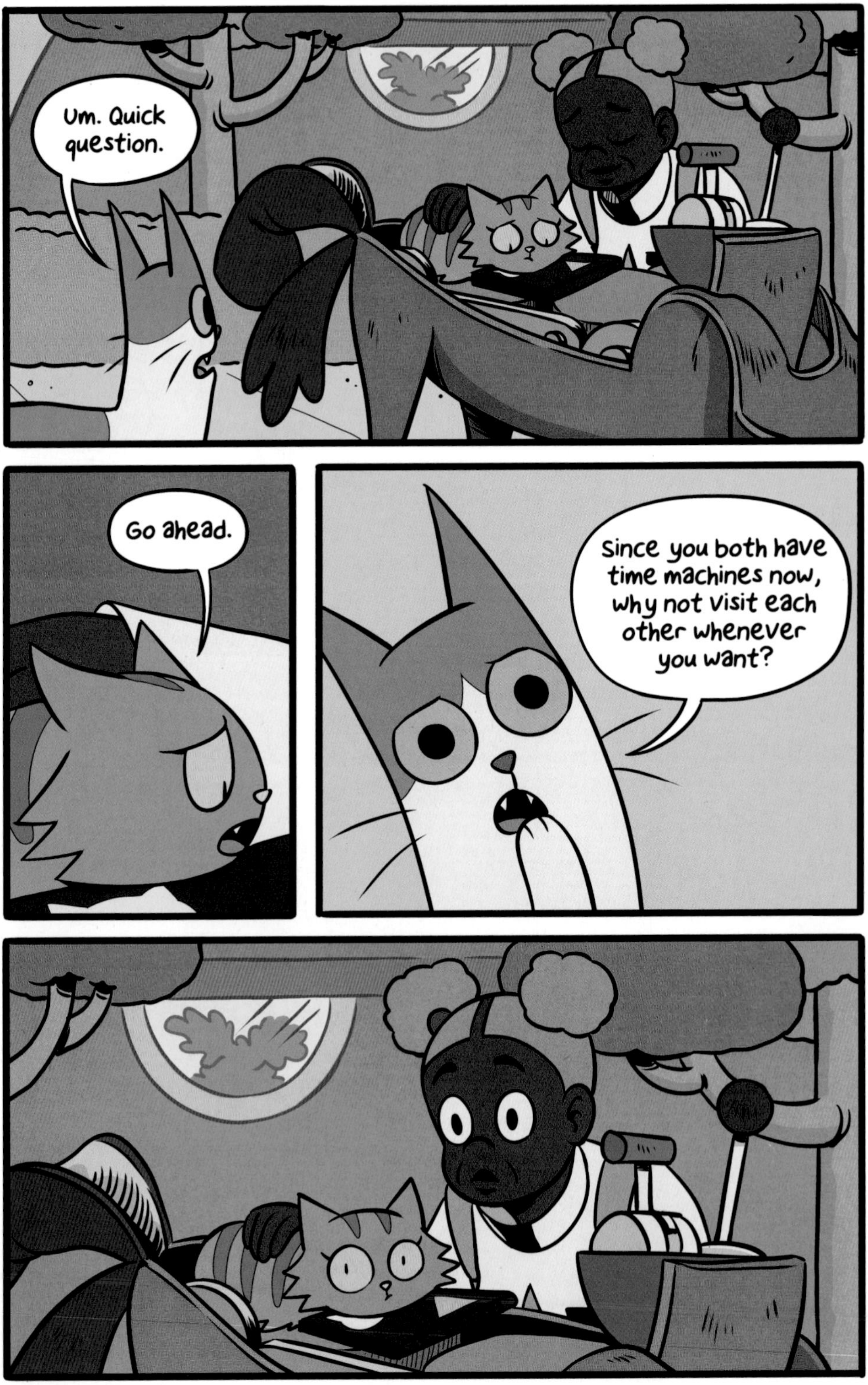
Um. Quick question.
Go ahead.
Since you both have time machines now, why not visit each other whenever you want?

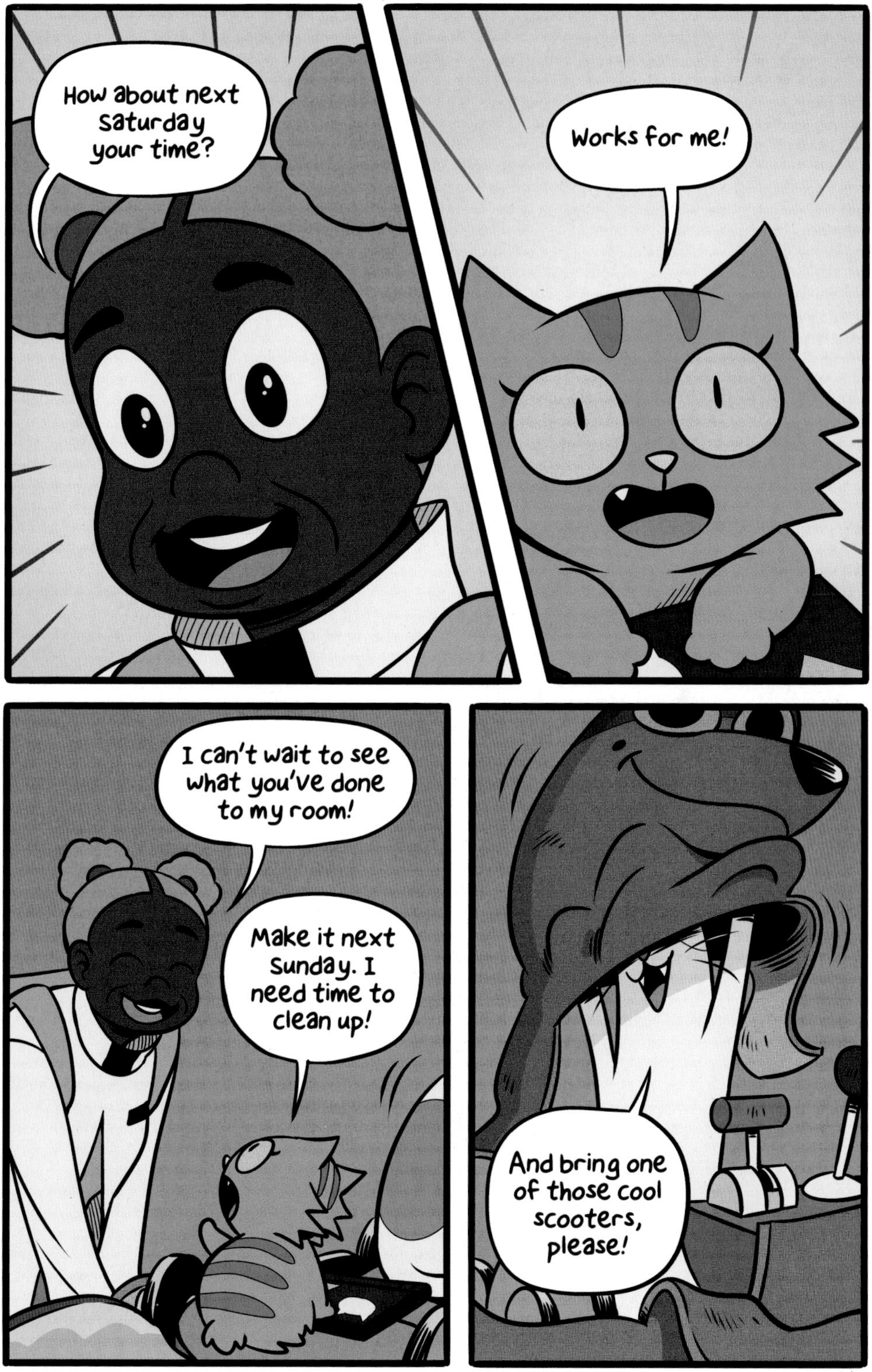
How about next saturday your time?
Works for me!
I can't wait to see what you've done to my room!
Make it next Sunday. I need time to clean up!
And bring one of those cool scooters, please!

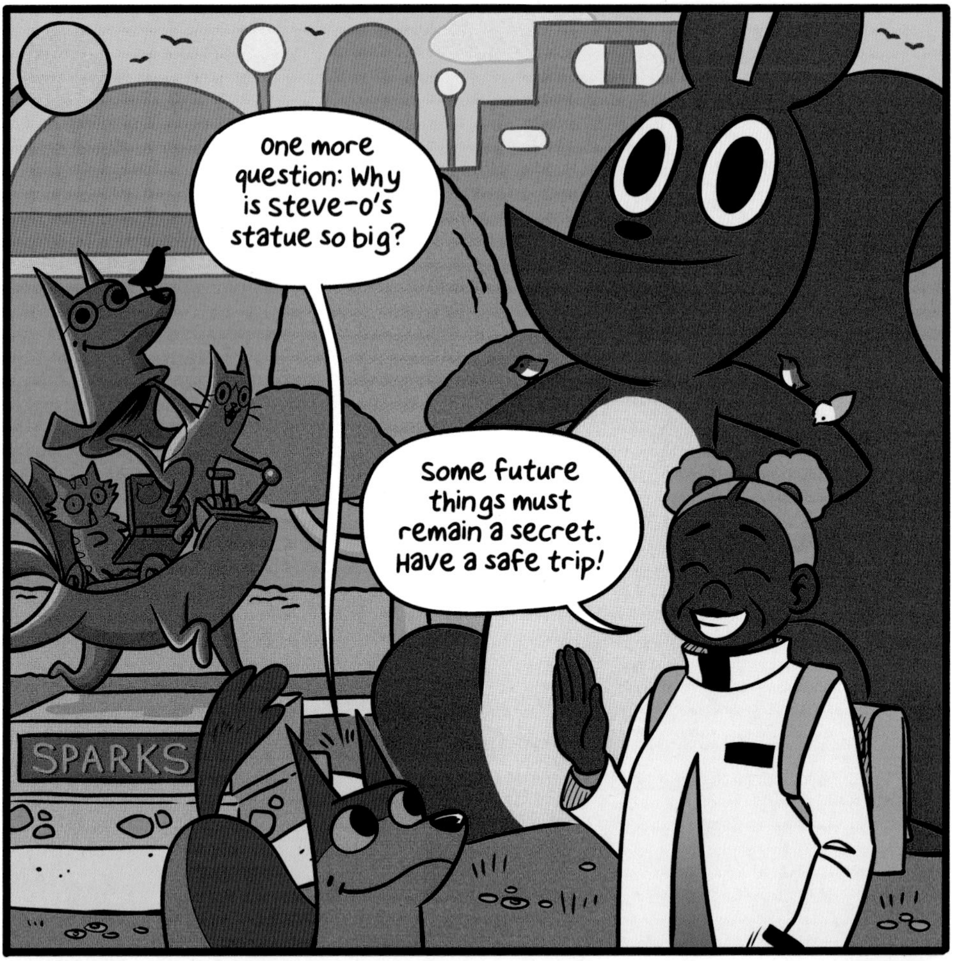
One more question: Why is Steve-O's statue so big?
Some future things must remain a secret. Have a safe trip!
SPARKS

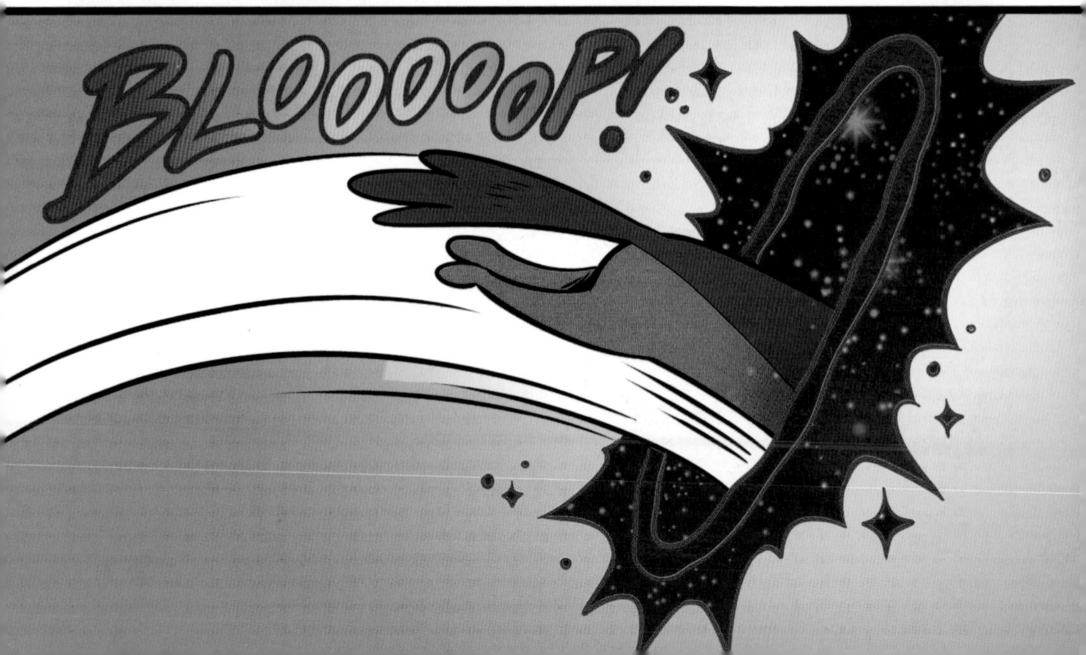
BLOOOOOP!

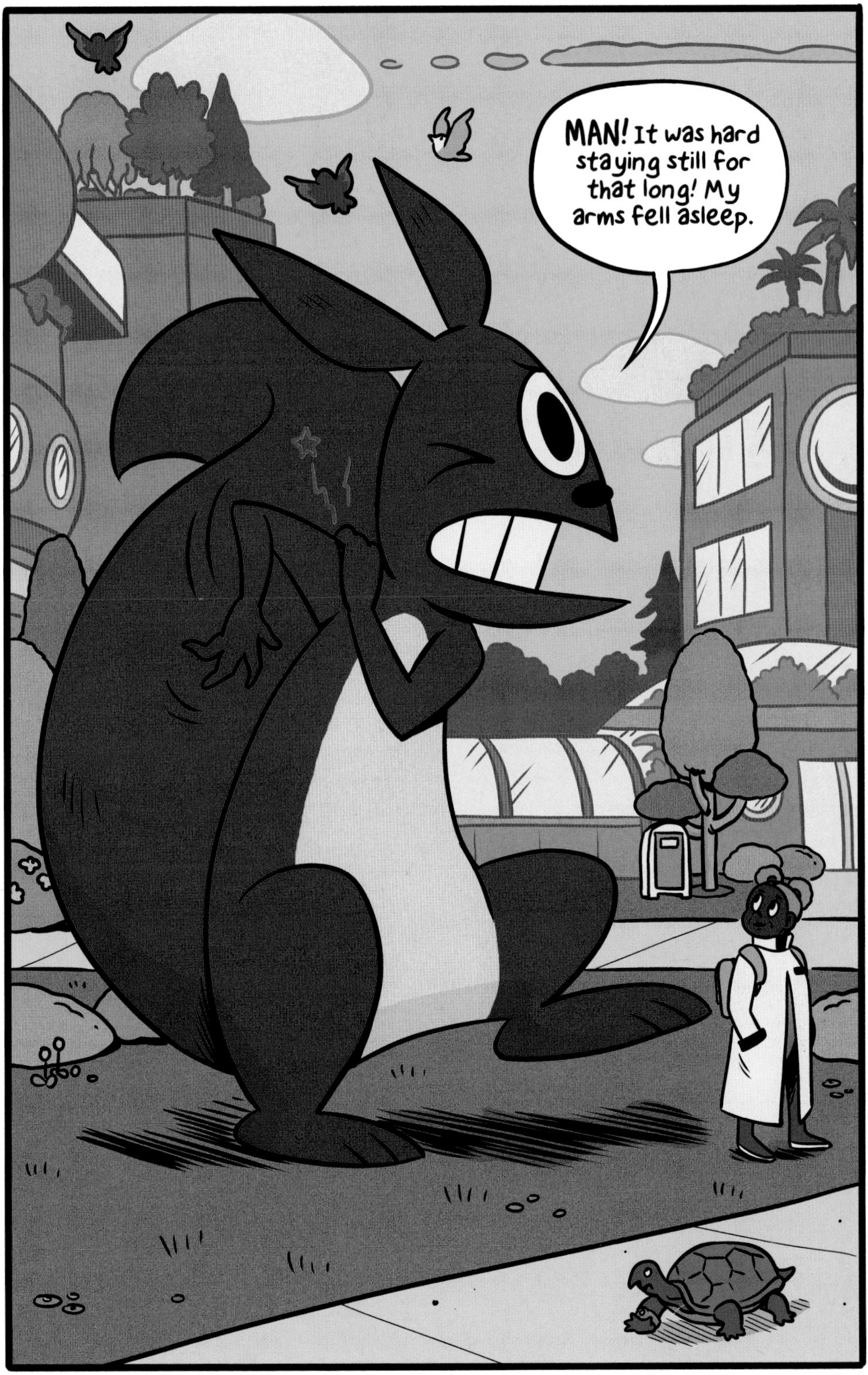
MAN! It was hard staying still for that long! My arms fell asleep.

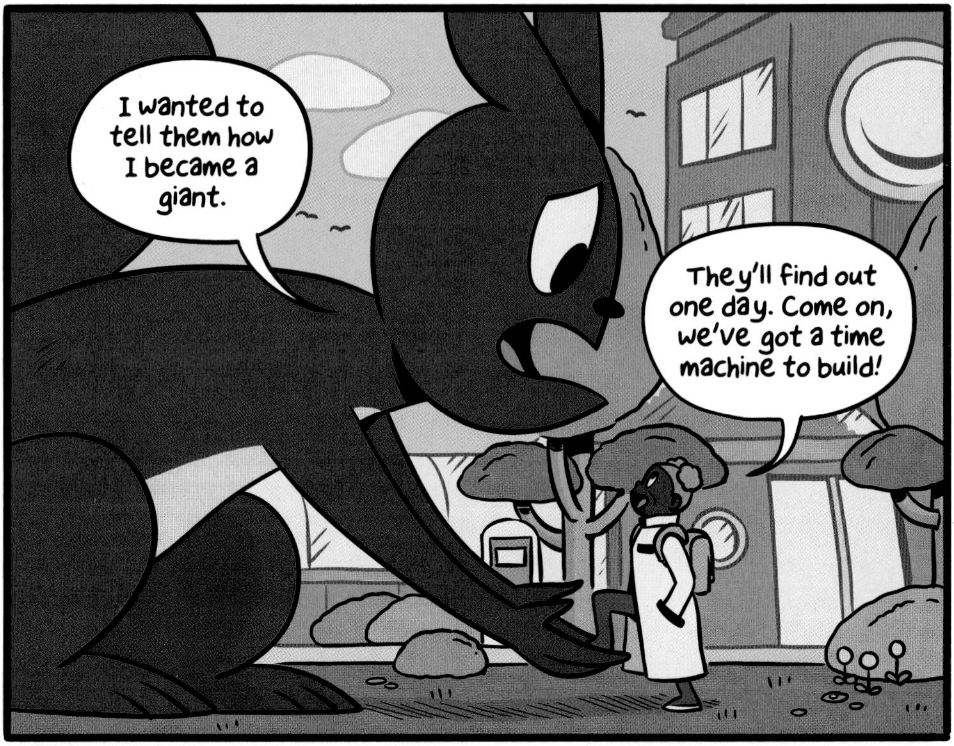
I wanted to tell them how I became a giant.
They'll find out one day. Come on, we've got a time machine to build!

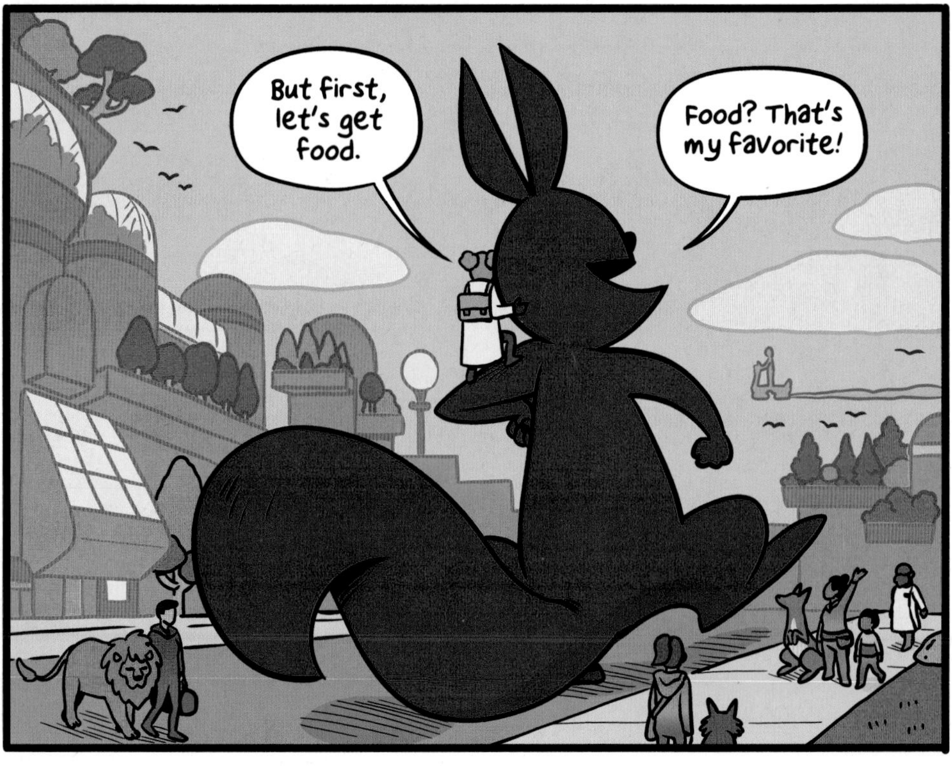
But first, let's get food.
Food? That's my favorite!

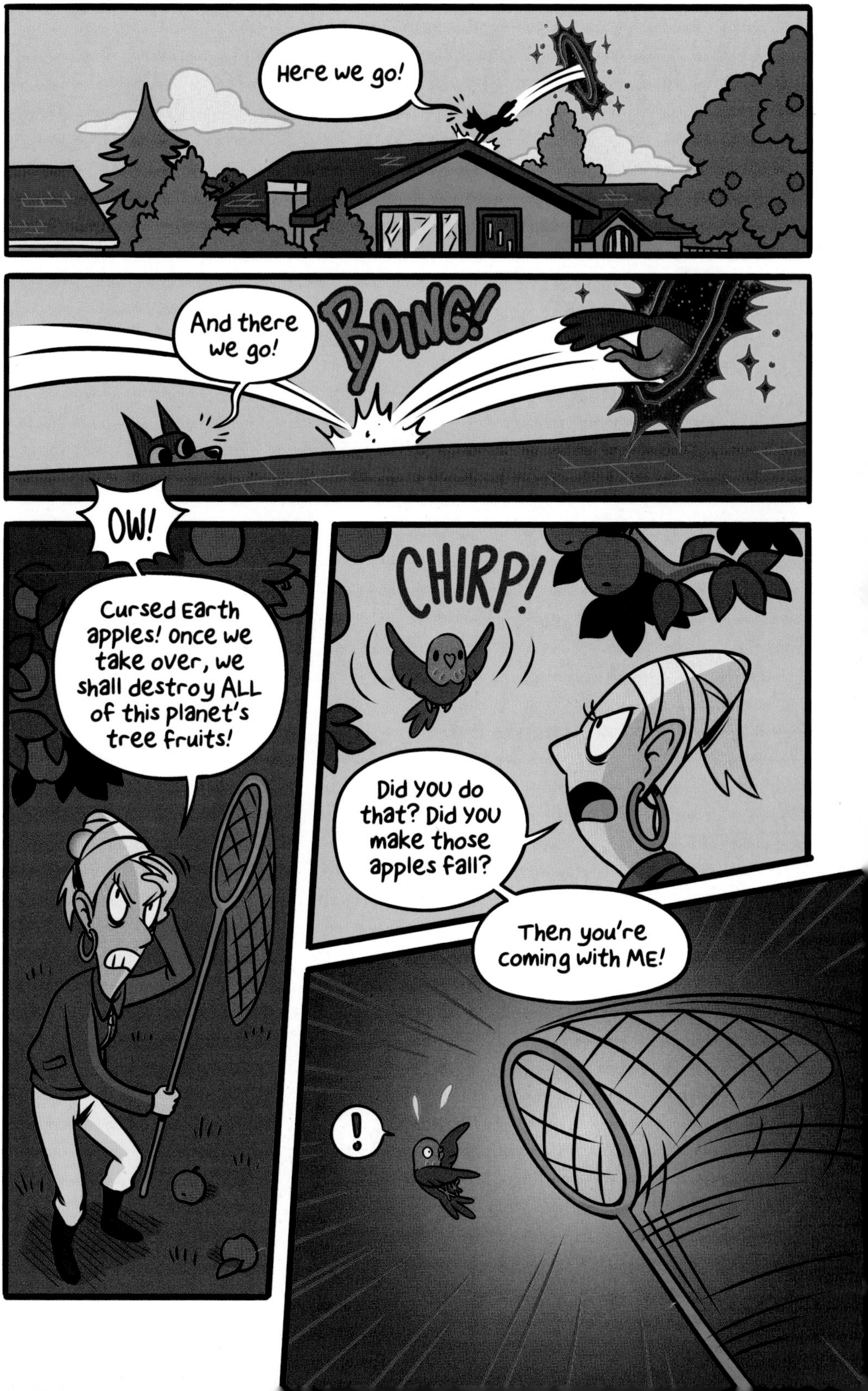
Here we go!
And there we go!
BOING!
OW!
Cursed Earth apples! Once we take over, we shall destroy ALL of this planet's tree fruits!
CHIRP!
Did YOU do that? Did YOU make those apples fall?
Then you're coming with ME!
!

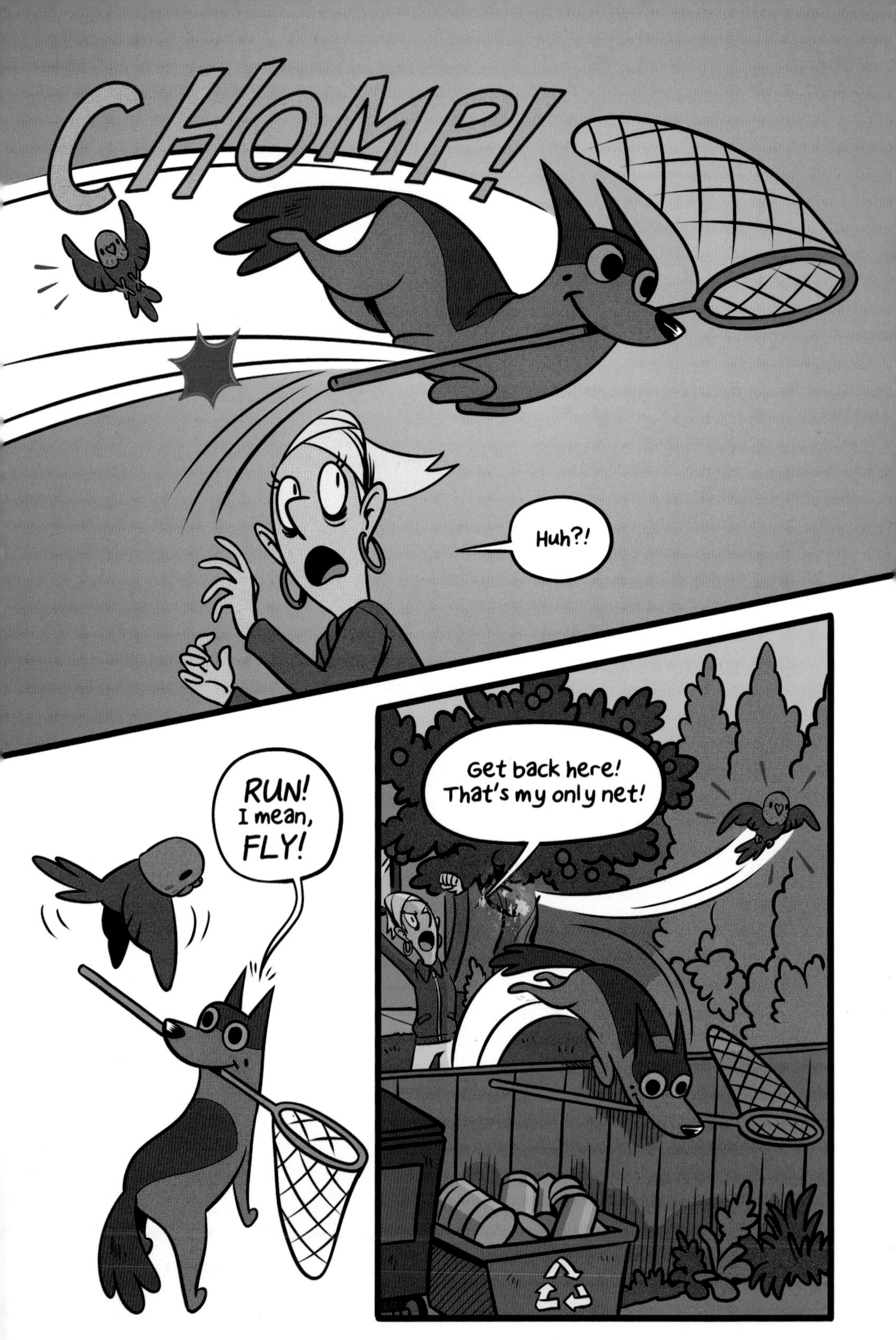
CHOMP!
Huh?!
RUN! I mean, FLY!
Get back here! That's my only net!

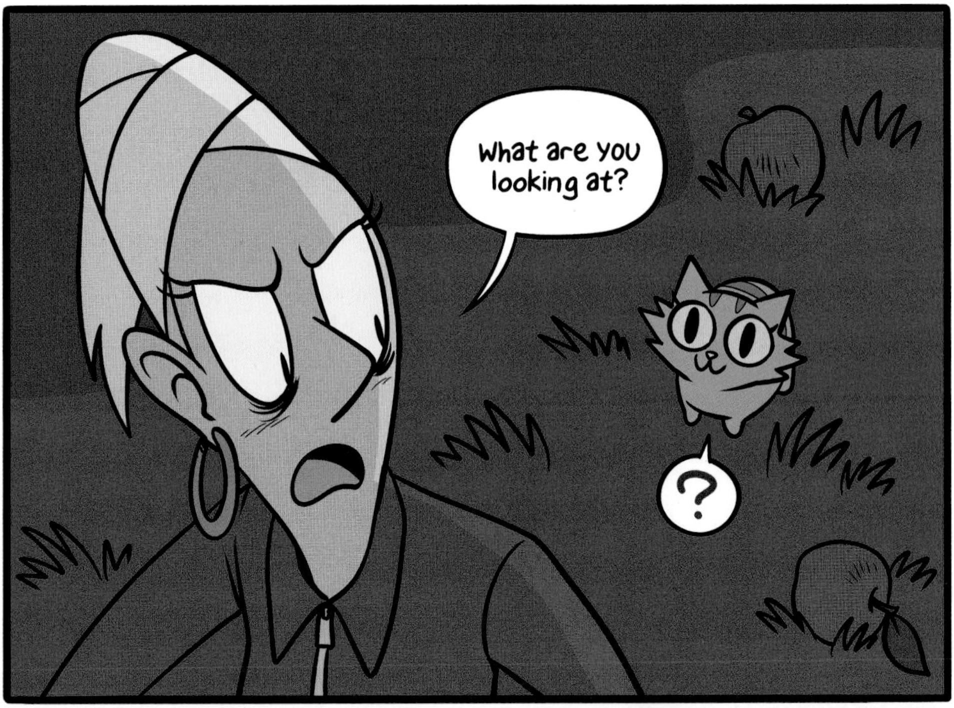
What are you looking at?
?

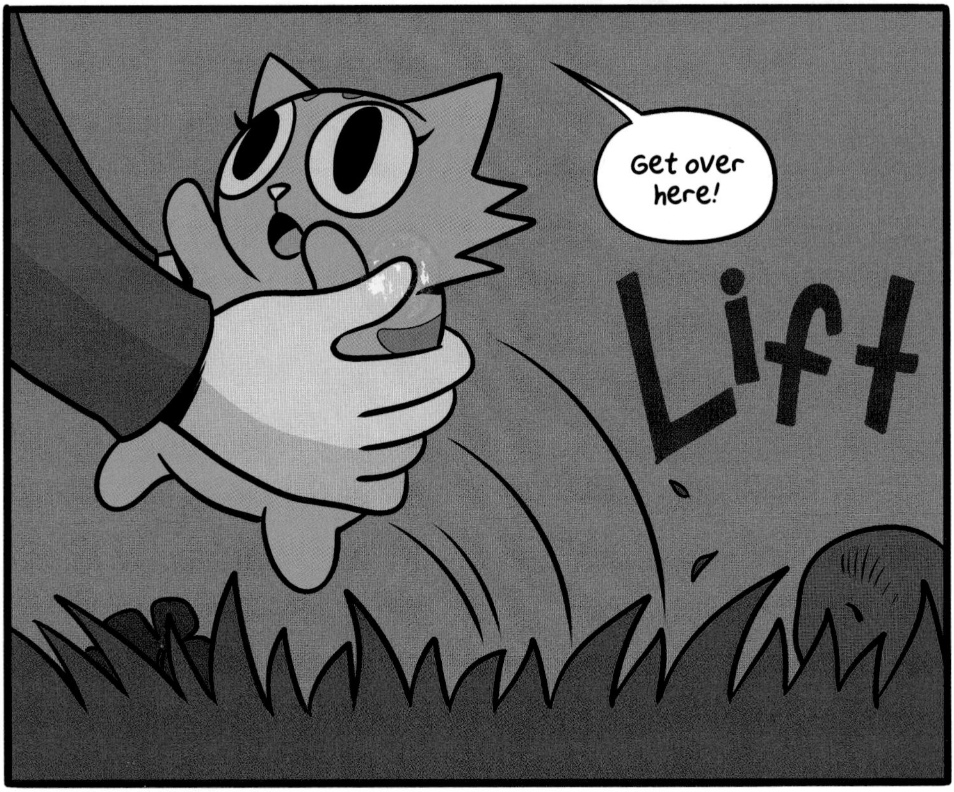
Get over here!
Lift

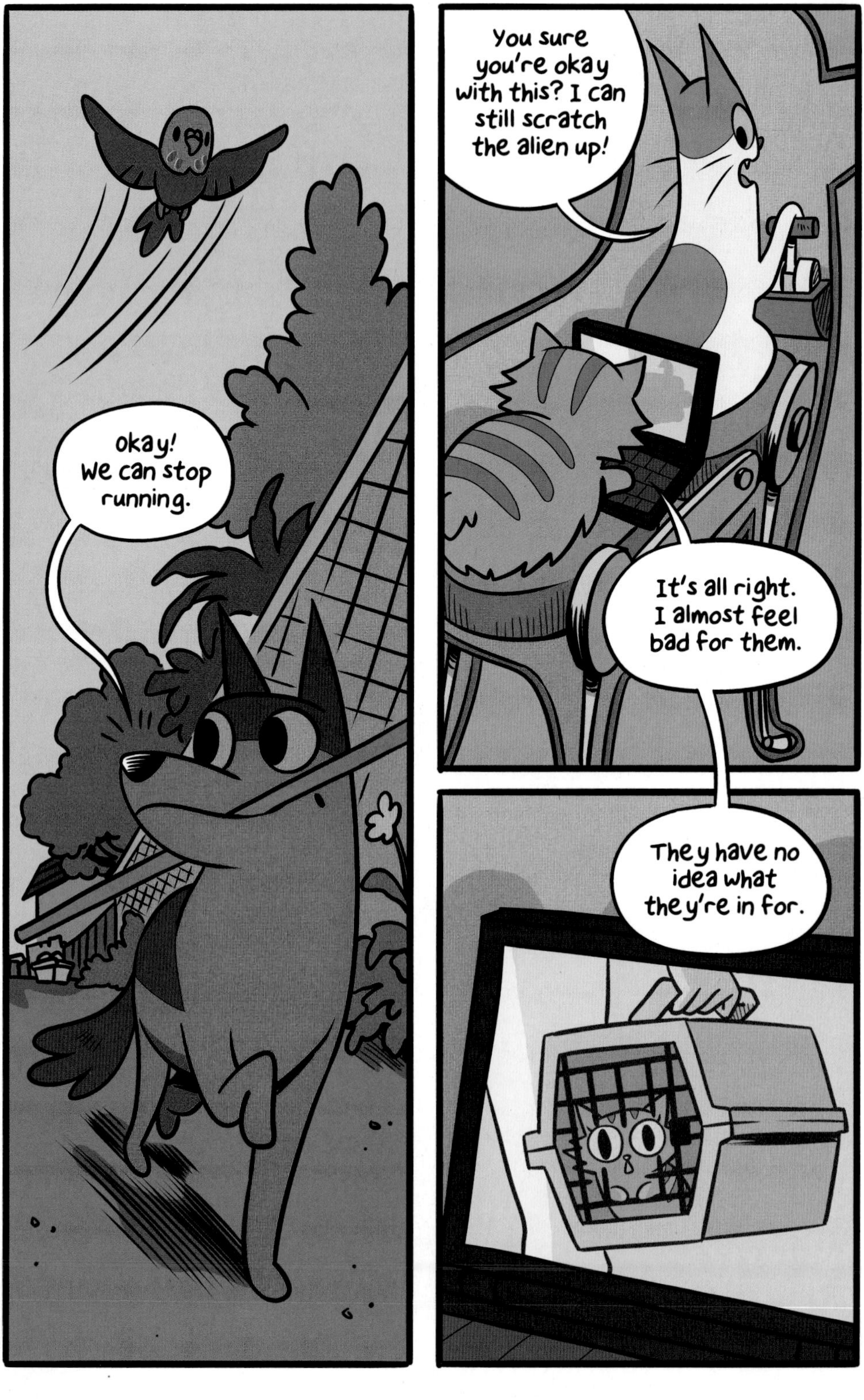
Okay!
We can stop running.
You sure you're okay with this? I can still scratch the alien up!
It's all right. I almost feel bad for them.
They have no idea what they're in for.

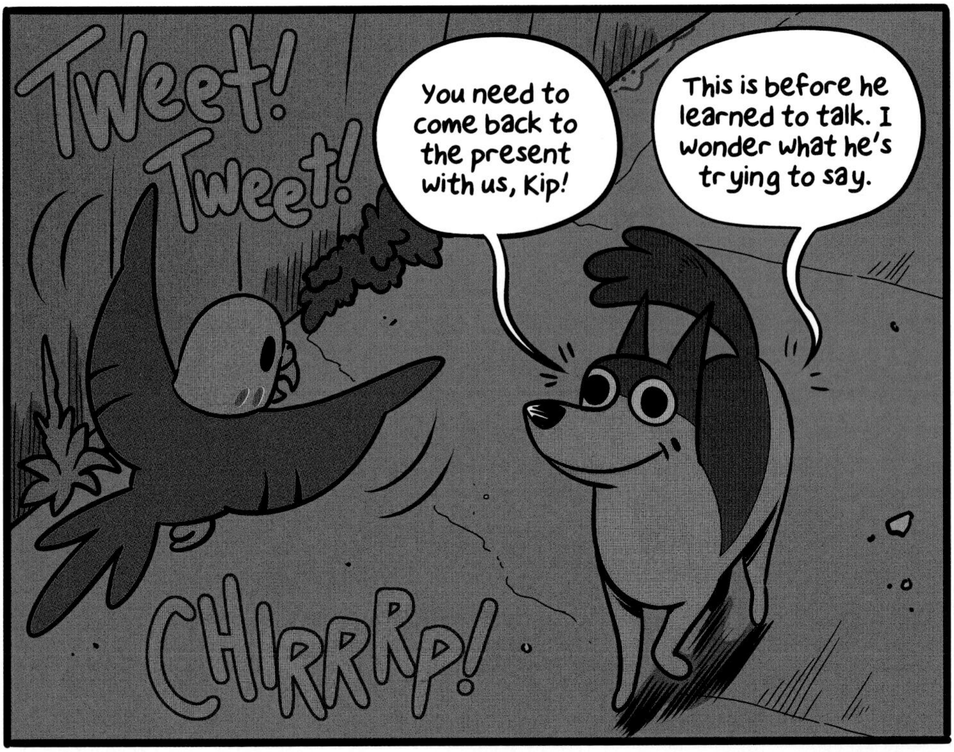
Tweet! Tweet!
You need to come back to the present with us, Kip!
This is before he learned to talk. I wonder what he's trying to say.
CHIRRRP!

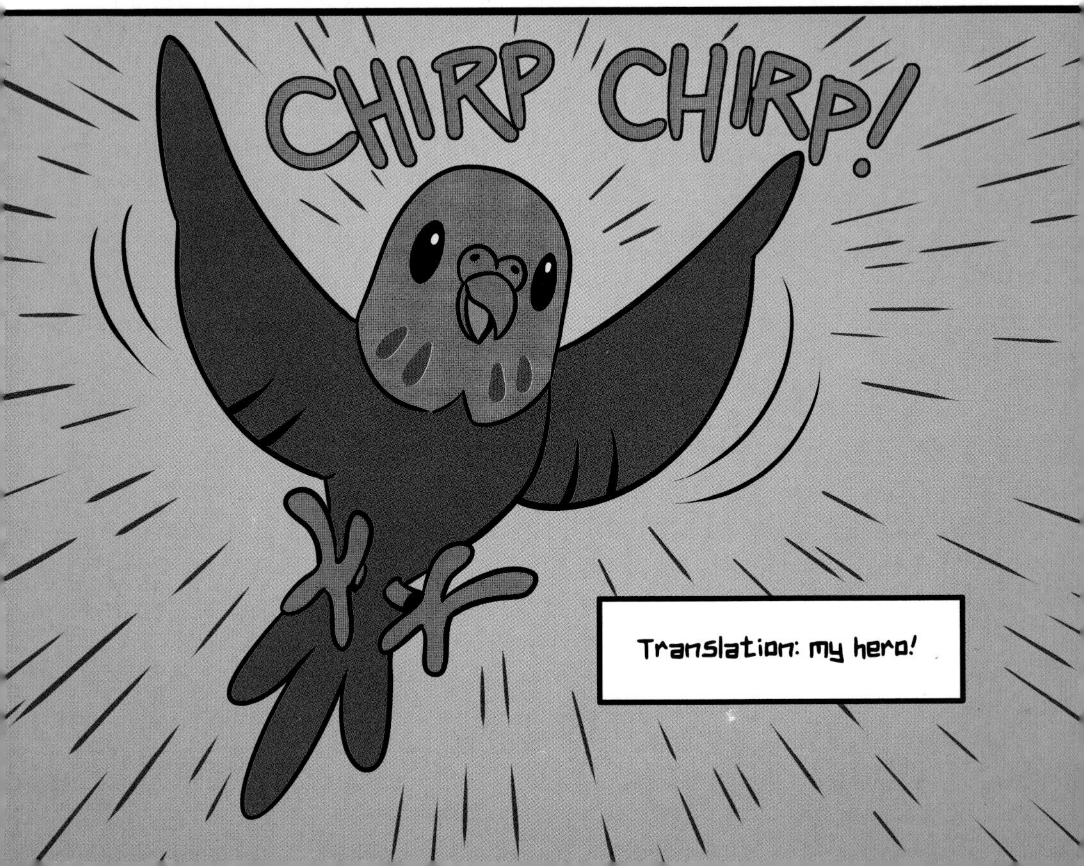
CHIRP CHIRP!
Translation: my hero!

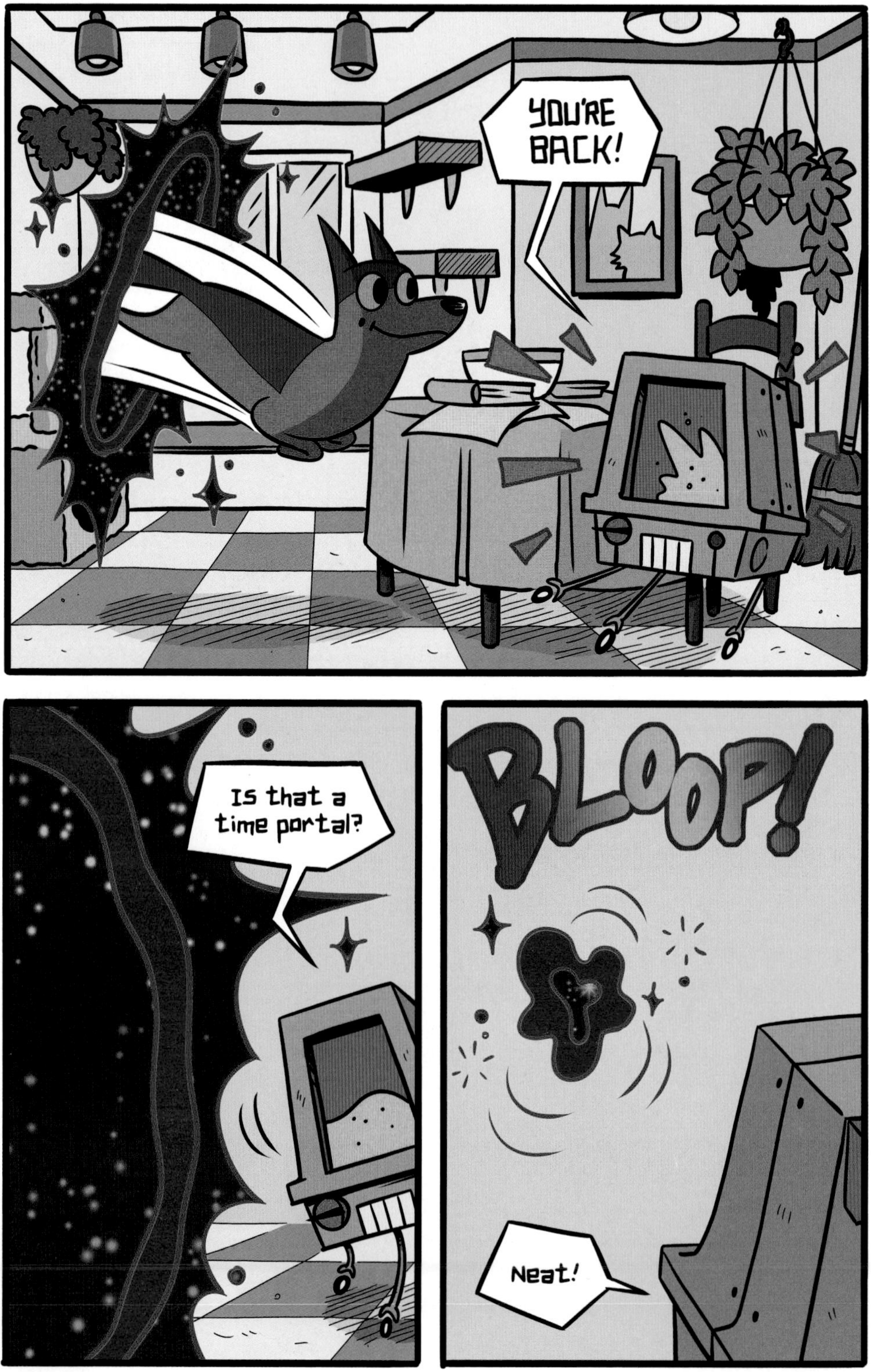
YOU'RE BACK!
Is that a time portal?
BLOOP!
Neat!

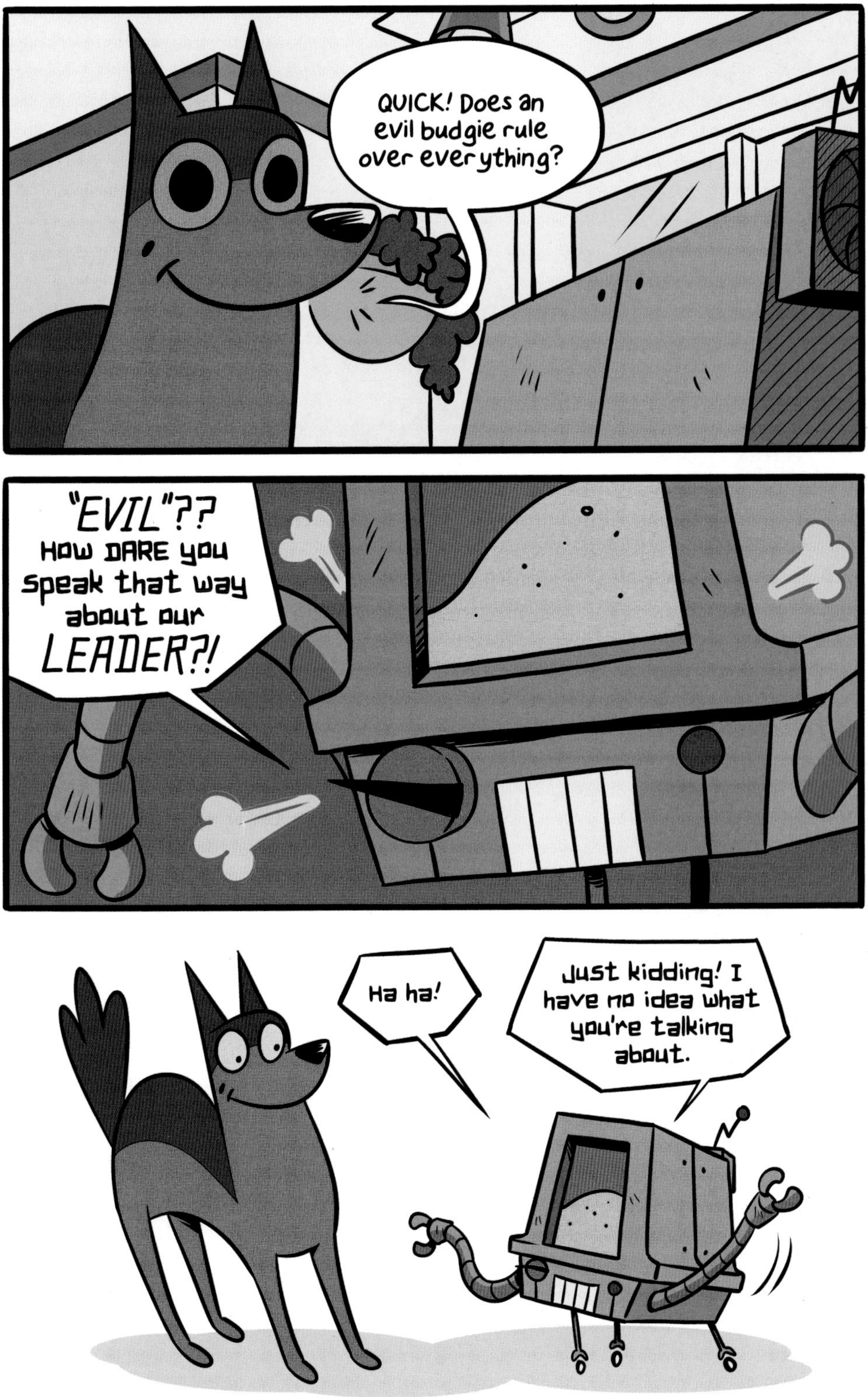
QUICK! Does an evil budgie rule over everything?
"EVIL"?? HOW DARE you speak that way about our LEADER?!
Ha ha!
Just kidding! I have no idea what you're talking about.

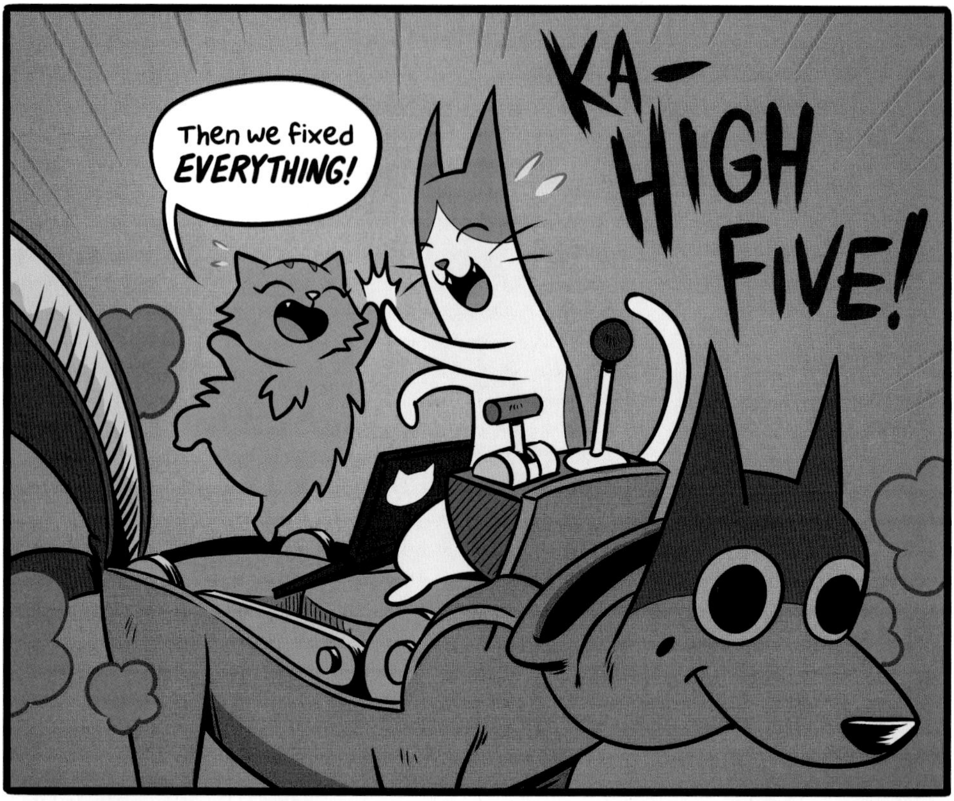
Then we fixed EVERYTHING!
KA-HIGH FIVE!

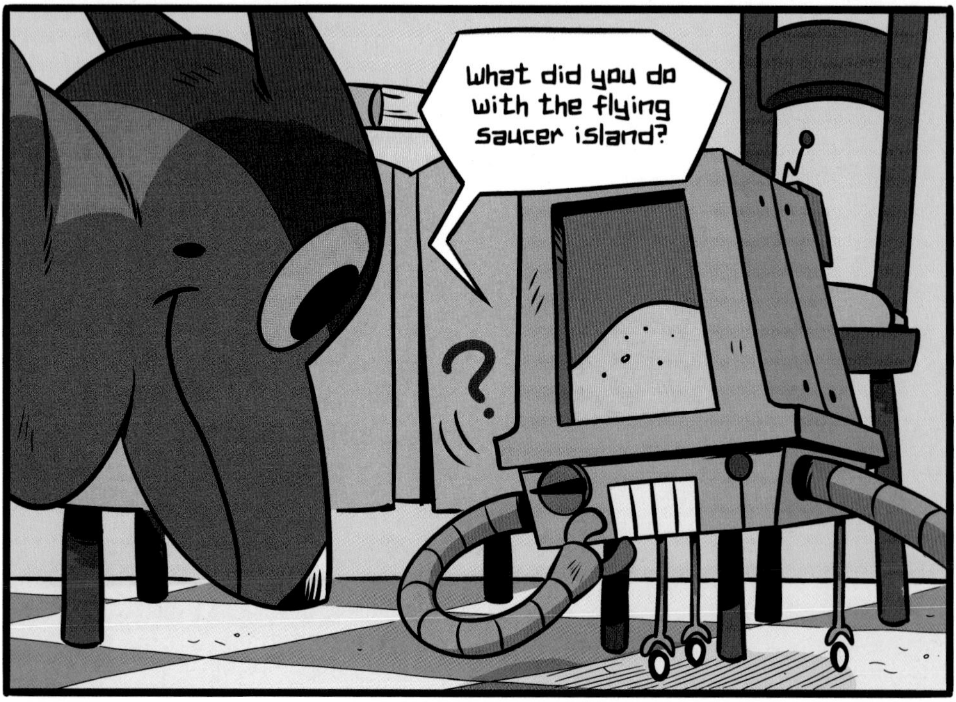
What did you do with the flying saucer island?
?

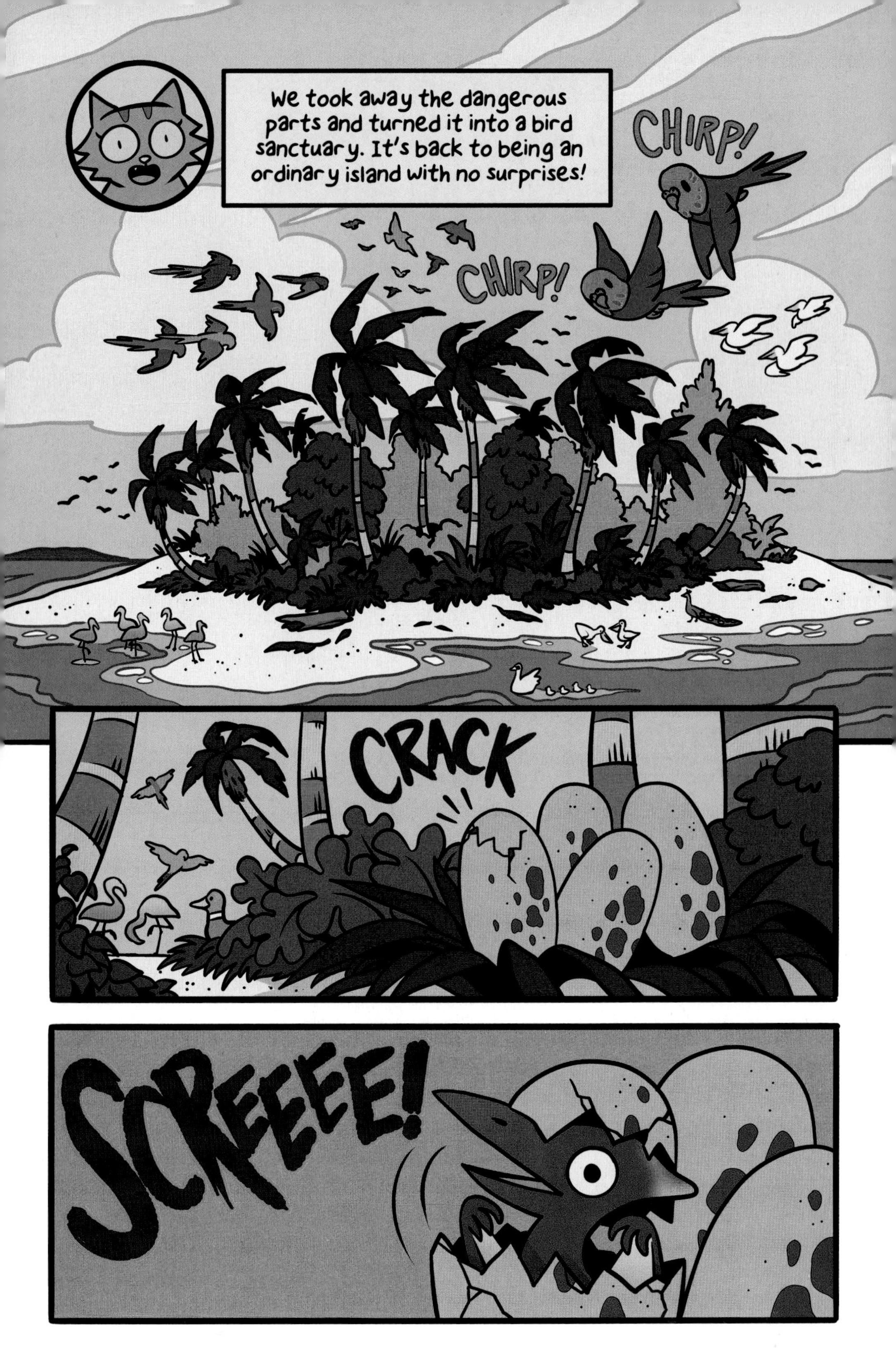
We took away the dangerous parts and turned it into a bird sanctuary. It's back to being an ordinary island with no surprises!
CHIRP!
CHIRP!
CRACK
SCREEEE!

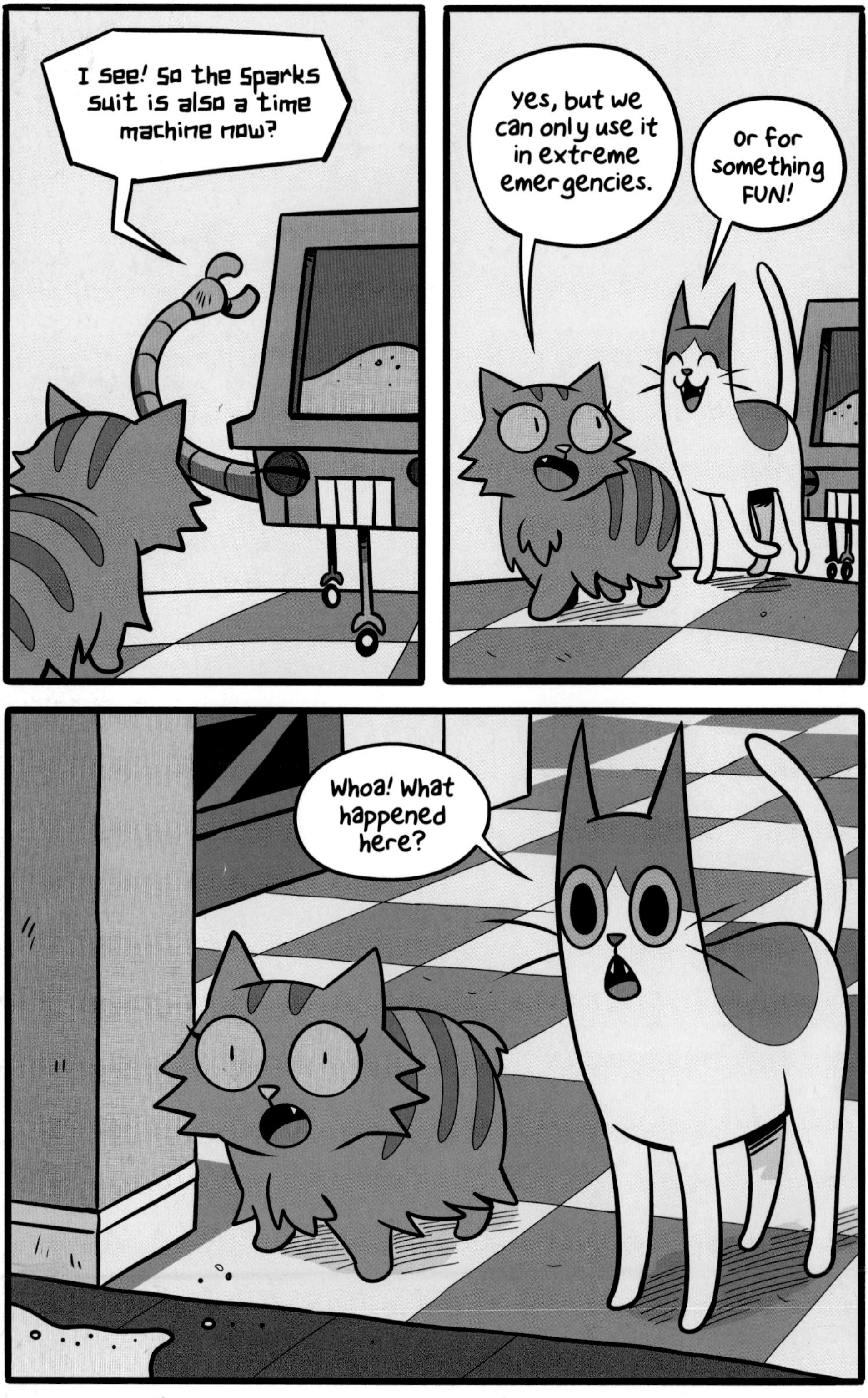
I see! So the Sparks suit is also a time machine now?
Yes, but we can only use it in extreme emergencies.
Or for something FUN!
Whoa! What happened here?

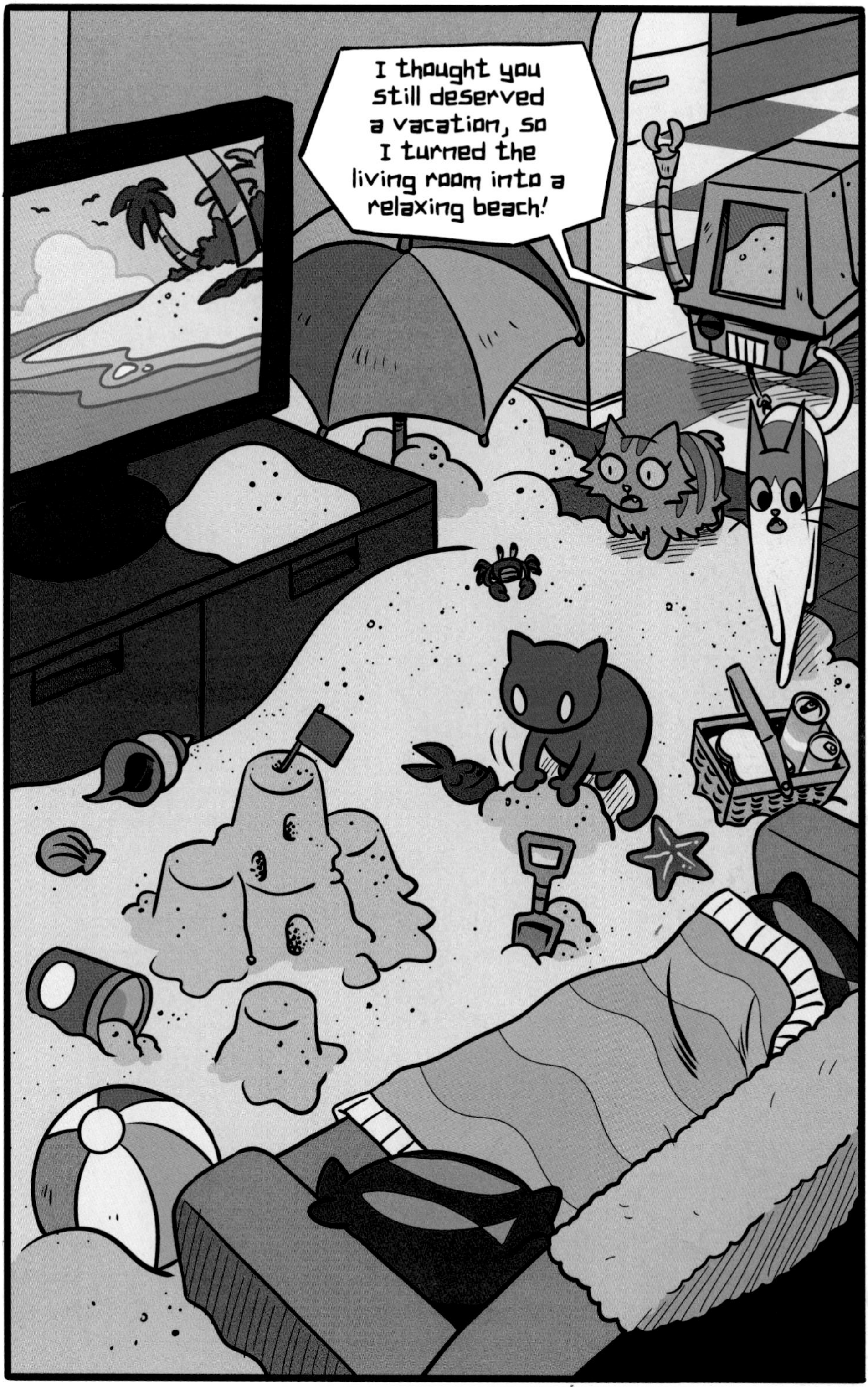
I thought you still deserved a vacation, so I turned the living room into a relaxing beach!

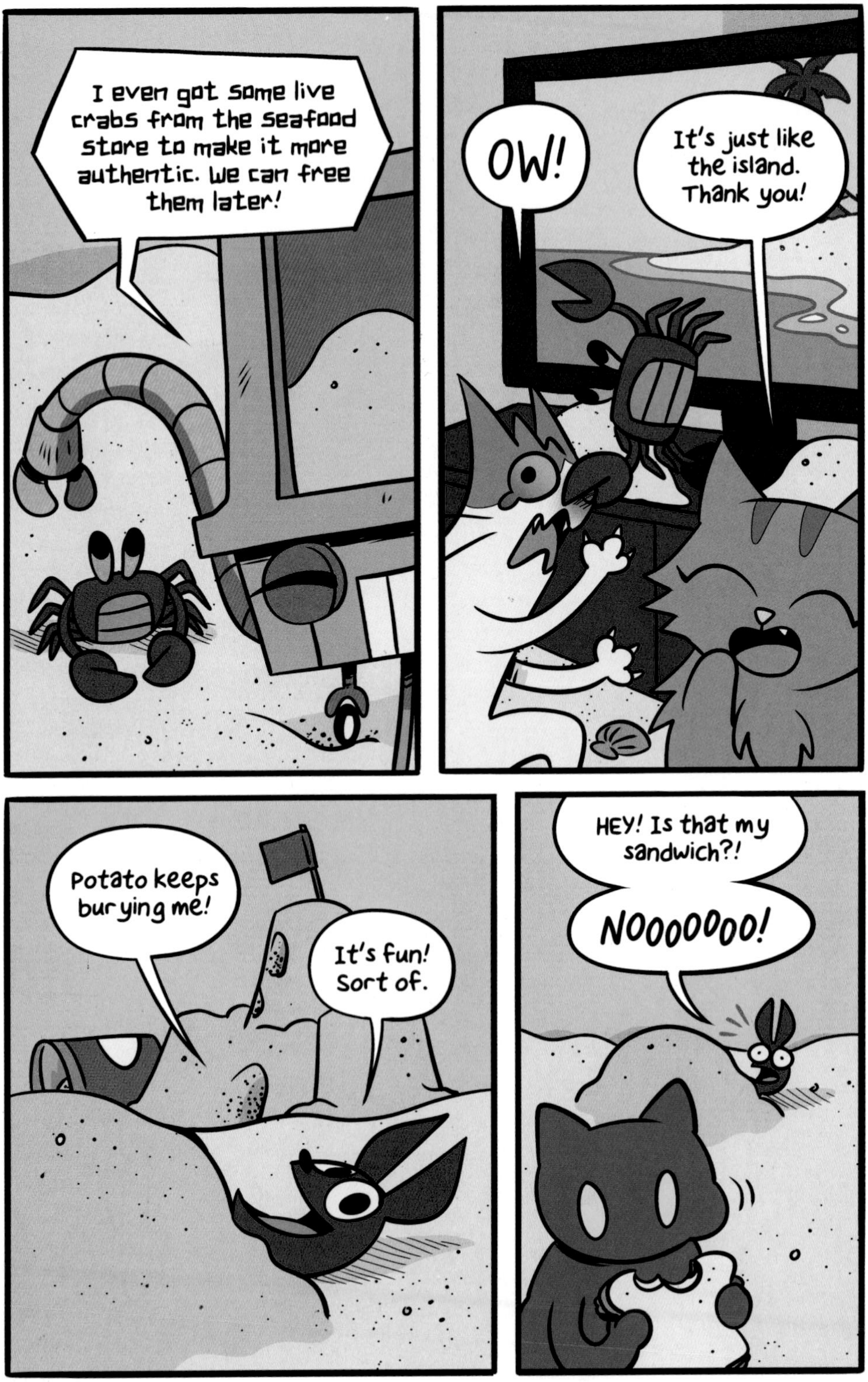
I even got some live crabs from the seafood store to make it more authentic. We can free them later!
OW!
It's just like the island. Thank you!
Potato keeps burying me!
It's fun! Sort of.
HEY! Is that my sandwich?!
NOOOOOOO!

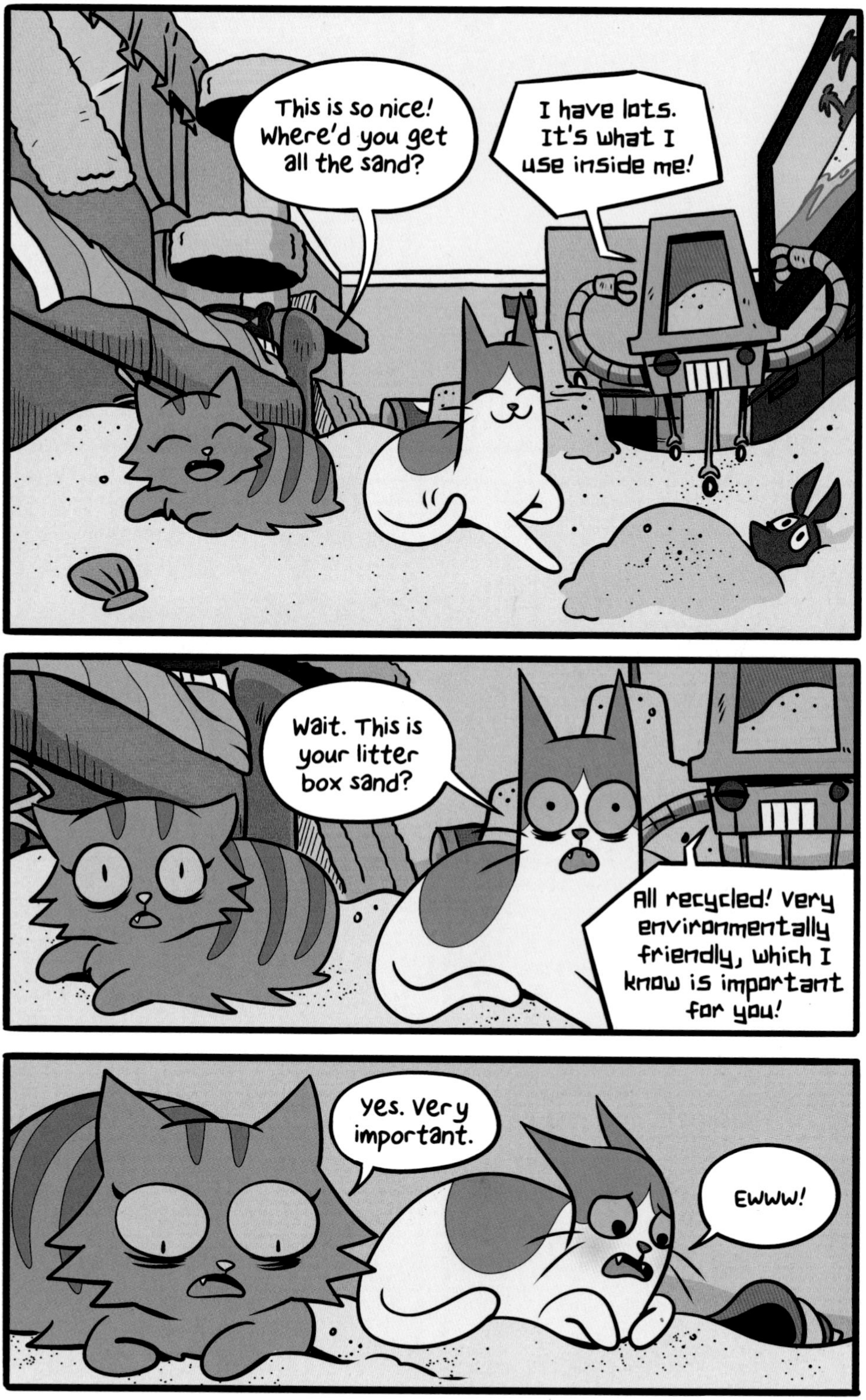
This is so nice! Where'd you get all the sand?
I have lots. It's what I use inside me!
Wait. This is your litter box sand?
All recycled! Very environmentally friendly, which I know is important for you!
Yes. Very important.
EWWW!

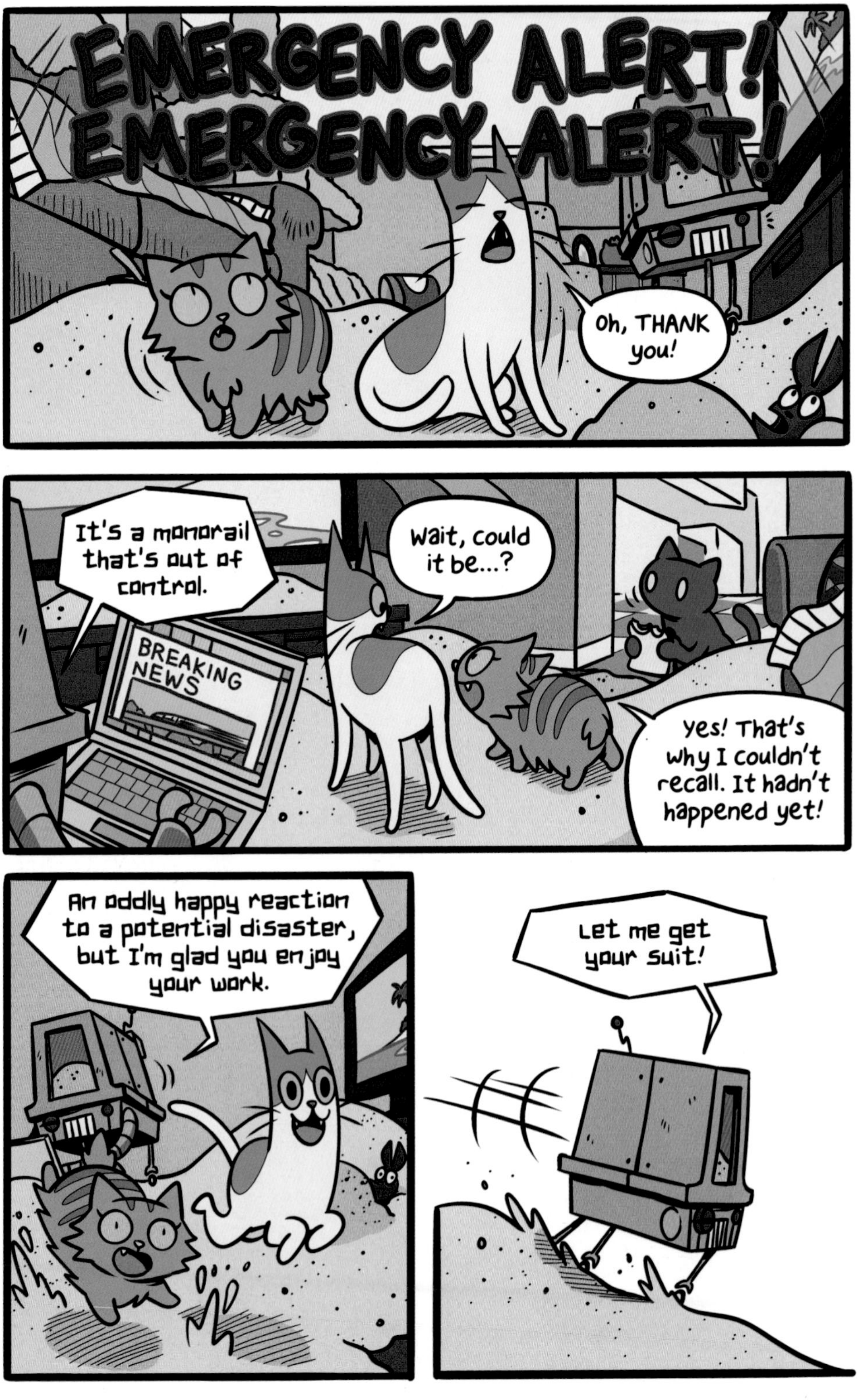

EMERGENCY ALERT! EMERGENCY ALERT!
Oh, THANK you!
It's a monorail that's out of control.
Wait, could it be...?
BREAKING NEWS
Yes! That's why I couldn't recall. It hadn't happened yet!
An oddly happy reaction to a potential disaster, but I'm glad you enjoy your work.
Let me get your suit!

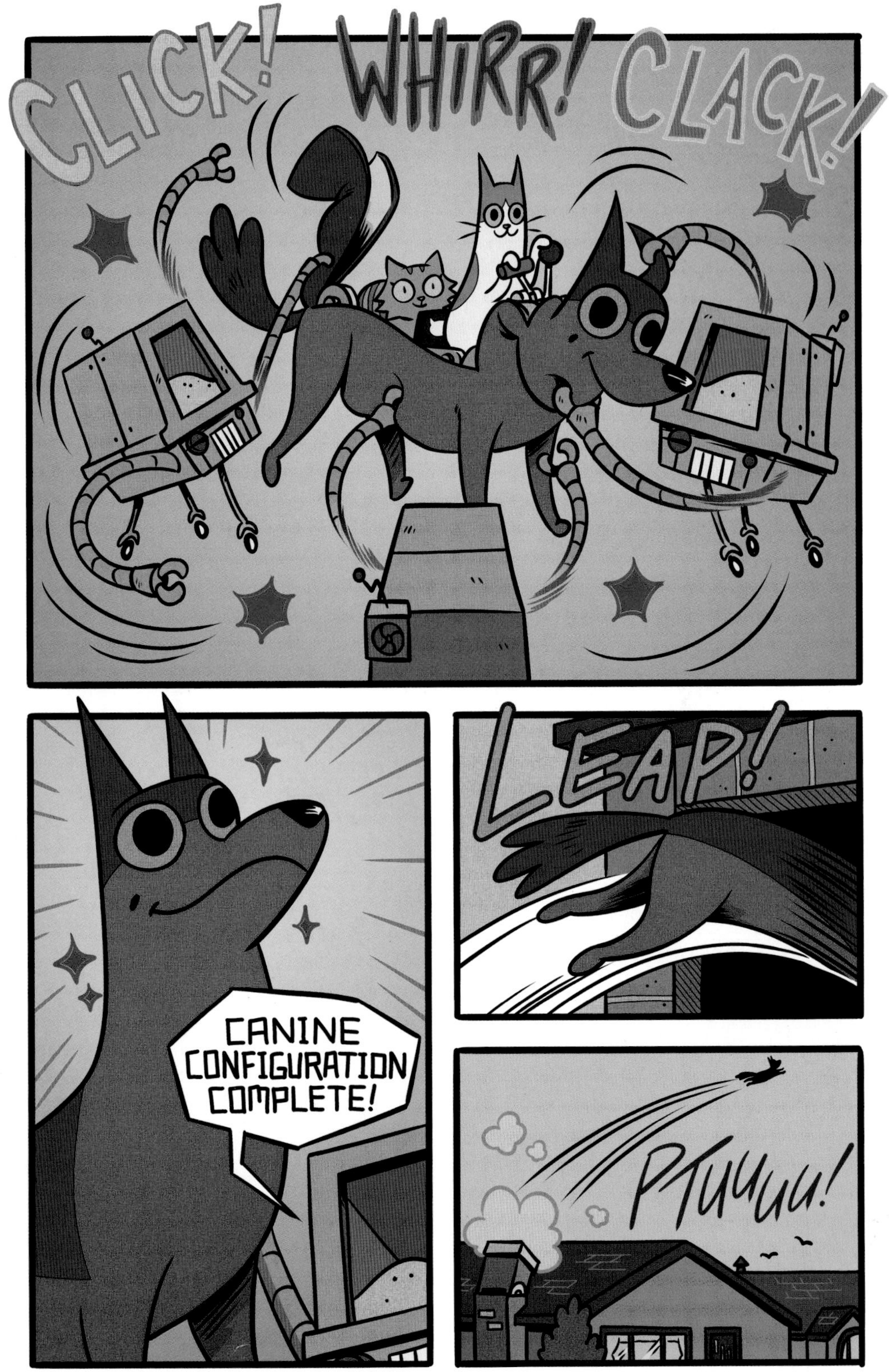
CLICK!
WHIRR!
CLACK!
CANINE CONFIGURATION COMPLETE!
LEAP!
PTUUUU!

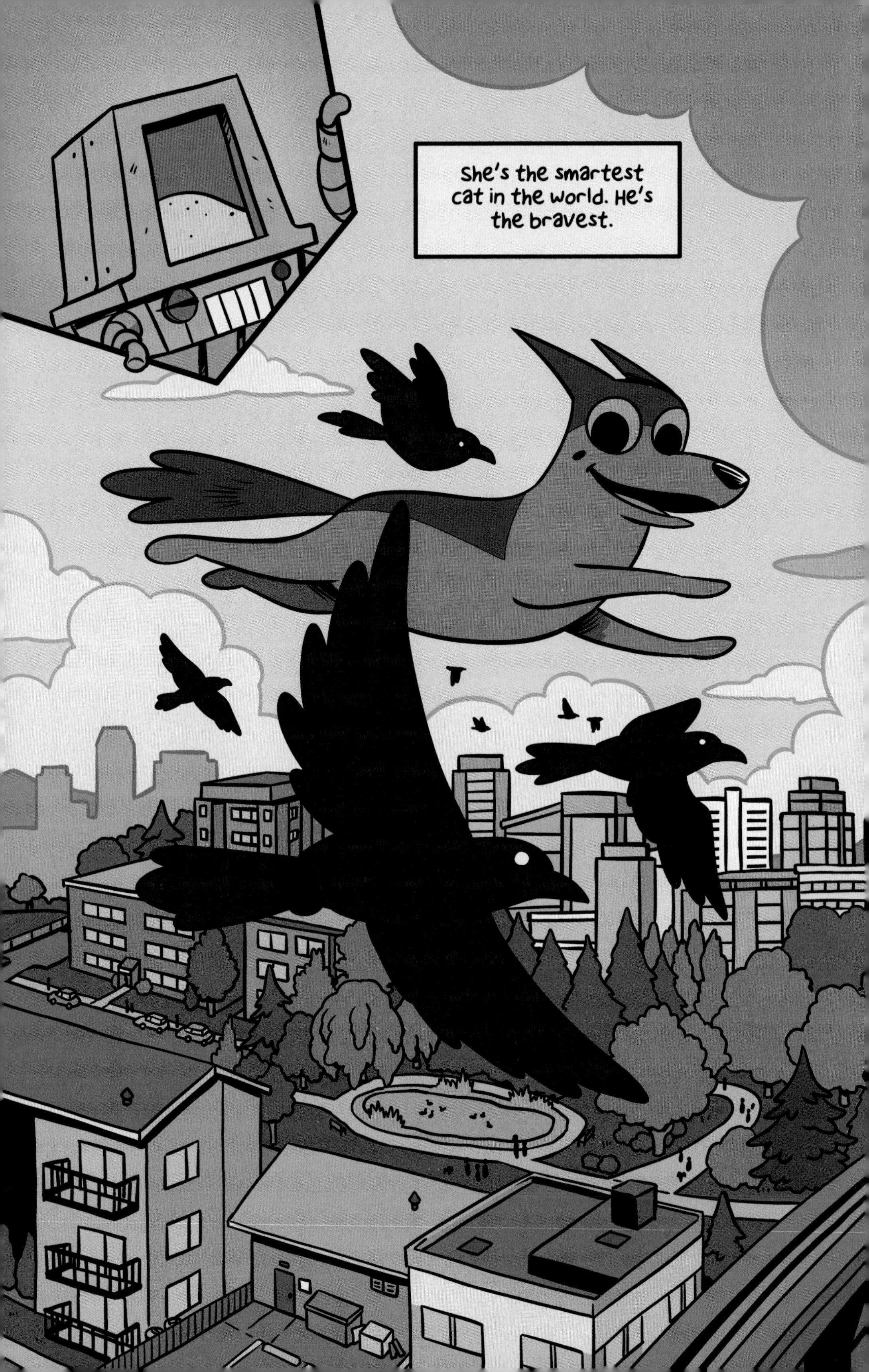
She's the smartest cat in the world. He's the bravest.

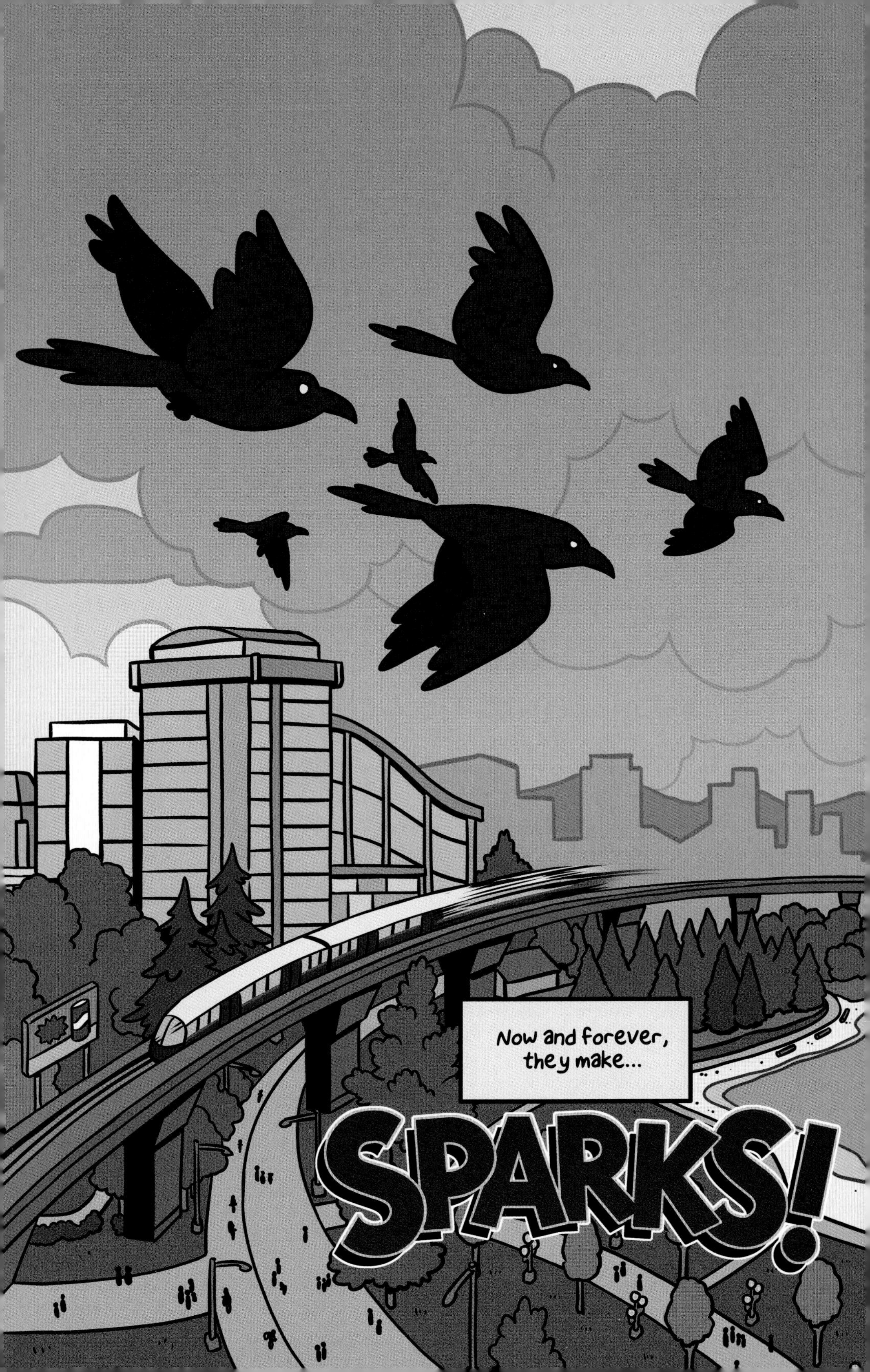
Now and forever,
they make...
SPARKS!

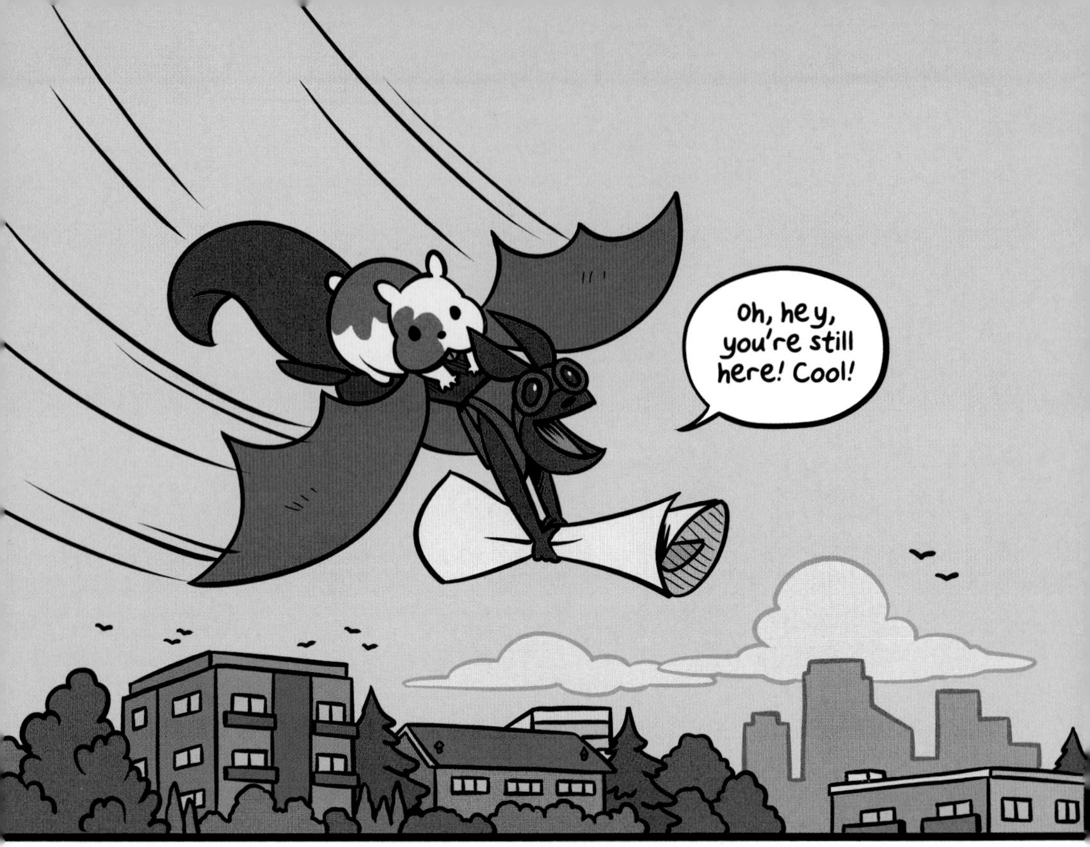
Oh, hey, you're still here! Cool!

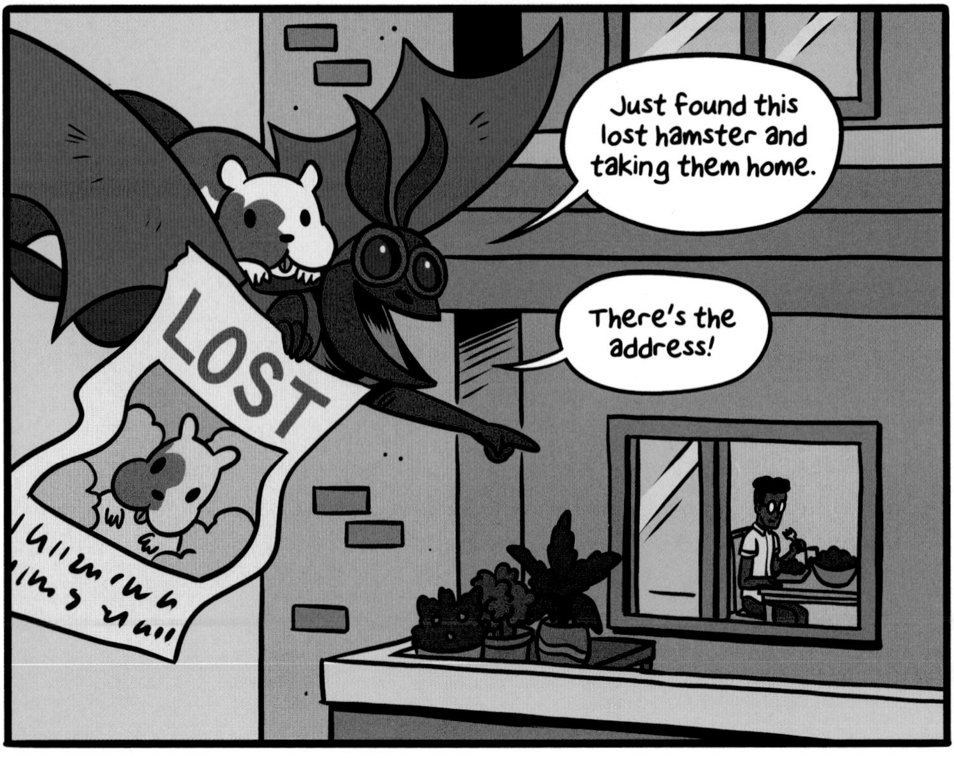
Just found this lost hamster and taking them home.
There's the address!
LOST

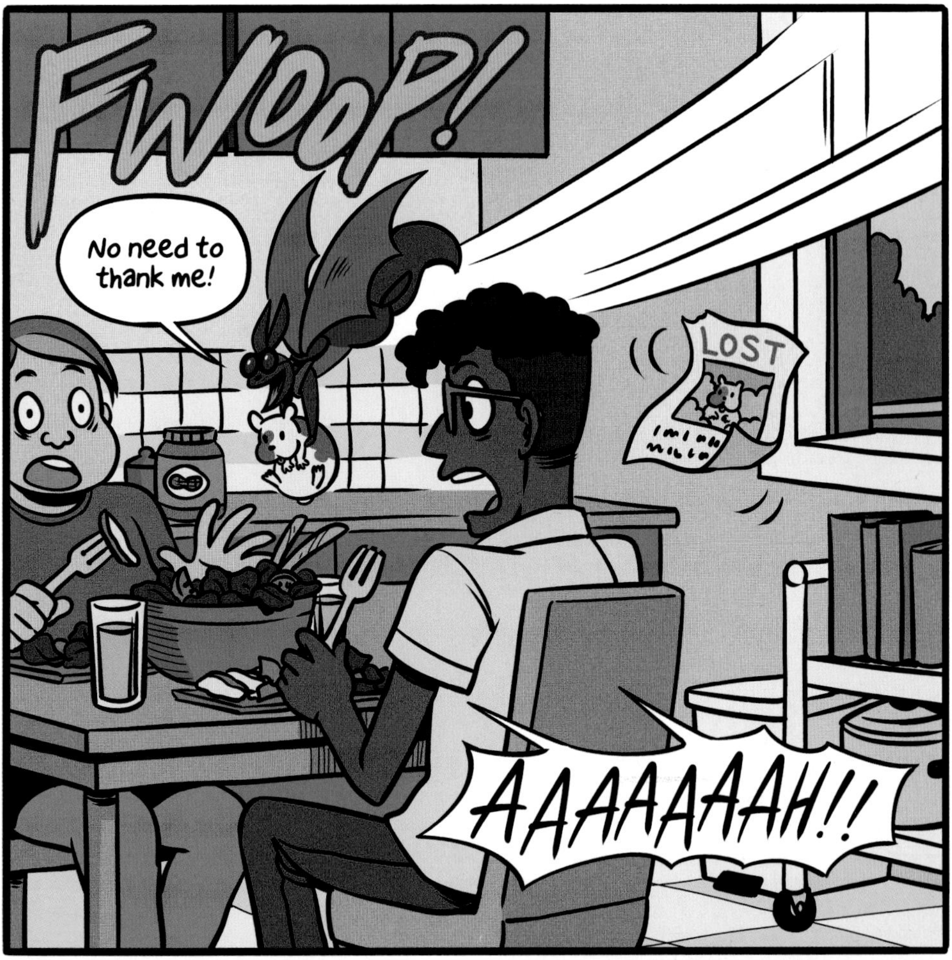
FWOOP!
No need to thank me!
LOST
AAAAAAAH!!

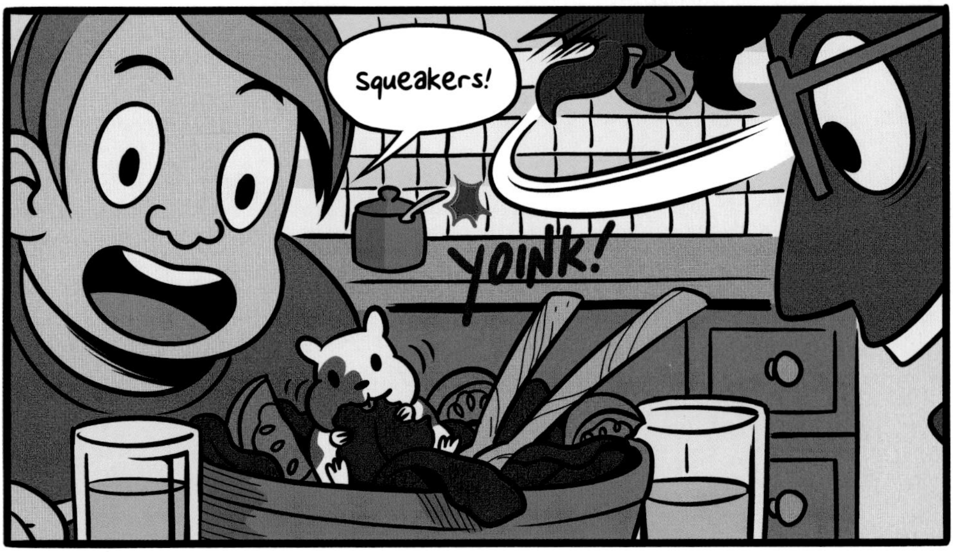
Squeakers!
YOINK!

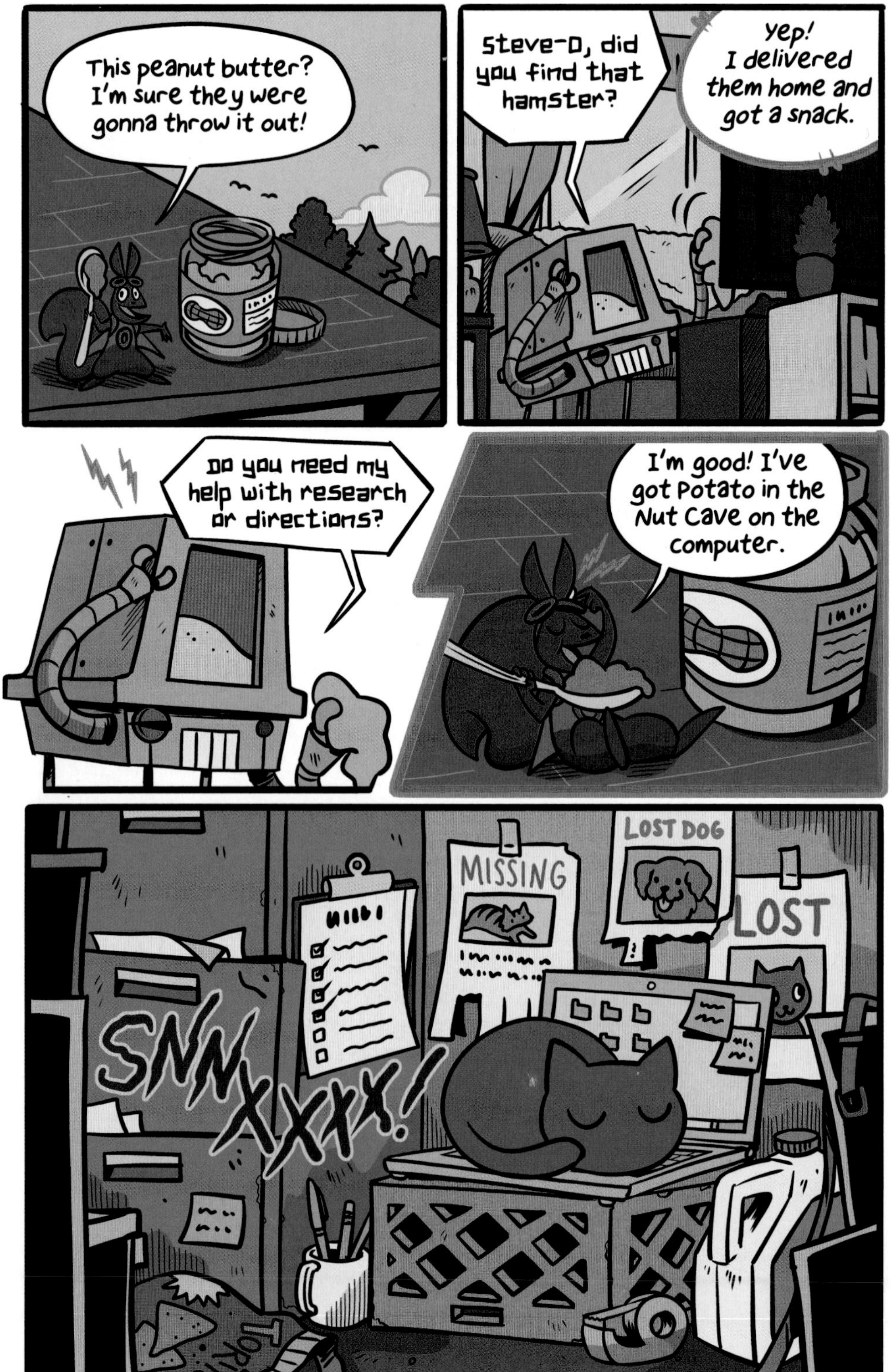
This peanut butter? I'm sure they were gonna throw it out!
Steve-O, did you find that hamster?
Yep! I delivered them home and got a snack.
Do you need my help with research or directions?
I'm good! I've got Potato in the Nut Cave on the computer.
MISSING
LOST DOG
LOST
SNNXXXX!

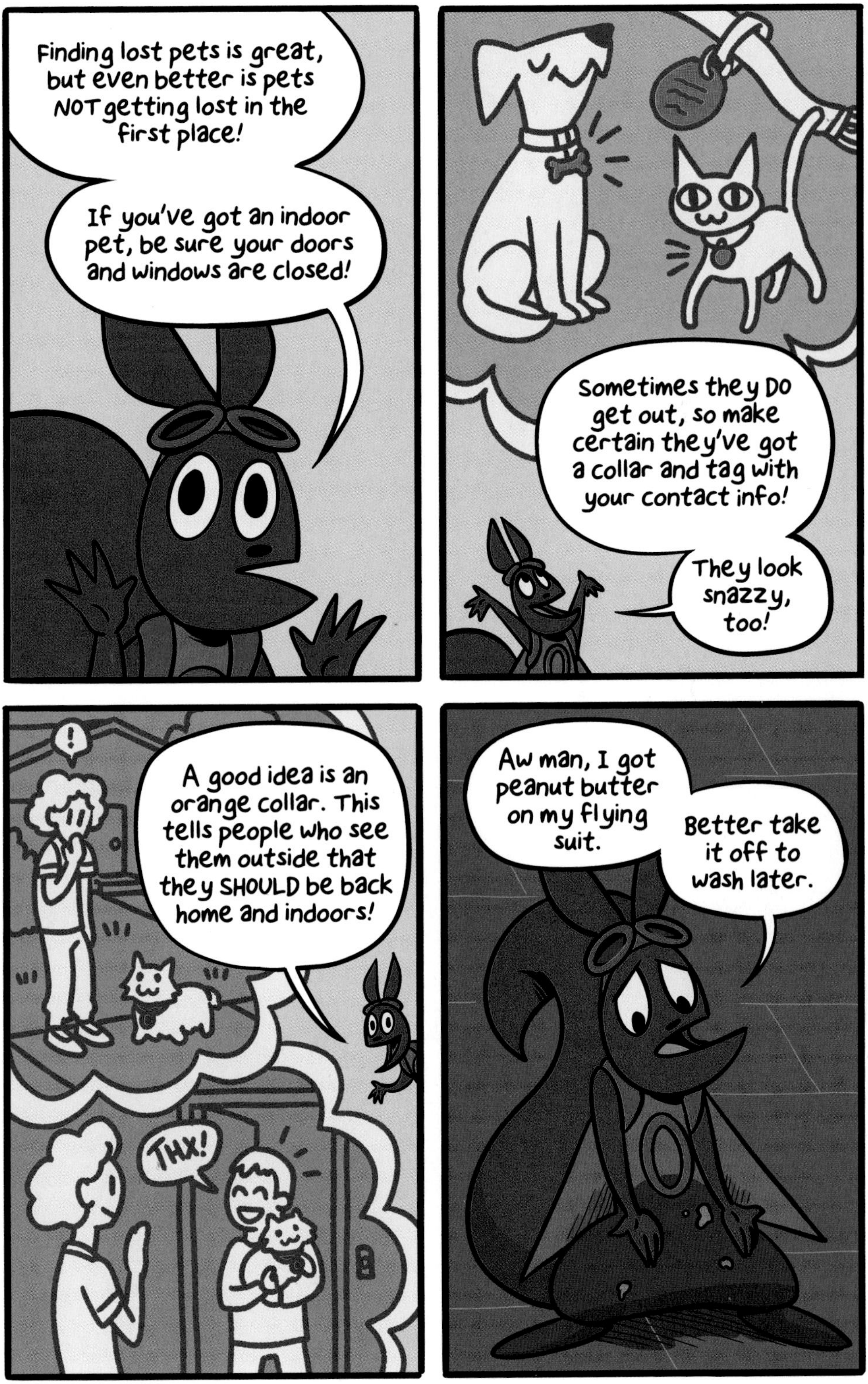

Finding lost pets is great, but even better is pets NOT getting lost in the first place!
If you've got an indoor pet, be sure your doors and windows are closed!
Sometimes they DO get out, so make certain they've got a collar and tag with your contact info!
They look snazzy, too!
A good idea is an orange collar. This tells people who see them outside that they SHOULD be back home and indoors!
THX!
Aw man, I got peanut butter on my flying suit.
Better take it off to wash later.

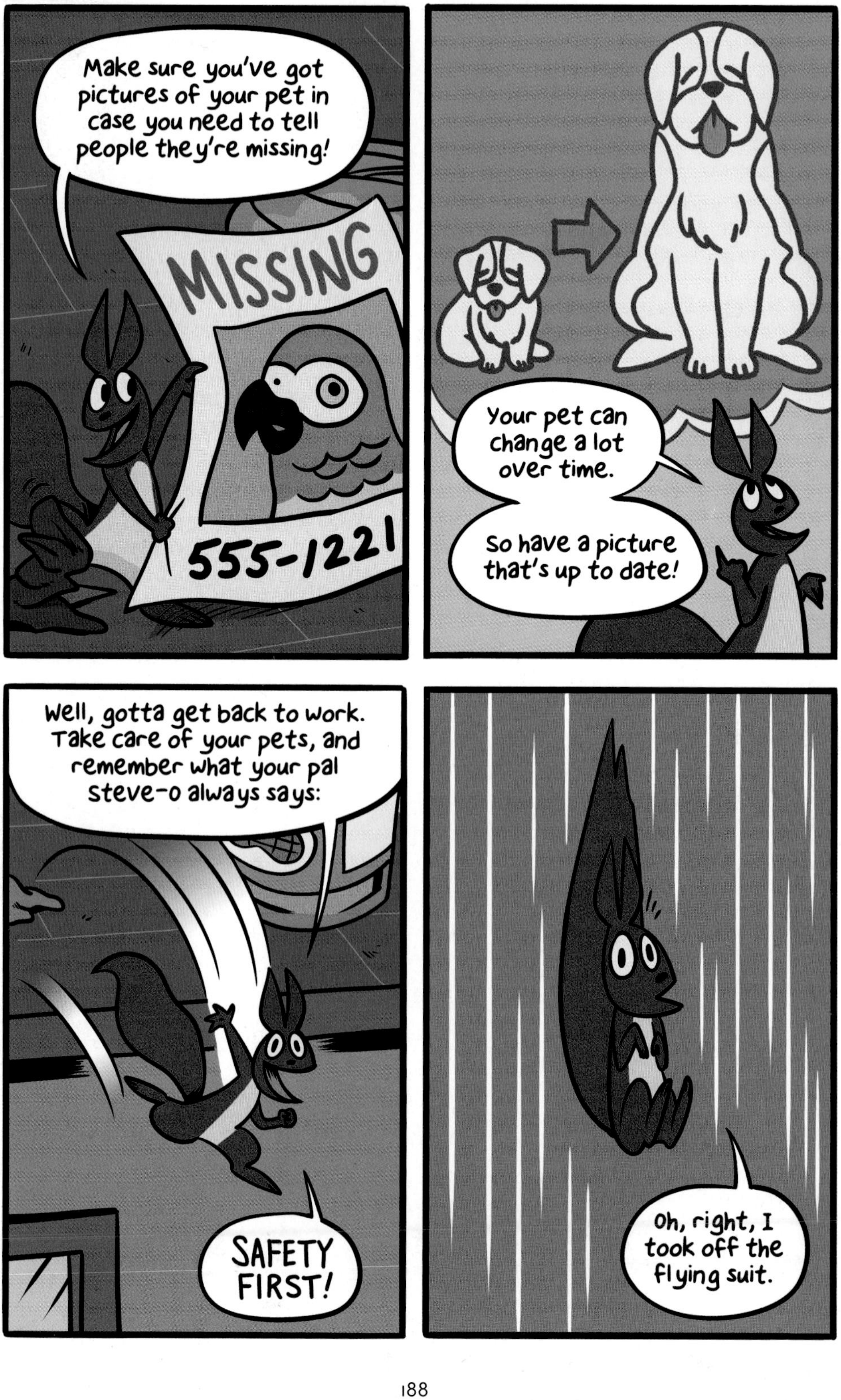
Make sure you've got pictures of your pet in case you need to tell people they're missing!
MISSING
555-1221
Your pet can change a lot over time.
So have a picture that's up to date!
Well, gotta get back to work. Take care of your pets, and remember what your pal Steve-O always says:
SAFETY FIRST!
Oh, right, I took off the flying suit.

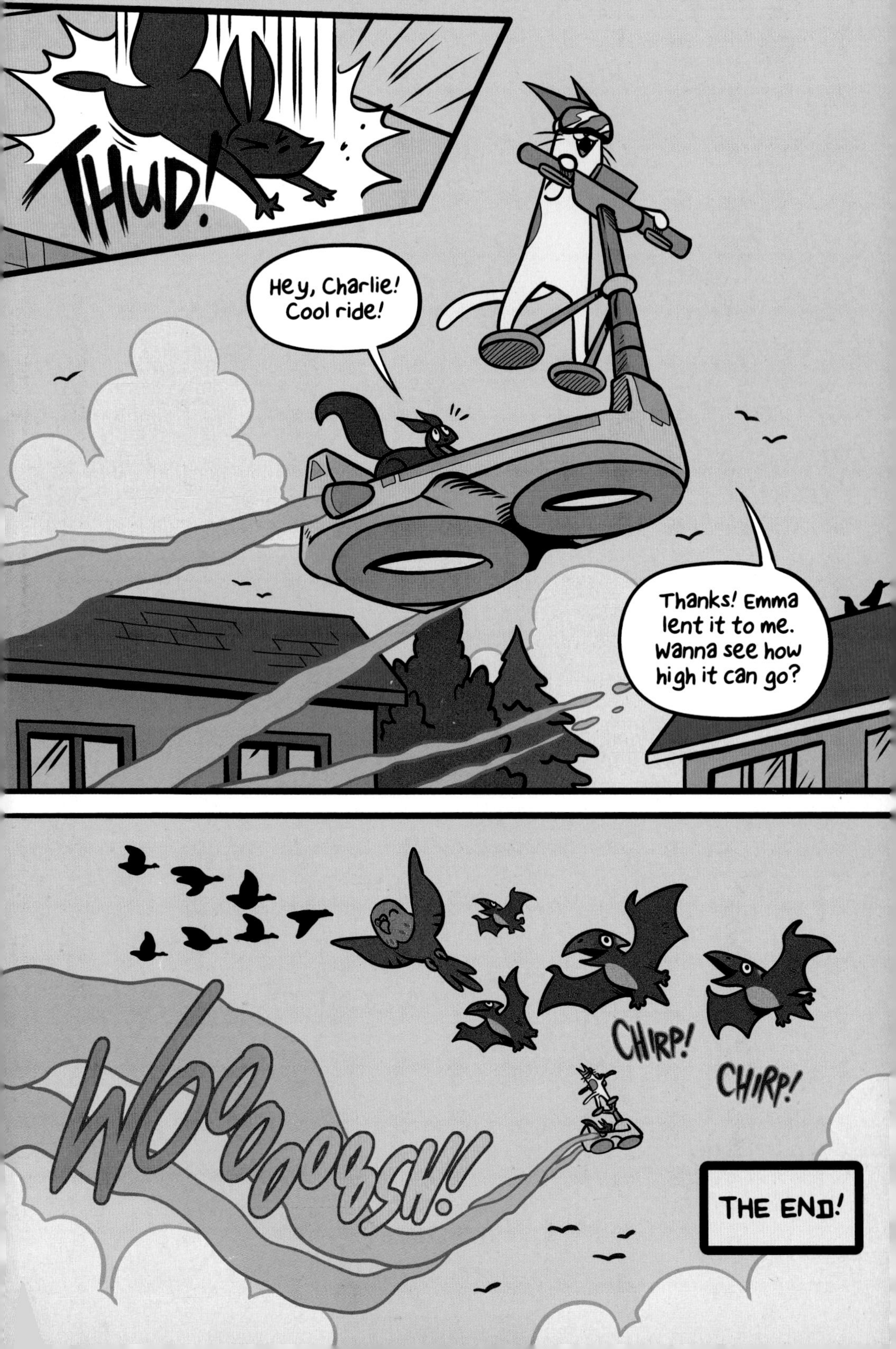
THUD!
Hey, Charlie! Cool ride!
Thanks! Emma lent it to me. Wanna see how high it can go?
WHOOOOOSH!
CHIRP!
CHIRP!
THE END!

IAN BOOTHBY has been writing comedy for TV and radio since he was thirteen and making his own comics since he was sixteen. Ian has written for *Simpsons* and *Futurama Comics*, as well as being a regular cartoon contributor to *MAD* magazine and *The New Yorker* with his wife, Pia Guerra. Ian has also won the Eisner Award for Best Short Story with his friend and Sparks! co-creator Nina Matsumoto. Ian loves cats but has a hard time drawing them.

NINA MATSUMOTO is a Japanese Canadian who designs video game T-shirts and merchandise for Fangamer. She has been drawing comics for over ten years — most notably for *Simpsons Comics*, which won her an Eisner Award for a story she drew written by Ian. She loves birds, and crows are her favorite.

DAVID DEDRICK has been writing and drawing funny pictures his whole life. He lives with his wife, two daughters, two dogs, one cat, one pony, and two chickens — but only some of them actually live in the house!